Since winning the Cath[...]
Fiction for her first nov[...]
Wood has become one of t[...]
in the UK.

Born in the mining town of Castleford, Val came to East Yorkshire as a child and has lived in Hull and rural Holderness where many of her novels are set. She now lives in the market town of Beverley.

When she is not writing, Val is busy promoting libraries and supporting many charities. In 2017 she was awarded an honorary doctorate by the University of Hull for service and dedication to literature.

Find out more about Val Wood's novels by visiting her website: www.valwood.co.uk

Have you read all of Val Wood's novels?

The Hungry Tide
Sarah Foster's parents fight a constant battle with poverty – until wealthy John Rayner provides them with work and a home on the coast. But when he falls for their daughter, Sarah, can their love overcome the gulf of wealth and social standing dividing them?

Annie
Annie Swinburn has killed a man. The man was evil in every possible way, but she knows that her only fate if she stays in Hull is a hanging. So she runs as far away as she can – to a new life that could offer her the chance of love, in spite of the tragedy that has gone before . . .

Children of the Tide
A tired woman holding a baby knocks at the door of one of the big houses in Anlaby. She shoves the baby at young James Rayner, then she vanishes. The Rayner family is shattered – born into poverty, will a baby unite or divide the family?

The Gypsy Girl
Polly Anna's mother died when she was just three years old. Alone in the world, the workhouse was the only place for her. But with the help of a young misfit she manages to escape, running away with the fairground folk. But will Polly Anna ever find somewhere she truly belongs?

Emily
A loving and hard-working child, Emily goes into service at just twelve years old. But when an employer's son dishonours and betrays her, her fortunes seem to be at their lowest ebb. Can she journey from shame and imprisonment to a new life and fulfilment?

Going Home
For Amelia and her siblings, the grim past their mother Emily endured seems far away. But when a gentleman travels from Australia to meet Amelia's family, she discovers the past casts a long shadow and that her tangled family history is inextricably bound up with his . . .

Rosa's Island
Taken in as a child, orphaned Rosa grew up on an island off the coast of Yorkshire. Her mother, before she died, promised that one day Rosa's father would return. But when two mysterious Irishmen come back to the island after many years, they threaten everything Rosa holds dear . . .

The Doorstep Girls
Ruby and Grace have grown up in the poorest slums of Hull. Friends since childhood, they have supported each other in bad times and good. As times grow harder, and money scarcer, the girls search for something that could take them far away . . . But what price will they pay to find it?

Far From Home
When Georgiana Gregory makes the long journey from Hull for New York, she hopes to escape the confines of English life. But once there, Georgiana finds she isn't far from home when she encounters a man she knows – who presents dangers almost too much to cope with . . .

The Kitchen Maid
Jenny secures a job as kitchen maid in a grand house in Beverley – but her fortunes fail when scandal forces her to leave. Years later, she is mistress of a hall, but she never forgets the words a gypsy told her: that one day she will return to where she was happy and find her true love . . .

The Songbird
Poppy Mazzini has an ambition – to go on the stage. Her lovely voice and Italian looks lead her to great acclaim. But when her first love from her home town of Hull becomes engaged to someone else, she is devastated. Will Poppy have to choose between fame and true love?

Nobody's Child
Now a prosperous Hull businesswoman, Susannah grew up with the terrible stigma of being nobody's child. When daughter Laura returns to the Holderness village of her mother's childhood, she will discover a story of poverty, heartbreak and a love that never dies . . .

Fallen Angels
After her dastardly husband tries to sell her, Lily Fowler is alone on the streets of Hull. Forced to work in a brothel, she forges friendships with the women there, and together they try to turn their lives around. Can they dare to dream of happy endings?

The Long Walk Home
When Mikey Quinn's mother dies, he is determined to find a better life for his family – so he walks to London from Hull to seek his fortune. He meets Eleanor, and they gradually make a new life for themselves. Eventually, though, they must make the long walk home to Hull . . .

Rich Girl, Poor Girl
Polly, living in poverty, finds herself alone when her mother dies. Rosalie, brought up in comfort on the other side of Hull, loses her own mother on the same day. When Polly takes a job in Rosalie's house, the two girls form an unlikely friendship. United in tragedy, can they find happiness?

Homecoming Girls

The mysterious Jewel Newmarch turns heads wherever she goes, but she feels a longing to know her own roots. So she decides to return to her birthplace in America, where she learns about family, friendship and home. But most importantly, love . . .

The Harbour Girl

Jeannie spends her days at the water's edge waiting for Ethan to come in from fishing. But then she falls for a handsome stranger. When he breaks his word, Jeannie finds herself pregnant and alone in a strange new town. Will she find someone to truly love her – and will Ethan ever forgive her?

The Innkeeper's Daughter

Bella's dreams of teaching are dashed when she has to take on the role of mother to her baby brother. Her days are brightened by visits from Jamie Lucan – but when the family is forced to move to Hull, Bella is forced to leave everything behind. Can she ever find her dreams again?

His Brother's Wife

The last thing Harriet expects after her mother dies is to marry a man she barely knows, but her only alternative is the workhouse. And so begins an unhappy marriage to Noah Tuke. The only person who offers her friendship is Noah's brother, Fletcher – the one person she can't possibly be with . . .

Every Mother's Son

Daniel Tuke hopes to share his future with childhood friend Beatrice Hart. But his efforts to find out more about his heritage throw up some shocking truths: is there a connection between the families? Meanwhile, Daniel's mother Harriet could never imagine that discoveries about her own family are also on the horizon . . .

Little Girl Lost

Margriet grew up as a lonely child in the old town of Hull. As she grows into adulthood she forms an unlikely friendship with some of the street children who roam the town. As Margriet acts upon her inspiration to help them, will the troubles of her past break her spirit, or will she be able to overcome them?

No Place for a Woman

Brought up by a kindly uncle after the death of her parents, Lucy grows up inspired to become a doctor, just like her father. But studying in London takes Lucy far from her home in Hull, and she has to battle to be accepted in a man's world. Will Lucy be able to follow her dreams – and find love – in a world shattered by war?

A Mother's Choice

Delia has always had to fend for herself and her son Jack, and as a young unmarried mother, life has never been easy. In particularly desperate times, a chance encounter presents a lifeline. Delia is faced with an impossible, heart-wrenching choice. Can she bear to leave her young son behind, hoping another family will care for him?

A Place to Call Home
When Ellen's husband Harry loses his farm job and the cottage that comes with it, he sets out to find a job in the factories and mills of nearby Hull, and Ellen must build a new life for her family on the unfamiliar city streets. But when tragedy threatens Ellen's fragile happiness, how much more can she sacrifice before they find a place to call home?

Four Sisters
With their mother dead, four sisters and their father form a close bond. But when tragedy suddenly strikes and their father disappears on his way to London, the sisters have no way of knowing what has happened to him – only that he hasn't returned home. With little money left, they're now forced to battle life's misfortunes alone . . .

The Lonely Wife
Beatrix is just eighteen when her father tells her she is to marry a stranger – a man named Charles, who shows little interest in her. Soon, the only spark in Beatrix's lonely life is her beloved children. But then Charles threatens to take them away. Can Beatrix fight against her circumstances and keep what is rightfully hers?

Children of Fortune
Following the untimely death of her cold-hearted husband, Beatrix and her three children are finally free. When her headstrong and independent daughter, Alicia, befriends the enigmatic Olivia Snowdon at school, they quickly become inseparable. But Olivia's past is shrouded in mystery and as the two families grow closer, secrets start to come tumbling out . . .

Winter's Daughter
James Ripley and his wife Moira have always looked out for the poor of Hull. When a shelter for the homeless floods, James rushes to help. Among those rescued is a young girl who speaks a language no one can understand. Some say that she came to the cellar with her mother, but no one knows where the mother is now. Concerned for the child's safety, James and Moira take her in, but will anyone claim this little girl as their own?

FOSTER'S MILL

Val Wood

PENGUIN BOOKS

TRANSWORLD PUBLISHERS
Penguin Random House, One Embassy Gardens,
8 Viaduct Gardens, London SW11 7BW
www.penguin.co.uk

Transworld is part of the Penguin Random House group of companies
whose addresses can be found at global.penguinrandomhouse.com

First published in Great Britain in 2024 by Bantam
an imprint of Transworld Publishers
Penguin paperback edition published 2025

A CIP catalogue record for this book
is available from the British Library.

ISBN
9781804996430

Typeset in New Baskerville ITC Pro by Jouve (UK), Milton Keynes.
Printed and bound in Great Britain by Clays Ltd, Elcograf S.p.A.

The authorized representative in the EEA is Penguin Random House Ireland,
Morrison Chambers, 32 Nassau Street, Dublin D02 YH68.

Penguin Random House is committed to a sustainable future
for our business, our readers and our planet. This book is made
from Forest Stewardship Council® certified paper.

With love to my family, who patiently understand my oddities as I enter another fictional world; and for Peter as always.

Author's note

Foster's Mill was written in the early years of my writing career, which began with my first novel *The Hungry Tide*, winner of the first Catherine Cookson Fiction Prize in 1993, closely followed by *Annie* and *Children of the Tide*; all were set in the 19th century. *Foster's Mill* was begun somewhere in the middle of these novels and intended to finalize the activities of the Foster family and bring them into contemporary times.

But it wasn't quite finished, and being set in the 1980s, when life was so totally different from that of the 19th century, and I was still hooked on writing of that earlier century, I tucked it carefully away in my late grandmother's old wooden chest, with other memorabilia that I cared for, and left it to mature.

All of my novels are fictional. The characters and places where they live are created totally from my imagination, though I often refer to real villages and towns close to my fictional ones and re-imagine how life would have been.

The Hungry Tide and eventually *Foster's Mill* were inspired by a real-life happening: the erosion of the cliffs on the east coast is fact, and since Roman times villages and even towns had been falling victim to the sea and disappearing for ever. The subject has been written about many times and maps drawn showing where once there had been a thriving community. It is the fastest-eroding coastline in Europe.

In the 1980s the small community of Mappleton was in great danger of losing their homes to the sea and appealed to the government of the time for resources to save their homes and livelihoods; in turn this appeal went on to the then EEC, who agreed and slabs of granite from Norway were shipped to our coastline.

This small village and its occupants were saved, but the effect of the 'Wall' pushed the erosion steadily onwards and affected other communities. The sea is forever hungry.

And so, in 2023, after celebrating a thirty-year re-issue of that much-loved book, and deciding to take a break, I opened up the old wooden chest and read once again the draft of *Foster's Mill*. It was tantalizing to read again of a 'fairly' modern Foster family and find out what they were doing with their lives.

There was a problem, however, which has been a complete challenge. I had written the novel on an old Amstrad, popular at the time, and it was copied on to a disk, but was completely useless for contemporary technology. After trying various means of copying, I came to realize that the best solution was to re-write *Foster's Mill* from scratch and get to know the family once again.

I have loved to re-engage with them and in some instances to re-connect the modern family with the old, to see the differences and yet the sameness that runs through all of us, the family traits we might describe that come from a time we don't know, yet with which, in some quiet times – hearing a sound, taking a breath – we might just re-connect.

Val Wood

CHAPTER ONE

1989

Liz paused and ran her fingers over the paint-spattered banister rail and looked up beyond the broken cracked cornices. As her breath slowed, she saw other scenes and heard more distant echoes. Were the whispering voices coming from upstairs, or the street outside the heavy front door? Or were they inside her head, strange and yet familiar, like the ones she used to hear when she was a child, when she was in another place and in another time?

'Come on, Liz, get a move on. I don't want to be here all night. Don't let the mess put you off.' Steve Black's voice broke into her thoughts. 'You won't know it when the builders have finished with it.'

'That's what I'm afraid of,' she muttered, gazing up at the high, cobwebbed ceiling of the once fine entrance hall. 'I hope they don't spoil it.'

'There's not much left to spoil,' he grimaced. 'The previous tenants couldn't have cared less. But you needn't worry.' He strode past her, taking two uncarpeted steps at a time. 'It's a listed building, so we're restricted in what the council will allow. There'll be conditions to adhere to.' He was taking a key from his pocket as he spoke, but paused before unlocking a door. 'Are you OK? You look a bit pale.'

'I'm all right.' She pushed a lock of red hair away from her forehead. 'I'm tired. It's been a busy week.'

'I'll say it has,' he agreed. 'I'll be glad to get home. I know it's late, but I wanted you to see this place. There're two units and we've got first choice, this one or the other downstairs. Come up and see what you think.'

The larger of the two rooms on the first floor had long windows facing on to the narrow and ancient High Street. One pane was covered over with cardboard; the frames were chipped, the paint blistered and peeling. Liz glimpsed white muslin curtains billowing against the glass and a bright fire burning in the grate of the fireplace, and caught hold of the door jamb to steady herself. *Stop it! Stop it!*

'You sure you're all right?' Steve's pale blue eyes narrowed as he turned and saw her face. 'You look ghastly.'

'Thanks,' she said. 'I'm tired, that's all,' she said again, and wrinkled her nose. 'Can you smell something fishy? Like cod liver oil or something?'

He shook his head. 'It's stuffy. I don't suppose the windows have been opened in years.' He put his hands against the frames and attempted to push them open. 'No! Jammed solid. It needs a jemmy or something to shift it.'

'What was this place?' She glanced at the bare patches of plaster on the walls where cupboards had been carelessly removed. 'Originally, I mean.'

He shrugged and ran his hands over his thick brown hair. 'No idea. It's been used for all kinds of trades: printers, offices, warehousing at the back by the river I expect, but probably a

2

private dwelling originally.' He shrugged. 'Most of these buildings belonged to shipping merchants, or so I'm told.'

For an estate agent he is remarkably uninformed, Liz
thought. Well, if he takes it, I'll make it my business to
find out.

The window in the office across the landing looked over
the Old Harbour, as many of the older residents of Hull still
called it, and Liz could hear the buzz of machinery coming
from outside. She knew that men would be working on barges
and mechanical dredges on both sides of the narrow waterway, and instinctively looked into the room, giving a quick
smile to the fair-haired man sitting at the desk facing her. 'Yes,
I'll like it here. Sorry, Steve, what did you say?'

The man disappeared as Steve spoke from the doorway.
'Shall we go downstairs and look at the other unit?' he
repeated, patting his pocket. 'I've got the key.'

'The kitchens.'

'What?'

'That's where the kitchens are – were. Below stairs.'

'Oh, yeh!' He looked at her, and then laughed. 'You're an
oddball, Liz. There can't have been kitchens here in decades.
Come on, then we can get off home.' He sighed. 'The traffic
should have cleared by now.'

The lower unit was claustrophobic. The basement space
had been divided into several small rooms by means of plas-
terboard, and with only tiny windows at pavement level was
devoid of natural light or atmosphere. On the ground floor, a
single room at the side of the front door was too small to be
used as a third office. She thought perhaps it had been a
receiving room where guests had waited to be invited in when
the building had been a private house.

'I prefer the upper floor,' she commented. 'If I'm given the
choice.'

'Well, you're going to be running the business from here,' Steve said, 'so the choice is yours. The front room can be the main office with the computers, fax and technical stuff, and the rear one that overlooks the river can be yours. How does that sound?'

'Sounds fine. But I'll need a junior, or an assistant; we can't leave the place empty every time I'm out showing properties to potential clients. I'll advertise for someone. We'll need more office furniture too – another desk and chair.' And I hope there'll be enough room for all of us, she thought, with the vision of the fair-haired man upstairs fresh in her mind. *I wonder who you are.*

She watched from the doorstep as Steve drove off at speed, the car wheels spinning in both gutters in the narrow street, and shook her head in exasperation. The street hadn't been built to take cars that tore up the cobbles, parked on the foot-paths or scraped the old brick walls as they hurtled past. Cabriolets, broughams and hand carts – stop it, she told herself again as she walked past the front of the house to where her car was parked on the staith side.

Tillington here I come, she mused as she strapped on her seat belt and moved off. I'm really ready for this weekend. I can forget about houses and building plots, take a breath of sea air, walk on the beach and unwind. She enjoyed her job, but it seemed as if everyone had wanted to find a house in these last few weeks: before summer was finally over, or before schools began autumn term, or even before Christmas.

She glanced at the clock on the dashboard: six thirty. She should be home in under an hour. The traffic would be less-ening on the main road, and once she'd left the eastern outskirts of Hull the country roads would be almost empty.

She slipped a cassette tape into the player and the strains of Mozart's *Idomeneo* drifted over her. She could hear the cry of gulls and wind in a storm in the music, and settled back to enjoy the drive.

It will be good to move out of that cramped office in the middle of town, she mused. I've never liked it. It's fine for showing photographs of the local properties we have on our books, and I understand why Steve wants to keep it, but he's keen to expand, and I can only set up a more efficient system if we have more space.

She thought back to the building they had just visited and the elegant room on the first floor with the muslin curtains and the paintings of ships on the walls. And the smiling man behind the desk in the opposite room.

Don't be such an idiot, she told herself. Stop it! She heaved a breath. The room was empty! You're just imagining things. But the man was very real. *I could have reached out and shaken his hand.* Off the main road now and reaching a village road she pulled into a lay-by, switched off the engine and closed her eyes. This hadn't happened in such a long time. Why was it happening now?

I remember my illusory childhood friend so well. She looked so much like me. It was like looking into a mirror, except that she dressed in strange clothes; the starched white apron over her ankle-length dress, her ankle boots and the bonnet on her red hair. I remember whispering to my mother about her. Whispering so that no one else would hear, as if it were a secret that no one else would understand, and Mum would bend her head so that it was touching mine, and smile and nod as if she understood, the smile lighting up her eyes, making them shine.

Then the little girl disappeared; it must have been about the time that Bill was born. And I can't quite remember when I saw her again. Except when Mum died.

*

She parked the car in the Ship's yard and strode through the door marked *Private*. 'Hi, Dad,' she called, tossing her brief-case on to a chair in the living room and shrugging off her jacket before sitting down.

Her father came into the room carrying a tray with two mugs of tea and a plate of biscuits. 'Good timing,' he said, putting the tray down on a small table and dropping a kiss on the top of her head. He glanced at the clock on the mantel-piece. 'I'll just have this with you and then go through.'

'Would you like a hand tonight? I'll need a shower and something to eat first.'

'No thanks, love. Jack and Dot are both in already. Besides, you've been at work all week. You'll be ready for a break.'

'It's been pretty hectic, I must admit.' She sipped the hot tea and nibbled on a biscuit, then leant her head back against the floral chintz. 'I'll take a long walk along the beach tomor-row. Have there been any more falls this week?'

'No, 'wind's been westerly. We'll be in trouble when it turns. Can you spare a couple of hours tomorrow lunchtime? Jack can't come in – got a dental appointment or something – and Dot'll be busy with lunches.'

'Yes, I don't mind. It'll give me a chance to catch up with the local gossip. Before you go,' she added as he heaved him-self from the comfort of his chair, 'do you know anything about the buildings in Hull's old High Street?'

'Which one? Wilberforce House or 'Transport Museum, do you mean? I used to know 'Old Black Boy inn when I was young. Everybody did.'

'No.' She smiled. 'Everybody knows them. You used to take us, Bill and me, to the museums when we were children. No, I meant the properties that used to be private houses. I've been in one today. They back on to the River Hull. Steve's probably going to rent one as an office for me.'

'Renovation? Steve Black must be loaded!'

'He's very successful,' she agreed diplomatically. 'He has plans for the new decade. The council are dividing this particular building into office units and retaining the original façade. We've been to have a look and it seems . . .' She hesitated. 'It seemed to be familiar.'

He shook his head. 'I haven't been down there in years. A lot of the old town was flattened during the last war, of course; the devastation lost Hull a great many historic buildings. I was onny a little lad – not even in school – but I remember my da taking me to look at it after 'war. Then they threw up some monstrous new buildings, and ruined 'whole place.'

'I'm inclined to agree,' she called after him as he went through an inner door to the bar. 'But it's still a fascinating old area.'

CHAPTER TWO

Liz rose early the next morning, showered, and dressed in a warm tracksuit and thick socks. Knowing her father would be still sleeping, she went quietly downstairs so as not to disturb him. She made a cup of coffee and drank it standing up, and then pulled on boots, scarf and a warm waterproof. The sun was shining, but the wind would be brisk on top of the cliff.

A green and yellow tractor pulling a trailer clattered towards her as she crossed the road and she raised a hand in greeting. From this distance, she couldn't recognize the driver, but she was confident she knew him or her, whoever it was. Everybody knew everyone else in Tillington.

Most of the residents of the village had been born here, or at least in the area; there were a few new ones, but not many, and those who had moved into the small housing development some twenty years ago were a hardy breed, coming to Tillington to escape from urban living, enjoying the challenge of pitting their strength against the elements or battling to grow their organic vegetables in the Holderness clay.

The sea was relatively calm; crests of water, silver shards beyond the sandbanks, breaking up into creamy white foam as they rushed towards the pale shore. *I'd love a swim. Is it worth the risk?* She knew for her it wasn't, though summer visitors who wandered down the long beach from the busier resort further up the coast, looking for somewhere quiet, often took a chance, not appearing to give any thought to the dangers lurking beneath the surface, or to sudden cliff falls.

She scrambled down the cliff path and walked along the sea edge, stooping now and again to pick up pebbles or shells which caught her eye and dropping them into her sandy pocket. There had been a fresh fall, despite what her father had thought: another step nearer to the village road, another win for the sea as it reclaimed the land.

She stood and gazed at the heaps and ridges of fallen clay at the bottom of the cliff, at the tufts of grass which lay newly repositioned on the sandy shore, and a feeling of melancholy swept over her. It isn't fair, she thought. This is our land and it's being swallowed up bit by bit and nobody cares; only the people who live here and they don't count.

She turned to look at the sea lapping close to her boots. 'It isn't fair, I said.'

There was a low laugh behind her and she turned, a quick response on her lips, an explanation as to why she was talking to herself, but there was no one there; just a long stretch of empty sandy beach to her right and left and only the swooping gulls disturbing the isolation.

She found a patch of dry sand and sat down, drew her knees up to her chin and waited; waited as she did when she was sixteen and her mother had just died.

'*Mum-my.*' It was a long-drawn-out cry, stretching the syllables into a childlike wail. Down here on the sands she could let go of her grief, not keep it bottled up for the sake of her grieving father and her brave young brother. She wailed again, releasing her sorrow, hearing the echo of her cry being carried away by the startled gulls as they rose up from the sands and screeched away from the shore.

She heard soft crying, but it wasn't hers; her illusory childhood friend was pacing the sands, backwards and forwards, to and fro, her long skirt wet and sandy around her bare feet, her hair, red like her own, but long, not short like hers, blowing tangled in the wind. She turned and gave a sad smile and Elizabeth saw that Sarah too had grown away from childhood, and now seemed more mature than she was herself.

Sometimes, during those long unhappy days, Elizabeth had seen her gazing out to sea, a lonely figure on the shore or cliff top, and had stood silently by her side, trying to both take and give comfort.

Then one morning, very early, she was drawn from her bed by a sensation of despair and she ran and ran, an urgency compelling her to be there; but there was no sign of Sarah, only an empty, desolate loneliness and a wild sea running high, crashing ferociously against the cliffs, and she wept and wept, crying for her mother and for herself and for her sad, lost, lonely friend; then she blew her nose and turned for home, and got on with her life.

Liz hunched herself into her coat, remembering that she'd gone back to the beach some time later, feeling less sad. Other friends had gathered round to comfort her in her loss, and she looked for the illusory girl, wanting to convey some solace and strength, but it seemed that Sarah had already found it. She didn't see her, but had felt the presence of love and contentment hovering around her like the warmth from the sun.

She waited now, but the reflective mood had gone and she watched a pair of fishermen, their bodies wide and heavy with woollen sweaters and yellow oilskins, trudging heavy-

booted up the sands, their rods and bait boxes, umbrellas
and thermos flasks clutched cumbrously in their arms.

They called to her: *Up later – hot soup – thaw us out*, and the
wind caught their voices, clipping their words into short fragments so that she had to guess at what they were saying. She
gave a thumbs-up, sand rasping down her jacket, and walked
on, her head down against the wind which flapped the scarf
around her neck, revelling in the icy sharpness which filled
her lungs and stung her cheeks and blew away her pensive
thoughts.

A trickle of sand and pebbles slid beneath her boots as she
climbed back up the low cliff, gathering up other debris in
their momentum down the incline and cascading into small
heaps on the sands. She paused to catch her breath and
looked out towards the horizon. The sky was blue and bright,
but an ominous band of grey clouds was gathering and heading towards the land.

She turned her back on the sea and walked quickly back
towards the village, not the way she had come but cutting
down a sandy strip where Tillington residents once lived in
comfortable homes. Now, the sturdy cottages and timber
houses stood in quiet abandonment and the wooden signpost
at the village end directing pedestrians to *The Seaside* lay rotting on the ground. The desolation was so familiar to her that
she cast no more than a cursory glance towards the empty
dwellings, but a surge of resentment swept over her as it always
did when she came this way, and with a set determination she
crossed the road again and headed past the church and on
towards the old mill.

The Reedbarrows' black Labrador barked at her as she
leant on the mill gate and stood for a moment gazing at the
decrepit structure. There was movement in the nearby mill
house and the angular figure of Carl Reedbarrow came outside and stood with his arms folded, watching her.

'Morning, Carl.' Her greeting was civil though not over-friendly, and he replied in a similar tone, a taunting grin playing about his unshaven face.

'We're still here, tha sees. Haven't gone away.' He laughed loudly at his witticism and she nodded slowly.

'Didn't think you would have.' She kept her voice light. 'Didn't think we would ever have been so lucky,' she murmured beneath her breath as she turned for home.

CHAPTER THREE

Chris Burton, Christopher only to his mother, put his thick parka on the back seat of the car with a thermos of coffee carefully propped up beside it and set off from outside his suburban apartment early on Saturday morning, his mind made up. He'd ringed an area on a local map giving him about an hour's driving distance from the college in the centre of Hull.

'There's no need for all that driving,' one of his colleagues had said when he'd mentioned his plans for the weekend. 'You'll find a place much nearer than that.'

But Chris had been used to taking an hour or longer to commute into work when he'd lived in London and it hadn't fazed him in the least, so now he didn't have the capital's huge amount of traffic to contend with he'd decided he could live further out, away from the suburbs and in a country district.

He'd driven to the west of the city when he'd first arrived to take up his new teaching position at the Hull college. The area was lovely: lush golf courses, well-laid-out parks, desirable bungalows and smart houses with trim gardens. Expensive price tags, too, though still much less than London's. But now he realized he wanted something different; remote, even. A bit run down, that he could renovate at weekends. So he'd looked at the map again and, decision made, on that Saturday morning he about-turned, crossed the River Hull which divided the city, and headed east towards the coast.

Not having explored this area before, he hadn't realized just how flat this part of the county was. It reminded him of Holland, of the central plains of France with their vast reaches of uninterrupted space, and of Kentucky too, where he'd spent several months between school and university; now he saw outstretched fields of golden wheat, a pale glow in the morning sun, punctuated only by rows of telephone poles marching like a disciplined army, and at some point on the horizon as he approached the coastal villages a solitary church, its spire pointing a perpendicular finger towards heaven.

Helena would hate this, he considered. She'd really hate this vast emptiness. But I don't. I feel as if I can breathe here. No barriers, no boundaries; and in any case I don't have to consider her opinion.

The road twisted and turned. It was not entirely flat, as he'd first thought, but meandered, riverlike, between the fields. Undulated would perhaps be a better word for it, he thought as he came to a junction. 'Tillington straight on,' he muttered beneath his breath, and thought the other road must lead to the sea, although it wasn't marked. Curious, he turned down the narrower road and saw a rough wooden board with the letter S painted on it in red displayed prominently on the grass verge. A few yards beyond the first board was another with a plump spherical O, and behind that yet another, tilted towards the ground, bearing another S.

SOS. Intrigued, he stopped and wound down the window to read another board on the other side of the road, which was now little more than a narrow track. SAVE TILLINGTON, it proclaimed in large letters. DON'T LET OUR VILLAGE DROWN.

He took a deep breath of sea air and could hear the sound of the surf dashing against the shore. As a boy he'd always been excited by his first glimpse of the sea, and as he felt the sharp tangy air on his face the childhood memories flooded back.

He recalled his summer holidays further up the east coast near Filey, where he'd stayed with his grandparents who had retired to a nearby village; idyllic days of crabbing and playing cricket on the wide sandy beaches, his skin steadily turning brown and his dark hair streaking blond in the sun and the salty air.

He glanced about him at the unmarked road with its deep uneven ruts, the dilapidated and abandoned holiday bungalows facing the pebbled cottages with their small overgrown gardens, the noticeboard advising of danger from cliff falls. Then he reminded himself why he was here and reversed back to the junction to drive on into the village, where he parked near a shop and reached for his coat. Locking the doors, he slipped the car keys into an inside pocket and turned up his collar. The brightness of the morning was rapidly disappearing and a chill wind was blowing strongly off the sea, sending grey rainclouds scudding across the sky and making him wish he'd brought a woolly hat.

A crowd of children were gathered about the shop doorway, swapping sweets and comics, oblivious of frowning and grumbling adults who were trying to get into the shop. 'Come on, lads,' Chris said in a brisk schoolmaster's voice. 'Make some room.'

Two elderly men, their shoulders hunched, dug their hands deeper into their pockets and looked on impassively as Chris waited for the boys to move. He caught their eyes and nodded. They nodded back and one of them eased his cap back from his forehead. 'How do,' he said. 'A bit brisk this morning.'

Chris bought a newspaper, tucked it under his arm and

wandered round the village. It wasn't very big and was fairly typical of others he had passed through. There was one main street, with a crooked lane leading off it on which he could see an assortment of terraced cottages and a couple of large square redbrick houses. At the end of the lane was a rundown smallholding with a tractor in the yard.

A neat cluster of newish bungalows was tucked away down another narrow side street, opposite a close of council houses, and beyond that, a few hundred yards away from each other on the main road, were two pubs. He walked down in that direction and paused at the bottom of a lane which ran along the far side of the Ship Inn. The lane was lined on both sides with massive horse chestnut trees, their huge branches touching to form a canopy. Their leaves glowed golden brown, and as the wind blew through them there came an occasional thud as the last of the knobbly green-encased nuts were shed on to the ground.

He walked up the lane to see where it led; as he passed he caught the smell of something cooking coming from the pub and thought he might try it later. There was a slight incline here, the nearest thing to a hill he'd seen since setting out this morning, and standing almost at the top of the lane like a sentinel on guard duty was the church he had seen from the main road; a very ancient one, he thought as he looked at the old brick, boulders and cut stone which made up its walls.

The churchyard gate creaked on its hinges as he opened it and passed into the neat and tidy burial ground. The grass between the graves was being cropped by two ragged old sheep that skittered away from him as he approached. The ancient headstones leant drunkenly towards the earth and the long-forgotten bones beneath them, and when he tried to read some of the names and dates they had once borne, most were worn away by the relentless effects of wind and rain.

He shivered and pulled up his collar. The wind was blowing

off the sea, and from where he stood on the higher ground he could just see the grey mass of water and the rainclouds scudding above. Not by any stretch of the imagination could this be called a pretty village, and yet it had an old-fashioned charm, an atmosphere of tradition and unshifting timelessness.

He walked back to the Ship Inn, and ducked his head as he entered the beamed and stone-flagged bar.

'Whoops! Mind your head!'

'I always do.' He smiled back at the red-haired young woman preparing the tables. 'I've had some nasty experiences with low doorways.'

'I bet.' She put down a tray of glasses and walked round to the back of the bar. 'What can I get for you, sir?'

'Bitter shandy, please. And are you serving lunch yet?'

'We will be.' She handed him the freshly pulled shandy. 'Ten, fifteen minutes and it'll be ready. Home-cooked, plain and simple.' She paused. 'Steak and kidney pudding? Game pie? Vegetarian hot pot?'

'All very tempting. I'll have game pie, please.'

She nodded. 'Are you new to the area?' She wrote down his order and slipped it through a hatch, then picked up a *Reserved* board and handed it to him, indicating that he should place it on a corner table set for two near the bar counter.

He grinned. 'However did you guess?'

'Accent,' she said wryly. 'You're not a Yorkshireman!'

'Is it so obvious? But I'm house-hunting, so I might turn into one.'

She laughed. 'I doubt it. Where are you looking? Somewhere round here, or Hornsea maybe?'

'Round here, or one of the other villages. On the coast; something oldish that I can renovate.' The bar was beginning to fill up, the door opening and closing as small groups of people, all dressed in warm coats and hats, began to arrive and find a table. Soon there was a hum of conversation; it was obviously a popular place. 'Are you local?' he asked quickly as she handed a brimming tankard to a man who hadn't needed to ask for his order. 'Would you know of anything?'

She nodded. 'I might,' she said, giving the customer his change. 'I'll speak to you in a minute.'

Chris went to his reserved table and took off his coat and scarf, hung them on the back of the chair and sat down to wait.

She was wearing a crisp white apron when she brought his pie and a dish of steaming vegetables. The meat was tender and the pastry light, the gravy thick with chopped onions and a hint of red wine, and though he was sated when he'd finished it he decided he'd have apple crumble nevertheless. The sweet white apple slices were spiced with a hint of nutmeg, and served with a separate jug of custard.

'Oh!' He breathed out when she came to take his empty dish. 'That was delicious. Did you cook it?'

Puzzled, she shook her head. 'No.'

He sighed. 'I was going to ask you to marry me if you'd said yes.'

'Dot cooked it, and she's still single. She's just gone home or I'd fetch her,' she teased. 'Although she prefers older men.' She smiled at the man wiping down the counter with a cloth. 'Isn't that right, Dad?'

'What?' He looked towards her, and then at Chris.

'Nothing.' She smiled. 'Just a joke. Would you like coffee?' she asked Chris.

'Please. Black. You've been very busy; is it always like this?' Chris aimed his question at her father, and saw a lounge area through an inner door behind the older man. It was fitted with beams and wooden floorboards, which to his carpenter's eye gave a comfortably old-fashioned feeling to the room.

Carriage lamps and horse brasses gleamed, and customers were sitting chatting at polished wood tables.

'Aye, generally, at 'weekend. We've a reputation for good food, and unless 'weather turns nasty we keep busy.' He turned his head towards a couple who were just leaving. 'Cheerio, Harry. See you, Annie.' Someone else waved at him, and he called 'Aye, right you are' in reply. The rush was over, apart from a few late customers who were settling into their corners and waiting for coffee to be brought. Chris heard 'Thanks, Gilbert' from a departing customer in the doorway, and 'Now then, Liz, you all right?' as the publican turned towards the hatch, where his daughter was putting pots of coffee on a tray. 'Tek your time; 'rush is done.'

Chris noted the accent. It was different from North Yorkshire, where his other grandparents had also lived, but it reminded him that his mother too sometimes let slip an odd word which marked her Yorkshire roots.

'Is this your regular job, or do you have another as well?' he asked Liz, sipping his coffee, which was hot and strong.

'Well, I live here with my dad.' She pulled out the other chair and sat down. 'It's our pub and I generally give him a hand at the weekend. I like the company. We get a nice crowd of people – mainly local, but regulars from Hull or Hornsea too.' She glanced at him quizzically. 'Are you serious about house-hunting? If you are, I might be able to help.'

'Really? Yes, perfectly serious. I've only recently come to live up here from London – I'm a teacher at Hull College. I'm in a rented flat in the city for the time being, but I'm looking to buy something a bit further out.'

'You might be in luck,' she said. 'I work for a Hull estate agency. We've a large range of properties in Hull and the East Riding, and some further afield too. If you tell me what you have in mind, I can look out some possibilities, and if there's anything you'd like to look at I'll arrange it for you.'

'That would be great,' he said. 'It must have been fate that sent me here instead of the other pub.'

'The Raven!' She laughed, and he noticed the flash of amber in her brown eyes. 'Their food's not as good as ours.'

Chris whistled softly as he drove back to town later that afternoon. Liz Rayner had offered to spend an hour on a whistle-stop tour of the area to show him some properties that were for sale, not all from the company she worked at.

She'd insisted on taking her car, and he'd noticed that she made a point of telling her father where they were going. Nothing he saw caught his imagination, but he felt that he was getting to know the district and with Liz to help him was on the right track to find the kind of property he wanted.

One of the cottages she'd shown him was practically on the cliff edge, teetering perilously as if waiting for the inevitable plunge down the crumbling cliff face to heap its remains in the oozing clay at the foot below. A rotting *For Sale* sign leant out over the edge, creaking mournfully.

'Mr Wainwright had to move out,' Liz said wistfully. 'He'd lived here man and boy, he says. He's been re-housed by the council and he's better off now than he ever was, but he comes here practically every day just to see if it's still here.'

'Well, it's not for me, thanks,' Chris said. 'I don't fancy waking up in the middle of the night with my feet wet.'

She'd driven him to two more nearby villages where other houses were on the market, but neither suited him, and then she'd taken him back to the Ship.

'I'm not in a desperate hurry,' he said as she pulled up outside the old inn. 'I've sold my London apartment, my furniture is in store, and the property I'm renting at present is not bad, so I can wait until the right thing comes along.'

'If you leave me your phone number, I'll let you know if anything comes on the market,' Liz said. 'I think I've got the idea of what might interest you. Nothing too modern, but something you can adapt to your own requirements.'

'I've got a better idea, though,' he said. 'Why don't you give me your phone number and perhaps come out for a meal with me?' He grinned hopefully. 'That is, unless you're married or anything?'

'No, I'm not "married or anything",' she answered. 'But I don't date my clients, especially not on a first meeting.'

'I'm not a client yet, am I?' he countered quickly. 'It's an enquiry.'

She wouldn't be drawn, but gave him the office number. He gave her his home number, told her the best times to reach him and reluctantly said goodbye, but added that he might be back next weekend.

He had just put his house key in the door when the phone began to ring and he ran up the stairs to answer it. It was Helena, and when the answering machine cut in she was not in a good humour. 'Damn,' he breathed; he'd fully intended to phone her during the week, but hadn't got round to it. He picked up the receiver. 'Helena, I'm so sorry,' he said. 'I really intended to ring this morning, but I went out early and I know you don't like to be disturbed too early on a Saturday.' He hesitated before adding, 'I've been house-hunting.'

'You really intend on staying there?' Her tone was incredulous and icy. 'I would have thought you'd have had enough by now. Wind and rain. I've seen the weather reports.'

'I've signed a contract, you know that. Besides, you don't know what it's like. You've never been this far north.'

'No, and neither do I want to. *This* is where everything happens, and where it happens is where I want to be. Anyhow, I just rang for a quick catch-up. I can't stop to talk; I'm going out to dinner.'

'Listen,' he said impulsively. 'Why don't you come up one weekend and I'll show you what it's like? Give you a chance to relax and breathe some sea air. That's where I've been today, to the seaside. It's so close.'

'You know very well that the only sea air I like to breathe is the sort that drifts over the side of a yacht in the middle of the Med. I'll catch you later.' She hung up on him and he thumped down the receiver in exasperation. Helena had no thought whatsoever for anyone else's feelings, and was always incredulous when her insensitivity was pointed out. She couldn't believe that anyone should care one way or another what other people's opinions might be, because she certainly didn't.

CHAPTER FOUR

Chris telephoned Liz at her office the following week, and although she didn't accept his offer of a meal out, she agreed to meet him to discuss his housing requirements.

'Thursday is my best day,' he said. 'What time do you close?'

He heard the hesitation, and then she said, 'We're a bit upside down just now as we're planning an office move, and I have another appointment on Thursday, but I could meet you at the Waterside hotel at five thirty. Do you know it?'

He said he'd see her there. He realized that he'd been rushing her with offers of meals out and decided to slow down, keep it strictly businesslike, but there was no denying he was very attracted to her. He had a sensation of suppressed excitement, like a youth on a first date.

You've been tied to one woman for far too long, he reflected as he made his way to the Waterside hotel on Thursday. He knew this was an exaggeration, but it was a fact that he and Helena had known each other a long time, although always without a commitment, especially on Helena's part. She had told him many years ago that they would only ever be friends; they had no obligation to each other whatsoever, for she didn't want to be tied down by anyone. He was fine with that, and friends they had remained ever since. The problem had been that no one else understood the nature of their bond, and even though there had often been friction in their relationship Helena had scared off anyone else who might have been interested in him.

He walked into the hotel, glancing around the reception area. It was very smart. The sofas and chairs he could see were mainly occupied, so he wandered into another room. It looked over the waterway, which was packed with yachts and motor vessels, and looked so interesting that he made a mental note that if Helena ever did come to visit, he would book her in here.

Liz was already there, sitting at a table by a long window with a pot of coffee and a pile of papers in front of her, totally absorbed and writing in a notebook.

He observed her for a few minutes before walking across. He'd had in his mind an image of a lively red-haired young woman in faded jeans and baggy sweater, as Liz had been when they'd met in the Ship Inn, and he wasn't quite prepared for the attractive young woman in front of him now. She was wearing a well-cut, honey-coloured suit, the jacket unbuttoned and showing a cream silk shirt beneath it. He noticed as he came closer that the colour toned with her skin, which was slightly sun-browned.

'Still working?' he said quietly.

She looked up and put out her hand. Her smile was wide and friendly. 'Hello. It's nice to see you again.'

Her hand was soft and warm, and when she removed it from his grasp he couldn't help but feel disappointed. She indicated the chair opposite. 'Come and sit down. I've not been here long but I thought I might as well finish off the day's notes.'

She stretched across the table and gathered up some papers. 'I've brought details of properties that might interest you. There's not much on the market just now, but these have been with us for a while, so there's a possibility that the prices will come down.'

He glanced through them and knew at once there was nothing that would interest him, but he nodded and said, 'I'll go through them when I get back to the flat.' He couldn't say home, for that it definitely wasn't, even though it held some of his belongings.

'Tell me what you have in mind,' she said. 'Are you sure you want to be out by the coast? The weather can be bad in winter.'

He gave her a grin; he certainly did, especially since meeting her. What an idiot he was, though; she might have a commitment already. She might not even live there, was perhaps just helping her father out at the Ship. What was it she had actually said?

'There's something about Tillington,' he said. 'I don't know what it is—'

'You know it's falling into the sea?' she interrupted. 'Anything you bought there would never be an investment. There'd be nothing to hand on to kids, or . . .' He heard a tremble in her voice and her words trailed away.

'I'm not married,' he said softly. 'I'm not committed to anyone. I applied for a job up here because I wanted a complete change from London. I was fed up with the constant hassle of traffic, and' – he paused for a second – 'needed to breathe in some good air, especially sea air.'

'But why here?'

'Initially I thought I'd go further north. Scarborough, or Whitby, maybe. My mother was born in Scarborough. But the job came up at Hull College and I took it and thought I'd come out and take a look at the coast.'

'What do you teach?'

'I'm a cabinet-maker by training and my intention was to set up in business somewhere, but then I read in the trade press that the college here was setting up various apprenticeship courses and would be needing staff, and it appealed to me. I thought that as this country is so short of craftsmen and there are so few apprenticeships I'd quite like to teach something worthwhile for a few years.'

He leant back in his chair, and when a waiter came by he asked for coffee and turned to Liz questioningly, but she shook her head.

'And have you teaching experience?'

'Yes,' he said. 'Fully qualified, but I've taught evening classes mainly so that I could continue with my other work.' His eyebrows rose. 'I don't think there were many other applicants for the job at the college and so I was offered the position.'

She smiled. 'I'm sure that's not true.'

'Well, maybe not, but my enthusiasm might have shown. I came a few days before the interview to look at Hull and I liked what I saw: a good art gallery, museums, notices of theatre events I'd like to go to. I looked at house prices too and they're much lower than in London, so when I was offered the job, I took it. Friends thought I was crazy coming north,' he added, 'but they had never been, so I didn't listen.'

Liz's back was to the window; the last of the sun's rays had dropped and glowed on her hair, increasing the fiery colour.

He blinked. 'I can't really explain why I felt I should come.' He didn't want to embarrass her with soul-searching, but he thought he knew the reason. It was a sense of belonging, a feeling of coming home; he'd felt it when he'd driven towards the coast and it had become even stronger since he'd met this smiling, responsive girl who was part of it.

'There's a house on the outskirts of Hornsea that might appeal to you,' she said. 'It's not that old, maybe fifties, but has potential for renovation. I've put the details there.' She indicated the pile of brochures and flyers she'd brought for him. 'If you're free at the weekend, I can show you. It's empty, so I have the keys. And there's another actually in Hornsea, but I'd have to phone the owners about that one first.'

'Well, all right, thanks,' he said reluctantly, 'though I still think I'd rather live in Tillington. There's something about the place. An old barn, maybe? Something a farmer doesn't use any more?'

She shook her head and laughed. 'Farmers don't have empty buildings standing about. They're all put to good use – for machinery, or hens, or for storing feed if nothing else,' she answered. 'It's an expensive, romantic notion, the idea of converting a barn into a house.' She sighed. 'But I'll put out a word. You never can tell. There just might be something, somewhere.'

It was cold and wet when he arrived in Tillington on the Saturday morning. Low grey clouds were being buffeted by the wind whistling off the sea.

'Are you quite sure you want to live here?' Liz joked. She'd been watching from the window of the Ship and came out to meet him, already dressed in her waterproof coat, woollen hat, gloves and sturdy boots. 'This is nothing to what we'll get once winter arrives. There are days when the mist rolls in to shore; others when the wind is so strong we can hardly stand up, or it's so cold you wish that you could be anywhere but here.'

'Yes,' he said, parking the car, knowing she'd want to use hers. 'I believe you, but I'm always up for a challenge.'

'*Allus*,' she corrected as she unlocked the doors.

'What?' He fastened his seat belt.

'Allus up for a challenge,' she said, backing out of her parking place. 'You'll have to learn the language if you come to live here.'

'Orless?' he said, and she laughed.

'Sounds like ollus,' she chuckled. 'I expect you'll learn if you're teaching youngsters in Hull, although there's a difference in dialect between Hull and Holderness.'

'Is there? Would I notice it?'

'Mebbe not. What you have to know is that Holderness is a mixture of nations; Teutonic, Saxon, Roman, Frisian, Celts – not in that order – and therefore our language is a jumble of each. Let's go to Hornsea first,' she went on, driving out of the village. 'I've arranged one viewing and I'll show you the other one as we pass. I have the keys if you'd like to look inside.'

'And when we come back I'd like to go on the beach,' he said, 'if I'm not taking up too much of your time?'

'I've told my boss I'm showing a client two houses this morning, so he'll be paying for my petrol.' She smiled. 'And our lunch.'

The bungalow they paused by was on the border of Hornsea, and in good condition, but on the edge of potential building land, with the implication that it might at some point be hemmed in by other houses. The other possibility was beautifully designed but very contemporary, so that didn't appeal either.

'Sorry,' he said on their return. 'I've taken up your precious weekend time.'

'Not at all,' she assured him. 'I hadn't anything else planned and I know now what you don't want. Shall I send you flyers if anything comes on the market that I think might be of interest?'

'Please, if you would. And would you mind if I called in to the Ship sometimes? To see you, I mean, maybe just have a chat? Would I be stepping on anyone's toes?'

She pulled into the pub car park, switched off the engine and unfastened her seat belt. Then she turned towards him. 'At the weekends, do you mean? Weekdays are generally busy for me, as I expect they are with you too.'

'Erm, yes – usually, but certainly not always. It's not as if I set homework, though sometimes I give out questionnaires.' He drew in a breath, unable to believe his luck that she didn't seem to be seeing anyone and hadn't rejected his suggestion; he was a stranger, after all. He daren't give her more than a few brief glances, yet wanted to gaze at her. What was happening? He'd never felt like this before.

'Do you still want to go down to the beach?'

'Sorry, what? Oh, the beach! Yes, please, if you have time. Are you not helping out with lunches?'

She got out of the car, closing and locking the doors after them. 'Not today I'm not; Dot is in. She wasn't well last week, that's why I was helping out on Saturday. Can you stay for lunch? Yes? I'll just go and tell her. The same as last time?'

He nodded. 'Please. Whatever's on the menu.'

He waited by the car until she came out again, feeling bewildered. Don't go blundering in, he told himself, just take things normally. But he didn't feel normal, he felt that something extraordinary was happening. He was house-hunting. He'd only ever had apartments before, and they'd never felt permanent, although he had bought the last one as an investment. He was putting down roots, thinking long-term; it was – what? He daren't voice it, didn't want to frighten her away, but it was a sense of belonging, and it was all due to this girl – no, young woman, who was her own positive person – walking towards him now.

CHAPTER FIVE

They walked out of the village, heads down against the battering north-easterly, and struck out along the road towards the cliff.

'There's a path here if you want to go right down to the beach,' Liz shouted against the wind. 'This was once a car park, but you wouldn't want to risk parking here now.'

He nodded; he'd seen the footpath when he came the first time.

'The cliffs are soft, especially after the rain,' she went on. 'Do you want to risk it?'

Along the top of the cliff were large crevices, deep fissures like cracks in a chocolate cake. One step on to the yielding surface and the unwary would find themselves hurtling down to the sands fifty feet below, but the path seemed stable and they scrambled down, grabbing for grassy handholds as they slipped and slithered on the oozing boulder clay down to the bottom.

'It's incredible.' Chris gazed up at the cliff. 'I wouldn't have believed this if I hadn't seen it for myself. All these cracks and crevices. The land is shifting, and slipping into the sea!'

'It's got worse over the last few years. There used to be a proper path with a hand rail when I was a child,' she said. 'All the schoolkids spent their holidays on the sands and we had visitors every summer, but the only people who come here now are dog walkers and fishermen, who take the wider footpath further along where the cliffs are lower.'

She gazed out over the sea and let out a soft sigh, and then looked north along the long sandy shore as if searching for something. Chris followed her gaze.

'We used to stay further up the coast every year when I was young,' he said. 'We stayed with our grandparents in Scarborough, but after they died we began going abroad. My parents wanted to be sure of the sun, but it was never as much fun as here.'

'Yes, you mentioned Scarborough before. So you're not quite a stranger after all?' She searched with the toe of her boot for a half-hidden shell.

'Not quite. My grandfather used to take my brother and me out fishing in his boat. It was a coble – one of the old wooden ones with an onboard motor – and we had a great time. Grandma used to pack a huge box of sandwiches and flasks of tea and lemonade and we would sit for a couple of hours bobbing up and down waiting for a catch. Grandpa always said that we'd catch mackerel one day, but we never did!' He smiled as he reminisced. 'Caught flounders once. There's nothing quite like the taste of freshly caught fish, is there? I haven't tasted anything like it in a long time.' He pulled a face. 'We weren't aware of pollution back then, of course.'

Liz agreed. 'Nowadays you'd throw back those that seemed dubious, but you can't always tell. It's almost a death wish, the way we're poisoning ourselves with chemicals and additives and polluting the very air that we breathe.' A note of cynicism crept into her voice. 'Yes, and sometimes we forget, because the air is good out here, and we think that because we can't smell or see the danger it isn't there. Sorry,' she apologized. 'I'm on my favourite soapbox. I was never out of the water when I was young, and now I never go in, so I feel deprived. But perversely' – she pulled a face – 'I eat the fish that my father catches. He says that our bodies will become able to deal with pollutants, but I don't think I believe that!'

They moved away from the cliffs and walked along the deserted beach close to the water's edge, Liz keeping her eyes peeled for the sea's treasure of pebbles, sea glass and shells. 'If you'd like to fish sometime, you might like to go out with my father,' she went on. 'He has a boat; keeps it up near Hornsea and takes it out when he has the time and the weather is OK. He never goes out if it's not. A friend loans him a tractor to pull the boat off the sands, and I'm sure they'd be glad of an extra pair of hands. There should be plenty of fish just now.'

'Really? That would be great. Life is getting better all the time.' He smiled at her. 'All I need now is somewhere to live.'

'You've only just started looking,' she said. 'Patience!' The wind was lessening a little, and she chanced a question. 'What do you do in your free time?'

He laughed. 'Now I'm going to sound really boring. My work is also my hobby. I love to work with wood, the feel and texture of it. That's why I want to find a house I can convert and have a workshop.' He moved away a couple of feet and pulled up a long piece of driftwood half hidden in the sand. 'Look at that! Such an odd shape. I could make something of that.'

The wood was dark and heavy with seawater, one end round and blunt with a hole pierced through it. The basic shape was curved, not straight, and tapered at the other end into a fin or a tail.

'It's a fish.' Liz took it from him to examine it.

'Or a seal,' he said, taking it back from her. 'Look; if it was softened and curved around the middle and the rough edges smoothed, make an eye at the opposite side and we have a seal.'

'You're an artist,' she said approvingly. 'We see seals here sometimes and often at Spurn Point, sunning themselves out on the flats waiting for the tide to turn. And have you ever heard of the drowned forest?'

'I don't think so.' He took his gaze off the wood and looked at her. 'Tell me.'

'Down towards the peninsula there are the remains of ancient forests that have been submerged in the sea for, oh, thousands of years – and at low spring tides you can sometimes see bits of tree stumps or pieces of bark protruding from the sand and clay.' She swallowed, a sudden tearful lump coming to her throat. 'I expect that's where Tillington will end up, just like Monkston, beneath the waves of the North Sea.' Conscious of his curious glance, she added quickly, 'Come on, let's see if Dot's got lunch ready for us.'

They scrambled back up the cliff face, and when they reached the top he said, 'I've been meaning to ask you who the old mill belongs to. I drove up the lane towards the church this morning. I don't know how I missed it before.'

'It's well hidden by the trees. I expect that's why you didn't notice it.' Liz spoke quietly, still subdued.

'So who does it belong to? It looks rather dilapidated.'

'The Reedbarrows live there. They're an old Tillington family.'

'The mill house needs a new roof,' he commented. 'There are a lot of missing pantiles.'

'Yes, it is a bit neglected.' She knew he was waiting to hear more, but she found nothing to say.

'So, would these Reedbarrows be willing to sell, do you think?' He stopped walking and turned so that she had to look at him or turn away herself.

'People don't just sell up because of a few broken tiles,' she said sharply. 'Not everyone is interested in making a quick sale for money's sake.'

He looked bewildered. 'I didn't mean . . . I just thought if they hadn't any money to spend on it . . . if maybe it was a liability, they might be prepared to sell. I'm sorry. I suppose if it's their family home they might rather stay with it falling around their ears than sell it to a stranger flashing his money about.'

'No, it's not like that.' She relented, sorry for her quick outburst. 'It isn't like that at all. There's . . . erm . . . a tricky situation here, and not one that I want to explain. But I can tell you for a fact that Foster's Mill is not for sale.'

'Foster's Mill? Not Reedbarrow's Mill?'

'No. Most definitely not.' Her mouth was stubbornly set, showing that she would not be drawn further.

Their conversation was rather strained as they walked up an easier slope towards the Ship. Chris felt he'd strayed into an area that was out of bounds with his questioning about the mill, but how was he supposed to know? There was obviously some conflict there, and he wondered whether to leave without waiting for lunch. He hesitated. Would he feel free to come back if they parted company on an issue that was nothing to do with him? Moreover, he was quietly amused by her dogged refusal to say any more and he liked the way her eyes flashed and her lips pouted when she was impassioned about something. What was it, he wondered.

'I'm glad you're back, Liz.' Her father looked up from behind the bar as they walked into the pub. 'Can you give me a hand with lunch? Dot's gone home; she's had another dizzy spell. I've told her she should go and see the GP, but you know what she's like!'

Liz took off her coat immediately and went into the kitchen, where they heard running water. 'Soup and cold meat?' she called through the hatch. 'There's some game pie left, and cheese flan. I'll make stuffed pancakes and a salad; that should be enough, don't you think?'

Chris turned towards her father. 'Can I help, or will I be in the way? I know how to pull a pint. I did some bar work when I was a student.'

'Well, if you wouldn't mind wiping down the tables and stacking some glasses it would be a great help. Thanks.'

Gilbert returned to serving the waiting customers and for the next hour Chris collected glasses, took orders for lunch and helped behind the bar when he could. He found he was enjoying himself, especially listening to the banter from some of the locals, who asked Gilbert where he'd found his posh barman. It was all very good-humoured and he wondered who it was who had fostered the legend of the taciturn Yorkshireman. There were certainly none in this bar.

When the pub had closed for the afternoon, the three of them moved into the sitting room and ate a late lunch of pancakes and salad and a pot of coffee.

'We don't have enough customers coming in to stay open all day.' Gilbert moved a curl of cress from his chin. 'Yes, they've changed 'licensing laws, but I can't afford to pay 'staff for hanging around twiddling their thumbs. It's different in 'summer, of course, when folk come to 'sands for a day out, but this might be 'last busy weekend for this year. It'll just be 'locals from now until next spring. I'm really grateful for 'way you mucked in, Chris. You were a big help.'

'Perhaps you'd take him fishing in return, Dad?' Liz asked. 'He wants to catch mackerel.' She smiled at Chris, raising her eyebrows, her humour apparently restored.

'Mm, I'm not sure about that,' her father pondered. 'You need to know what you're doing; there can be some rough weather blowing out there. I'm going out in 'morning, though,' he added. 'Weather's fairly calm at 'minute.'

'I've fished before, though not for a long time, and I'm a

strong swimmer. And,' Chris emphasized, surprising himself, 'if I manage to find a place out here, I'll think about buying a boat; a coble, probably.'

It was a startling idea, but it seemed right.

'You could stay the night,' Liz murmured when her father had gone into the kitchen for more coffee.

Chris grinned. 'That's the best offer I've had in a long time.'

Liz laughed and shook her head. 'No! But if you're still here in the morning, Dad'll ask you if you'd like to go with him if he thinks you'd be up to it. We've plenty of room,' she added. 'We used to take summer visitors when Mum was here, and still do occasionally. There's generally a bed made up.'

He nodded. 'I'd like to, and I could go on with my search for a property in the afternoon once we're back.'

She seemed to have forgiven his blunder over the mill; at least he hoped so. He really did want to know her; he was intrigued by her, and it was a fact that he hadn't ever felt like this before. The remark about continuing his search for a property was merely a ruse, for he hadn't previously been in any hurry at all to find a place to buy. But he definitely did want to get to know Liz.

CHAPTER SIX

Liz told her father that Chris was staying the night so that he could continue his house-hunting the next day.

'Is there a room made up?' Chris thought that Gilbert glanced rather suspiciously at him, and guessed that he was a protective father. Perhaps they didn't often get single males staying the night.

'Apart from the bed,' she replied. 'Mum only made the beds up when they were needed, so that they smelt of fresh lavender from the airing cupboard.' She smiled at her father, and he nodded.

'Well, if you're stopping, you can come fishing in 'morning if you've a mind to,' he told Chris. 'We'll be out for a couple of hours if 'weather stays clement. I can loan you some wet weather gear, but you'll have to be up early. No later than five.'

There was a fire lit in a small sitting room which was kept mostly for guests; it was furnished with comfy armchairs, a small dining table suitable for four, a bookcase filled with popular books and local magazines, and a television set. Chris saw a telephone and directory available for use on a shelf.

'You can have this to yourself, if you like,' Liz told him, showing him the room. 'Or you're welcome to sit in with me and Dad in our sitting room.'

He chose to sit with them; he was keen to get to know Liz and this seemed to be a perfect opportunity, though he was anxious not to come on too strong. He found her both appealing and intriguing, quite different from anyone else he had ever met. The rain came down in a steady torrent for the rest of the afternoon, gushing over the gutters and streaming down the windows, and he spent the time leafing through some brochures that Liz had in her briefcase. As the day drew on her father fell asleep, and she built up a wood fire in the grate before taking off her shoes and curling up in an armchair. 'I hope you don't get bored,' she said. 'You can watch television, if you like, or the newspapers are over on that chair.'

He shook his head. 'Unless you have other things to do, I'd rather talk to you.'

When she answered 'Not right now, I haven't', he stretched out his legs and relaxed. The room was warm and the furniture comfortable: deep armchairs with soft downy cushions that wrapped themselves around him. Pictures of ships in harbours or at sea decorated the walls, and there was a clutter of books in no particular order littering a wall of shelves.

A Chinese-style vase filled with chrysanthemums stood on an old wooden dresser, the rich heavy scent drifting across the room. He felt warm and sleepy, and drowsily he murmured, 'Who would have thought that only a few weeks ago I was driving along King's Road, dodging cyclists, sitting in queues of traffic and arriving home tired and wrecked?'

She nodded. 'London is such an exciting place to be, and has so much to see and do, but it's exhausting. I worked there for a couple of years. I thought at the time that I needed to get away from Yorkshire, to spread my wings, but I actually missed home and my dad more than I expected. I missed the sea too, the sound of it as much as the sight. I didn't feel as if I belonged in London at all, even though I had made friends. Then my brother – he was not much more than a schoolboy then – did the same thing and went off travelling, and I came back to be with my dad.'

She seemed pensive. 'Our family, the Foster Rayners, have lived in this district for such a long time, over a century now, but Dad and I are probably the last. Much of the land has disappeared over the edge, and it's – well, for some of us at least, in spite of that, it's as if we've been drawn back; as if there was some force compelling us to return.' She gave a slight shrug of her shoulders and raised her eyebrows. 'I expect that sounds rather other-worldly?'

'A bit,' he admitted, 'but it doesn't matter if it's important to you.' He had noticed when he first arrived that there was a feeling of agelessness in the village, almost as if time had slowed down. 'You've done the family research, I expect?'

'Some,' she said. 'I'd like to do more, but it's so time-consuming. I know that both the Fosters and the Rayners came from Hull originally. The first Foster I found was a whaling man who drowned at sea, but out at the village of Monkston, not at the fishing grounds. His daughter married a Rayner, but she kept the Foster name.'

'Really? Wasn't that unusual in those days?'

She smiled. 'That's what I thought. Sarah must have been a strong woman to do that!'

'Sarah?' he quizzed. 'You found her name?'

She nodded. 'And her brother and sister, but I lost sight of the sister. It was her brother Tom who built the mill here at Tillington.'

He sat up in his chair and glanced at her father, who was still asleep. 'So that's why it's still called Foster's Mill?'

'Yes,' she admitted. 'Dad is a direct descendant from the original Foster, who was called William. William was the miller

Tom's father, and Tom in turn had three sons, one of whom he named Thomas, and *he* married his cousin Sarah Rayner, which was how we got the name!' She laughed at his confused expression. 'It's all right, I'm not going to test you. I won't expect you to remember the lineage.'

'I daren't even mention the name Reedbarrow,' he confessed.

'No, please don't,' she said. 'That's a longer story, and there's no reason for you to be in the least interested.' She glanced up at the clock. 'Dad?' she said. 'Dad, it's five o'clock. Chris, can you lean across and give him a little pat on his arm?'

Chris did as he was bid and Gilbert shifted and opened his eyes. 'Have I been asleep?'

'Yes, Mr Rayner.' Chris smiled. 'There's something rather nice about a nap in the afternoon.'

'Mm.' Gilbert shuffled. 'Gilbert will suffice,' he said. 'Or Gil, but not Bert, if you don't mind.'

'So is Gilbert a Foster Rayner name too?' Chris questioned.

'I don't know,' Gilbert said, looking across at Liz. 'I don't really know or care about that sort of stuff. Liz and her mum used to trawl through 'records. We've all come from some-body or other, after all, and I expect we're bound to have got some of their genes and characteristics.' He shrugged and got to his feet. 'We are what we are,' he said pragmatically. 'Warts an' all.'

When Gilbert and Liz went through to the bar Chris sat gazing into the fire, rearranging his thoughts and making premature plans; he could hear another voice, a woman's, and then a man's: staff, he thought. Then he gave a sudden start. He should have telephoned Helena. He hadn't spoken to her for over a week, not since she'd hung up on him the last time; he'd left messages on her answering machine but she hadn't returned his calls. Perhaps he should phone her now, but she'd be sure to be going out. She always did at the weekend. But then, maybe not.

Helena could be so derisive; she'd scoffed when he told her he was thinking of taking a position at a school in the north. 'Why would you want to do that? There'd be no career advancement for you there. London – or the south at least – is where you'd make progress, surely?'

'You have no idea how education progresses,' he'd retaliated. 'And in any case, I'm looking for somewhere quieter than London; I'm fed up with the traffic and the crowds. I want a more peaceful life than I have now.'

'That's all very well,' she'd snapped back, 'but you don't have to travel so far. If you want to be nearer the coast, you could go to Brighton or Worthing.'

She told him that he was turning into a middle-aged man, and it was this comment that made up his mind. He was not yet thirty; he was going to make the move.

Liz came in as he was pondering. 'I'm thinking of getting a mobile phone,' he said. 'Do you use one? It seems like a good idea.'

'I don't, but Dad wants me to. He thinks that women should have them for when they're out on their own,' she said. 'But they weigh a ton, don't they?'

'I was thinking for convenience. It can take ages to find a telephone box sometimes – well, in London it does – and if you're driving you can't always find a place to stop; but yes, I think you should, and I will too.'

'If you want to use our phone, there's one over there.'

'Erm, no, it's fine. I'll wait until I get back to the flat. I was going to call a friend, but there's no hurry. Just a catch-up call.'

She nodded. 'Will you want dinner? Shall I set you a table, or have you made other plans? Some of the other villages have pubs that serve food, and a couple of places in Hornsea, but you'd probably have to book.'

'Oh . . . am I being presumptuous, or may I take you out to dinner? I'd like to,' he added quickly. 'You've been very generous with your time, showing me around the area, as well as arranging bed and board!'

She laughed. 'That wasn't too difficult,' she said. 'I know the area, and,' she added slyly, 'if we take you on our books and find a property for you—'

'I know,' he butted in. 'You'll earn commission!'

'Exactly.' She smiled. 'Well, Dot is in tonight, and Jack too, so I'm not needed, but to be honest I'd rather like a quiet night in. It's been a busy week; my boss is planning on moving office and most of the organizing will be on my shoulders, so I thought I'd cook an omelette or something in our own kitchen and have a glass of wine and read a book.' She hesitated for a second. 'If you'd like to join me you'd be very welcome, but if you'd like to go off and explore the local night life for yourself, that's fine too.'

She'd flushed slightly as she'd spoken, but he answered immediately. 'I'd love to join you, if I'm not intruding. Let me buy the wine, please.'

She requested a red, and when he'd bought it from Jack, who opened it for him, and said hello to the comely fair-haired woman he gathered was Dot, he went up to his room to wash and tidy himself. He hadn't brought a change of clothes, not knowing he would be staying out, so it was a very few minutes later that he went down again to find Liz chopping mushrooms.

She'd put out wine glasses and he poured the wine. 'It's great to be here,' he said, handing her a glass and raising his in a toast. 'It really is. Thank you. It's strange, but I feel very much at home here, as if I've known you a long time.'

Liz raised her glass in salutation and took a sip before

saying, her voice light but a gleam in her eyes, 'Perhaps we met in another life?'

He gazed at her. 'Who knows?' he said, and in that instant realized that he very much wanted to know her even better. Heavens, he thought, I've only just met her; how has this happened?

'You know,' Liz was sautéing mushrooms in a pan, 'I have to say in all honesty that you should think twice about buying a property in Tillington, even if one came up. There isn't much on the market, as you will realize, and what there is is underpriced, even compared with Hull. Conclusion: there must be something wrong with it. Oh, dash it. I haven't peeled the garlic.' She pushed two cloves towards him.

'I'll get a bargain whatever I buy,' he said, as he stripped off the thin skin, 'coming from the south.'

'Yes, but I think it's only fair to tell you the reason, even though my boss would think I'm crazy. I've tried to give you a hint, and anyway you'd find out sooner or later—'

He pressed the peeled garlic cloves with his thumb and dropped them into her pan. 'You're not telling me the plague's still here, are you?'

She laughed, but it had a hollow ring. 'It might just as well be, because we can't ever get anyone out here to listen to our problems.'

'So are you going to keep me in suspense? Is there a need to know?'

'You must have realized? You've seen it. The erosion! How can anyone sell or buy property here when the village is falling into the sea?'

'You can't be serious? It won't reach the village for decades, surely?'

She took the pan off the heat and faced him, her eyes wide. 'That's just what I mean. Nobody ever takes the situation seriously!' There was a catch in her voice and she took another drink from her wine, a longer one, until her glass was half finished. He topped it up.

'We're losing three metres of land a year. Matt Wilson across the road has lost nearly half of his paddock in the last three years but he only keeps hens and goats, so what does it matter, you might think? It matters to *him*. You've seen the old track – I showed it to you. My grandmother used to live in one of the cottages down there, her home all her life. Now they're all abandoned, desolate, waiting for the sea to swallow them up. But does that matter either? They're only bricks and cobbles!'

Her face was flushed with emotion, and he took the spatula which she was clutching so fiercely from her hand and impulsively kissed her.

'You're very passionate,' he said softly. 'Do you ever direct that passion elsewhere?'

CHAPTER SEVEN

Chris didn't sleep at all well that night. Liz had shown him to a guest room at the side of the building. 'This is the oldest part of the pub,' she'd told him. 'It dates back to when it was a coaching inn. I've put you in here because it has the biggest bed.'

The room was indeed dwarfed by the old-fashioned mahogany bed, which was draped with a brightly coloured patchwork quilt. Chris had sunk into the comfy mattress, but sleep wouldn't come, so he got up and looked out of the window into the yard, where a single lamp cast a moon-like circle of light on to what looked like a stable block. The rain, which had been steady, had now stopped, leaving the brick and concrete stable yard clean and shiny. A slight breeze was clearing the clouds from the night sky and revealing myriad stars.

He got back into bed and lay listening to the relentless, leaden thud of the sea and eventually drifted off into an uneasy sleep; a sleep disturbed by dreams where alone in a small boat he was tossed about in a sea of enormous waves which threatened to engulf him. The boat was being drawn nearer and nearer to a huge forest in the middle of an ocean, and at the edge of the forest was the figure of a woman, wailing and waving her arms and urging him to go back.

Liz carried her breakfast of tea and toast into the downstairs sitting room on a tray, spread the Sunday papers across the floor and settled down to enjoy the solitude. Her father and Chris had gone out early; she'd been vaguely conscious of low voices as she drowsed and had turned over, enjoying the comfort of the duvet and the satisfaction of being able to stay in bed for as long as she wanted. But at seven o'clock she got up, her sleepiness disrupted by meandering thoughts.

She paused in her reading of an article on the narrowing house price divisions between the north and south of the country, which she didn't believe, to lick a spot of marmalade from her finger.

Perhaps I was too hasty in saying I'd show him around, and as for inviting him to stay – he must have thought me pushy and I'm not! He's nice, though. The way his eyes crinkle at the corners when he laughs. Do everybody's do that? And that kiss! I know I laughed it off, but phew! And mobile phones? What was that about – just random? I'll bet it was a woman; bound to be – an attractive man like him!

The sun suddenly broke through, sending a flood of light into the room to highlight the yellow chrysanthemums on the dresser and reflect a scintillating flash across the glass of one of the pictures on the wall. She narrowed her eyes. Of course – those paintings I thought I saw in the office in High Street. These are the same scenes. She got up to look at them more closely. How strange that you can live with something all your life and never really see it, she thought.

Some of the pictures were original oils or engravings, some were old prints, but all were of ships. Whalers marooned in frozen waters, their masts and rigging covered in ice, and small stiff men standing on the floes with clubs and harpoons in their outstretched hands. Some were of schooners with their sails billowing; her father's favourite, a copy of Turner's gallant *Fighting Temeraire* with the golden sunset behind her. Whitby cobles beached for repair, their solemn masters caught in immortal pose gazing impassively at the artist with their hands dug deep into baggy trouser pockets and clay pipes in their mouths.

She moved across to another wall and gazed at the family photographs. There was one of her great-grandparents' wedding, the bride looking about sixteen in a dropped-waist gown of lace with a bandeau and veil on her head, and her new husband with a thick head of hair and shaggy moustache, wearing spats and looking much older than his years.

Everyone in the grainy picture stared solemnly and stiffly at the camera except one. It had been said by older relatives of her father that it was a young Tom Foster, except no one was sure which one, who peeked, grinning, over the top of a bridesmaid's shoulder.

She heard keys turn in the inn's front door and Dot singing slightly out of tune. 'Anybody up?' she heard her call and answered back, 'Yes, in here. Dad's gone fishing.'

Dot put her head round the sitting-room door. 'I was up early, so thought I might as well get started on 'pastry for lunch. I thought we'd have chicken and tarragon pie. I took three chickens out of 'freezer yesterday and they'll have thawed overnight, so I'll put 'oven on and get cracking. Roast potatoes and mash, carrots, Yorkshire pudding – I'll see what we've got. What do you think? Stuffed aubergine?'

'What would you stuff the aubergine with?'

'Rice . . . mebbe garlic.'

'Sounds lovely. Would you like a hand?'

'No thanks, love; you know I like to work on my own. Mebbe later if we get busy.'

Liz heaved a sigh of relief and cleared away her tray. I think I'll take a short walk, she thought as she went back upstairs.

Showered and dressed, she dried her hair, put on a trace of foundation and darkened her fair eyebrows. A tinge of sadness briefly enveloped her. *Summer's gone; my freckles have almost disappeared.*

She put on her coat, slipped into her trainers, called to Dot that she was going out and went out of the back door, leaving it on the latch.

A group of worshippers were leaving an early service as she passed the end of the church lane. She stopped briefly to talk to some of the congregation and pass the time of day, and then on impulse turned back and walked up to the mill.

With any luck, Carl might be out, she thought as she lifted the gate latch, but if he isn't I'll have to think of a reason to be here. The dog came bounding; he didn't bark at her but wriggled his rear and sniffed her boots.

'Funny that you don't bark when your master's out, Ben,' she said, fondling his ears. 'You're not much of a guard dog, are you?'

There was movement behind the dingy curtains when she knocked and Ben dutifully barked, but no one came to the door. She knocked again and found that it was open, so she pushed it cautiously and called out, 'Are you there, Jeannie?' There was no answer, but she caught sight of a movement in the kitchen. Ben did too, and with a grunt of pleasure he pushed past Liz and confronted the woman lurking in her hiding place behind the door.

'What do you want?' Jeannie stayed where she was, half hidden, one hand on the kitchen door as if about to close it.

'Nothing. I just wondered how you were. I haven't seen you about for ages.'

'No. Well, I don't get about much. I'm busy. I don't have 'time to stand and gossip like some folk.'

'Can I come in for a minute?' Liz eased herself into the small hallway, pushing to one side the muddy boots and broken tools and boxes of firewood which cluttered the floor, and refraining as far as possible from breathing in the aroma of stale fat and burnt toast emanating from the adjoining kitchen.

She tried to hide the gasp that came to her lips as the thin, dejected woman faced her. Jeannie's right eye and cheek was a swollen contusion of many shades, from scarlet spreading to mauve, to deepest purple.

'He always knows when to stop, doesn't he?' Liz's mouth trembled as she spoke. 'He never breaks anything, not even the skin.'

'I don't know what you're on about,' Jeannie answered sullenly. 'I tripped and fell.'

'You fell,' Liz repeated. 'Again? You should see somebody about all this falling. One of these days you really will hurt yourself.'

Jeannie didn't answer, and for a moment they both stood in silence before bending simultaneously to stroke Ben's head. Their hands touched and Jeannie snatched hers away with a sudden intake of breath.

'You can't go on like this, Jeannie,' Liz said softly. 'He'll kill you one day if he doesn't control his temper. What's upset him this time?'

Jeannie shook her head. 'No, he won't. It's like you say – he always stops in time.' She backed into the kitchen behind her. 'It's not his fault, you know; he can't help it.'

She's always protected him, Liz thought. That's why we didn't know anything was wrong; never suspected even when she worked for Dad at the pub and would suddenly grimace whilst vacuuming. Just a stitch, she'd say, it's nothing. Not until Dot, who always noticed what was going on around her, realized that there was something seriously amiss and told Liz and her father.

'Leave him,' Liz hissed now. 'Pack your bags and go.'

'Leave? Where would I go?'

'There are shelters for women in your position.' Liz was emphatic. 'I know there are. I'll find one for you.'

'You'll do no such thing! Mind your own damned business.' Jeannie began to cry. 'It's nowt to do wi' you or anybody else, and anyway, he'd onny find me and bring me back to this godforsaken dump.' She caught Liz's glance at the peeling wallpaper and shabby furniture. 'And I'm not just talking about 'house either. I wish 'whole damned village would fall into 'sea.'

'You don't mean that, Jeannie,' Liz said quietly. 'It's not a bad sort of place. Most of the people are all right; you just haven't got to know them.'

'It's all right for you to say.' Jeannie blew her nose on a tissue. 'You belong here,' she sneered. 'One of 'villagers.'

'There are other newcomers here,' Liz said defensively. 'They've learnt to mix, that's all. Look, why don't you come down to the Ship one night? When the bruising has cleared up,' she added hastily. 'It might cheer you up.'

Jeannie shook her head. 'I can't. Carl says I haven't to go near your place again. I don't know what he's got against you and your dad, but I daren't cross him.'

They both jumped as the door was suddenly flung open and Ben, mindful that he was out of bounds, shot out of the kitchen between Carl's legs and disappeared into the yard.

'What the hell is *she* doing here?' Carl glowered at Liz as, startled, the two women stared at him.

'I – called in for a chat,' Liz said nervously, trying to keep her voice steady. 'I haven't seen Jeannie about much recently.'

'She hasn't time for socializing, especially not wi' you and your kin, so clear off and don't come back.'

'I'll only leave if Jeannie wants me to.' Liz's temper began to rise. 'She's entitled to have friends call if she wants to.'

'You what? She's entitled to nowt unless I say so.' He pushed his face into hers and she backed away. 'This is *my* house.' He turned to Jeannie contemptuously. 'She's onny here for one thing. Don't think 'red-haired schemer's just being friendly like.' He laughed. 'She thinks she's a right to be here.' He wagged a finger a hair's breadth from Liz's nose and she backed away. 'Don't think I don't know what you're up to! But you've no chance. No chance at all.'

'You'd better go,' Jeannie said flatly. 'There's no sense in staying.'

Carl opened the door wider and stood aside as Liz passed by him, animosity showing in his narrowed eyes. Ben barked at her, showing his mettle, and escorted her to the gate. 'Oh, shut up, Ben,' she said irritably, and with a reproachful look from his soft brown eyes, the dog slunk away.

'Hey! Hey, come here, I want you a minute.' The old man beckoned her from the churchyard.

'Hello, Mr Wainwright. How are you?' The encounter with Carl Reedbarrow and Jeannie had shaken Liz and she wanted to be going on her way, but he was leaning on his stick waiting for her so she walked towards him.

'Well, I could be a lot better, I suppose,' he answered, 'but I could be a lot worse. You have to put up wi' things when you get to my age.'

'But you're keeping warm, are you? Plenty to eat?'

'Oh, I don't eat much. Not like when I was working; and I've got to cook for meself now that 'wife isn't here to do it for me.' He stroked his straggling droopy white moustache. 'I never know what to do for a change.'

She waited patiently for him to finish. 'Are you going to see your old house?' she asked.

'Aye, in a minute. If it's still there. But I wanted to have a word wi' you. To ask what you folks are going to do about it.'

She stared at him, uncomprehending. 'Er – hm. What do you mean? About what?'

He stared back at her, his eyes watering. 'Don't you understand English? I thought you'd had 'benefit of a good education?'

She didn't take offence. She'd known him all her life and many a time caught the sharpness of his tongue as well as the warmth of his generosity. But she sighed; something else to shatter her equilibrium, the pressure still prickly. 'Well, short of standing there all the winter holding it up, I don't know what I can do.'

He tutted. 'Well, I don't know! You young folk. Don't you know what I'm talking about?'

'I do know what you're talking about, Mr Wainwright, and I'm sorry, I really am.' Her face was deadly serious, her eyes anxious. 'But I don't think there's any chance at all of saving your house, and I believe that you're going to have to accept it. At the next big storm I'm afraid it will go over. But you've got a nice bungalow; you'll be safe there.'

'I know all that!' He banged his stick in exasperation. 'But what about 'rest of village houses? Are you going to let that happen? Are you going to let 'sea win?'

She faced him as he threw down the challenge. 'You know we've tried. We've tried as hard as we can to drum up support.' Her voice cracked. She was already highly strung up with emotion; this was one more thing to add to it.

'I made signs for the road,' she said defensively. 'We wrote to the council. Not that any of it did any good – nobody ever listens to us,' she added, feeling tears gathering behind her eyelids.

'I know you did,' he admitted. 'But time is running out; I don't mean for my house and some of 'others near by it's too late for them. Some of 'em are halfway over already.' He swung his stick in a wide arc. 'Everything will go: 'road, 'church, houses and farm land, everything. Mark my words, Elizabeth: in fifty years' time there'll be nothing left.'

Liz put her fingers to her brow and briefly closed her eyes as a sense of *déjà vu* swept over her. When she opened them she became aware of movement behind Mr Wainwright. Beyond the shadow of the lych-gate and his stooped shoulder she could dimly see two people standing in the shade of the church porch. The woman turned towards her and Liz gave an impulsive smile of recognition, which slowly faded as the pair grew dim and seemed to disperse in a thin trail of mist.

Mr Wainwright turned round and glanced towards the church to see what she was staring at, then looked questioningly back at Liz. 'Are you listening to what I'm saying, Elizabeth?'

'Yes. Yes, I am,' she answered vacantly. Mentally she gave herself a shake. 'You're absolutely right. We shouldn't have given up. We must start again.'

'Not *we*,' he said sharply. 'I'm too old. You young people, you're the ones to do it; start campaigning again before it's too late. You especially, Elizabeth. You must do it for them that's already in here as well as them that come after.'

She opened the gate and joined him and they wandered around the churchyard together. He had been tidying up his wife's grave and had placed poker-straight blue irises into a pierced bowl; he followed her towards a far corner where some of the gravestones were so old that only a few letters and the faintest of dates remained legible, whilst the newer ones, including her mother's, were still shiny and polished.

'This is where all you Foster Rayners are' – he pointed – 'and over there 'Reedbarrows.' He peered down. 'This one was drowned at sea, *Lost in the sake of Love*. What name does it say, Elizabeth? I can't read it.'

She leant towards the roughly etched stone. 'Joseph Reed-barrow,' she murmured. 'This is a Monkston grave,' she told Mr Wainwright. '*A much loved son and friend*.'

'They've all been here a long time,' he said. 'Longer than anybody else. Brought ower from 'owd Monkston church, I reckon.'

'Yes,' she said, suddenly overcome with emotion. 'And you're right: we can't let them down. Something must be done.'

CHAPTER EIGHT

It was nearly lunchtime when her father and Chris arrived back from their fishing trip. Chris seemed exhilarated, and her father anxious to know if the Ship had survived without him.

'We've not been all that busy,' Dot said through the hatch from the kitchen where she was making sandwiches. 'Though it might pick up now 'weather's clearing.'

'You all right, Sal?' Gilbert asked. 'You look a bit peaky.'

Chris raised his eyebrows at Liz as he removed his waterproofs. 'Sal?' he said.

Liz gave a slight shrug. 'Sarah Elizabeth,' she said. 'Yes, I'm all right,' she answered her father, 'but—'

'She was always Sarah,' Gilbert interrupted. 'Then one day, she was onny little, mebbe five or so, she announced that she was to be called Elizabeth.' He laughed. '"So we don't get mixed up," she said.'

Liz wrinkled her brow. *Yes, that was why. I'd almost forgotten. We'd arranged it between us as we sat on the stairs. My friend was called Sarah too, but it was the only name she had, whereas I had – have – two.* For some reason, she remembered the woman in the churchyard this morning.

55

'I've had rather a fraught morning, Dad. A confrontation with Carl Reedbarrow.'

Her father frowned, his eyes sharp. 'What's he been up to?'

'I suppose he thought I was interfering, which' – she hesitated – 'I probably was, but with the best of intentions.'

'What?' her father asked critically.

'He's given Jeannie a black eye, and bruised her face dreadfully.' She drew in a breath. 'She looks awful. I had to say something!'

'Why does she stay?' Gilbert raised his voice in anger. 'I don't understand. Why? I'd like to give him a taste of 'same. He was always a bad 'un!' He stopped as if he'd said too much.

'This is the couple at the mill,' Liz explained to Chris, who was looking bewildered.

Gilbert's face was flushed. 'Best not go there again,' he told Liz. 'I'll ask Dot to pop in and see if Jeannie's all right. He'll not say owt to her.'

He seemed about to say more, then shook his head as if in resignation, muttered something and sat down. 'Well, we had a right good morning, didn't we, Chris? He's got 'makings of a fisherman,' he told Liz. 'But we'll see how he shapes up when we go out again.'

'It was great,' Chris enthused, rubbing his hands together. 'I really enjoyed it. I'm marked out for flounder but we caught a couple of bass and whiting and your dad nabbed some cod, so not bad at all.'

Preoccupied and only half listening as the two men discussed the morning's success, Liz turned over in her mind the problem of Jeannie and whether she should get involved, and the conversation that Alf Wainwright had brought up.

She watched as first her father and then Chris closed their eyes and drifted off into a light doze, her father making soft puffing noises from trembling lips, his jaw slack and eyebrows rising and falling with each breath, whilst Chris lay perfectly still, his head against the chair back and his eyes closed.

She gazed at his dark curly hair, his straight nose and strong slim fingers; he suddenly opened his eyes and caught her looking at him. Leaning forward, he reached for her hands and took hold of them.

'Penny for them,' he said softly.

The movement disturbed her father, who humphed and cleared his throat as he sat up and rubbed his eyes. 'I must have nodded off. I should be going into 'bar.'

They both sat up as if caught out in a misdemeanour, and Chris's mouth turned up whimsically as he held her gaze. Liz looked away and spoke directly to her father. 'The other thing I wanted to tell you,' she said, conscious that Chris's eyes were still on her, 'is that Alf Wainwright has asked me to organize another petition to save the village from drowning.' The attention of the men was caught immediately, and she added, 'I've decided to call a public meeting.'

Gilbert rubbed his chin as if testing whether he needed a shave, which he did after his early morning start, then nodded. 'Right,' he said. 'I'll speak to 'other parish councillors at 'next meeting; in fact I'll call an extraordinary meeting. It's time we did something again. We've waited too long. We might almost be too late.'

'So it's really bad?' Chris asked. 'The village is in real danger?'

'It's not only one small village,' Liz told him. 'There's the road to think of; the main road along the coast that cuts through it. If that goes – and it will if the sea isn't stopped – then other villages, farms and land will go over the edge too. Hornsea will lose its livelihood.'

'We've had petitions before,' Gilbert broke in. 'We've had borough councillors here to take a look, and county. We've had experts and scientists from various universities, and they've all come up wi' ideas to stop the erosion, from a wall of tyres to dumping thousands of tons of shale waste. Everybody recognizes that there's a problem, but the biggest problem is that there isn't any money available, not for a little place like Tillington. We've got to make them look at 'bigger picture.'

'I suppose you've used the press?' Chris asked. 'It's absolutely essential to have media coverage on your side, plucking at the heartstrings and stressing the plight of local villagers about to lose their homes to the sea.'

Liz nodded. 'The press usually come, but the whole thing has gone off the boil over the last few years. Everyone is always busy with something else personal to them, but what's more personal than losing your home?'

She gazed into space and thought of the couple in the churchyard. Was that what happened to them? You can't tell just from a few words on a gravestone. She looked up. 'If we're going to do it again, we must get everyone on our side – Joe Public, newspapers, TV, everybody. We'll press for a meeting as soon as possible. This might be our last chance.'

Chris saw how fired up she was, how her eyes gleamed as if a spark hid within; you could almost say she had the bit between her teeth, he thought, but I'd really be mixing my metaphors then. Nevertheless, if anyone can succeed, I'm sure that she can. The downside, I fear, is that she won't have any room for a stranger hanging around and making demands on her time. I'll have to take a step back.

CHAPTER NINE

'Liz?' She'd just made herself a coffee and was about to take a bite of her lunchtime sandwich when Steve called across the room to her. 'Be a sport and go down to the High Street, will you? I want to know if the painters have finished yet, and if they haven't, tell them to get a move on! Then we can get the flooring down.'

She was tempted to tell him to send one of the junior secretaries, but she was curious to see how the work was progressing, so she agreed she would go when she'd finished her lunch. A few minutes later she put on her jacket, and leaving King Edward Street behind cut across the paved pedestrian areas towards the city centre, where Queen Victoria on her plinth reigned supreme over the citizens of Hull.

It was a sunny October day during the schools' half-term break, and there was almost a holiday atmosphere. The raised gardens at street corners were still massed with fading summer flowers, and the hanging baskets suspended from lampposts and shop doorways were garlanded with trailing ivy and orange and yellow nasturtium, bright red geranium and petunia.

The old shopping street of Whitefriargate, where once the white-robed monks had walked, was packed and she quickly cut down it, not looking in shop windows but turning towards the open market, which, she soon decided, was a mistake. She should have walked straight up and into the quieter Silver Street, rather than having to push her way through the crowds jostling round the stalls selling everything from tracksuits and sweaters to boots and shoes, pot plants and garden shrubs. Young mothers pushing prams dragged protesting children into the melee, whilst teenage youths and girls sprawled on benches with bags of chips or packets of crisps or melting ice cream, enjoying their days of freedom.

It was cooler once she had crossed over the road and through the narrow cobbled old street into High Street, and she fastened the top button of her jacket as she mounted the steps of the building they were to occupy. The door was open and she called out, but no one answered; perhaps the decorators had slipped to the pub across the road for a sandwich, she thought, though she could hear voices coming up from the floor below.

She called up to the top of the stairs and the floor they would be occupying but there was no reply, so she looked about her to assess the progress of the work. The painting seemed to be finished, and the rooms just needed to be cleared of rubbish and made ready for the office furniture to be put in place.

She went upstairs and was disappointed to see that a pile of newspapers and rolls of old flock wallpaper was scattered at the bottom of the loft ladder as if it had been thrown carelessly down from above and left where it lay. Making a mental note to advise Steve to remonstrate with the contractor, she started to riffle through the mess. Some of the yellowing newspapers looked very old, and the prices of the various goods mentioned in the advertisements made her smile, they were so ridiculously low. She put a few to one side, intending to take them back to the office to read, but the rest she simply pushed with the rolls of wallpaper into a heap for disposal.

One roll, though, seemed much thicker than the rest, and on inspection she discovered that it wasn't wallpaper but wrapping paper, which surely would be the thinner of the two. Curious, she put it to her eye and saw that inside was a cylinder and in the cylinder was the rolled edge of something of a quite different texture. Easing carefully on the loose edge, she kept on unwinding, and pulled.

It was as if all sound had stopped; as if she had suddenly lost her hearing. The hammering had ceased and the traffic was hushed; there was simply a murmuring of distant voices, a faint rattle of wheels on the cobbles outside, as the painting of a boy's face emerged.

She took it into the front room where there was more light, the better to see what she had found, and she caught her breath as the boy gazed searchingly at her from the cracked canvas. He was, she thought, just emerging into manhood; his skin was as fair as any young girl's could be, but his features already portrayed masculine strength, his blue eyes discerning and intelligent.

The artist had depicted him sitting relaxed, hatless, with a soft cravat wound around his throat above the high-cut velvet collar of his coat; a riding whip was held in one hand, his legs were clad in knee breeches and his boots were casually crossed.

'I know you,' she breathed. 'We've met before.' His face was so familiar to her it was like meeting someone she knew well, but whose name and habitation she had temporarily forgotten.

'Of course,' she whispered. 'It was here, wasn't it? The first time I came here. Only you were older; a grown man.' She smiled down at the painting as she remembered again the face of the fair-haired man seated at the desk in the back room overlooking the Old Harbour. 'Somewhere else also, but where?'

The front door banged and the sound of feet running up the stairs disturbed her. Hurriedly, she slid the thin canvas under the newspapers she meant to keep, and put them next to her bag.

A grey-haired man clad in overalls looked into the room. 'Hello? Have you come to help?'

'No, I haven't.' She grinned. 'Steve Black asked me to look in and ask when you think you might be finished.'

'Decorators have finished. They'll be back with the van later today to fetch their stuff. I'm the electrician. I've been up in 'loft to check 'electrics and everything's OK up there. Plumber's been and gone, so I'll just go up and close 'hatch and I'm done.'

When he came down again he indicated the pile of discarded papers with his foot. 'I threw this lot down,' he said. 'Beats me why folk keep so much rubbish. They don't seem to realize what a fire hazard it is. I'll clear it up afore I go and put it into 'skip with 'other stuff.'

Relief poured over her that she'd got there in time. 'I've kept some of the old newspapers to read, if that's all right? I'll take them back to the office if nobody wants them. You should see the house prices,' she added. 'Steve won't believe them.'

'Aye, well, most folk couldn't afford to buy a house on 'wages they earned pre-war and just after, you know; everybody rented. Amazing how things have changed, never mind that most of 'reading in them old newspapers seems like onny yesterday to some of us old fellas.'

She found a plastic bag in a cupboard and put the newspapers she was keeping in it, and whilst the electrician was clearing away the rest carefully placed the portrait between them. With suppressed excitement, she called out 'Cheerio' and left, walking swiftly back to where she had parked her car.

I'm taking you home with me, she deliberated, as she carefully put the bag into the car boot. The last place you'll go to is the skip!

'Tell you what, Liz.' Steve tapped her desk with a pencil as she cleared it at the end of the day. 'Can you stay in town? We need to discuss the move, so what about something to eat?'

'When? Tonight?'

'Well, we have to get a move on if we're to be in in a fortnight.'

'There's not that much to do,' she objected. 'We're on top of most things; at least I am.' She sighed. She knew him of old, asking her out on the pretext of discussing business, but he'd been in the middle of divorce proceedings then and she had always managed to keep him at arm's length. 'Are you sure there's no ulterior motive?'

'Well, there might have been,' he said disarmingly. 'I'm a free man now. But no, no ulterior motive, though I promise you won't have to pay for your dinner.'

She gave him a derisory glance, but reluctantly agreed. 'Shall I book somewhere?' At least then I can choose the time and place, she considered. 'What about Louis? He'll be open in an hour. I mustn't be late, as I told my dad I'd give him a hand in the bar.' Which was a downright lie, but a useful ploy.

'Good idea. I fancy a large dish of pasta and a bottle of red.'

'Well, it'll be tonic water for me. I'll be driving, and the nights are getting darker much earlier.'

He nodded. He lived west of Hull and could call a taxi if need be, but he might not; he was a chancer, was Steve, and she wasn't.

'By the way,' he said, 'did anything happen with that guy who turned up wanting something out your way?'

She took a second before answering and assumed a vacant

contemplation. 'Erm, Chris Burton? No, there's nothing on the market to suit him. He wants something to convert.'

'Hm! There must be something. He's got money available, has he?'

'I believe so. He's sold his own property.' She was reluctant to discuss him. He had left after the weekend he'd stayed, leaving her his telephone number to ring if anything turned up, but nothing had so there'd been no reason to call. It was almost three weeks now and she had heard nothing from him. There was no reason why he should call, of course, but she had thought . . . well, what had she thought? Just because he'd been an overnight paying guest was no reason to expect him to be in touch.

'We don't want him going elsewhere, do we?' Steve said thoughtfully. 'We must see what we can find.'

'There's nothing,' she said. 'I've looked. He's told me exactly what he wants and there's nothing!'

'What does he do? His job, I mean.'

'He's a teacher,' she said briefly. 'Woodwork.'

'Oh, boring!' he said dismissively. 'Come on then, get your coat.'

CHAPTER TEN

She'd made him wait whilst she phoned the restaurant to make the booking and then rang her father to tell him she'd be late, but not too late. It was not quite six o'clock so she reckoned she'd be home by ten.

'You go on, Steve. I'll catch you up,' she said, knowing that he'd try to persuade her to stay later if he were driving.

He was waiting outside the small Italian restaurant when she walked up after parking her car. 'That's a waste of petrol,' he said. 'You do know that, don't you?'

'No, it's not,' she said, indicating he should open the door to let them in. 'We live in different directions.'

It was fortunate that they had booked, she thought, as contrary to expectations the restaurant was busy, even though they had come early. Most of the tables were full, mainly with families with children who were vigorously tackling banana splits and zabaglione.

'Oh, no! Is it a school holiday or something? I didn't expect to see all these kids here.' Steve was disgruntled as he stared around the room.

'They will be leaving soon, sir,' the proprietor told him. 'We have a special menu on for children today, but soon they will be tucked up in bed and we will be quiet again.' Louis passed them each a menu. 'A bottle of Chianti for you, sir?'

Steve nodded, grimacing. 'A few of them will be sick before then, too, by the look of them.' He cast a glance at a small girl at the next table with ice cream lathered around her face. She saw him watching her and opening her mouth wide she wiped her tongue around her lips, successfully scooping up the creamy froth. Steve shuddered and looked away, waiting for his glass to be completely filled when the wine was poured, whilst Liz put her hand over hers when it was only half full.

She laughed. 'It's pretty obvious you'll never make a family man.'

'You're dead right,' he said. 'Marriage doesn't work for me, so from now on it's no strings. Love 'em and leave 'em.' He leant over and put his hand on her knee. 'I'm convinced there are many women who feel the same.' He gave her a wink. 'Only they daren't admit it.'

She removed his hand. 'You might be right,' she said. 'But it's manners to ask. Now what about work? Isn't that why we're here?'

He sighed. 'You're such a spoilsport, Liz. You never give me any encouragement.'

Their table was in the middle of the restaurant and Steve's chair was facing the door, and she sensed his attention wavering from time to time as he observed other diners coming and going. One of the things that annoyed her about him – in fact one of many, she thought – was that although he could be charming and studiously considerate, his attention was often elsewhere. Now she saw his eyes widen and his mouth purse in an appreciative sigh.

'Wow', he breathed. 'Will you take a look at that!'

Obligingly Liz swivelled round. A tall blonde woman, her hair swinging straight and shiny to her shoulders with not a single strand out of place, wearing a black jacket with a skirt just touching her knees on legs that went on for ever, had come through the door. As if knowing that all male eyes were fixed longingly upon her, she gazed provocatively around the room whilst the waiter found her a table. Liz's face froze as she saw her escort take her by the elbow and usher her forward in response to the waiter's signal.

'There's something about a blonde,' Steve began; then he looked at Liz and saw her expression. 'Do you know her?' he asked hopefully.

'Him,' she said. 'That's Chris Burton. He's the one who wants to buy something in Tillington.'

Her mouth was suddenly dry and she took a sip of wine. *I might have known he'd have good taste in women.* She watched him pull out a chair for his companion and then sit down himself, and as his gaze ran round the restaurant she looked away and gave Steve her undivided attention.

'He won't settle in Tillington with a bird like that,' he murmured admiringly.

'Don't be coarse, it doesn't suit you,' she replied cuttingly, although she knew that her boss's opinion of women as a whole was low. His professed admiration of her stemmed, she knew, only from her efficient business capabilities – and he paid her well for those – and her ability to keep his amorous advances at bay. Yet, in spite of his low schoolboy wit and his arrogance, she felt a grudging humorous fondness for him. His pretentious brashness, when he was in the right mood, could be coupled with a preponderance of charm.

He turned on the charm now as their order was brought, and smilingly observed, 'He's coming this way, Liz. I think you might have scored. Perhaps he'll introduce us to his friend!'

'You are a pain, Steve.' She smiled a yes to the waiter for extra parmesan on her lasagne while murmuring 'I don't know why I tolerate you' under her breath to Steve, and waited for the moment she could look up in surprise and greet Chris

Burton. When it came she was pleased after all that she was in the company of Steve, who in spite of everything else was confident and self-assured, and well dressed in his grey business suit. He had unfastened the neck of his striped shirt and put his tie in his pocket, and as he rose to shake hands with Chris as Liz introduced them he was almost, but not quite, as tall as Chris was.

Chris looked rather drawn, she thought, and ill at ease as he glanced towards his table. 'I have a friend from London staying for the weekend.' Awkwardly he rattled some coins in his pocket. 'If the weather holds I thought we might drive over to the coast. She wants to compare Tillington with Brighton.'

Liz laughed. 'No comparison!' She glanced significantly at Steve. 'I'm not sure if I'll be there, but call in at the Ship if you happen to be passing.'

'Thanks, we will.' He turned to leave, then glanced back at her. 'How is your friend, by the way?'

'My friend?' She was puzzled.

'The one at the mill. I wondered how she was.'

'Oh, Jeannie! I think she's all right. Dot has been to see her.'

He nodded and moved away, then looked back at her. He looked pensive, and too late Liz thought she knew why.

I haven't given Jeannie a thought since I last saw her and yet someone who doesn't know her is concerned.

'What was all that about?' Steve was curious. 'I didn't know there was a mill in Tillington.'

'Yes,' she said vaguely. 'It's very old.' She knew he wouldn't be interested in its history, only its value. She took a deep breath. 'And the man who lives there is an intimidating bully who beats up his girlfriend.' She pushed away her plate. 'I seem to have lost my appetite.'

'And is there land with this mill?' He was about to pour her more wine, but she placed her hand over the glass.

'I have to drive home. I daren't risk another. There are too many deep ditches in Holderness.'

He smiled and took her hand. 'Just a few minutes ago I got the feeling that you might not be going home tonight. That you might be keeping me company?'

She smiled back and placed her other hand over his. Leaning towards him so that her lips were close to his ear, she breathed softly, 'I don't know how you could be so mistaken.'

Damn. Damn. *Damn!* Chris weaved his way back through the tables. Frustration knotted his insides and, glowering, he sat down.

'Well?' Helena's eyebrows arched.

'Well what?' *I hope she's not going to start again.*

'Who's your redhead?'

'She's not *my* redhead. I told you: she's an estate agent. She's trying to find me a house.' He ordered their food and a carafe of house red. 'I just wanted to say hello, that's all.'

'Taking a personal interest, is she?' Helena looked across the room from beneath her long lashes. 'Who's the guy she's with?'

'Ha! I might have known you'd take an interest there! Liked the cut of his suit, did you?'

'I did. I can smell money, and he wasn't wearing anything fake!'

'Well, you'd know about that if anyone does.' His mood was disintegrating. He'd had misgivings over this visit, but Helena had been so enthusiastic on the telephone that he'd felt his qualms were unjustified. Unfortunately, from the moment she had arrived on his doorstep nearly two hours late and in a furious temper over the amount of traffic, the goddamned state of the roads and the difficulty of finding his flat, tucked away as it was in the middle of an avenue miles long where none of the houses were numbered, or only some of them, she had gone on and on, and it hit him once more just how disruptive and provoking she could be.

'I told you to take the A1,' he'd said when she'd arrived, as he'd ushered her into the hall and then upstairs. 'The traffic is always bad on the M1.'

But she hadn't listened; she'd demanded a drink and a shower, and he was out of gin and the shower was temperamental and the water was cold. He'd put his arms around her to give her a hug, because he really was very fond of her, but she'd pushed him away. 'Don't rush me, for heaven's sake. I've only just got here,' and he knew they were in for a fraught weekend, just like so many others.

He'd planned to cook her dinner, he'd bought food and wine – flowers, even, for the table – and thought she would like the chance to relax and chat, but on second thoughts had decided that it would be better if they went out. At least they wouldn't argue if they were somewhere public, and there were some good restaurants and bistros in the area that he thought she would like.

He'd felt a sudden uplifting of spirits as he'd come into the restaurant and seen Liz; her back was to him but he would have known her red hair anywhere. But his mood had taken a nosedive when he'd noticed her companion, and sank even further as he took his seat at the table and glanced casually round, only to see that they were in lively conversation, as if they knew each other well. And obviously they did. He'd seen that look between them when he mentioned going to Tillington, and the gleam in the guy's eyes as if he'd been promised a treat.

'Well, are you going to talk to me or are you going to sulk all night?' Helena flicked a long strand of hair behind her ear, showing an ornate silver and amethyst earring which hung almost down to her shoulder.

'I am *not* sulking.' He tried to catch the waiter's eye.

'You are sulking – and don't order another house wine. It's vile. Get a Chianti – if they have it,' she added peevishly.

'Sure, if you like, though the house red seems OK to me.' He shrugged. 'I can get drunk on Chianti as fast as I can on house plonk.'

'I'm ghastly, aren't I?' Helena suddenly reached out and touched his cheek. 'I'm sorry, Chris. You deserve someone nicer than me. I just can't help baiting you. You leave yourself wide open.'

She looked so beautiful: her pale oval face, large guileless eyes, perfectly shaped mouth. He watched her and felt sad. There was something missing. It was as if an artist had caught a perfect likeness on canvas and yet had failed to find the essential pigment which would give the subject an essence of humanity, the warm breath of life.

'No. No, you're not,' he said wearily, the fight suddenly gone out of him. 'You're not ghastly, at least not all of the time, but you just don't care about anybody or anything, and – and I've had enough of squabbling and arguing, that's all.'

She gazed at him for what seemed like a long moment. 'You're wrong, Chris. I do care. I care about you, and I know that sooner or later I shall hurt you and then you'll hate me and I don't want that. You're my best friend.'

'Is that it, then?' he said lightly. 'The end of a perfect relationship?'

She closed her eyes, and when she opened them she was smiling. 'What arguments we've had; what fights, and I've enjoyed every one of them, whilst you, poor darling, have hated every minute. Perfect relationship? What a laugh!'

The waiter brought their food and Chris ordered Chianti and clean glasses and the waiter poured for them both. Helena lifted her glass and gazed at Chris over the rim, her eyes holding only amusement, no hint of remorse. 'If you're going to catch your redhead, you'll have to get a move on.'

'I told you, she's not my redhead,' he retaliated. 'I hardly know her.' Nevertheless he felt faint stirrings of pleasure until he followed Helena's prompting gaze and saw Liz whispering into Steve Black's ear.

CHAPTER ELEVEN

'It's a dry night; we should get a good turnout.'

Liz nodded in the darkness as she and her father strode towards the village hall, catching up with other villagers all busily discussing the issue which one way or another would affect their lives.

'Will you open the proceedings, Liz,' her father went on, 'seeing as you called the meeting? Introduce the councillors and suchlike?'

'Can do, if you like, and then what? Can everyone have a say?'

'Well, if we're not careful things could get out of hand and we'll have a shouting match. Feelings are running high, so what I'd suggest is that after you've made 'introductions and told everyone why we're here, you ask 'parish chairman to speak next, and then 'borough councillor. He can ask 'county representative for his views and then we'll throw it open to 'hall.'

Alf Wainwright was already at the door, urging people to come along inside and waving his walking stick like a doomsday prophet. The hall was already half full, some people jostling for particular seats whilst others leant against the walls, either to see better or to make a quick getaway. Liz smiled and nudged her father when she saw Mr Wainwright's tweed cap saving the middle chair of the front row.

A tall thin man in a waxed jacket with a camera round his neck and a notebook and pencil in his hand was talking to George Bennett, the parish chairman. He looked her way as Mr Bennett pointed her out and came straight across to them. 'Hello. I'm Jim Jackson – we spoke on the phone. Can I have a word with you after the meeting? I'll need names and photographs to add to the report.'

Liz nodded in agreement. She was beginning to feel nervous. There were more supporters here than she had anticipated. *I feel sick. I've set the ball rolling, but what now? What if it comes to nothing like last time? Will they blame me for being incompetent?*

She climbed the steps to the stage and stood waiting for people to settle. Practically all the chairs were taken, and people were standing at the back of the hall as the councillors and other officials made their way on to the stage and took their seats. Liz remained standing, and gazed down. *They're not all Tillington people. There are some I don't know, but there's the butcher from Hornsea, and the cobbler from Aldbrough.*

She saw other familiar faces from neighbouring villages, coastal and inland, and was gratified and a little emotional when she realized that word had already got around and Tillington wasn't standing alone.

She moved to the front of the stage and wished she had a microphone. Why hadn't someone thought of that?

'Ladies and gentleman.' She had a good clear voice. 'Thank you all very much for coming tonight, and special thanks to the people I see who are not from Tillington, but good neighbours from near by who have come to give us their support because they too are aware of the impact the present situation could have on all our lives.'

Gradually her diffidence faded away. Gaining confidence

as she saw the expectant faces turned up towards her, she went on.

'As you are all aware, the problem of erosion has been around for a long time. For most of our lives, in fact, certainly for mine, my parents', my grandparents' and great-grandparents' too; and as you already know, our villages have been lost, succumbing to the sea since Roman times. But now it's time for us to fight back, to save our homes, our church, our village school, and the livelihoods of all who live here.' She licked her lips and turned to the councillors seated behind her. 'We have tried petitions before, and we are mindful that officialdom is aware of our situation . . .' There were a few disgruntled rumblings from the body of the hall, and she raised her voice. '. . . but we need action *now*, before it is too late.'

Calls of 'Hear hear' and clapping erupted round the room and she held up her hand to quieten them. 'The sea has a voracious appetite and we know from our family histories that many villages where our ancestors were born and raised have been washed away by the power of the waves to lie forgotten at the bottom of the sea.' She looked across the hall. A woman was wiping her eyes; Mr Wainwright was vigorously blowing his nose. Carl Reedbarrow leant languorously against the wall, a limp unlit cigarette drooping from the corner of his mouth; to the left of him was Chris. So he did come after all.

The audience watched her silently; even the children were quiet. Sarah smiled gently at her from the middle of the hall, as did the fair-headed man at her side. Liz faltered and looked again, but her own eyes were misty and she could no longer see them.

She took a deep breath and continued. 'Those villages, each of which once had a heart and a community, are now remembered only as names of offshore gas fields.' She paused for effect. 'Are we going to let this happen to Tillington? Is our village going to be forgotten too?'

A great shout of 'No! No!' went up. She was startled by its intensity, its fervour, and sat down abruptly in some confusion, quite forgetting to introduce the chairman. Fortunately, George Bennett rose to his feet unprompted and nodded his thanks to her. His short portly figure seemed to swell as he launched into a vigorous message of support from the parish council. He seemed to have been inspired by Liz's speech, and promised to lead them to victory in the struggle ahead. 'But we at the parish council can't do it alone,' he ended in ringing tones. 'We must have your full support! Your commitment to fight with us! You must be the foot soldiers as we lead you forward through the battle lines of county hall and government bureaucracy!'

'As long as you're in 'firing line, George, we're right behind you,' a lone voice shouted through the cheers. A ripple of laughter and sly jokes about joining-up papers, uniforms and rifles filtered up to the stage and Liz bent her head to hear her father whisper, 'George allus thought of himself as officer material, but he didn't get further than corporal.'

'Well, he's about to get himself an army now,' she whispered back. 'They're very enthusiastic.'

Next came the borough representative, who pledged their support but warned that there was little money available. The county council official stated that there would certainly be some money on offer but not enough, and they would have to look elsewhere for grants.

'Unofficially I can tell you that the more pressure you bring to bear, the more noise you make, the more likely you are to succeed. If you give up, then nobody's going to help you.'

A man leaning against the back wall stood forward. 'It's all very well you saying that,' he said, jabbing a finger. 'But we elected you to work for us, not to sit on your backsides all day in County Hall while we do all 'ruddy donkey work.' He looked round at his neighbours for support, his face flushed.

'That's right,' shouted another. 'I pay my taxes like everybody else here; it's time we saw summat for our money. They'll be asking us to build our own damned wall next, let alone find 'money for it.'

Build our own wall. Build our own wall. Build our own wall. The words pounded in Liz's head like surf on the shore and she pressed her fingers to her ears to stop it.

Gilbert stood up. 'Nobody is asking anybody for money; money isn't what we came here for tonight. We don't have anything like 'kind of money that will be required for the project that we are asking for. What we must have is total commitment from everybody. No half-hearted support. We must have a pledge, a guarantee from you all, that we will all work together to achieve our goal. Otherwise it's like Liz says: we'll finish up being rehoused elsewhere and 'village will be at 'bottom of 'cliffs.'

Voices were raised, urgent questions being asked. He held up his hand. 'Just a minute, please. You can all have a turn, but can we hear Mr Wainwright first? He is our most senior resident and as such should be listened to. Mr Wainwright – Alf – you wanted to say something?'

The old man had been bobbing up and down, trying to attract attention. 'It's like I said to somebody 'other day. You young people have to do it. Likes of me can't. I wish I could, but I'm too old now, so you lot have to do summat for all of us, for yourselves and for 'young bairns who'll come along after.'

His voice was thin and people strained to hear. 'Never mind asking folk at County Hall to sort it out while you sit comfortable by your firesides,' he went on. 'You'll nivver get owt done that way. It's up to all of you to start 'ball rolling; that's what my old da used to say, and he was a Tillington man and proud of it. Do it for these young bairns that have come tonight. Think o' them, cos if you don't they won't have a fireside to sit by in their old age, not in Tillington anyroad!'

He sat down abruptly, reaching into his coat pocket and bringing out a clean white handkerchief. There was a poignant silence and then the sound of a single pair of hands clapping, then another and another, until everyone in the hall was clapping and stamping their feet and Mr Wainwright was blowing his nose even more vigorously as people leant towards him to pat his arms, grip his shoulders. Liz felt a tear trickle down her cheek and daren't look at her father, always a demonstrative man. Instead she looked across the hall and saw Chris watching her. He smiled as she caught his gaze and gave her a thumbs-up, and her tears flowed in earnest.

'I'll have to go, Liz.' Her father shrugged into his coat. 'With a bit of luck they'll all be flocking down to 'Ship.'

'You go, then. I'll help to put the chairs away.'

'Nice bit of publicity there.' Chris came across to her as she watched Alf Wainwright perched solidly on his chair, his chin determinedly set and a hand firmly clasping his stick, with the four-year-old Johnson twins standing on either side of him as he posed for the journalist.

'Yes,' she murmured. 'The new and old generations. I hope they get the headline right.'

'You should write it for them; you're very good. That was a rousing speech you made, and there were a few wet eyes around.'

She was embarrassed. 'I only said what I feel.' She hesitated. 'Someone, can't recall who, said we should play on other people's emotions. They were right, I think.'

He nodded, and picked up a couple of chairs to stack with others at the side of the hall. 'I'll walk back with you when you've finished,' he said. 'My car's parked at your pub.'

A sea fret had rolled in whilst everyone was inside; it hung cold and damp, shrouding the buildings and clinging in wet strands around the streetlamps. Chris pulled his coat collar up around his ears. 'I'll have to get a flat cap if I come to live in Tillington if this is the sort of weather to expect.'

'And a whippet,' Liz countered. 'Are you still keen? I wasn't sure you'd still want to come.'

'Why not? There haven't been any cliff falls recently, have there?'

'N-no. Did your friend like Tillington?'

'No, she hated it. She thought it was desolate and that I was mad to even consider coming here. But I knew she wouldn't like it. She's a city girl, always has been. We didn't call in because I took her up to see Hornsea.' He grinned. 'She didn't like that either.'

'Oh!' She felt strange stirrings in the pit of her stomach. 'I saw you at the top of Church Lane when I came back from the beach that day.' I saw you, she thought, and walked round the village again, killing time, hoping you would have gone by the time I came back; I thought you were showing her the village as a potential place to come and live. 'Were you looking at the view or the mill?' she asked. My mill, she thought.

'The mill,' he said. 'I wanted to show it to Helena, but she wasn't impressed. We saw your friend Jeannie, though. I don't think she was too happy about us peering over her gate.'

They were at the entrance to the pub yard. Liz put her hand in her pocket for the key to the side door.

'Could I persuade you to invite me in? For a cup of tea?' He stood over her, his hair damp and curly, a winning smile on his face.

'All right, but I shan't let you stay long. We move to our new office tomorrow and I have to be in early.'

'I promise I won't overstay my welcome.' His smile grew wider, and the sensation inside her grew stronger, her senses tingling as she fumbled with the lock on the door.

They sat in the warm kitchen, shaking off the dampness in front of the Aga, drinking tea and eating biscuits, not speaking much.

'Did you—?'

'Was there—?'

They both laughed. 'Go on, you first,' she said.

'I was only going to ask if someone or something was bothering you whilst you were up on the stage?'

'No. Why did you think that? I was a bit nervous, I suppose; there was a lot hanging on that meeting.'

'It was just that at one point you seemed to be a little uncertain, almost as if you were looking for someone.' He smiled. 'I was sort of hoping you were looking for me!'

'I'd already seen you,' she answered, too quickly.

'So you *were* looking for someone? Was someone bothering you?' A crease appeared just above his nose, between his dark brows. 'Not the fellow from the mill?'

'No. He was standing next to you in the hall, leaning on the wall, a cigarette in his mouth. Unlit,' she added quickly.

Chris looked thoughtful. 'Oh, that was him, was it? Someone else, then?' he persisted.

She shook her head. He was obviously not going to give up. 'It was nothing really. I just thought I'd seen someone I knew, but when I looked again they'd gone.'

'Disappeared into thin air?'

She looked away, a flush coming to her cheeks, and Chris frowned. 'I'm sorry. I didn't mean to pry. It's just that you seemed . . . well, you looked . . .' He searched for the right word. 'Bewildered.'

'How observant you are,' she answered flippantly. 'Do you suppose anyone else noticed?'

'I shouldn't think so,' he said softly. 'Unless they were watching you as closely as I was.'

She reached across to put down her empty cup and he caught hold of both her hands, staring down at them, stroking them with his thumbs. She felt a pulse race, a persistent hammering in her throat whilst the rest of her body remained still, waiting.

'Will you tell me who it was?' he asked. 'I'd like to know. Someone from your past turning up out of the blue? Someone you want to see again – or not?' He gazed at her steadily.

'No,' she whispered, her voice hoarse. 'It was no one.' She looked down at her hands lying loosely in his and instinctively stroked her fingers against his. 'You'll think I'm weird,' she said, keeping her eyes averted. 'But sometimes I think I can see people who aren't there; people who don't exist.'

She looked up to see if he was laughing at her, but his face was perfectly serious. His eyes searched hers. 'Ghosts, do you mean?'

'I don't know what I mean. There's someone I've always been aware of. A little girl no one else saw – Sarah – who I called my friend when I was little, and then I saw the same girl, grown up, when I was grown up. And now – now I've seen her lately with someone else – a man – and I've seen him separately, too, and not here.' She swallowed hard. 'I think I'm probably going crazy, because I don't know what it means.'

He stood up and pulled her to her feet and cradled her face between his hands. She blinked, and stared at him, but didn't pull away. 'You're not going crazy,' he said softly, 'and I'd like to kiss you.'

Her eyes widened and she gave a little nod and so he did, on her forehead, which she thought was sweet and not what she'd been expecting.

'You're also very sensitive.' He kissed her again on both cheeks. 'And intuitive,' which she thought was an improvement, but even so – and he bent his head and she smiled and closed her eyes as he said, 'and probably a witch,' and kissed her again, only longer this time and on her mouth and she didn't resist.

'And I'm so relieved,' he whispered; 'because I thought you'd spotted someone really special, and if there really isn't anyone, except perhaps in another sphere, then maybe I'm in with a chance?'

CHAPTER TWELVE

His eyes crinkled at the corners when he smiled, as she'd noticed before; his hair was thick and dark and curled at the nape of his neck, and there was a faint shadow down his jaw. She swallowed and reluctantly pulled away. 'And erm, what about your friend Helena?' she asked lightly. 'How would she feel about it?'

'I couldn't begin to explain our relationship,' he said, and she thought she'd touched a nerve. 'She's a very special friend – we've known each other since we were very young – but we're not involved emotionally now, though we once were. She's so contentious, she really irritates me; I think she does it deliberately, just to wind me up. But I'm very fond of her.' He sat down again and gazed at her. 'And she said I should move fast if I wanted to catch *you*.'

She turned swiftly to look at him. 'I'm not sure that I want to be caught,' she said briskly. 'I have a full life, we do have culture in this part of the world, and I don't know if I'm ready for complicated emotional ties.'

'Who said anything about complications?' He sat up to look at her, clasping his hands together. 'I'm a straightforward sort of person; a teacher, pretty boring really, and not at all complicated.' He grinned and shrugged.

'But I'm not. Straightforward, I mean. I'm very complicated.' She gave a short rueful laugh. 'It's not your average person who sees people who aren't there, and gets passionately roused over past injustices and lost birthrights and events that happened before they were born.'

'It's no use trying to put me off,' he said, folding his arms and leaning back into the chair. 'The more I hear the more interested I am. If you could bring yourself to tell me, I'd like to hear.'

She glanced at the clock on the mantelpiece. The bar wouldn't empty for another hour, so her father would be busy with customers. 'Yes, I'd like to tell you. I need to talk to somebody.'

They moved into the downstairs sitting room and Liz switched on a lamp on a low table and another in a corner alcove, bathing the room in light and warmth.

'This is such a lovely room,' he said. 'It's so welcoming and comfortable.'

'Thank you. I brought you in here because I wanted to show you something.' She knelt on the carpet and rummaged under some bookshelves, bringing out a pile of yellowing newspapers in a carrier bag. Carefully, she smoothed them out, though some were torn and creased, and parted two of them to reveal a canvas. The boy in the painting looked up at her.

Chris carefully picked up the canvas by the edges and held it towards the light. 'This must be very old. You ought to get it professionally cleaned – perhaps have the creases taken out if you can. Where did you find it? In the attic?'

'Yes, but not here – in the old building in Hull's High Street the company I work for is moving into tomorrow. The newspapers and the picture and other bits and pieces were going to be put in the skip, so I rescued them.'

'But what was it doing there? Did your family have connections in Hull?'

She stared at him. 'What do you mean – my family?'

He didn't immediately answer, but gazed at the portrait and then across at her. 'There's a slight likeness about the mouth, but the eyes are definitely your father's, and if that's a photograph of your brother' – he nodded over to the table where the lamp lit up the photograph of Bill – 'it's him to a T.'

'What are you talking about?' She took the painting from him. 'It's just a picture that had been rotting in the loft in our new office – nothing to do with us.' But as she gazed at Bill's photograph to compare them she felt dizzy, for apart from Bill's dark hair, so like their mother's, his face could have been a carbon copy of the boy in the picture. 'That's incredible. That's why the painting was so familiar! Perhaps I'm not crazy after all.'

Chris lifted his hands in bafflement. 'I don't understand you. Are you going to tell me what you're talking about or not?'

She began in the middle, when she had seen Sarah at the meeting, then broke off to describe the illusion of the man seated at a desk in the office in High Street, and started again about the days when her mother used to take her to the mill.

'Ah! The mill. I had a feeling that the mill would come into it somehow.' Chris nodded. 'You were very reluctant to talk about the mill and its occupants.'

'That's because they shouldn't be there,' she said fiercely. 'Not by rights! But I'll try to explain.'

She sank back into a chair. 'When I was very young my mother took me for a walk there. We went by the churchyard; I can remember that she was carrying flowers. Sometimes . . .' she hesitated, 'sometimes I think I can smell them.' Her voice slipped into a whisper. 'A fragrance that comes from nowhere. Anyway, there we were at the mill gate and my mother was talking to a woman I didn't know and the woman was crying. When we came away, Mum was angry about something, and she said that one day – one day we would get back what was ours.

'I didn't know then what she meant, but I can remember my mother and father arguing and then Dad telling her to leave it and not to meddle.'

A faraway look came into her eyes. 'It's strange how it's stuck in my memory. I don't ever remember them quarrelling about anything else. My dad is and always was the least quarrelsome person I've ever known.'

Chris nodded. Gilbert Rayner was a most mild-mannered man.

Liz gazed around the room, seemingly unseeing, and went on. 'It was about the same time that the little girl came. I thought she lived with us. We played together, ate together, slept in the same bed. It was only later that I realized that I was the only one who ever saw her.' She lifted her shoulders, embarrassed. 'Silly, isn't it? Children's imaginings.'

'Go on. What about the mill?'

'I subsequently learnt some of the history. There's nothing from before the Fosters; they seem to be the only family who have owned it, so maybe they built it, but we'll never know. It came down from father to son and they all seem to have been called Tom from the beginning of the nineteenth century. Tom and Elizabeth were the first Fosters who lived here,' she said wistfully. 'And the last Foster had a spinster daughter, Mary, and her father left the property to her with the proviso that if she died without heirs the property would go to the Foster Rayners. However . . .' She leant towards him. 'Are you getting bored?'

He shook his head, his lips twitching, and looked at his watch. 'No. Please go on.'

'Well, Mary turned the tables on them all by marrying one of the Reedbarrows and producing a son who eventually became the grandfather of Carl Reedbarrow. At least, I think I've got that right, and you did ask!' She sighed. 'It's very complicated. My mum did most of the research, even though she wasn't a Foster Rayner herself, and worked out how the mill and the house passed out of Foster hands and into the Reedbarrows'.'

'If you feel so strongly about it, why don't you do something? You could ask him if he would think of selling.'

'Because, for a start, my father would never ever discuss it. It's the one thing guaranteed to raise his blood pressure, and that's really bad for him. Besides, Carl wouldn't sell to us on principle anyway. He just doesn't like us, the same as his father didn't, and I don't know why.'

Chris shrugged. 'Perhaps he feels threatened. If it's legally his, yet he knows you want it . . .'

'I want it back for continuity's sake. I know it's an obsession, but the property was built by a Foster and has always belonged to the Fosters, and my dad and I are Fosters.'

'Well, you could say that Carl Reedbarrow is a Foster too. His great-grandmother was a Foster before she married, didn't you say? He could call himself Foster Reedbarrow if he wanted to, though it's a mouthful.'

Liz looked taken aback and paled. 'But he doesn't care about it in the way that we do,' she whispered. 'He would sell it if he could. He'd knock down the mill and build an estate of houses on the land; he cares nothing for the history, or the people who have lived there.'

He was silent, and then gently stroked her hands. 'You are so . . . complex. Elusive perhaps I mean, or other-worldly, maybe. I'm almost afraid that you'll disappear into some other sphere before I can catch hold of you.'

She gazed through him, lost in thought. 'But of course you're right. He does have Foster blood.' Her voice dropped low. 'He's my kin whether I like it or not. Strange that I've never thought of him in that way before.'

'Oh, come on! How far back are you going? He can't have more than a drop, a mere speck.' He gave her a gentle shake on the shoulder. 'Come on; even I might be related to you, and where would that leave us?'

She gave a faint smile. 'I don't know. I'm confused. Where would you like it to leave us?'

He whispered into her ear and she pushed him away. 'Under my father's roof? You must be joking. Go home. I'm exhausted with all this talking.' Hesitantly, she touched his arm. 'But thank you for listening.'

She waved him off from the door and went back to the sitting room, too drained to think of going up to bed. When her father had locked the door behind the last customer and came to join her, she silently passed the painting to him.

He looked at it. 'Where did you get this?'

'I found it. It had been in the loft of our new office in High Street. Chris thinks it looks like Bill.'

He pursed his lips. 'Why did he think that? He's never met Bill.'

'The photograph.' She nodded over to the table. 'He thought it was a family portrait. Thought there was a family likeness.'

'Can't see it myself.' Gilbert tapped his fingers on his chin, pondering. 'Those buildings you were talking about, in 'High Street. Well, I've been thinking about them. Some of them belonged to 'shipping merchants at one time; they backed on to 'river.'

She nodded. That much she had discovered.

'They'd have had easier access for loading goods; and some of 'em would have lived there.'

She listened to him, but more intently to the sounds inside her head: her father's voice superimposed on others, layers of echoes, murmurings and whispering; faint footsteps too, but not in here.

'It's quite possible that we might have had some connection; my grandfather used to talk about 'men in 'family being whaling men in 'old days, and when that died out going into trawling. But mebbe further back in 'past somebody came into 'country, to Monkston, which ironically is now under water. We've allus been seagoing men or farmers. Strange combination, isn't it?'

'Until your father,' she said. 'Grandpa.'

'Aye, well, he allus hankered after going to sea. But his father bought 'Ship Inn when farming was at a low ebb and seagoing was allus a dangerous livelihood, and I suppose he allus knew there would be a living in a hostelry on 'coast. Folk liked to be here afore they discovered abroad. I would have stayed at sea too if it hadn't been for your mother.' He smiled wistfully and Liz felt a lump in her throat as he went on. 'I'm glad that I didn't, though. Glad that I came ashore. We didn't have that long together.'

He glanced at her and she waited for him to say more, but he cleared his throat and got up from his chair. 'I'm going up now. We're all locked up.' He bent to kiss the top of her head. 'G'night, love.'

She lay awake in her bed for what seemed like hours, her thoughts switching from the public meeting and the falling cliffs to the portrait of the boy, and the mill, and then back to the office in High Street where she had a lot to do when she got back to work after the weekend.

Turning over so that she could see the dark sky from her window, she thought of Chris and the proposition he had made and smiled in the darkness. Maybe another time. Yes, most definitely another time. But maybe he won't ask again, she thought sleepily, on the edge of a dreamless sleep, but then do I want him to? I don't know what I want, but I will be very disappointed if he doesn't.

CHAPTER THIRTEEN

Chris gritted his teeth. He'd circled Aldwych and the Strand three times in a vain attempt to find a parking place. He'd had a good journey from Hull, rising early and leaving at six, and apart from the build-up of traffic at various city intersections he'd made reasonable time into London, but now! He swore under his breath. He'd forgotten in the short time he'd been away how he hated the sensation of tension as he sat in a jam of stationary traffic, listening to the constant hum of engines, the revving of motorbikes, the cacophony as impatient drivers sat with their elbows pressed against their car horns. It was almost an hour and a half before he had finally found a space to park and was running up the six stone steps to the glossy red door that was his objective.

When he was last here, the cool green squares of Lincoln's Inn Fields had been littered with the limp forms of office workers and students as they lay absorbing filtered sunlight and traffic fumes; the men with their sleeves rolled up and canned drinks in their hands, and the women and girls with shoulders bare and faces upturned to the sky. Now the gardens were strewn with plastic tents and cardboard boxes, tree branches draped with old curtains for privacy, held down by broken bricks and battered suitcases; home and shelter for the homeless and destitute, all looking for their own pitch before winter set in.

A few brisk and solitary figures hurried purposefully across the grass with their coat collars turned up about their ears and their eyes averted from anyone who might halt them in their progress with a 'Got a coin for a coffee, mate?' or 'Got a cig, man?' while bedraggled pigeons pecked at crumpled crisp bags and scraps of silver paper and gave their throaty coos. Chris had slowed down as he passed and glanced across at the cardboard city; there were many more people gathered there than he remembered seeing before. It's because Christmas is coming, he thought; they're booking their places with their tents and clobber, and looking for company too as much as for the soup kitchens. What a reflection on today's society.

He rang the bell of the handsome Dickensian building that now housed the offices of a smart firm of solicitors, and asked the receptionist who admitted him if Helena was free.

'Would you take a seat for a moment, Mr Burton, and I'll ask if Miss Graham can see you. I know she has several clients this afternoon.'

He sat down and waited, then rose to his feet when he heard Helena's voice from an inner room. 'Come on through, Chris. Trust you to pick my busiest day.'

The receptionist held the door for him and gave him a brief smile as he went into Helena's office. Helena's desk was over-flowing with piles of papers and crammed files and she waved a nonchalant hand over them.

'As you see,' she drawled, 'nothing changes. The stacks don't get any smaller, in fact they grow ever higher, although the contents are not necessarily the same as when you were last here.'

He shook his head in incredulity. He never could come to terms with the fact that the elegant, haughty Helena, who looked as if she should be on the international catwalks of Paris or Milan, had chosen such a demanding profession as the law. But she was razor sharp, her mind cool and calculating, and she was very successful. Today she was wearing a crisp white shirt and a black knee-length skirt, with her long blonde hair coiled into a neat chignon. 'I have a client at two o'clock; we've just time for a sandwich if you're hungry. Are you staying over?'

'Yes. I hoped you could give me a bed for the night.'

'You've got a nerve.' She rose from her desk and flipped a black wool jacket from the coat stand. 'I don't hear from you in weeks, then you drop in out of the blue demanding a bed! Come on, let's go!'

'I wanted to ask you something,' he said as he ran after her down the steps and across the square, through narrow winding passages and back into the Strand, where she pushed her way into a crowded pub.

'I'll order; you'll never get served.' She signalled to a barman without asking Chris what he wanted. 'Two ham sandwiches, a pint of bitter and a black coffee; and don't be long, will you, Tony? I'm absolutely flying.'

The order came back in five minutes. 'Go through to the back room,' Tony whispered, giving her a nod. 'There's a table free. Do you want this on the slate?'

'No she doesn't,' Chris cut in. 'I'll pay.' He took the tray from the barman and followed Helena into another smaller and darker room, where the timbered walls were black with age. He put the tray down on a small table and removed several used glasses to make more space. 'This place doesn't change,' he said, unbuttoning his coat. 'It just gets busier.'

She nodded, and breathed out a deep sigh. 'I'm shattered. I'm ready for a break.' She leant forward, sipping her coffee. 'So! What have you been up to? How's the redhead?'

Chris tried to suppress the smile which bubbled up inside him, spreading to his mouth in a lopsided grin. 'She's fine.'

Helena bit into her sandwich. 'Don't tell me you've really fallen for her?' She stared at him as he didn't answer but gazed down into his headless beer. 'You have!' she said with her mouth full, and removed a curly strand of cress from the corner of her lips. 'I can tell. I don't believe it. Not you of all people.'

'Why not me? Why do you say that?'

She took another bite of her sandwich. 'I don't know. I suppose I expected you to come tearing back to London. I thought you'd get fed up with the quiet life.' She smiled mockingly. 'You're besotted, aren't you? Yes you are, you're absolutely besotted!'

'Never mind about that.' He wasn't going to discuss his feelings for Liz with Helena. 'I wanted to ask you something. Inheritance, contracts in the nineteenth century, that sort of thing.'

'This is my lunch hour, for heaven's sake.'

'Well, I'm going back to Yorkshire tomorrow to finish off a few things, and then coming to spend Christmas in Surrey. I just thought I'd mention it whilst I'm here.'

'Ah! How is your mother?'

'OK, I think.' All the better for not seeing you, he wanted to say. His mother was not fond of Helena. All of his friends had been welcome at his home during his teenage years, with the exception of Helena.

'This inheritance thing,' she said. 'It's for her, isn't it? Your redhead.'

'Her name is Liz— Elizabeth. Will you stop calling her my redhead!'

'Sorry, I'm sure. If you're going to get touchy I shan't help you.'

They both laughed and he shook his head ruefully. 'Why is it you always rub me up the wrong way?'

'I enjoy it,' she admitted. 'I like to watch your reaction. You rise to the bait every time; you'd be useless in a witness box.' She leant back against her chair. 'So what do you want to know?'

He told her about the mill and the Foster Rayner connection.

'I remember the mill,' she said. 'Decrepit-looking place; can't think why anyone would want it unless it was for the land. Even so, just because she thinks they've a right to it doesn't necessarily make it theirs. Would she try to turn the occupants out if they made a case for it?'

'No,' he said swiftly. 'It's not like that.' He was anxious that she shouldn't see Liz as someone mean or acquisitive. 'She doesn't even know that I'm making enquiries. I thought if I could come up with some sort of evidence of a contract, if it had come down the line of Fosters as she says, it would settle the ownership question once and for all. What they did about the Reedbarrows living there would be a different issue altogether then.'

Helena pursed her lips. 'There's always the General Register Office in St Catherine's House, but I think that the best thing for . . . Liz? . . . to do would be to get in touch with her local land registry office. If there was a contract they would have details of it; there's something called a Trust in Perpetuity. But I doubt that's what happened. It's more likely to have been willed, in which case she doesn't stand an earthly, I'm afraid. I can't say more than that without knowing more details.'

She told him where he would find the GRO and left to go back to her office. Chris sat on after she'd gone, glumly swirling the remaining liquid in his glass and watching the sparse bubbles frothing and popping. I think I've developed a taste for Yorkshire bitter, he thought, though the thick creamy head had taken some getting used to. Abruptly he put the glass down, paid the barman and strode out of the door, heading towards Kingsway and St Catherine's House. He joined the crowds of people thronging the population censuses and surveys office and edged his way through, to enquire of an attendant where he would find the files for the name of Foster.

CHAPTER FOURTEEN

'Is everything working OK, Liz? No hiccups?' Steve came into the new office mid-morning on the day after they'd moved in. 'Sorry I wasn't here earlier,' he went on, 'but it's as if a bomb has gone off at the other place. It's chaos!'

'It takes time to organize everything, but it shouldn't be long once we've got the advertising boards in place and the window displays up. People will be curious, so I'd guess there'll be a lot of interest. But don't ask me to come back, will you? Sharon and Caroline know what to do there and I've plenty to be going on with here, but yes, everything is all right, or it will be.' She swung round and looked with quiet satisfaction at the almost-organized office. It smelt of wet paint and new carpeting, but it looked like what it was, a modern commercial business.

In the front office her new assistant, Susan, older than her and married, was organizing herself. Liz had known on first meeting her that she would have no truck with Steve's philandering manner, which was why she had offered her the job. She had also given Caroline and Sharon quiet instruction on how to deal with Steve when she was no longer there. 'Begin by always calling him Mr Black,' she said. 'And I don't mean only when clients are here, I mean each time you need to speak to him. And don't allow him to lean over your shoulder when you're at your desks and need to ask him something. You're both intelligent young women and he'll come to rely on you, but don't let him become too familiar; his flirting is innocent enough but it has no place in a professional office.'

A couple of days later both girls had changed their style of clothing and were wearing suits, as she was, with navy jackets and skirts but different-coloured shirts. It seemed that now they were going to be running the old office without her, they were showing their efficiency in style of dress and manner.

Steve walked across to the window and peered out. 'Oh, yuck,' he said. 'What a dismal outlook; it's pouring with rain. Just look at the river. It's like mud.'

'It is mud.' She glanced up. She'd positioned her desk so that she could look towards the window; she couldn't see the river when seated but she could see the sky. 'The rain is churning it up, but it's not dismal. There's always something going on; it's a busy old harbour.' She too got up and went to look out. Bright red barges were lying low in the water as they were loaded with sand and gravel from the heaps on the bankside. She sighed. *I'll never get any work done.*

'I have to go out,' Steve said, turning around. 'I won't be back until later in the day. Nothing you need me for, is there?'

'N-no, don't think so. Where are you off to? Anything interesting?'

'Erm – just here and there, a few calls to catch up on,' he said vaguely. 'I've had a whiff of information about some land.'

'Oh!'

'It might not come to anything.' He didn't volunteer more, and made his departure. He had fingers in many pies and this might not have had anything to do with housing. She was sure he would have said, if it had been, so she carried on with filling drawers and cupboards with the contents of various boxes brought from the city centre office and carefully labelling them.

She ate a home-made sandwich and made a cup of tea, calling through to Susan to ask if she'd like one. She came through and said she would. Susan too had brought her own lunch and asked Liz if it was all right if she worked through her lunch break and left a bit early.

'Yes, of course,' Liz agreed. 'I'm going to slip out myself in a minute. I need to go to the central library and I think it will be quiet as it's so wet and miserable today. I don't think anyone will come in, since we haven't advertised our move yet, but if anyone does, refer them back to the city office or ask them to wait. I won't be out long.'

The rain was drizzling steadily, so she cut through one of the larger stores and out the other side and put up her umbrella as she crossed over Queen's Gardens, the sunken garden which had once been one of the biggest docks in the country and whose flower beds were now bare and bereft of colour. The fountains were stilled in the ponds, where rain spattered and splashed instead, and mallards upended as they searched for food amongst the duckweed. She slowed to watch as a pair raced back and forth across the grass, shaking their glistening plumage and simulating flight as they flapped their clipped, outspread wings.

By the time she reached the library she was soaking wet, and as she pushed open the swing doors of the local history department she could smell the warm steam rising from the clothes of other library users, which mingled with the odours of faded old books and wax polish on the wooden drawers and cupboards. She lingered for a while, looking through glass doors at the ancient titles whilst she waited for an assistant to become free, then gave her request and filled in a card and waited whilst books and pamphlets were brought for her.

'This is a reprint of a Hull directory,' she was told. 'If you know the name you're looking for you might find it in here.'

Liz thanked her, found a corner to sit in, and carefully began to turn the pages. There were several Fosters listed and one Rayner, but none of the professions or the street names fitted. There were chandlers and fruit sellers, victuallers and masons, most of whom had been situated around the old town area in squares and courts and yards before any further developments had begun or had disappeared because of the devastation of the last war.

She glanced at her watch: she was late, very late. Hurriedly she returned the books and pamphlets to the desk. 'I've run out of time,' she said. 'I'll have to come again.'

The rain had almost stopped and she hurried back across the town, dashing through the pedestrian area and colliding with a young woman with a pushchair hurrying in the opposite direction. 'Sorry . . . I'm sorry,' she gasped.

The woman glared at her, and accidentally or not jarred Liz's ankle with the pushchair. The child in it looked up briefly from a crisp packet and went on crunching, a sprinkling of salt crystals around its lips. 'Why don't you look where you're going?'

'Ow!' Liz snapped. 'I said I was sorry.' As she felt her scraped ankle and peevishly watched the hostile retreating back, her eye was caught by a glass-enclosed poster hanging on the railings of the triple-domed Town Docks Museum.

She limped towards it to have a closer look. The poster was advertising the whaling section and depicted a ship sailing up the Davis Strait, her canvas sails spread and chunks of hummocky ice floating in the cold green sea. Ghostly forms of towering icebergs loomed on the horizon ahead. It was similar to a picture they had at home, and as she looked, perception dawned. Yes, she thought intuitively. This is where I must look. This is where I will find you.

The telephone behind the Ship's bar rang and Gilbert picked it up. 'Ship Inn,' he said. 'Gilbert Rayner speaking . . . Yep. Where are you? Right; I'll be half an hour, mebbe forty minutes. Wait there – I'll be as quick as I can.' He put the phone down and turned to speak to the bartender.

'Can you manage for a couple of hours, Ted? I have to go to Beverley. I don't think there'll be many folk coming in this morning. There are egg and cress sandwiches and sausage rolls in 'fridge if anybody wants them. Tell 'em we don't do lunches on a Monday.'

The man behind the bar, polishing glasses and filling the optics, nodded. 'No hurry,' he said, 'my time's me own. You should tek a day off anyway. Take Dot out for lunch!' He raised his eyebrows significantly above the rim of his glasses. Gilbert grinned back at him and went to fetch his coat and car keys. 'Shan't be long,' he called as he left. He wasn't keen on leaving the pub in other hands, but he knew that Ted was honest and capable, and he thought as he hurried to the car that he himself really was ready for a bit of time off.

In Beverley, he parked near the cattle market and went to meet Dot in the pub in the Market Place where she was waiting. An empty coffee cup lay on the table in front of her and several overflowing shopping bags and parcels were scattered about her feet.

'Thanks, Gilbert. I wouldn't have bothered you, but . . .' Her round face dimpled and in her smile he saw the young girl she had once been.

'But?'

'Well, I couldn't have managed all this shopping on 'bus, and besides, I thought it was time you took me out to lunch.'

He shook his head. 'You've been colluding with Ted. That's what he told me to do.'

She tutted. 'Cheeky devil! I haven't. And I was being discreet.'

'There are no secrets in our village; you should know that, especially when you work in a pub.'

'Ted doesn't gossip, you know he doesn't, and we're only having lunch. Not that it should matter anyway; we're both free. Well, I am,' she added.

'And so am I,' he retaliated. 'But I don't like folks' tongues wagging. I wouldn't want anybody discussing us, or our relationship. It's nowt to do wi' anybody else.'

A fleeting shadow of annoyance drifted across her face and she began to pick up her parcels from the floor and place them on the spare chair. 'What you mean is you don't want Liz to know.'

He shrugged, offhand. 'I wouldn't know how to tell her. She's my daughter. I couldn't discuss it with her.'

'But I could.' She smiled, her humour returning. 'She's a big girl now, she knows about these things; and you forget, I've known her all her life. Those kids were practically mine when Nina was ill.'

'I know.' He patted her hand and held on to it. 'I haven't forgotten, but I think she still misses her mother.' He squeezed her hand. 'We've been through a lot together, haven't we? Losing Nina and then Gordon. Come on, let's go.' He pulled her out of the chair and picked up a few shopping bags. 'Don't let's get maudlin. Pass me 'rest of your parcels and we'll go and eat. Where do you want to go?'

She handed him another bag and sighed. 'Nobody'd possibly guess we were having a passionate affair,' she said, and Gilbert looked around in alarm to see if anyone was near enough to hear. 'It's so disappointing,' she went on. 'Does nothing for my ego. We look like an ordinary married couple, not a lover and his lass.'

He raised his eyebrows and shook his head. One thing about Dot, she always made him smile. 'Come on,' he said, smiling back.

As they drove homewards in the afternoon, she put her hand on his thigh. 'Thank you for my lunch,' she said with a smile in her voice, and he lifted her hand to his lips. 'Watch out!' she shouted as a sleek white car flashed round the corner on their side of the road.

Gilbert swerved to avoid it and ran on to the grass verge, leaving a long muddy skid mark. 'Idiot,' he hissed. 'Just as well I wasn't driving fast.'

Dot exhaled a huge breath. 'Frightened me to death. I was sure he was going to crash into us. Folks don't understand our Holderness roads; they don't think that there might be other folks driving just round 'corner.'

'I know that car, I'm sure I do,' Gilbert muttered. 'Where've I seen it before?' He drew up outside Dot's house and got out to unload her parcels.

'I don't know, darling,' she said as she put up her hand to be heaved out of the passenger seat. 'But let that be a lesson to you. Keep your eyes on the road and both hands on the wheel. That could have been tricky.'

He laughed, and putting both arms around her gave her a bear hug. 'You do me the world of good, Dot, do you know that? Here, give us a kiss and to hell with the neighbours.'

CHAPTER FIFTEEN

'The official erosion meeting won't come up until the end of January, Liz,' Gilbert said. 'I've had a call from George Bennett.'

Liz was stretched out on the sofa reading the local paper. 'Oh, no!' She put down the newspaper. 'Why so long?'

Her father shrugged. 'There's always something more urgent on the agenda.'

Liz sat up and folded the paper. 'I'll phone the press office on Monday and tell them we've been delayed and are praying for a mild winter. It'll keep us in the public's mind.'

'Good idea,' he agreed. 'Though I don't think we'll get one; a mild winter, I mean. It's really cold this morning. I bet we get snow before Christmas.' He glanced enquiringly at her. 'What do you want to do for Christmas?'

'What do you mean?' She looked up at him, surprised. 'We'll do what we always do, won't we?'

'Well, I . . . erm, I just thought that you're seeing Chris quite a lot and I wondered if you wanted to invite him here, or what?'

'No.' She picked up another section of the newspaper. 'He'll be going to his mother's, I expect. She lives in Surrey.'

She peered over the top of the page and grinned wickedly. 'I don't know him well enough to invite him for Christmas, Dad.'

Gilbert threw a cushion at her, flattening the paper. 'What rubbish. You and Bill have always invited friends here.'

I know, she thought, but Chris is becoming special, and if I ask him to come I won't want him to leave. 'No,' she said. 'Just you and me.' She sat up and stretched. 'And I expect we'll get a phone call from Bill and of course we'll have Dot; we can't have Christmas without Auntie Dotty!'

'Are you sure?' he said anxiously.

'Of course I'm sure! She's practically family, isn't she?' Her eyes were wide, inviting him to confide.

'Almost,' he said, picking up a section of the newspaper and sitting down with a sigh. 'I'll just order a small turkey and a couple of pheasants, then. And by the way, I was talking to Kevin from 'Raven earlier. He wants to be involved in 'erosion meeting, and said he was willing to hold 'next one in 'Raven.'

'Oh, no,' she said, dismayed. 'He'll only waffle on, and besides, he's not been here long enough to care. Probably won't stay long enough to be affected either.'

'Well, he's never very busy, that's true, but he has different customers from us, so he might gather up new folk. Don't see how we can refuse his offer.'

'No, I suppose not,' she said reluctantly, and sighed. 'We can't be exclusive. Maybe he'll have contacts who can help spread the word.' But she wasn't pleased about it.

Chris telephoned that evening. 'Is it all right if I come up tomorrow? I've got something to tell you, and I want to bring you a token Christmas present, because I won't be able to get up again before Christmas. I've a few things to finish off before we break up on Thursday, and I'll be heading off early on Friday to try and miss the traffic.'

'Oh! I didn't think you'd be going just yet.' She tried to hide her disappointment.

'Will you miss me?'

'Erm, let me think,' she said casually. 'Possibly. But I haven't seen you for nearly two weeks and I managed!'

'Ah, yes. I'll explain about that when I see you—'

'I'm joking,' she said, though she had wondered. 'I expect you've been busy winding things up before the holiday.'

'Yes. The students have been finishing off their projects; they've done very well, most of them. So can I come tomorrow?'

'Of course you can,' she murmured. 'Bring rubber boots and we'll go on the beach. There might not be many more opportunities.'

After she rang off she wondered if she should have got him a Christmas present too, but there was no time left. I'm always last minute, she thought. I was going to shop next week, but after tomorrow I won't see him until the new year. I wonder if he'll see Helena – will she be part of his Christmas ritual? They've known each other a long time, he said. I suppose they're bound to meet. But I'm only guessing, and anyway, do I care?

Well, actually, she pondered, yes, I do.

The next morning she was only just out of the shower and drying her hair when she heard the back doorbell ring. *He's never here already!* She listened and heard her father's voice inviting someone in and then calling up the stairs. 'Lizzie? Are you decent? Chris is here,' and then a mumble of conversation.

'Five minutes,' she shouted back, then quickly put on a warm sweater and her jeans, gave a final brush to her hair and darkened her fair eyebrows, and was on her way down, drawn by the smell of the coffee that her father was making.

Chris turned to greet her and she saw the smile that lifted his lips and creased the corners of his eyes. He moved towards her, giving her a brief kiss on each cheek. 'You look – and smell – lovely,' he murmured. 'I wish I wasn't going away.'

'Stop for lunch if you like' – Gilbert turned from reaching for the coffee cups – 'though we're open to 'public today.'

'I'm very tempted,' Chris said, and Liz realized that he was still holding her hand. 'Unfortunately, I still have some marking to do.'

'Never mind,' Liz found herself saying. 'There'll be other times, perhaps.'

'Are you going to spend Christmas with your mother?' Gilbert asked.

'Yes. Father's work was in Surrey, and my mother moved to Dorking after he died. She seems settled there, though it's quite a drive from up here.'

'Ah.' Gilbert nodded and poured steaming hot coffee into three cups, the rich aroma filling the room. 'But you've decided to stay on at the college, have you?'

'That's the plan.' Chris smiled and squeezed Liz's fingers, but she gently pulled them away before her father turned round to set two of the coffee cups down on the table.

'If you don't mind, I'll tek my coffee into 'bar,' he said. 'Dot'll be here in a minute to cook lunch and she'll need a hand.'

Liz fetched the biscuit tin and Chris took a chocolate digestive, so Liz found him a small white plate. 'I'm sorry you're off so soon,' she said. 'I thought I might see you again before you left for London.'

'I'm not going to London,' he said. 'Only to Surrey. I went to London last weekend; I was on a mission. That's what I want to tell you.'

She licked her lips. What was he going to say? If he'd been to London where did he stay? Did he see Helena?

It was as if he was listening to her thoughts. 'I went to see

106

Helena. I told you she was a lawyer, didn't I?' He didn't wait for an answer, but went on, 'I wanted to pick her brains.'

'About what?' she asked, taking a sip of coffee.

'To ask her about land registry and inheritance contracts in the nineteenth century. Did I do right, or was I sticking my nose into something that is nothing to do with me?'

She swallowed. She couldn't believe that he'd travelled all the way down the country for that reason. She wondered why he hadn't talked to Helena on the telephone, but she supposed it might be unprofessional for lawyers to discuss such matters on the phone.

'Anyway, we had lunch at her local pub, and then she went back to her office, but she'd reminded me that St Catherine's House was near by – you know, the public records office? I hope you don't think I was interfering in something that was nothing to do with me, but I went there and asked if I could look up the name Foster.'

She stared at him in astonishment. 'There must have been thousands!'

He nodded. 'More than – and I didn't have any dates, so went right back to when records began, 1837 I think it was, and ploughed right in.'

'Why?' she questioned. 'Why did you do that? Such a mammoth task.'

He shrugged. 'Well, to start with I'd asked Helena if she knew anything about contracts in the nineteenth century, thinking about the mill, you know, but it doesn't work in the way I thought it did. Seemingly property could only be handed down through a Will; there's something called a restrictive covenant.'

She looked puzzled. 'I still don't understand . . .'

'It's just that I thought if there had been some kind of business contract—'

'No,' she said, 'I don't mean that. What I don't understand is why you went to so much trouble to find out about the Fosters.'

He took up her hand again. 'I wanted to find your friend Sarah,' he said softly. 'I wanted to find out if she ever existed.'

Her eyes widened. 'So you believe me? You don't think I'm making it up, or it's my imagination?'

He shook his head. 'There has to be a reason for it. I thought that if there once was such a person, maybe somebody – your grandparents or someone like that – had talked about them when you were a child and you stored it away in your subconscious or subliminal mind.'

'Do you believe in that kind of thing?' she asked breathlessly.

He gazed at her. 'Let's say I don't disbelieve it. Most of the Fosters from this area were male. Thomas and William, a Mark and a couple of Georges; then there were some Elizabeths and Marias, a Sarah early on, and a Sarah Maria born in 1862, I think it was, so that might be her.'

'It might,' she agreed. But it wasn't, she thought. I would know.

'And oddly,' he went on, 'I looked up Rayner and there were marriages between Fosters and Rayners even though they were related. It will take some working out who's who. I've made notes for you,' he added. 'You can see what you make of them for yourself.'

'Thank you,' she said, and impulsively kissed his cheek.

'There's a lot more, so you must look through and see what you want to keep. I took a brief look at Reedbarrow, too; I thought it was such an unusual name. I found some from this area and they seem to have been here as long as your family. I found a Paul, but I couldn't find Carl, though I was restricted in any case as to what I could look for.'

'But don't all registrations go there?' Liz asked. 'I thought they did.'

Gilbert had come into the kitchen as Chris was speaking, and now he broke in. 'Why are you doing this, Chris? What's the point of it?'

Chris was startled by the question. 'Initially I was looking for the Fosters, for Liz, though she didn't know. The Reedbarrows – that was simply their interesting name.' He returned Gilbert's gaze. 'But I couldn't find much, and besides, the place was on the point of closing. Does it matter?'

'It might,' Gilbert said. 'People's names are important to them.'

'But – I'm not gossiping about it. It was just an interesting name,' he repeated.

'I dare say,' Gilbert mumbled. 'But if Carl found out that he isn't registered, for instance, it might make him angry; angrier than he usually is.'

'But, Dad,' Liz broke in. 'We certainly wouldn't tell him, and I'm sure Chris won't.'

'No, I don't think he would, but some things are best left alone. You seem to have inherited your mother's curiosity and it won't do, Liz. It really won't.'

'But this was nothing to do with Liz,' Chris protested, 'and I'm sorry if you think I've interfered. It wasn't my intention, and I apologize.'

Gilbert lifted a hand in exoneration. 'It's all right. But the Reedbarrows are a sensitive lot and you've got to know how to handle them. So let's forget it.'

He went out of the room, and Liz and Chris gazed gloomily at each other.

'I've put my foot in it, haven't I?' Chris mumbled. 'I'll be told never to darken his doorstep again.'

Liz laughed in spite of herself. 'He'll be fine eventually; he doesn't stay cross or angry for long. You'll see, he'll be apologizing to you.'

'I am sorry, though,' he said seriously. 'I never thought of it as prying, but I suppose it could be construed that way.'

'I really don't know why he got so uptight.' Liz pondered for a moment. 'Or defensive about Carl. I mean, he's nothing but an absolute pain as a rule.'

Chris's mouth twitched. 'Your father?'

'No, silly.' She began to giggle. 'Carl Reedbarrow.'

CHAPTER SIXTEEN

'I'll have to go soon,' Chris said. 'But first I want to give you your present. It's not the kind that can be wrapped in Christmas paper and it's in the car boot.' He got to his feet. 'I'll just fetch it. Won't be a tick.'

She smiled. *What is it? It's not going to be something like perfume or shower gel; that would be too personal, and anyway, he doesn't know what I like.*

Her father looked round the door. 'Are you staying for lunch, Chris? Oh – he hasn't gone, has he?'

'No. He wouldn't leave without saying goodbye. He's only gone to get something from his car, but I don't think he's staying for lunch, Dad. He's got things to do before he goes off to Surrey on Friday.'

'Ah!' Gilbert nodded, and she knew his earlier irritation had passed.

Chris came through the kitchen door with a very large parcel wrapped in brown paper and tied with string. Gilbert raised his eyebrows and disappeared back into the bar.

'Good heavens,' Liz said. 'Not something for my dressing table, then?'

'Hardly, and as I haven't seen your dressing table, I wouldn't know what to buy.'

He sat down with the parcel between his knees and slowly began to untie the string; Liz sat cross-legged on the floor and watched him, intrigued, as he began to peel off the wrapping.

The first time she had taken him down the cliffs to the beach, when he'd picked up the odd-shaped piece of drift-wood and told her what he could make of it, he'd carried it back and put it in the boot of his car. Now, as he took off the last piece of brown paper, Liz saw it transformed; carved, shaped and polished into the shape of a seal, the neck and head lifted high and given a trace of fine whiskers and a tear stain below each dark eye. The back and belly were smooth and curved, the fore flippers close to the body and the stubby tail jauntily flipped.

'It's *beautiful*,' she whispered. 'Absolutely beautiful. How clever you are! Thank you.' She leant forward and kissed him on the cheek. 'Thank you.'

He kissed her back, pleased with her praise. 'I got so much pleasure from watching it come to life. I had to do it at college, of course; there's no room at the flat. I must find somewhere to buy soon.'

'I'm still looking,' she said, 'but now isn't a good time and people in Tillington rarely move anyway, especially now they're waiting to find out what's going to happen about the erosion plans.'

She told him that the next meeting had been put back, and Gilbert came in again as Chris was saying that it gave them more time to plan their campaign and Liz agreeing that they could do the posters themselves, and get the schoolchildren involved with something eye-catching. Gilbert bent down to admire the seal.

'We'll start straight after Christmas,' Liz said, wanting to include him in the conversation. 'Won't we, Dad? And drum up support from outside the village.'

'Sounds great,' Chris agreed. 'You're on your way. Tillington's last stand.'

'Hey, I like that.' Gilbert grinned and raised his fist triumphantly. 'That's good. Tillington's Last Stand.'

The next few days went quickly, and on Christmas morning Gilbert unlocked the back door and put on his coat to fetch Dot. Liz came downstairs in her dressing gown and started preparing coffee for the three of them; she took smoked salmon from the fridge, sliced up lemons and cracked eggs into a bowl, giving them a quick whisk so they'd be ready to cook when her father and Dot arrived for breakfast.

Odd how we make these regular occurrences into a habit, she thought. Dot could easily stay here on Christmas Eve rather than go home alone, because we have plenty of space – she could even have her own permanent bedroom, leave some of her own stuff here, and yet she and Dad continue with this charade that they're just good friends and she still goes home at night. Dad's been widowed for – how long since Mum died? Seven years, and five for Dot. They've known each other since childhood. Is it because of us? Me and Bill? They surely know we wouldn't mind; that we'd like to see them both happy.

She noticed that her father had already put the oven on for the turkey; he always cooked the roast, and she and Dot worked together to prepare everything else. The stuffing was ready: chopped chestnuts stirred into sausage meat, sliced onion with herbs and juniper berries, and a fresh egg blended into the mixture. Potatoes had been peeled the previous evening with the rest of the vegetables; the pressure cooker was in place for the Christmas pudding, which was already cooked and awaited only re-heating. The sprig of holly to be placed on top was on a saucer in the fridge, and a bottle of brandy was waiting for the final splash and a match to be lit.

They ate breakfast when Dot and Gilbert came back from Dot's house, laden with parcels which tradition dictated be opened in the afternoon when they were replete with Christmas dinner.

At one o'clock, whilst Dot prepared gravy and her father opened wine, Liz laid a crisp white tablecloth over the dining table and then a festive paper one over the top of it; in the centre of the table she placed a red candle in a brass candlestick and carefully surrounded it with sprigs of golden winter jasmine and the flat-petalled Hellebore niger, or Christmas rose as it was often called, which flowered every winter to Liz's utmost delight.

She stood back to admire, and then opened the cutlery drawer to finish setting the table. Dot was draining potatoes prior to placing them in the roasting tin. The turkey was resting, its skin crisp and golden, and Gilbert was about to open another bottle of bubbly.

The telephone rang. They all looked at each other. 'Are we taking bets?' Liz said, and then she and her father made a dash for the telephone in the hall.

Liz got there first. 'Hello,' she called out. 'Ship Inn.'

'There's no need to shout,' said the voice at the other end. 'I'm not a million miles away.'

'Well, where are you, then? Happy Christmas. Are you somewhere exotic? Warm and sunny? Dad, here, say Happy Christmas. It's Bill. Dot, it's Bill. Come on.'

'Will you be quiet for a minute, Liz? I can't hear what he's saying! What do you mean set another place?' Gilbert screwed up his face to listen. 'Here, Liz, talk to him. I think he's joking but he might not be. He says he's at Hull station!'

She took the receiver again and listened. 'I'll come and fetch you.' Her voice was high-pitched with excitement. 'No? Well, all right, if you're sure. Yes. We'll see you soon. Bye.'

She put the phone back in its cradle. 'He said it's taken him hours, but I don't know where from, cos there aren't any trains on Christmas Day, are there? He's hired a taxi. It'll cost him a fortune!'

'He won't mind!' Gilbert picked up his glass and reached for the wassail bowl on the dresser where the sliced apple and oranges still floated on the depleted red wine. 'Well.' He blew out a breath. 'This calls for a celebration.'

Dot took the glass from him. 'Tell you what. Why don't you make us a pot of tea and we'll sit down for a bit? Dinner won't spoil if we turn 'oven down for half an hour or so; we're going to have a hectic time once Bill gets here and you'll be upset if you miss anything by getting plastered before 'day is half over.'

He pulled a face at her but complied, and forty minutes later as Bill's taxi pulled up at the door they were relaxed and smiling, the turkey still warm in the bottom oven, the roast potatoes crisp and hot, the sprouts and other vegetables waiting for their turn to be cooked and the red wine all the better for having breathed steadily for the last half hour.

'It was a sudden decision and I wasn't sure if I could get here in time.' Bill leant back from the dining table. 'I didn't want to tell you in case I couldn't and that would have been so disappointing, but I was dead lucky. I met a bloke on the plane to Gatwick who was being picked up and driven to York, so I offered to go halves if I could share the trip and then managed to hitch a lift all the way to Hull.'

He grinned. 'I was basking in the Sydney sun just over two days ago and I suddenly got a yen for an old-fashioned Christmas dinner with all the trimmings.'

'Well, you almost missed it.' Dot brought in the blazing Christmas pudding, the brandy on top burning a blue haze, the holly sprig blackening. 'Another half an hour before you called and we'd have started without you.'

'But you didn't fly all that way just for Christmas dinner?'

Liz began, but the look in her brother's eyes made her falter, 'Even though Dot makes the best pudding in the world. It's *delicious*, Dot, but I'm absolutely stuffed.'

'No, of course not,' Bill said. 'But I haven't been back for nearly twelve months and I didn't want you to forget what I looked like.' He squeezed Liz's arm and winked. He's different, she thought, he even sounds different; a strange sort of accent – a drawl which he didn't have before – and he seems remote somehow, as if he's grown away from us, which is inevitable, I suppose. A sadness seemed to draw close around her; he has, after all, done his growing up away from home, in other lands and with other people.

Chris rang her in the evening as she had hoped he would, but she couldn't talk to him properly. Bill had put on some loud music and was whirling Dot around the room, bending her over backwards as she instructed him in the art of an improvised tango, and just as Liz put down the phone they crashed in a tangled heap of arms and legs on the floor.

'Oh God, I won't be able to move in the morning.' Dot collapsed on to the sofa next to Gilbert. 'I'm too old for this sort of caper.'

'Not you.' Gilbert smiled at her. 'You were always 'best on the floor.' His arm was resting along the top of the sofa and Liz saw his hand steal gently behind Dot's neck, caressing softly with his fingers; Dot's eyes closed for a moment, and then she opened them to gaze back at him. Liz saw the almost imperceptible rise of her father's head and Dot's silent, willing acquiescence before she said it was time she was going home.

'Aren't you staying, Dot?' Bill turned to her in surprise.

'Some of us have work in 'morning,' Gilbert said. 'Come on then, Dot, I'll walk you home.'

Dot kissed Liz and Bill goodnight, and as Gilbert followed

her to the door he called back, 'Better lock up after me, Liz. I'll take a walk around 'village. I've got my keys.'

'All right. I'm going off to bed soon,' she answered, playing the game along with him. 'I think I'll have a sleep in in the morning.'

'What is it with those two?' Bill laughed, after they'd gone. 'Who do they think they're kidding?'

Liz shrugged. 'It doesn't matter, if that's the way they want it. It's their way of being discreet.'

Christmas Day was the one day in the year when the Ship was closed, but on Boxing Day it was business as usual, and while he prepared the bar Gilbert suggested that Liz take Bill off for a walk. 'He looks as if he could do with some fresh air,' he said. 'He's a bit pale under that suntan.'

They all looked pale in comparison with Bill's deeply tanned complexion; even his black hair was in marked contrast to his sister's and father's.

'You look like a gypsy.' Liz took his arm as they left the pub through the back door.

'I am a gypsy,' he said. 'I always was. I always want to be moving on.'

'But sooner or later you'll settle,' she said persuasively. 'What are the clichés? Come into harbour; cast anchor; make port?'

He gave a non-committal shrug. 'Come on, let's go down the Old Road. I want to see what's left of it.'

There was a blistering wind blowing off the sea as they walked down the puddled, broken road and Bill drew in a sharp breath. 'I'd forgotten just how blooming cold it is in England.'

'You've gone soft,' Liz said teasingly, brushing her hair back from her face. 'Swanning around in those hot climates, your backbone's melted.'

'Too right it has. I couldn't stand this now. Give me a soft warm breeze any day.' He hunkered down into his coat and shivered.

'Your accent! I've been trying to place it. You've picked up an Aussie twang.'

'That's because I've got an Aussie girlfriend. Nadia. That's another reason why I came home; I wanted to tell you and Dad about her. She would have liked to come with me to meet you both but she couldn't get away. She helps run her family's farm, and they're always short-handed around Christmas time.'

Liz looked enquiringly at her brother. 'Is she special?'

'Sure is; we're going to get married in April when my next leave is due.'

Liz stopped in her tracks. 'Married! Aren't you rushing things a bit? You're only just twenty-one.'

He shrugged. 'What difference does that make? And she'll keep on living at the farm whilst I'm away; there's an annexe which her dad says we can have, we just have to do a bit of decorating. It's great, Liz – you'd love it. It's just outside Victoria, great tracts of countryside, miles and miles of sky; just like here, only blue and warmer.'

Liz felt a lump growing in her throat. 'That means we shall never see you, and if you have children we won't see them either.'

'Sure you will. You'll have to come over, meet the family; you'll get on well with Nadia and her folks; everybody does. You might even think of staying. It's a great country!'

'No,' she said sharply. 'You know I can't do that. You know how I feel about this place.'

'Where's your spirit of adventure? There's a lot of world out there, just waiting to be seen.'

'Waiting to be seen?' she repeated. 'But I don't want to just look at a place, a country – I need to be a part of it, to belong. I thought you understood that?'

'Sure I do, but if people like Nadia's forebears hadn't packed their bags and gone to look at fresh fields, then Australia or the States wouldn't be what they are today.'

'That's different,' she said passionately. 'People then were escaping from poverty and hardship; they were pulling themselves out of dirt and squalor, searching for a better life for themselves and their families; somewhere they could put down roots.'

She stopped walking and put her hands over her ears. She could hear an echo of her own words in her head as if she had said or thought the same thing before, or had caught the emotions of someone else saying them.

She looked down over the broken edge of the road and saw that more chunks of cliff had slumped down and lay like a wide grassy green shelf twenty feet below. The tide was full; dashing spumes of dun-coloured water thundered and broke against the base of the clay cliffs and the colour changed into milk chocolate brown and frothy cream. Out towards the horizon sky and sea merged, and she blinked and stared as a phantasm of obscure and various shapes shifted and broke before her eyes, became constant so that they were almost recognizable and then tauntingly reshaped themselves, faded, and vanished.

'Well, then, aren't we talking about the same thing?' Bill's voice was irritable. 'Liz.' He glanced at her. 'Liz, are you OK? You're not having one of your funny turns? Don't tell me you're still on with all that stuff?'

She stared at him vaguely.

'You don't still think you see things, for God's sake? Haven't you got over that yet?'

Liz shook her head to clear it. 'What were we talking about?'

Bill snorted impatiently. 'You used to scare the pants off me when we were kids: "Let's go and find Sarah" you used to say,' he mimicked a childish voice. 'And there was never anyone there.'

'Yet you used to say that you'd been playing with her when I was in school.' She smiled at the recollection. 'I never really believed you.'

'That was only because I didn't have anyone to play with,' he said. 'I was jealous, I suppose, of you being at school when I wasn't, so I used to pretend that I had seen her, but I felt really creepy even talking about it.' He gave a slight shudder. 'Still do.'

'She's very real to me.' Liz spoke softly, knowing that he wouldn't understand, that he never had understood. They retraced their steps down the lane after Bill decided that it was too cold to walk along the cliff and too dangerous. 'You shouldn't walk out here alone,' he said. 'You could catch your foot in one of those cracks, or the edge could give way . . . You could lie there for hours and no one would know.'

'I'm always careful,' she said. 'I know where not to walk. I know every inch of this path, every new crack that appears.'

They stopped at the gate of one of the derelict cottages. 'Shall we go into Granny's?' said Bill.

Liz hesitated. 'I don't know. I never do. I still miss her.'

He lifted the gate; one of the hinges had come off and it leant lopsidedly on one side. The gravel path to the door had long since been submerged by earth and nettles, and thorny fingers of dead brambles reached out from the small front garden and tore at their clothing.

'I don't know if this is a good idea.' Liz was hanging back.

'There's no harm in it.' Bill looked through a crack in one of the boarded-up windows. 'I used to come after school with some of the other kids; we used to climb in through a window at the back and have a smoke.'

'How could you?' Liz said reproachfully.

'Only at first. I didn't come after Gran died.'

Such a pity, Liz thought. She would have lived so much longer if she could have stayed here. She thought with affection of her grandparents, of her grandpa's shiny bald head and bristly ginger moustache, which he used to rub on the back of her neck to make her laugh, and of her tiny grandmother, who sat her at her table on a tall stool where she swung her legs and waited for warm bread and home-made jam, and then jokingly made her promise not to tell her mother. *But Mum always found out, of course – the tell-tale sticky mouth gave the game away – and then she would complain to Dad that Granny was spoiling us.*

'I often wondered why she didn't come and live with us after Grandpa died,' Bill said, trying the door. 'Shall we go round the back? I mean, we had plenty of room at the Ship, and it had been her home before we had it.'

'Maybe that's why she wouldn't.' Liz followed him round the side of the house to the back door. She knew that the reason their granny wouldn't come and live with them after the council had decided that the road was unsafe, and the cottages a danger to the occupants as the foundations were subsiding, was because she didn't like her son's wife Nina, mother of Liz and Bill.

When her grandfather retired from pub life, Liz's father took over the running of the Ship and her grandparents moved into the cottage which overlooked the sea and was where her grandmother had been born. Her grandfather helped out in the pub when they were busy, did odd-jobbing for local farmers, chopping and delivering wood, but was happiest of all when he was digging in his vegetable garden or wrapped up in thick hand-knitted jerseys and woolly hats to go fishing from the shore.

Liz still remembered that summer evening when her granny

went to the cliff edge to call him in for his tea. She'd heard her say that she'd called and called, but he didn't answer, so in her exasperation she climbed down the wooden steps, hurling lively abuse at his tardiness, his deafness, his inability to tell the time, and found him sitting perfectly still in his old canvas chair, with the rod in his hands and the sea lapping around his boots, gazing with sightless eyes at the remote horizon and hearing nothing.

'She never seemed lonely, did she, all those years on her own?' Bill said. 'Or maybe she just never said.'

Liz didn't answer. The old lady was always busy, making and mending, baking pies and scones and giving them all away, spring cleaning an already spotless home, and welcoming anyone who called.

I sometimes took Sarah with me, she thought; we played in the garden. I remember the smells of summer, bright blue forget-me-nots and yellow daffodils, apple blossom and primroses, the perfume so heady and sweet that I wanted to drink it, so penetrating in its intensity that it almost overpowered me.

'I'm a Foster too,' *said the little girl, jumping up and down, both feet coming off the ground, a beaming smile on her face and tendrils of red curls bouncing under the frill of her bonnet. Elizabeth took hold of her hand and jumped and skipped with her amongst the flowers and tried to explain that her surname was Foster Rayner, but she became out of breath with jumping and her words got jumbled and Sarah looked puzzled and wrinkled her freckled nose and didn't understand her.*

'I don't want to go in,' Liz said quickly when she saw the panels of the back door yielding under Bill's weight. 'Let's go.'

Bill hesitated for a second and then he too turned away, haunted perhaps by similar memories. 'Only a year after she went into that home, wasn't it?'

'Yes, but it was her choice, her decision; there was no arguing with her.' She shivered, not with the cold but with the memory of her grandmother uprooted from her birthplace, her once busy hands still, her small body like a flower deprived of water visibly shrinking day by day, patiently waiting for the end.

'Do you want to go up to the mill?' she asked as they came to the end of the lane.

'Not particularly,' he said in surprise. 'I'd rather go home for a hot toddy.'

'If you go to live in Australia permanently you'll lose your chance of ever getting the mill.' It was a vain attempt to rekindle childhood aspirations.

'You've got to be joking.' He looked at her squarely. 'Wake up, Liz. I never wanted to live there, not after Carl Reedbarrow threatened to throw me off the top!'

She gasped. 'I never knew that!'

'Well, he did. He asked me if I wanted to look at the view from the top floor. I was about eight or nine at the time. I think his mother was out and he was being really friendly. I knew we'd been told not to go there on our own, but I thought it would be good fun.'

Liz nodded. She remembered her father shaking his finger and telling them that the mill was out of bounds, never mind why.

'Anyway,' Bill went on, 'I looked back when we were halfway up and he was right behind me, and I saw he had a length of rope in his hands. I began to get a bit panicky, and said I'd changed my mind and wanted to go down, but he kept pushing me up, poking me in the back, and he had this scary grin on his face and then he pushed me towards the hatch where the sails used to be.' He faltered. 'I still have nightmares about it sometimes. He made me lean out, said he was going to hold on to the other end of the rope and swing me; he kept saying "You'll enjoy it, Bill; don't worry, I won't let you fall."

'Well, I was kicking like mad and trying to shout, but he had one hand over my mouth so I couldn't, and he was very strong even though he looked such a wimp. And then, suddenly, he let go of me. His father had just driven into the yard. I didn't see him but Carl had heard the motor, and I tell you, Liz, I'd thought I was scared, but I wasn't as scared as he was; he was shaking like a jelly, and he unfastened the rope and said if I ever told anybody he really would push me over.' Bill squared his broad shoulders and laughed mirthlessly. 'I feel better for telling you that; maybe I'll go over and ask him to try it again.'

'I had no idea.' Liz was shocked, lost for words.

'So your daft ideas about inheritance and all that rubbish never did mean anything to me. I wouldn't have the mill if it was handed to me on a gold plate; that was your dream, Liz, never mine.'

She stared at him. 'But we used to talk about it; plan what we would do when it was ours. Or was that just a game?'

'Of course it was; I never did think of it as anything else. It was you and Mum, Mum especially; she was always telling us that it really belonged to us, the Foster Rayners. She shouldn't have done that, Liz. It wasn't true. It belongs to the Reedbarrows; it came down to them legitimately through marriage, and there's no getting away from it.'

He put his hand on her shoulder, her younger brother who was such a realist; a practical man with solid dreams, not delusional ones like her own. 'Come on,' he said. 'Let's go back. I'm frozen stiff.'

'You go,' she said. 'Go and talk to Dad; tell him about Nadia. I'll stay out a bit longer.' She smiled sweetly. 'I'm a lot tougher than you.'

He shook his head. 'No you're not; you've got your head full of dreams. It's time you came back to the real world, Liz, and stopped pretending.'

When he had gone, compulsion led her up the lane to the church and into the churchyard. She wandered about amongst the gravestones, looking at the fresh flowers and holly wreaths that had been placed there; she saw her mother's grave and the yellow chrysanthemums that her father had brought, and she thought about what Bill had said.

Why had her mother made so much fuss about the mill? It wasn't as if she were local, not like Dot who had been born in Tillington and had her roots here. Two things about her mother had remained vivid in Liz's mind for seven years: she violently disliked all the Reedbarrows, and she had been a vigilant, possessive protector of what she believed to be her children's rights.

'I don't know what to do, Mum,' she whispered. 'You've insinuated this obsession into me and I can't shake it off.'

Whispered sounds in the churchyard filled her head as the ghosts of the past embraced her. The wind blew through the old yews, which creaked and groaned as their branches rubbed against each other, and she walked silently, watching and listening, wandering through the familiar yet unknown landscape like a transcendent spirit.

'Elizabeth.' Sarah beckoned to her. She was standing in the lane outside the church gate, shadowy and unsubstantial, yet real and earthly. She beckoned again, and Elizabeth followed her—

'Elizabeth.' The voice was persistent and slightly irritable. 'Elizabeth.' Slowly Liz turned, remote and preoccupied, and found herself at the top of the lane near the mill. She breathed in a shaky breath, and saw Alf Wainwright, his short bent figure leaning against the mill gate, waiting for her. 'Are you a bit deaf?'

She shook her head. 'No.'

'You're in a world of your own, then. I've been trying to get your attention for 'last five minutes!'

'Sorry. I was thinking about something.'

'Hmm. Or somebody. You'll have been thinking on yon chap that's been hanging around, I reckon?'

'I don't know what you mean.'

'Don't you? Well, I don't miss much. We don't all go deaf and daft when we've logged up a few years, you know. Anyway,' he conceded, 'he seems a decent enough fellow.'

Liz sighed. She hadn't realized that Alf Wainwright had ever met Chris. Probably he hadn't, but that didn't mean he didn't know about him. There wasn't much worth knowing that the old man *didn't* know about.

'Come over here,' he said.

She moved reluctantly towards him. A slight tremor ran through her.

'You're all right, 'dog won't bite you; he's harmless enough.'

Ben had ambled up to the gate, his tail wagging, and she put her hand through the bars to stroke him. It wasn't Ben who had made her shake, nor even the thought of Carl Reedbarrow, but her friend Sarah, who had drifted through the gate and into the yard towards the mill just before Alf Wainwright's voice had intruded upon her. The dog sniffed her hand, then suddenly backed off and sprinted across the yard with his tail between his legs.

'Now, then, what's up? Summat's frightened him.' The old man gave a wavering whistle towards the dog, who was now hiding in his kennel.

'He's probably been told to keep away from me,' she said mildly. 'I'm not exactly welcome here.'

'Well, never mind about that now. I wanted to show you where your grandfer and me used to play when we were lads.'

Liz frowned slightly. Was this all he wanted, to reminisce? Still, she thought, if he hadn't seen her he would have kept his memories locked away; she should feel privileged to be allowed to share them with him. She looked up at the mill.

'Did you play inside?' She thought of Bill's fear of Carl Reed-barrow's bullying antics.

'Play inside? Play inside? Course we didn't play inside. We'd have been given short shrift if we'd attempted to. No! There was still some milling being done; they'd had a new engine put in a few years before, mainly for animal fodder, but your grandfer and me . . .' He paused for a minute. 'What was I saying? Ah, that's right. We used to come sometimes to help out in 'yard, filling sacks and loading 'wagon and such like, but what I was going to tell you about was when we swung on 'sails.'

'You swung on the sails?'

'Aye, we did.' The old man started to chuckle, and she could see a trace of boyish mischief on his wrinkled cheeks.

'Anyway,' he went on, 'we'd finished our jobs and were just going to fetch off home when 'wind got up and started to turn 'sails, and your grandfer – he was allus one for a lark – dared me to catch hold and swing round.'

She looked up and saw the white canvas sails turning against the skyline. Pink-etched clouds romped across the sky, blown by the buffeting wind, and in the yard shadowy figures moved about their business: men with laden sacks which they stacked under cover of a barn; a woman with a pail of corn which she scattered to scratching fowl; and grubby children who played in the dirt without any admonishment from their elders.

'Anyroad, not to be outdone, I said I would if he would,' Alf went on. 'So we pushed 'cart over to stand on, cos we weren't very big and couldn't reach, and on 'count of three we jumped and then we were up and away and, by, we were that scared but exhilarated at 'same time; 'wind was blowing quite hard and we had to hang on for all we was worth. We went round three or four times and then, just as sudden, 'wind dropped and we were stuck.'

He started to laugh. 'By, I nearly cried. We couldn't jump cos we were too far off 'ground. We just hung there, our legs dangling, cramp in our arms and our hands red hot, and we just 'ollered as loud as we could for somebody to come and rescue us. Anyway, missus came out to find out what all 'din was about, and she fairly burst her sides laughing to see us. But it was a different matter when 'miller came out: he had to haul on 'ropes to fetch us down. He was that mad, said we could've broken our necks, never mind 'frames, but we never thought of that; it was just a lark.' He rubbed his behind. 'I can still feel 'sting from 'leathering I got when I got home.'

'You got a hiding, did you?' Liz grimaced at the thought.

'Oh aye, we both did. Old miller had to tell of us; we might have been killed if we'd tried again. We used to boast to 'other lads what we'd done and that we'd do it again, but we never did; we were too scared of another leathering.' He pulled up his collar. 'It's getting a bit nippy standing here. I'd better be off. I don't want to catch cold. Nice to have a chat, Elizabeth.'

She watched him as he walked down the hill. His stick seemed to swing with an extra jauntiness, and she smiled at the thought of the young boy living on in the old man's body. Perhaps memory does linger on after we've gone, she mused. And perhaps some of us are permitted to look in on other people's memories to recapture a bit of the past.

She turned to look at the mill again. The yard was empty except for Ben, who had come out of his kennel and was standing looking back at her and wagging his stumpy tail.

CHAPTER SEVENTEEN

Chris took the right-hand junction on the M18 and headed for the eastern section of the M62. He watched in his driving mirror as the traffic behind him veered off towards Leeds, leaving only his car and a few lorries travelling in the direction of Hull.

Shall I go straight to Tillington, or should I go to the flat first? I don't know if Liz will be home; she might be out with her brother if he's still there. I should have phoned.

He'd telephoned Liz from his mother's on Christmas Day. He'd wanted to say that he was missing her, but she was full of the news that her brother had turned up from Australia and it hadn't seemed appropriate. He could hear laughter and music in the background and he put down the phone feeling deflated, as if he was missing out somehow. It was quiet with just his mother and him; she even seemed a little edgy and he felt that perhaps she would have made other arrangements if he hadn't come to spend Christmas with her.

The weather was mild. There had been rain that morning but it had cleared quickly, and now a pale sun hovered over the Humber estuary. As he approached the Humber Bridge the silver light touched its span and highlighted its slender tensile delicacy; he slowed down at the curve in the road and glanced at the old whiting mill on the foreshore, black and stark and lonely against the colourless sky and glinting water.

When he had first come to the area he had read an article about the East Riding which mentioned the hundreds of mills which lined this coast and riverside in the eighteenth and nineteenth centuries; almost every village had at least one corn mill to provide the farmers with a service and the inhabitants with flour. There are so few left, he thought; I must say the idea of a conversion appeals to me. Should I have a word with Carl Reedbarrow and see what I can find out? There's definitely something odd there.

He decided to keep on driving to Tillington, and when he arrived he parked his car at the back of the Ship. The garage door was drawn up and he saw Gilbert's old estate car, but Liz's car wasn't there and he felt a pang of disappointment. He stayed where he was for a moment, wondering what to do, but then he got out of his car and walked into the pub.

'Hello, Chris! Good to see you.' Gilbert reached across the bar and shook his hand. Dot turned from putting logs on the fire and gave him a wide smile; he smiled back, feeling comfortable with these people. 'It's nice to see a real fire,' he said, moving towards it, 'even though the weather isn't really cold today.'

'Ah, that's it, isn't it?' she said, sweeping up the ash with the hearth brush. 'Folks like to see the glow, especially in a pub; it makes everyone more cheerful. They gather round and chat and then while they're chatting they drink more beer!'

He laughed with her, then turned questioningly to Gilbert, who shook his head. 'She's out,' he said. 'She's taken Bill into Hull to visit their mother's relatives, and I don't know when they'll be back. They'll probably be asked to stay for a meal.'

'I should have phoned first,' Chris said. 'I just kept on going after I came off the motorway – I haven't even been back to the flat yet.'

'Well, stay and have something to eat with us.' Dot looked at Gilbert for confirmation. 'I was going to throw something together for Gilbert and me.'

'No, no I won't, thanks. I'll just take a walk, though, before I go back to Hull. I need to stretch my legs after sitting in the car so long.'

'I'll make you a sandwich,' Dot insisted. 'I'll bet you've nothing in your fridge for when you get home!'

He agreed that he hadn't, but said that his mother had packed him enough leftovers to last for a month so he knew he wouldn't starve, and went off for his walk.

Closing time at the Ship was half past two, but when he walked past the Raven at almost three o'clock he saw through the window that customers were still standing at the bar. On impulse, he turned in at the door. 'Are you still serving or am I too late?'

'Sure.' Kevin Warner got up from his stool behind the bar and stabbed out a cigarette in an ashtray. 'We're not so busy that we turn customers away just because it's out of hours, not that that seems to matter much nowadays.' He was a big man, taller than Chris and twice as broad. His dark hair was cut short, and his long nose had clearly been broken across the bridge.

Ex-rugby player, Chris thought; I bet he doesn't get any trouble in here.

'Where have I seen you before?' Kevin pulled him the pint of bitter he asked for. 'You've never been in here, have you?'

Chris shook his head, 'No, but I've got friends in the village.'

'He's having it off with Rayner's lass. That's why he's here.'

Chris swung round. Carl Reedbarrow was leaning against the fruit machine tossing a coin in his hand, a bedraggled hand-rolled cigarette between his lips. The lights from the machine glowed green, red and yellow, highlighting his pinched cheeks and turning his eyes as red as if caught in a camera flash.

'What did you say?' Chris put down his glass, but as he did so, he felt a restraining hand on his shoulder.

'Leave it.' Kevin Warner jabbed a warning finger at Carl Reedbarrow with his other hand. 'I've warned you before about stirring up trouble, and this is the last time I'll tell you, mate: once more and you're out of here for good.'

The door to the toilets opened, squeaking on its spring, and Alf Wainwright came out. Everyone looked towards him as he fastened his jacket and picked up a half-finished glass of beer from the end of the counter. He drained it, then took a handkerchief from his pocket and carefully wiped the corners of his mouth, looking at each man in turn as if realizing that he had interrupted something significant. He sat down at the nearest table, crossed his arms over his chest and waited.

'It's not me that's causing trouble.' Carl came away from the fruit machine and leant his elbows on the counter, an arm's length from Chris. 'Rayner's lot think they own 'village.'

'That's nowt to do with us,' Kevin Warner chipped in. 'I'll not have you upsetting my customers, and if you get banned from here you'll have to go to 'next village for your beer, cos you'll not be welcome at 'Ship.'

As if he hadn't heard a word, Carl stared moodily at his reflection in the mirror behind the counter, the Christmas fairy lights winking in bright white, harsh yellow and scarlet.

'They want my place, you know.' His top lip twitched in spasm as he turned towards Chris. 'Rayner's wife, the one that's dead; she was allus after it. She was a greedy tart, always going on at my mam, but they'll never get it, I'll see to that! Just because it used to belong to their family. Even if there'd been a contract, it wouldn't hold up in a court of law; stands to reason, dunnit?'

'And was there ever a contract?' Chris spoke quietly, trying not to break the man's train of thought, but Carl suddenly opened his eyes wide and looked around, then pushed away from the counter and headed for the door. 'Mind your own bleedin' business.'

When he had gone, Chris raised his eyebrows and laughed ruefully. 'How did I walk into that?'

'He's always having a go at the Rayners.' Kevin Warner sat back on his stool and lit a cigarette. 'And if you're a friend of theirs, you're going to catch it as well. I shouldn't bother too much, though; he's not all that bright.'

'Don't be too sure about that.' Alf Wainwright got up from the table and leant across for his overcoat, which was folded neatly over the back of a chair. Chris stood up and helped the old man into it, pulling a long scarf out of the sleeve.

'Will you have another drink?'

'No I won't. I've had my ration for today.' Alf wrapped the scarf around his neck and tucked it inside his coat, then turned up his collar. 'But don't go judging yon fellow; he might not seem right sharp but he'd make a bitter enemy.' He contemplated the landlord for a minute, then picked up his cap and jammed it on his head. 'I'll see you Friday.'

'These villagers always stick up for each other, have you noticed?' Kevin indicated towards the door as it swung to behind the old man. 'They can say what they like about each other, but they won't let outsiders like you or me say owt. Anyway, I still think Reedbarrow's a bad lot; for a start he never lets his wife out of the house. Nobody ever sees her. Another pint?'

Chris got up to leave. 'No thanks. I'm driving back to Hull. Just like Mr Wainwright, I've had my ration!'

'One pint.' The landlord was reluctant to let him go. 'One pint Monday, Wednesday and Friday, and he goes to 'Ship Tuesday, Thursday and Sat'day. He's done that for years, they say, shared out his custom.'

'What happens on Sundays?' Chris reached for the door handle.

'He stays home, has a couple of whiskies and watches television!'

The Ship and the Raven stood on the same side of the main road, with Church Lane and several village houses separating them, and as Chris set off back to the Ship he saw a white car travelling fast towards him. He was about to cross Church Lane when the car swung in front of him, its tyres squealing as it turned up the lane, racing past the church and up the incline towards the mill, where it came to an abrupt halt.

Carl Reedbarrow's got some rich friends, he thought, as he tried to see who was getting out of the car. Anybody who mistreats an expensive car like that has to be loaded.

Dot and Gilbert had waited for him before eating and the three of them sat in the kitchen and had soup and trencherman sandwiches. Chris confessed that he'd been into the Raven and had a beer. 'That's why I'm late back. I'm sorry if you've been waiting for me, Dot.'

'I should think so too, patronizing the opposition. What's 'latest gossip? Kevin Warner doesn't miss much.'

'I didn't stay long. Mr Wainwright was there, and Carl Reedbarrow.'

'It's Carl's local; he never comes here, never did,' Gilbert said. 'I expect his father stopped him.'

'Why would he do that? Is there a family feud? He said something about the Rayners always wanting his place.'

'Did he now?' Gilbert's face flushed. 'Well, Carl Reedbarrow should keep his mouth zipped if he knows what's good for him; I'm getting a bit fed up with him and his innuendos.'

'Sorry. Perhaps I shouldn't have mentioned it, though I think I'd rather know if somebody was spreading rumours about me.'

Dot shook her head at Chris as if to say *Drop the subject*, but Gilbert pushed his plate away and continued: 'I know it's not all his fault. He doesn't know the facts, and he's been fed on untruths since he was a young lad and everything's got magnified. God knows,' he muttered, 'I've done my best for them.'

Dot looked annoyed and stared at Gilbert for a moment; then, glancing at Chris, she got up from the table and started to clear away. 'We're guaranteed to get indigestion if we talk about 'Reedbarrows at mealtimes; shall we change the subject? Anyone for apple pie?'

Both men declined and Chris said he'd have to get moving. 'Will you tell Liz I'll ring her tomorrow? I hope I'll get a chance to meet her brother.'

'He's leaving tomorrow,' Gilbert said. 'Liz will be dropping him off at 'station; perhaps you could catch them there? I don't suppose you'll be back at 'college for ages?'

Chris smiled; everybody assumed that college lecturers had masses of holidays. 'Another week and then we start. Is Liz doing anything special for the New Year, do you know?'

A grin flickered around Gilbert's mouth. 'You'll have to ask her. We're having a fancy dress party here at 'Ship, so perhaps she'll invite you. Or you could buy a ticket and come anyway; the money is going towards our demo. You know – for the wall.'

As it was, he could have asked her immediately, for he was about to pull out of the Ship's yard when she drove in, but in the flurry of greetings and introductions he forgot all about it.

'Won't you come back in?' Liz asked. 'Do you have to go now?'

'It's your brother's last night at home. I don't want to intrude on a family gathering.'

'Don't worry about that.' Bill's reply was swift. 'Come on in, mate. I've had my fill of family gatherings; I could do with some lively company.'

'Thanks,' Liz snapped. 'I've just spent the whole day trailing you around to all the relatives and listening to you spouting all that claptrap about your travels while they hang on your every word, and you've the cheek to say that!'

Bill grinned. 'They loved it, didn't they? Oh, crikey, the tears when they heard I was going to live in Australia for good.'

'And you couldn't care less, could you?'

Chris heard the catch in her voice, but Bill heard it too and put his hand on her shoulder. 'Come on, Liz, you know I'm only joking. I shall miss you all, you know that.' He glanced at Chris. 'She's a sensitive soul is Liz, gets hurt real easy. You'll remember that, won't you?'

I don't need a raw youth like you to tell me that, Chris thought; you don't need to be related to someone to know their singularities. But he nodded agreeably and kissed Liz on the cheek and told her he wouldn't stay, but would ring her the next day.

He climbed back into the car and drove out of the village; it was already dark and he put the headlights on dip until he reached the main road. In his mirror he saw a car coming up fast behind him, the headlights on full beam. He pulled away to shake it off, or at least remind whoever was driving that he was being dazzled, but the car caught up and with a sudden thrust of power overtook him, forcing him over on to the verge.

'Idiot!' he shouted and put his own lights on full beam, catching the spoilers, racing stripes and twin exhausts of a familiar white car. In retaliation the driver stood on his brakes to flash bright red lights before switching on his glaring rear fog lights and pulling swiftly away.

CHAPTER EIGHTEEN

Liz was opening the mail in the back office when she heard footsteps on the stairs.

'Oh! I didn't think you'd be in today.' Steve looked surprised to see her and just a little taken aback. 'I said you could take the rest of the week off.'

'Yes, I know, but I've just dropped my brother off at the station so I thought I'd look in to see if there was anything urgent waiting.'

'You're so conscientious – how would I manage without you?' Steve made a grab and pulled her towards him. 'Are you going to give me a kiss for the New Year?'

'No I am not. Get off or I'll report you for sexual harassment!'

He moved back a step. 'Liz! Give me a break; it doesn't mean anything.'

'I dare say, but you just might try it on somebody who'll take you seriously and then you'll find yourself in real trouble.'

'No I won't,' he said sulkily. 'I only do it with you. I thought you were fond of me!'

She raised her eyebrows in exasperation. 'Clear off, will you, and leave me in peace so I can get finished and go home. Anyway, why are you here? I thought you were going away.'

'I am. Look at me.' He opened his arms wide and gave a slow twirl. 'I'm in my country gear; didn't you notice?'

He was dressed in beige corduroy trousers, a wool sweater and a dark green shooting jacket, with a tweed cap and leather boots to complete the look.

'Is your dog in the car?' she asked innocently.

'What? I haven't got a dog!'

'Then you'd better get one,' she said. 'That's the only thing that's missing; otherwise you're the perfect country gent.'

He looked at her suspiciously. 'I'm never sure when you're winding me up. Have I left a cheque book? I need to get some cash.'

She searched in a desk drawer and handed it to him. 'Are the banks open?'

'I hope so. I need a fair bit. I'm hoping to do a deal, but the guy wants cash.'

'Well, don't forget a receipt,' she said. 'You'll need it for the books.'

'OK. I'll see you next week. Have a good New Year.' He closed the door behind him, and then, opening it again, he puckered up his lips, closed his eyes in mock ecstasy, and said, 'One thing you can't do, Liz, is stop me thinking.'

'The man's a fool,' she muttered as his feet clattered down the stairs. She lifted the blind and looked out of the rear window; a group of tourists was strolling along the riverside walkway. Some had cameras, and were taking photographs of the silent yellow cranes with their empty buckets lying idle against piles of sand on the opposite bank, and of the red barges moored alongside.

She narrowed her eyes and stretched her neck to look up the waterway towards the swing bridge and the crush of traffic crossing it; in the distance she could see the tidal surge barrier at the mouth of the Hull and its confluence with the broad Humber. When she looked back the tourists had gone and the walkway was empty, yet she felt conscious of great activity and the sound of muffled voices reached her ears; there was the clattering of wood and metal, the rumbling of iron wheels on cobblestones, and an oily, heavy smell which permeated the building.

She dropped the blind and returned to her desk, putting the morning mail in a tray and locking the drawers before picking up her handbag and briefcase. She closed the door behind her and went into the front office.

The fax machine was switched on but there were no messages, and she wandered across to the window and looked out. The street was dim and full of shifting shadows; the buildings opposite, which were tall and narrow, excluded much of the daylight, and as she breathed in she put her handkerchief over her nose to keep out the fetid, nauseating smell.

She felt the beginning of a headache, and pressing her fingers to her temple she turned away from the window.

Something light, like muslin, touched her face and she brushed it away and turned towards the fire and the man standing beside it, who appeared to be waiting for her. He politely indicated her towards a chair and she slowly moved towards it and sat down, feeling the heat of the flames. She looked up at him and saw intensity in his blue eyes and felt the pleasurable sensation of enduring emotion.

He was about to speak and she lowered her eyes; she felt vulnerable, though not afraid, defenceless and compromised and yet assured of his regard and protection. Her mind was sinking into a subliminal state, and reason was suspended. She looked down at her hands, and they were hers; she looked at her feet and thought vaguely that her boots looked small and unfamiliar.

She lifted her head and opened her mouth to speak. She wanted to ask him, Am I here because of you? Or am I part of your life already? A life that I have mostly forgotten and can only remember in small fragments or see in slivers of reflection as though in a broken mirror.

There was something else she wanted to say, but she thought

he had understood her unspoken questions; and then he was gone and the door was open and someone was standing there.

'It's all right. It's all right. I'm so sorry – I didn't mean to frighten you. Didn't you hear me come up? I called out.'

Liz shook her head; she couldn't speak. Her mouth was dry and her heartbeat thumped so loudly she could feel it in her throat.

'What are you doing, sitting here in the dark? Where's the light switch?' Chris fumbled on the wall and pressed the switch, and a fluorescent tube flickered a few times and then filled the room with its cold blue light.

Liz shivered and looked down at the boarded-up fireplace. 'They used to light fires in here.' Her voice was a whisper.

Chris frowned. 'I expect they did. Have you finished here?'

She nodded and swung slowly off the typing chair.

'Come on, then. We'll go and have a coffee.' He glanced at his watch. 'Or lunch if you like.'

'Is it only lunch time?' she asked vaguely. 'I feel as if I've been here all day.'

'I've just seen that prat of a boss of yours,' he said as she locked the doors behind them. 'We passed each other just now on the street. He stopped me to say he was still looking for a property for me.'

'He recognized you?' Her head was aching, her thoughts hazy and indistinct. 'He's only seen you once, hasn't he? That time in Louis' place. Why do you call him a prat?'

'Because he almost had me off the road last night, coming back from Tillington. I recognized the car just now when he got in it.'

She didn't answer; she wasn't really in the mood for discussing Steve or his fast cars. She felt decidedly shaky.

They lunched in a café in the marketplace and looked out of the small-paned window across to Holy Trinity church and the empty square.

'No market today?'

'No,' she said vaguely. 'Tuesday, Friday and Saturday.' She put her chin in her hands and gazed out. 'I think I've had a paranormal experience.'

He didn't answer, but gazed at her over the rim of his cup.

'It was so strange. I felt as if I was in another time, or living a dream; even now, sitting here with you, talking, I feel misplaced . . . as if I belong somewhere else.'

'Which time?'

Dimly she stared at him. 'What?'

'You said you felt that you were in another time. Which time were you in? Past or future?'

'Oh – past, I suppose, judging by our clothes.'

'Whose clothes?'

'The man's and . . . mine, I think.'

She looked into space. *It didn't occur to me that I was wearing different clothes; why did I say that? But my skirt felt long about my ankles and there was something odd about my boots.*

She crossed her legs beneath the table and felt the filmy resilience of nylon beneath her knee-length skirt. 'The man – he was wearing a shirt with a frill, a cravat or something, I think, and breeches as you'd expect; and the girl was wearing a long dress and a bonnet.'

She stopped. *The girl? So it wasn't me? Was it Sarah? Why did I think it was me?* Chris was watching her. 'It can't have been me after all,' she said weakly. 'I must have thought I'd seen two people.'

'I don't know anything about this sort of thing,' Chris said.

'Do you think I'm crazy, seeing and hearing things?'

He shook his head and caught hold of her hands across the table. 'Listen, I don't know about these things, but I think it's quite possible that some people do have links with the past; look at mediums and people who go to séances. Oh, I know that there are charlatans, but there are a lot of people out there who believe that there is another sphere, another layer of life, as well as this one.'

She withdrew her hands from his and linked her fingers together. 'Do you think I ought to talk to someone about all this?'

'Who? A psychologist, do you mean?'

She kept her eyes averted and didn't answer.

'No, I don't. I think that when all is said and done, there might be some rational explanation. You're probably a bit overwrought. You've been busy over Christmas, Bill has just gone away, you're probably thinking about the weekend . . .'

'Oh, New Year! We're having a fancy dress party. I'd forgotten. I have to choose a costume.'

'There you are, then. What did I tell you?' His eyes crinkled into a smile and she smiled back, a warmth running through her as she realized how much she'd missed him.

'When you look at me like that . . .' he began, his voice low, and stopped.

'Yes?' she said, watching his lips.

'I really want to kiss you.'

He'd kissed her cheek before, when greeting or leaving her, but only then; when he'd given her the wooden seal she had kissed him as if they were friends, which she thought they now were. She leant in towards him. 'So why don't you? Are you waiting for permission?'

'I suppose I am,' he said softly. 'And also, there are quite a lot of people in here.'

'They won't mind, or care,' she whispered. 'Let's dare.'

CHAPTER NINETEEN

'OK, switch off all 'electric lights except for 'tree and 'bar,' Gilbert called through to Jack in the other room. He adjusted the wick of a paraffin lamp, carefully lit it, and hooked it up on to a beam, then just as carefully took it down again. 'That's too low; somebody'll crack his head on it,' he muttered. 'Put 'lights on again for a minute, Jack, while I see where to put this lamp.'

He wandered around the room trying it in different corners, and finally settled for a shelf out of the way of any draught and too high for awkward elbows. 'It stinks a bit,' he mumbled, 'but maybe it'll burn off. Right – put 'lights out again ready for when people come in.'

He looked around with some satisfaction. It had been his idea to add an extension to the small snug, but his father had resisted any change, and it wasn't until the old man died and the property came to him that he was able to do as he wanted. Now only an expert could tell what was old and what was new, for the new had mellowed and blended with the original except that now there was room to accommodate extra tables for the customers who had heard of their good food, and there were comfortable chairs to relax in and efficient plumbing in the washroom.

Jack came through from the lounge where he had been lighting the candle lamps on each table. He'd dressed in a long cotton smock and had tied string beneath the knees of his baggy cord trousers. Two handkerchiefs were knotted together and carefully arranged on his thinning grey hair, and through the knots he'd pushed several pieces of straw.

'You look like a ruddy porcupine with that on your head,' Gilbert said. 'Just who are you supposed to be?'

'I'm a country yokel, aren't I?'

'Well, there's no doubt about that.' Gilbert grinned. 'No doubt at all. I'm just going to get changed; I'll be down in ten minutes.'

'Well, what you going to wear?' Piqued, Jack peered at his dim reflection in the mirror on the wall.

'It's a surprise,' Gilbert called back as he went through the door into the private quarters. 'You might not even recognize me.'

'In that case don't be surprised if I charge you for your drinks!' Jack shouted back.

Dot breezed in through the front door. 'I'm sorry I'm so late; I intended to be here to help get everything set up. Where's Gilbert?'

'He's just gone up to get changed.' Jack watched her as she took off her coat. 'Who've you come as?'

'Can't you guess? I'm a barmaid, of course – a serving wench.' She opened a shopping bag and brought out a large jug, which she balanced provocatively on her hip. 'Look, I've brought a jug to serve the ale.'

She delved into the bag again, pulled out a mob cap fashioned out of scraps of gingham, and pressed it on to her fair curls. Moving to the mirror, she took out her lipstick and made a circular spot on each cheek, rubbing them in with her finger. 'It's a bit dark in here, isn't it?'

'Well, that's what I thought, but this is how Gilbert wants it.

144

By, you look smashing, Dot.' Jack's eyes brightened as she joined him behind the bar. 'I like your frock.'

Dot's eyebrows shot up at the compliment. 'I'll probably catch pneumonia, but never mind; it'll please 'customers.'

She looked round appreciatively. Gilbert had draped small fishing nets studded with cleaned and scraped crab and lobster shells above the bar counter, and above them a large notice pronounced that newcomers were entering Neptune's Cave.

'It looks good,' she said, and then laughed as she surveyed the full glory of Jack's outfit. 'Been rolling down 'haystacks have you, Jack?'

The inner door opened and Liz came in. Dot looked at her admiringly. 'You look lovely, Liz. So demure and graceful. So, so – right, somehow.'

Liz was wearing a silvery grey dress with a low neckline and a long skirt that swished about her ankles. Over it she wore a white cotton apron and on her head, with a few wispy tendrils of red hair fetchingly escaping, was a white linen cap, both found amongst her grandmother's things years ago, and had now been washed and starched until they were crisp and crackly.

Smiling mischievously, she returned Dot's compliment. 'And you'll have to watch out tonight, Dot. No man will be able to resist that neckline!'

'Yes, you're right.' Dot adjusted her cleavage, pushing a white handkerchief down the bodice. 'I only hope my neck doesn't go red.'

Liz glanced around the bar and lounge and went to inspect the large Christmas tree with its glittering stars and flickering candles. Pine needles were dropping rapidly on to the red sheet beneath it, and Liz breathed in the pungent aroma. Christmas has been and gone, she thought. I wonder what next year will bring.

Customers started to come in, first the older regulars in groups of two and three, who settled themselves at their favourite tables near to the fire and the bar. Most had made some effort at fancy dress, including one man who had whitened his face like a clown and kept dropping on to his knees and singing until his embarrassed wife, who was not in costume, told him to shut up.

Matt Wilson was still recognizable, dressed as an onion-seller with a navy blue striped sweater and a Breton beret crooked over his ear and followed by a woman dressed as a schoolgirl in a minuscule uniform and black suspenders on her shapely thighs. There was a policeman who kept bending his legs, knees akimbo, and several sailors in various kinds of uniform which didn't appear to belong to any particular navy. Following them through the door came Alf Wainwright in a thick white guernsey beneath his navy jacket, an unlit pipe clenched between his teeth and a telescope under his arm. His trousers were tucked into heavy-duty socks and wellingtons, the tops of the socks turned over the rims of the boots, and on his head he'd rakishly angled a naval peaked cap.

'Well done, Alf,' someone shouted, and sporadic clapping broke out as he took his place at the bar. 'I just hope you're not going to light that pipe.'

Alf took the pipe from his mouth and looked at it. 'No I'm not. I haven't smoked a pipe since 'doctor said I had hemphysemey. This isn't mine; it was my da's. You can't get them like this any more.'

'You should grow a beard,' someone else called out. 'You'd really look like an old salt then.'

'I used to have a full set 'til a year or two back,' he told them, rubbing his chin, 'but I thought it were mekkin' me look old, so I shaved it off.'

'I wish your dad would hurry up, Liz,' Dot muttered. 'We're going to be busy by the look of it.'

Liz laughed. 'I think he might be having a problem with his outfit; maybe I'd better go and give him a hand.' But before she could move Dot put her hand to her mouth and burst out laughing.

'Oh my goodness, who's this?'

Gilbert stumbled through the door, his entrance impeded by a large metal trident which had a realistic plastic fish skewered to it. On his head he wore a tatty long grey wig and a lopsided silver crown draped with seaweed, and around his chin was plastered a wet and straggly cotton-wool beard.

His chest was covered by a string vest through which he'd put one arm only, leaving one freckled shoulder bare; round his neck was a necklace of shells which Liz recognized as coming from her old toy box.

Dot and Liz fell about laughing, there were hoots and whistles from the crowd, and Jack, turning to his customer at the bar, said, 'And I thought I looked daft.'

Liz went to help out with the buffet, where plates of sandwiches, both turkey and chicken, hot sausage rolls, quiches and mince pies were included in the price of the tickets. She kept glancing towards the door, watching for Chris, hoping that he wouldn't be long. She'd felt so mixed up that last day at the office, so emotionally strung up over the incident that she couldn't explain, and then Chris turning up as he did when she wanted nothing more than to feel his arms around her, keeping her safe. But, as always, he had held back, even though she felt that he wanted that too.

Having driven home after picking up her dress from the costumier's, she had been in such a feverish state of churning frustration that she snapped at her father over something quite trivial, and to his consternation had gone off on a long walk on the cliff top in the gathering dusk to work off some of the restless energy that was overwhelming her. She had apologized to him when she came back, but remained unsettled.

At last, leaning over a table, she felt Chris's arms around her waist and heard him whisper in her ear, 'Fair maid, prithee bring me a jug of ale, for I've galloped many miles to be with you tonight.'

She turned to look at him. 'You look very handsome, sir,' she began, just as Dot called from the bar, saying 'That's a shapely pair of calves if you'll pardon me for saying so', and raised a glass to him.

He laughed. 'I'm not very comfortable; I can hardly walk in these boots.' His legs were encased in tight riding boots over white breeches, and he wore a dark green velvet tailcoat with a white frilled shirt and swirled a tricorn hat on a finger. 'I drew the line at wearing a wig, which is what the girl in the shop wanted, and settled for a ribbon instead.' He turned his head to show her.

'I feel very strange dressed like this, too,' Liz said, 'especially in here with the lights out, and just the glow from the lamps and the fire; it's very atmospheric. Don't worry,' she added hastily as a look of concern crossed his face. 'I'm not going to have hallucinations or anything.'

'Well, that's a relief.' Chris exhaled a sigh. 'I don't want you disappearing into thin air when I've only just got here; it took me long enough to get ready. There's no wonder the gentry had to have servants to get them dressed – I can't wait to get back into my jeans and sweater.'

Later, when the evening was almost over, Liz waved a prearranged signal to her father, who nodded. His face was hot and flushed, and he reached for a glass of beer on the shelf behind him and took a long swallow, before picking up the trident and banging it hard on the wooden floor. 'Can I have your attention, please!'

A general groan went up. 'You're too early, Gilbert. It's only quarter to. I thought we had an extension 'til half past?'

'Can we have some quiet, please? I only want to say a few words.'

More good-humoured banter followed, implying that he couldn't possibly say only a few words once he'd got the floor, but eventually they were ready to listen.

'In another ten or fifteen minutes we shall be entering another year, another decade, and as you know, 'main purpose of our function this evening, apart from 'obvious one of enjoying ourselves, is to add to 'funds of the Save Tillington Project. But that isn't 'only reason we're here. We also need you to show your support by your enthusiasm and your commitment to 'cause.'

Liz looked round the room. It was lit by the warm glow of the candle lamps on the wooden tables and the flickering flames of the fire reflected in the copper pans and horse brasses. There was a smell of wax polish and the sweet perfume of the hyacinths that sat on the deep windowsills, and as she watched she saw that people were listening intently, watching over the rims of their drinking glasses and nodding their heads silently in agreement. A crowd had gathered in the doorway of the lounge, craning their necks and shushing those who, out of sight, were still talking.

Gilbert pushed the wig further back on his head and wiped his forehead with the back of his hand, his crown tilting over one ear. 'What I want to suggest is that you set up your own working committee, one that isn't bound by rules and regulations like 'parish council, but can get on with a scheme that 'powers that be will listen to.'

'You're dead right, Gilbert,' voices shouted out. 'Absolutely spot on. That's what we want. But who's going to set it up?'

'Well, I'm going to put Liz on to you and you can sort it out between you, because as a parish councillor my hands are tied.'

Liz came towards the bar and Chris lifted her up on to it so that everyone present could see her. She looked at the clock on the wall; she had less than eight minutes before it struck midnight and she wanted to catch their emotions at precisely the right moment.

'There are not many residents in Tillington,' she began. 'Most of the younger generation, people of my age, are moving away. Why? We haven't had an influx of new houses or new people the way other villages have. Why? Does anybody know?'

She didn't wait for an answer but plunged right on. 'I'll tell you why, because everybody out there' – she waved her hand vaguely inland – 'thinks that we're finished; they think that Tillington will end up in the sea – and they're right! Tillington will fall into the sea unless *we*, the remaining residents, do something about it.'

People were starting to stand up. Hands were being raised, earnest discussions started in small splinter groups, and questions were being called out.

'What Tillington needs is a wall!' Liz had to shout to make herself heard. 'What Tillington needs is a wall to keep the sea back!'

The woman in the school uniform, only slightly inebriated, stood up. Raising both arms above her head and wiggling her hips, she sing-songed, 'Tillington needs a wa-all! Tillington needs a wa-all.'

'Tillington needs a wa-all!' The onion-seller grabbed her round the waist and congoed her towards the bar.

Laughing, everybody except the very elderly or staid put down their glasses and caught hold of their nearest neighbour, and soon a snaking line of spirited Tillington inhabitants and their friends was winding its way into the lounge past the glittering Christmas tree – some remembering to duck their heads under the low ceiling and others not – towards the far door, which someone was conveniently holding open, and disappearing into the night.

'Heck! I hope they come back.' Jack gazed round the half-empty room.

'They'll be back in a minute.' Gilbert wearily poured himself a whisky. 'Apart from 'cold getting to them they'll remember 'free wine at midnight.'

They could hear the carousing coming closer again. Chris propped open the door, Gilbert, Jack and Dot poured wine into the glasses standing ready on a side table, and at one minute to midnight the crowd was back, faces flush from exertion and the biting cold air.

'To Tillington,' somebody shouted, holding up a glass as the chimes of Big Ben on the radio struck twelve. 'Happy New Year. To Tillington,' eager voices called back, and hugs and kisses were exchanged. 'And to our wall!'

Glasses were washed and dried, tables wiped over with damp cloths.

'You get off home now, Jack. And thanks a lot – you've done well.' Gilbert finished cashing up.

'OK, Gilbert. I must say I'm ready for my bed. It's been a good night. I'll see you all tomorrow.' Jack took the handkerchiefs from his head and smoothed his sparse grey hair and put on his coat.

'I'd leave them on, if I were you,' Gilbert grinned. 'Suits you. Besides, you might catch cold without 'em.'

Jack grunted. 'G'night, everybody. Or good morning. And happy new year.' He stepped outside and then put his head back in the doorway. 'I reckon there's a storm brewing up; that or we'll have snow in 'morning.'

Chris put his arms around Liz. 'You're not going to send me home, are you?' he whispered into her ear. 'You heard what Jack just said.'

She smiled and glanced towards her father, who was leaning heavily on the bar counter, his head propped up in his hands.

'Besides,' he said coaxingly, 'I've got something to tell you.'

'What?'

'Something I found out when I was in London.'

'Oh,' she said, faintly disappointed, but unsure why.

Gilbert stood up. 'Well, another year gone by, Liz.' He took off his wig and crown, tossed them under the bar and poured himself another whisky.

'You'll not remember much of this one if you have any more of that.' Dot slid the bottle away from him. 'You'll be a cup too low.'

'If I want another I'll have one,' he said flatly, moving the bottle back towards him, not looking at her. 'I'll go to 'devil in my own way.'

Dot turned away, a tremble on her lips.

Liz left Chris's side and sat on a stool near the bar. Her father leant his chin in his hand, staring down at the counter, then sombrely looked up at her and tweaked her cheek. 'What time is it in Australia?'

'I don't know, but I'm sure Bill will phone tomorrow – today, I mean.'

He nodded absently. 'Aye,' he sighed. 'Yep, another year gone.' He took a handkerchief from his pocket and blew his nose noisily, and Liz felt her eyes grow hot. This was a ritual they went through every New Year, ever since her mother had died.

'Dot?'

Dot had appeared with her coat on, her normally smiling mouth pinched and tight. 'I'll be going now, Liz.'

'No. No, don't go, Dot,' Gilbert appealed, his words slurred. 'Stay for a bit. Please! You know what I'm like.' He got up from behind the bar, came clumsily towards her and tried to put his arms round her, but she pushed him away. He looked puzzled and hurt. 'What did I do?'

'You forgot. That's what you did.'

'Forgot what? What did I forget?'

'If you can't remember then it isn't important.'

'Won't you stay, Dot?' Liz asked quietly. 'It's a bitter night.'

Dot's eyes met hers. 'No. I'd rather go home.'

Liz nodded understandingly and then gave her a hug. 'I know,' she said softly.

'I'll walk you home, Dot.' Chris got up from the chair where he had been a silent observer.

'Bless you, no. It's only a step.' Dot put up her coat collar and wrapped a large scarf around her head. 'I can manage on my own.' She took a deep breath. 'I've been doing it a long time.'

Gilbert suddenly screwed up his eyes and clenched his fists. 'What an idiot! Dot! Wait – please. I'm sorry.'

She hesitated at the door, her eyes wet. 'I'm not staying, Gilbert.'

'No. Wait. I'll get my coat – just a minute.'

She'd walked away when he came back, trailing his coat and a sweater.

'She's gone,' Liz said. 'You'll have to dash.'

'It's all right. I'll catch her up.' He pulled the sweater over his head. 'Erm, can you help Liz to lock up, Chris? You'll be stopping?' He patted his coat pocket. 'I've got my keys. I'll just see that Dot's all right, and then mebbe I'll have a walk round 'village. Have a breath of air.' He gave a sheepish grin. 'I'll see you in 'morning.'

'What was all that about?' Chris shot the two heavy bolts on the front door and turned the old iron key.

'Dad always gets worked up at the New Year. It's a busy time and then he thinks about Mum.' She bit on her lip. 'And he forgets that it's a difficult time for other people too, especially Dot.'

'Why Dot in particular?'

'Because it was New Year's Eve when her husband died, suddenly, two years after my mum.'

'Poor old Dot,' Chris murmured. 'And she's always so cheerful. Let's hope he catches up with her.'

'He will.' A smile flickered about her eyes.

'What about the back door?' he asked as they went through to the living room. 'Shall I just check the lock? Will your dad come in that way?'

'Bolt it,' she said, with her hand on the light switch. 'He won't be back tonight.'

CHAPTER TWENTY

'I'm going out.' Liz wrapped a long wool scarf several times round her neck and pulled a beret on her head; the week after the New Year the weather had turned bleak and bitterly cold, and a thick covering of snow in the city streets had crunched into splintering, leg-breaking furrows. 'If Steve comes in will you tell him I'm taking an early lunch? And if there are any calls for me to deal with, I'll ring back later.'

Susan nodded. 'Will do.' She had proved herself to be reliable and conscientious and Liz had no qualms about leaving her in sole charge.

It had been quiet most of the morning, with only an occasional phone call about properties that had been advertised. Steve hadn't been in at all, nor even telephoned, and Liz felt quite justified in taking an extended lunch hour; there had been many times when she'd barely been able to down a cup of coffee, let alone go out into the city, which was her destination now.

She cut through the narrow cobbled street leading out of the High Street; it was only just wide enough for a car, indicating a very different age. She crossed towards Holy Trinity Church, pausing and turning as she always did to look at the shifting, vacillating image of it in the bronze mirror-clad curtain walling on the building behind it.

The wind caught her full blast, its raw bite stinging her cheeks and making her gasp for breath as she came out on to the open space opposite the liner-shaped shopping centre which floated on the still waters of one of the old town docks. She resisted the momentary temptation to enter its haven of warmth and music and commercial splendours and pressed on, crossing the city square towards the whaling museum.

She thought about the notes on her ancestry that Chris had copied from the record office and which were still lying unread in a large brown envelope in her bedroom. It was like a Pandora's box tempting her with the secrets within, beckoning her to take a look and find the answers she sought, yet some cautionary diffidence, a sense of trepidation, had made her resist.

Do I really want to know who Sarah was? Will I be sad to know that she was alive and now is not? Whereas now . . . I feel as if she still exists: and if I find her, will I know my own self better?

The questions had tormented her for days; was it more desirable to keep her illusions or seek out the truth and risk discontent?

Then, this morning, as she drove carefully over the icy terrain into Hull, she had come to a decision, knowing she couldn't put it off any longer. She would go to the whaling museum and find out who had lived in the High Street building, and tonight after work she would read through Chris's notes.

As she pushed open the double doors of the museum she was assailed by a recording of the plaintive, emotive sound of the whales' song, and immediately recalled when her father had brought her and Bill here during their school holidays and she had stood in front of the paintings of whaling ships and the skeleton of a whale and had suddenly felt dizzy and faint. Her father had had to take her outside for some air, half carrying her through the door and sitting her down on the steps, anxiously patting her bowed head until she recovered, whilst Bill, embarrassed and scornful of female inadequacies, stayed inside to examine the thin blades of the flensing knives, the blubber forks, the whale spears and barbed harpoons under the watchful eye of an attendant.

She hadn't been inside since, though she had passed its doors countless times. She had blotted out the incident, for she didn't know why she had felt so strange and only knew that her head had been full of shapes and sounds that she couldn't explain.

But here I am now, she thought as she looked up at the wide curving staircase, and I still feel strange, though I think I can cope this time. She followed the directions and looked at the paintings of the whaling ships, the *Swan*, the *Truelove*, the *Diana* and another that seemed vaguely familiar but whose name she couldn't make out because of the angle of the light shining above it; she read the copies of the old commercial posters produced by the whalebone industry in another age, advertising brushes, window blinds, bed bottoms and corset stays.

She climbed a sloping ramp and stared into the glass cases filled with tools and delicate scrimshaw work which the seamen had patiently carved on to whale teeth and walrus tusks as they lay icebound in their trapped vessels, waiting for the Arctic ice to open and release them.

Why did I come, she wondered, and ran her hand absently along the prow of a longboat. What was my purpose? Her legs felt unsteady, the wooden floorboards seeming to dip beneath her feet and the sound and surge of the sea washing over her. She was cold, so cold that her fingers were numb, her breath white and vaporous. The whale song floated mournfully, sobbing, blowing, an inherent echo in her mind from a distant inaccessible sphere.

'Are you all right, miss?'

She was sitting in another room where the sorrowful lament was the loudest, the resonance of the refrain ringing between the walls and pulsating like a heartbeat through her body. *Poor whale. Poor whale. Poor whale.* On one of the walls was a large chart plotting the route to the whale fishing grounds: to Greenland, to Davis Strait and Baffin Bay, and it was at this she was staring when the attendant spoke to her.

'Erm, yes, I think so, thank you.' She blew her nose and felt tears on her cheeks. She couldn't remember coming into this room or sitting down.

'You've been here ages,' he said. 'I was a bit bothered about you.'

'Sorry.' She got up, holding on to the chair. 'It's the sound, I think. It makes me feel rather strange.'

He nodded and made to move off, then turned. 'You can get a cup of tea upstairs if you want one.'

She hesitated, not sure what she wanted, but – yes, there was something. 'If, erm, if I wanted to find out about someone, where would I look?'

'Somebody in whaling, do you mean?'

'Yes, perhaps, or to do with shipping.'

'Well, we've plenty of books. If you come through to the desk I'll show you.' He led her back into the entrance hall and showed her the booklets and pamphlets piled on the information desk, and then pointed to the bookshelves on the wall behind. 'You might find what you want there, and if not have a word with the curator; he'll put you right.'

Vaguely she looked at the titles on the slim green and yellow books until she came to a paperbacked volume entitled *Hull Ships and Their Owners.* She pulled it out from the shelf and flicked through the pages. It was an easy-to-read book, written for the layman, and it dealt with shipping merchants and their trade from 1500 until the nineteenth century.

There's that ship again. She looked down at the picture of a whaler embedded in ice, her bows staved in by the pressure, her masts and rails covered in frost and ice, and in the background another vessel, her sails set ready, heaving a way through the narrow open water, and towering behind it a massive iceberg. *The same ship again that I've just seen.*

'Have you found anything?' The attendant spoke from behind the desk.

'I might have; I'm not sure.' She took the book across to him. 'This ship. Is it the same one as in the painting down the corridor?'

'Yes. It's the same picture. There were several paintings of that ship and her sister ship; they're from the Masterson fleet.'

She followed him back down the corridor until they were facing the painting again. He shielded the light with his hand. 'There's the name, see, at the bottom. The *Northern Star.*'

This was the original painting, and the artist had captured the bright white ice, the stark etching of rails and rigging garlanded with frost, and a pale grey sky dotted with ominous white clouds. The mountainous iceberg, crystal blue and threatening.

'Thank you,' she murmured. 'Yes. I see it now.'

Swiftly she thumbed through the index of the book, searching for M – 'Here we are, Isaac Masterson, shipping merchant, High Street. That's it,' she whooped.

Two schoolboys chewing on their pencils stared at her as they slouched past, but ignoring their snorts of mockery she dashed back to the desk to pay for the book and then ran up the stairs to the café, where she took a table by the window overlooking Queen's Gardens.

Isaac Masterson, she read hurriedly, was an enterprising and successful master mariner and shipping merchant, who in the late eighteenth century built up a fleet of ships which plied the Arctic waters in search of whale. She shuddered slightly but read on; this was a different world entirely from the one in which she was living now.

His ships, she read, were among the first to use the New Dock – she looked up briefly to view the present-day gardens there – and his home and office in High Street, as she was now certain, overlooked the Old Harbour, once the chief waterway of the town.

That's it, she repeated under her breath. It's got to be. That's why I'm getting these feelings. But where's the connection? She looked out of the steamy windows down on to the gardens. The flower beds were bare but for the stumpy, leafless rose bushes, and the sinking paving stones were wet with scuffed snow; in the distance at the eastern end was the sky-high monument to William Wilberforce which stood in the forecourt of the Hull College of Higher Education, where even now Chris might be working behind those blank windows.

So this is where it began. Maybe even where I began, but I'll probably never know. She sighed and turned the page. The Masterson fleet continued to expand, the following paragraph went on, even more so when Masterson's energetic nephew was made a partner in the company. The company name was changed to Masterson and Nephew, and when Masterson retired to become a farmer in the country district of Monkston on the Holderness coast, to Masterson and Rayner.

The words blurred on the page and she drew in a gasp as the implications hit her. Rayner! Could it be? It must be! Why didn't we know? Why did no one bother to find out? Perhaps no one ever felt the need. With an ancient island history like ours we all know that our heritage is inseparable from shipping and the sea.

'Are you ready to order?'

She jumped as the waitress stood in front of her, her order book open and her eyes fixed in the middle distance beyond the window. Liz ordered a pot of tea and a sandwich and then slowly turned the page of her book. She was expecting to find other articles about shipping merchants, but found instead a print of Isaac Masterson, showing a strong-featured old man wearing a frock coat, his hands firmly grasping a wooden cane. Below it was a picture of his nephew and heir, John Rayner.

He's exactly as I first saw him. The revelation warmed her, comforted her. Sitting at his desk, the way he had been, and his left hand resting on an ivory paperweight, the frill of his cuffs showing beneath his coat sleeve; and the same whimsical smile. He wore no wig, unlike his uncle, but his fair hair was tied back with a ribbon, and his clothes were sober and sensible, befitting a prosperous businessman about to begin a day's work.

John served his apprenticeship on board the *Polar Star*, she read, and on his first voyage almost came to an untimely death when he fell overboard into the Arctic waters and was rescued by one of the crew. This did not deter him from seagoing, the article went on, and he spent much time in the whaling grounds, including on the ill-fated *Northern Star* which sank in the Lancaster Sound with much loss of life.

He was a popular figure in the town and in the country district of Monkston in Holderness, where he made a controversial marriage to the daughter of one of his uncle's employees, Sarah Foster. The marriage was a success and lasted over forty years until his death. They had several children.

Her mind was numb; she was unable to comprehend what she had just read. *Sarah Foster. Sarah Foster.* 'I'm a Foster too,' the little girl had said; and then she became a Rayner. But she hadn't given up her name; or at least she had given it to their children and it had passed on down through the generations to us.

The tea went cold in the cup as she stared vacantly out of the window. She saw a tall figure amongst a group of people, striding down the footpath between the flower beds, and with a sudden start of recognition she jumped up, scraping her chair noisily on the floor. She grabbed the book and her handbag, scrabbling in her purse for change for the bill, leaving the untouched sandwich and cold tea on the table.

'I'm sorry, I'm sorry.' She jostled a customer waiting at the cash desk. 'I have to go. The money's right.'

She ran down the stairs and through the swing doors, almost falling headlong into Chris's arms. 'Oh, Chris!'

Tears of relief started to flow and she sobbed against his chest, feeling the coldness of the zip on his jacket against her forehead.

'What on earth? Where have you been?' He held her away from him. 'What's happened?'

She could hardly speak. 'I've found her. Chris, I've found her.'

CHAPTER TWENTY ONE

'I knew we had a long connection with shipping.' Gilbert and Liz sat over the remains of their supper. 'But I hadn't realized we went so far back. Early eighteen hundreds, you say?'

Gilbert got up and began to clear away the dishes. 'It's incredible. What luck you going into 'museum and finding that book like you did.'

'Yes, wasn't it? Leave the dishes, Dad, I'll do them. Listen, I'm going to look through the notes that Chris did for me and you're not to mind. He did them because he wanted to help. He understands how I feel.'

'I only wish I did.' His face creased and he chewed on his lip. 'I don't care for you searching into the past, Liz. Why can't you accept things as they are?'

'I'm only looking into our ancestry. I'm not looking at anybody else's.'

'All right! All right!'

'All the same, I do wonder why you're so protective of Carl Reedbarrow. He's a bully, and he's very intimidating.'

'Don't talk like that, Liz. I don't like it, and besides, there's a lot you don't know.'

'But if there are things I don't know and you're not willing to explain, how can I be expected to understand?'

'I can only say that I made a promise to *my* father a long time ago, and *he* made a promise to Carl's mother.'

'Good heavens! And I thought I was the only one tied to the past! But Carl's mother? Have you seen her lately? Is she still in that residential home in Beverley?'

He nodded. 'Aye, 'same one she went into after Carl's dad died. Poor old lass, she needed somebody to look after her for a change. She must have been sick of being at 'beck and call of them two and never getting any thanks for it. Dot and I go to see her now and then, and others from 'village do too.'

Liz got up from the table and gave him a kiss on his cheek. 'You're a funny old stick, aren't you? Perhaps you'll take me with you one Sunday?'

She thought she saw a fleeting shadow of apprehension cross his face, but he just nodded and said nothing and went through into the bar, leaving her to browse through the dates and records of the Fosters and the Rayners.

Chris had made concise notes in his large clear handwriting, indexed in date order on several sheets of paper, and she became lost in time as she pored over the names of her predecessors: William, Richard, George, Sarah Maria, Victoria, Ellen, Thomas, Mark, Elizabeth . . . so many, she thought as she ran a pencil down the list. Her father's name was there; another Thomas – what did they all do? But the one she was looking for, Sarah, wasn't there.

I remember why I became Elizabeth; it was because I had two names and she had only one. The recollection came flooding back. *I told Mum and Dad I wanted to be called Elizabeth, then we won't get mixed up I said, and Dad laughed and I didn't understand why.*

The windows rattled as a wind suddenly rose, and she got up to close the curtains. She could hear the sea as it dashed against the cliffs, and she wondered idly what the weather forecast was. I hope it isn't bad tomorrow, or nobody will turn out for the meeting.

She'd been looking down at a list of names taken from records of births, and it wasn't until she picked up another sheet that the name she was looking for jumped out almost in greeting. Recorded dates of death. Have I been avoiding this? Don't I want to admit that you are dead, Sarah? That you no longer have the breath of life? Has part of me died too? A great sadness overwhelmed her and she closed her eyes to still the brimming tears.

I don't know what's wrong with me, she thought. She blew her nose. Why am I so preoccupied with what has gone before? Why do I feel so desolate? I know that we're vulnerable mortals; that our time is measured.

But is it? Or do we come back, like Sarah does? And *why* does she? Does she come back when she's unhappy or does she come when I am unhappy, like when Mum died? Or – and I haven't thought of this before – is she an inherent part of me? Am I – or was I – Sarah?

She sat cross-legged on the floor, gently rocking, oblivious of time, her arms folded across herself, and when she felt calmer she glanced down at the date recorded. *1859. I wonder if you lived to be an old lady, Sarah. Did you have a good life with your John? How do I know this is you?* She stared into space. *I don't know. But know it I do.*

She was woken several times during the night by the rattle of dustbin lids being blown about in the yard. Once the slithering of roof tiles above her bedroom disturbed her, and she propped herself up on her elbow, listening. The gusts were getting much stronger, whistling and howling around the building, and her thoughts went out to the North Sea ferry on its nightly crossing between Rotterdam or Zeebrugge and Hull, and the passengers on board who wouldn't be getting much sleep tonight as they were tossed in their bunks.

She got up to go to the bathroom and met her father on the landing, his sandy hair standing in tufts and peaks and his eyes bleary through lack of sleep.

'What a night,' he croaked. 'It's a real blow out there. Sounds like a north-westerly.'

The next morning she got up late, feeling wrecked; it was Saturday, and she'd taken the morning off work to attend the meeting at eleven. She put the kettle on to boil and looking through the kitchen window saw her father out in the yard clearing up the debris that was scattered about. The wind was still very wild, and she watched him as he picked up a tile and placed it on top of the dustbin to hold the lid down and then looked anxiously up at the roof.

'There's allus another job,' he grumbled when he came in. 'You think you're on top of everything and then summat else crops up. Well, I shan't be able to get a roofer to go up until 'wind drops. We'll not get many outsiders at 'meeting if it doesn't ease up.'

He washed his hands at the kitchen sink. 'Have you heard 'news? Two tankers have collided somewhere near Flamborough. There's a twenty-mile oil slick heading this way.'

'No!' She held the bread knife poised in mid-air and stared at him.

'It was on 'seven o'clock news.' He glanced at the clock. 'It should be on 'local radio now if you switch it on.'

She reached over and pressed the button, then searched for the local wavelength until she heard the familiar tones of the regular newscaster. 'It maybe won't be as bad as we feared,' a guest's answering voice said. 'If these high north-westerly winds keep up, the oil slick will break up by itself. If they

subside and the winds veer to the east, then it will be a major
environmental disaster for this area, particularly for the birds
feeding on Spurn Bight.'

'And are any departments considering the use of detergent
to break up the slick?' came the question.

The guest's voice paused. 'Yes, they are considering it, but
that also brings problems, so it's six of one and half a dozen
other snags, really. The detergent itself can cause enormous
difficulties, as we know, because although it can disperse the
oil into millions of smaller slicks each going their separate
way, it is also a poison and can kill seashore animals, like crabs
and worms and so on. But at the moment, because of the
weather—'

Liz switched off. 'What are we doing? Just what are we doing?'

'It was an accident.' Gilbert took the bread knife from her
and sliced the loaf. 'It's pretty rough out there.'

She clenched her fists and shut her eyes tight. 'It makes me
feel so powerless. You know it's a dump out there! There's the
sewage that's constantly being spewed out and the rubbish
that gets thrown overboard; the oil drums, the plastic bottles,
it all ends back on our laps, back on the land. The fish are
dying and so are the seals – and those are the dangers we can
see; the ones we can't see are even worse. The chemicals, the
pesticides!'

'Well, what can we do about it?'

She struck the table with her fist. 'That's just it. This is the
price we have to pay. It sickens me to think about it. We're all
so complacent. None of us, not one, would give up our elec-
tricity, our cars, our luxuries of twentieth-century living, so
choose instead to live alongside a sewer.'

Gilbert shrugged and sighed and sat down to his breakfast,
but Liz went into the back hall and grabbed her old coat and
scarf and climbed into her wellingtons. She heard her father
calling out not to forget the meeting, and banging the door

behind her she ran out across the yard and the road and down towards the old rutted lane that led towards the sea. The power of the wind broke her furious momentum; she could hardly stand up, so violent was the buffeting, and she had to bend almost double as she battled the gale. She came to the end of the lane but daren't stand near the edge in case she was blown over.

A huge tide was running, crashing so high against the cliffs that she could feel the spray. *This is no ordinary high tide! I've never seen it like this before.* This was a vicious, spiteful, devouring sea, urged on by the strength and fury of the wind above it. Spumes of white water leapt and pitched, smashing against each other, a boiling explosion of awesome force bent on destruction.

A powerful raging surge of emotion rose within her, seething up through her feet so she curled her toes against it; forcing its way into her body so she clenched her buttocks and abdomen, coming up through her tightened throat and into her open gasping mouth.

She grasped her head with her hands, clutching her tangled hair. 'Get back,' she shrieked. 'Get back.'

A slithering, squelching, rumbling reverberation brought her to her senses and she felt the ground shake beneath her. She turned her head towards Alf Wainwright's derelict cottage and watched the cliffs falling around it. Tons of precious earth, a plunging mass of mud and grass and ancient glacial clay, slipping and sliding down into the waiting waves.

She ran back down the lane, her heart hammering, her breathing coming fast, and as she reached the main road she saw Alf Wainwright hesitating on the other side, heading as usual towards his cottage.

'Mr Wainwright! Alf! Wait, wait!'

The old man looked up and stood leaning heavily on his stick, waiting for her. 'Now, then, Elizabeth,' he called, his voice wavering as the wind caught it. 'What's up? Aren't you going to 'meeting?'

She crossed over to stand with him where he waited for her. 'Yes.' She breathed heavily. 'Yes I am. But don't go down the lane. It's too dangerous. The whole lot's going over!'

'My house?'

She nodded. 'It hasn't gone yet, but it's on the edge. Please don't go; you'll be upset.'

'Nay, lass, I won't. I've been expecting this to happen for years. It had to come. It'll be a relief in a way. It'll be done with, won't it?' He took a large handkerchief from his pocket and wiped his watery eyes, but whether it was emotion or the effect of the blustery wind that made them glisten she couldn't tell.

'You won't be able to stand up in this,' she said. 'It's too wild. Will you come back home with me? I have to make a phone call, and then we can go to the meeting together.'

'Aye, all right. It is a bit of a blow.' He took her offered arm as they walked back to the Ship. She left him talking to her father whilst she dialled the number that Jackson, the journalist, had given her.

'If you want front-page news, you'd better come straight away and bring a photographer with you,' she told him. 'I'm going to ring the television companies too . . . Yes, I've got contacts, thanks. You'd better be quick; the cottage will go over any time, if it hasn't gone already – it was hovering on the edge ten minutes ago . . . You can sit in at our meeting; eleven o'clock this morning. Oh, and it's to be held at the Raven, not the Ship . . . Yes, indeed. The whole village is united in this, there's no rivalry. We're in this together, and for the long haul.'

She put the phone down and went into the kitchen, where her father was making coffee and Alf was sitting drinking a mug of tea. The adrenalin that had made her race down the road to the lane and aroused a positive response in Jackson was fading. Now all she felt was a cold determination to get the campaign moving – and fast.

She claimed her father's attention. 'Dad, if the wind is north-westerly, I don't understand why the sea is so wild. I can't remember seeing it running so high!'

'It's a surge tide,' he said. 'There's a strong spring tide running, and it's surging down the coast towards 'Humber. Because it's so high, it gets trapped and can't get away before 'next tide comes in. The road at Spurn will be breached, no question.'

'Aye,' Alf murmured. 'I'll second that.'

CHAPTER TWENTY TWO

Much to Liz's surprise, when they arrived at the Raven they found that Kevin Warner had everything ready for the meeting. He'd put out a long table with chairs down both sides, two carafes of water and glass tumblers in the centre, and notepads and pencils for those who required them.

'Don't think we'll need all these chairs, do you, Liz?' Gilbert murmured.

'I don't think so. We'll get plenty of support, but maybe not many will want to be on the committee.'

As it turned out they were wrong, for about thirty people arrived ten minutes before the meeting was due to begin. Some chose to stand at the back, others leant on the bar, but if they were hoping for a free drink they were disappointed, for a handwritten notice clearly said *Bar closed until 12 noon.* The rest sat on wooden benches.

'I don't want to be on 'committee, Liz,' a man called from the back of the room, 'but I'd like to vote for who goes on it.'

'That's fair enough,' Kevin replied before she could respond, 'We'll all have a chance to speak once the meeting is officially open.'

Liz was impressed by his assurance; he was clearly used to taking command. She glanced around, but Jim Jackson hadn't arrived yet. If he was coming from Hull – or maybe Beverley; she didn't know where he was based – he could well be snarled up in traffic. She saw Chris come through the door and lifted her hand in greeting, and then Kevin asked her if she'd like him to open proceedings.

'Five minutes,' she said, 'and maybe the press will arrive in time.'

'OK,' he said, and asked in a clear voice if everyone would be seated so they could start in five minutes.

Which they did exactly on time. Jim Jackson still hadn't appeared, but Liz thought it didn't matter too much as long as he arrived before the committee meeting began.

Kevin Warner greeted everyone and thanked them for coming, and then introduced Liz by saying that she had begun the campaign and was present to give them the details and invite them to form a committee.

Liz stood where everyone could see and hear her, and she too welcomed them and thanked them for their interest in such an important issue. 'This is going to be an informal committee,' she explained, 'but nevertheless we should vote in a formal and proper way so that there is no doubt as to who is doing what. To start the ball rolling I would like to propose our host today, Kevin Warner, as chairman if he is willing?' He said that he was, and several people put up their hands to second the motion.

'Thank you,' he said. 'I'm not a local man, as you'll know, but my business is here and it's important to me that this campaign succeeds so we can all get on with our lives. What we need is a team of people willing and able to commit to putting in sufficient time and effort to get things moving.'

The man who had spoken earlier put his hand up again. 'I want to vote for Liz; she began this campaign and we know she won't give in.'

'I'll second that.' Dot put her hand up, as several others did too. 'And if you want any typing doing, I've got a typewriter.'

Liz smiled. 'I'll vote for Dot as secretary,' she said firmly, knowing that Dot was extremely organized. 'Can we have another to second the proposal so it doesn't look like a family affair?' Several other hands were raised, and as it seemed no one else owned a typewriter Dot was voted in as secretary.

Liz raised her hand. 'I'll be glad to be on the committee, and if everyone is agreeable I'd like to be publicity officer. I've already taken it upon myself to invite the press this morning, and I've telephoned our local television people to suggest they raise public awareness of what is happening to the cliffs.'

'Over here!' A hand was raised at the back of the room, and she saw Jim Jackson and another man standing near the door.

'Good thinking,' Kevin Warner said. 'Is it agreed, then, that Miss Liz Rayner is voted in to be publicity officer?' Practically every hand went up, and a few people clapped. 'A majority vote, then,' he went on, turning to Liz. 'And quite right too. We wouldn't be here without you,' and more people clapped, and a few cheered.

'Thank you for your support,' she said. 'Together, we can win, but ideally we need three more members on the committee, and one I would like to propose if he is willing is Mr Alf Wainwright. He has lived here in Tillington longer than any of us and has lost more than anyone. I think he would be a valuable asset to us when we are pleading our cause.'

She knew he would be pleased with the gesture, and she genuinely felt he would add some sage wisdom and stability to the committee, but also that she could use him to good effect in publicity campaigns. Many hands went up in support, and Alf rose from his seat and went to the committee table, where he sat back in his chair and crossed his arms, waiting for business to commence.

'Do you think we should have one more member?' Kevin tapped on the bar counter with his pencil. 'Gilbert?'

Gilbert declined, as did some of the other parish councillors. George Bennett, the chairman of the council, would have accepted but no one proposed him; others from outside the village shook their heads, and finally it was left to Matt Wilson, who had lost considerable acreage including a huge chunk that very morning, to agree to stand.

A committee meeting was then arranged to formalize that morning's decisions in fifteen minutes' time, and everyone was invited to attend if they wished, regardless of whether they'd been nominated or not.

Liz went across to speak to Jim Jackson, who had indicated discreetly that he would like a private word.

'Do you think Mr Wainwright would be willing to have his photograph taken by his cottage?' he asked. 'If it's still standing? I've been to have a look, and we've' – he gestured to his colleague with the camera – 'taken photos in case it goes over before we get a chance.'

'I don't know,' she said. 'It's so wild he won't be able to stand up.'

'I could take him in the car – as far as possible, I mean – and then he wouldn't be out long.'

When the question was put to Alf he agreed, but on Liz's insistence Chris went home with him first to ensure that he changed into his sea boots and a warm scarf.

When the article appeared in the newspapers a few days later, his photograph was on the front page with the headline *Ol' Man o' the Sea*. He was shown staring out to sea with his hand to the peak of his naval cap and his father's pipe firmly clenched between his teeth, and close by the home of his childhood teetering on the edge of the cliff.

The article described his life as a seaman fighting to save his country during the Second World War, and how when he should be enjoying a well-deserved retirement he was still fighting, this time to save a village from the cruel sea which on several occasions had almost claimed him.

How can we let this happen? the item concluded. *The people of Tillington ask only that they be enabled to live on in their peaceful village as their ancestors did, and not see it become just another name in the history of the lost villages. They require only a wall to save them from the ravages of the sea. It doesn't seem a lot to ask! Ms Liz Foster Rayner, the prime mover of this campaign, said, 'We will march on Westminster if necessary. This time we will win!'*

'We sound rather prehistoric, don't we!' said Liz, after reading the article out loud to her father, Dot and Chris.

'Did you really say that, about marching on Westminster?' Chris leant over her shoulder to read the piece again.

'I don't recall saying those exact words.' Liz laughed. 'But someone asked, in front of Jim Jackson, if we would appeal to the government, and I might have said it sounded like a good idea!'

CHAPTER TWENTY THREE

The house phone rang before Liz left for work; it was Dot for her father. 'Can you tell him I've sprained my foot? I fell over the cat last night when I came home. He was that anxious to be inside he just shot through my legs and I tripped over him. My foot's so swollen this morning I can't put it down. Tell your dad he'll have to get Jack in tonight.'

'You haven't broken it?'

'I don't think so.'

'All right, Dot, I'll tell him. Just put your foot up and take it easy. Have you got some ice for it? Dad's not up yet, but I expect he'll be round to see you as soon as he is. I'll go and tell him now.'

Her father was in the bathroom, but opened the door, his chin covered in shaving foam, when she tapped to give him the message. That done, she collected her briefcase and hand-bag, and carefully placed the campaign poster she had been working on until half past one in the morning on the back seat of the car and drove into Hull, calling first at the print shop they used for office flyers and asking them to make a dozen copies.

Her morning was busy. Caroline had telephoned to say she wouldn't be coming in as she had a streaming cold, and

Sharon was constantly ringing through from the other office with queries she couldn't answer herself. A big advertising campaign had been promoted during the weekend and they were inundated with enquiries.

'Where's Steve anyway?' Susan came into Liz's office to ask during the afternoon. 'He's never here when we need him.'

'Oh, he'll be around somewhere,' Liz said. Wheeling and dealing, she thought privately as she put the phone down once more on Sharon.

There were footsteps on the stairs and Steve came up. 'He's here,' Susan said before disappearing back into the front office.

'Speak of angels,' Liz said. Steve sat down opposite her and put his feet on her desk.

'I need to talk to you,' he began.

'Do you mind!' She batted his feet with her hand and straightened the papers he'd dislodged. 'I've just sorted these out.'

'Sorry.' He got up from the chair and peered out of the window.

'Was there something in particular?' she said caustically. 'Because if not we are quite busy!'

'Sorry. Er, yes.' He came back from the window and perched on the edge of her desk so he could lean towards her. 'You know that mill house in your village – the one you've talked about?'

'Yes,' she said briskly. 'There is only one.'

'Well, I've just done a deal with the chap who owns it. I've been working on him for weeks – a few sweeteners – and I've finally clinched it this weekend. I couldn't tell you before because he asked me not to. He wouldn't say why, but said if I told you the deal was off. There's some kind of feud, isn't there?'

She didn't answer; couldn't answer, because shock and rage were locking her throat.

'He hasn't signed up yet, but I've paid him a deposit, so I thought I could mention it now. I know,' he added quickly, 'I'm sort of breaking the rules and I might lose if he backs out, but I really want that land. If the village gets its sea wall then it'll be prime building land, and the whole village will open up for development.'

I don't believe it. But yet why shouldn't I believe it? she asked herself. Steve's in the business of buying land suitable for development. That's what he does.

'The mill?' she asked weakly.

'Oh, the mill! Well, I expect it will have to stay. I should think it has a preservation order on it. I phoned your friend Chris Burton last night to ask if he was interested in buying it. I think he might be.' He leant across the desk. 'Is he still your friend? He's not your type, you know; you need someone more extrovert, somebody to make you zing.' He put his hand under her chin and lifted it so that she had to look at him.

'Mind your own damned business.' She slapped his hand away. 'And keep your creepy hands to yourself. Why you think you're the answer to every woman's prayer I can't imagine. Women don't get a thrill when they find your hand up their skirt, so don't for a moment think that they do.' She grabbed her coat and bag and glared at him as he sat in open-mouthed astonishment. 'And if I should hear so much as a whisper that you've been harassing any of our female staff' – she shook a finger at him – 'I shall report you, make no mistake about it.'

'But, Liz, wait! Where are you going?'

'Home!' she shouted, and slammed the door behind her. Her voice echoed up the stairs. 'And I might not come back.'

She took the docks road home, thinking that it might be quicker, even though it was a longer route. With fewer cyclists and pedestrian crossings than on the inner road, no mothers hovering on the footpath with children and pushchairs, no pedestrians dithering on the edge of the pavement waiting for a break in the traffic, she thought she'd be able to drive at forty.

But she'd mistimed it. The traffic was heavy. Articulated trucks, transporters and consignment lorries were all hurtling towards the docks to catch the North Sea ferry. She got into a wrong lane and found herself behind stationary traffic with winking right indicators and sat fuming, drumming her fingers on the steering wheel, unable to proceed until they moved on.

She began to feel intimidated as lorries bore down on her in a crushing melee of spinning wheels and grinding steel, and the stink of diesel and petrol seemed worse than usual; but as she left the docks behind, the smell changed to the sweeter, cloying odour of cod liver oil which floated on the vinegary-scented air round the illuminated industrial palace of Saltend.

It looks like fairyland, she thought as she approached the massive chemical complex; a dreamlike fantasy. In the gathering dusk the light sparkled and glinted from every building and walkway, from every tower and chimney; a scintillating tinsel town whose brightness lit the early evening sky with a rosy dawn . . . and it's such a contradiction in terms, she told herself crossly. It's just a man-made nightmare.

Her anger, which she'd kept in check as she'd battled with the traffic, threatened to erupt again as she thought about Steve and the mill. She felt vaguely regretful about the way she had roared at him, because she knew that came from what he had told her about the mill, and not from moral outrage as she had claimed. She could handle him perfectly well, though recognizing that his behaviour had to be restrained before he found himself in real trouble.

She felt like turning round and boarding that ferry, just clearing off and leaving; giving up on the cliffs, the village, everything. She'd had enough.

Turning left at a roundabout she was immediately on the country roads that would eventually lead her to Tillington, away from traffic and industry. The contrast was so instantaneous that to a stranger it would be surprising. No straggling industrial estates, no minor commercial sprawl, just a spread of green touched by a hovering frost, stretching wide and boundless.

She glanced in her mirror at the cooling towers looming behind her and the industrial lights flickering. The lorries had gone, leaving only two or three cars in the distance. She sighed, and though resentment still simmered she felt calmer; the landscape always had that effect on her. The panorama which she perceived as infinite and enduring was surely more permanent than the seething road she had left behind, carrying its frantic, death-rattling mob.

She drove along the narrow, twisting road, past an ancient church and on once more, down a dip and up again, raising her eyes to glance in her rear-view mirror. She saw two church towers on the darkening skyline, and driving to a remembered lay-by drew to a halt and got out of the car.

The two church towers, one in the ancient town of Hedon and the other she had just passed in Preston, were two miles apart, but from this particular point in the hummocky landscape they appeared to stand side by side, whilst to their right in marked twentieth-century contrast the cooling towers sat blowing hazy, innocent clouds of steam.

A car zoomed towards her as she leant her elbows on the car roof. It stopped and a man, maybe in his sixties, wound down his window and leant across. 'Do you need any help?'

'No thanks,' she said. 'I'm just enjoying the view.'

He looked through his rear-view mirror and then turned to her. 'That's not a view! Scotland's a view. The Lakes are a view!'

'You must be a stranger, then,' she answered, and opening her car door got in and fastened her seat belt.

He leant towards the window. 'I've lived here for thirty years,' he said. 'And I've never seen a view yet.'

She engaged gear and smiled in sweet condescension. 'Then that's your misfortune.'

CHAPTER TWENTY FOUR

'You're home early. No work to do?'

'Plenty,' she answered, and flung her handbag over a kitchen chair. 'Decided not to do it!'

'All right for some.' Her father glanced at her, weighing up her mood. 'You must be well in with your boss.'

'He gets more than his fair share of work out of me,' she countered. 'I'm entitled to take time off now and again.'

Her father inhaled. 'Oh! Feeling like that, are we? Better put 'kettle on. You've obviously been having a hard time.'

Tears were very near the surface, she felt so full of misery. She fiddled with the buttons on her coat but didn't take it off. 'Dad. I've something to tell you.'

He turned to face her, his expression anxious. 'What's up, love?'

'The reason I'm home early, well, I've had a row with Steve. I shouted at him, though it wasn't really his fault – well, it was in a way, though he didn't know . . .'

'Didn't know what?'

'He's going to buy the mill house. Foster's Mill.'

Her father looked at her, his eyes wide, sandy eyebrows raised. 'You what?'

She nodded and reached into her pocket for a paper tissue

to wipe her nose. 'He's only told me today; that's why I left the office. Apparently Carl insisted that I wasn't to be told, no one was to be told or he'd cancel the deal.' She took a deep, shuddering breath. 'Anyway, Steve decided to tell me. I suppose he guessed I'd find out eventually. I can't bear to think about it. Steve said he'll build on the land.' Tears filled her eyes. 'I can't bear it,' she said again, the words catching in her throat. 'What—? What's the matter? Why are you laughing?'

Gilbert put his head back and roared, his shoulders heaving. 'You can't be serious. Steve's paid him money? In his hand?'

'Well, sometimes it's done; people can pay cash, though it's risky. Don't laugh,' she shrieked. 'It isn't funny!'

'Oh, but it is. It is.' He wiped his eyes and then went off in another peal of laughter.

'You've never understood, have you?' she railed at him. 'Never cared about it the way that Mum and I did. And to cap it all, Steve phoned Chris to ask if *he* was interested in buying the mill house, went behind my back to ask him, and Chris never even phoned me to tell me. Some friend *he* is!'

She suddenly burst into tears, and Gilbert stopped laughing. He put his hand to his mouth. 'Liz?'

'Don't even talk to me,' she sobbed. 'Just don't say a word. I don't want to hear your sweet reasoning, your whys and wherefores. Carl Reedbarrow has done this deliberately just to spite us. I can only think that he has one great big grudge over something.'

The door shuddered as she slammed it behind her. Coatless, she ran out of the yard and down the road, not towards the sea where she might have gone for comfort, but towards the house where Dot lived.

*

It was almost an automatic response when she thought about it, which she did when she slowed to a walk as her passion diminished and only slow tears fell. She always ran to Dot whenever she was in trouble: when she was a wool-gathering child and a rebellious adolescent; when she couldn't measure up to her mother's exacting standards or when her father would jokingly try to lighten her mood and she wanted to be serious.

Dot would always listen no matter what she was doing. Would never comment or advise unless asked to do so, but would always be ready with a sympathetic ear and understanding.

'Who is it?'

'It's me, Dot. Liz. Can I come in?'

'Just a minute.'

She heard a lop-sided shuffling and a rattling of chains and Dot opened the door, one foot in a fluffy slipper held off the floor. 'Don't know why I bother with all these locks. Nobody's going to want anything I've got – more's the pity,' she added with a laugh.

'Oh, I'm sorry. I'd forgotten about your poor foot. How is it?'

'It's all right. On the mend. Come on in and sit down. Get off there, you rascal.' She tipped a sleeping cat off a chair by the fire. 'He's the one that tripped me up. Cats' home for you,' she said, stroking under his chin as he jumped on to her knee as soon as she sat down, and curled up, tucking his tail around him. 'Cup of tea?'

Liz shook her head. 'My boss has given me some news. Carl Reedbarrow is selling the mill house, and Steve is buying it. He'll re-sell the land for building.'

What's the matter with everybody, she thought. Dot's eyes had narrowed and Liz could have sworn that there was a faint glimmer of humour there, but she could have been mistaken.

'Selling it, is he? Well, well. Has anything been signed yet?'

'No, I don't think so, but Steve has paid him a deposit.'

'Has he now? I would have thought a man in business would know better than that.'

'Good building land is hard to get hold of, and Steve probably thought that Carl wouldn't keep to a bargain without money changing hands.' She put her chin in her hands and leant towards the fire. 'I'm so miserable, Dot, and angry. I stormed out of the office. Shouted at Dad.'

'Just like the old days,' Dot murmured.

Liz looked up. 'What do you mean?'

'Your mum and dad used to have some unholy rows about 'same subject.' Dot's mouth lifted in a wistful smile. 'And then one or other of them would come here to get it off their chest.'

'If you came and lived with Dad we shouldn't have so far to go.'

Dot didn't answer, just continued to stroke the cat.

'Why don't you, Dot?'

Dot raised her head and gazed at Liz from wide blue eyes that had just a trace of laughter lines around them. 'I haven't been asked, that's why.'

'But you know Dad. He just hasn't got round to asking you. You know what he's like.'

'You wouldn't mind, then?'

'You know I wouldn't, and neither would Bill. You've been like a second mother to us.'

'I allus did come second, though.' She raised a hand and added swiftly, 'I'm not complaining, just saying. I've got over that hurdle.'

Liz put another lump of coal on the fire and pushed over a stool so that Dot could put her foot up and waited for her to continue.

'Did I ever tell you? No, I'm sure I didn't – that your gran and my mother always intended that your dad and me should get married?' She gave a rueful laugh. 'They planned it when we were both in our cots. They were good friends, and your gran was a good friend to me, even afterwards.'

'Afterwards?'

Dot gazed into the fire. 'We did everything together, your dad and me, right from being babies. Nursery school – even at senior school we were real good pals, and I never went out with any of 'other lads, even though I was asked. I only ever wanted Gilbert as my friend and he was 'same about me. It was all innocent, of course.' She looked up. 'We didn't go in for anything else. Some did,' she added, 'but most of us were innocent in them days.'

'So what happened?'

'Oh, we were too young. We didn't ever discuss the future; it was a sort of joke which we inherited from our mothers. Except that our mothers were deadly serious!'

She stretched her foot and winced. 'Then when Gilbert went away to sea I was really miserable and I didn't know anybody else, cos it had allus been just 'two of us. I knew then that there'd never be anybody else for me.' She gazed again into the fire and Liz didn't know whether or not to break the silence.

Dot took up the tale again. 'But then he met Nina – your mum. It was funny, really. He was on leave and we were going to go dancing at 'City Hall in Hull, only I'd caught 'flu and couldn't go, and I persuaded him to go with some of his pals. He didn't want to, but I made him – we had tickets already – and that's where he met your mum, and that was it. I knew immediately that I'd lost him. He didn't say anything at first, but I could tell. I knew him so well, you see; every whim, every mood. Knew him as well as I knew myself.

'When his leave was over, I didn't hear from him for weeks. I knew he was plucking up 'courage to tell me about Nina, though I didn't know her name then – I just knew he'd met somebody.

'I do go on, don't I? You don't want to hear this old story; you came with problems of your own.' Dot made to get out of her chair. 'I'll mek us a pot o' tea.'

'No, you sit there, I'll make it.' Liz went into the small neat kitchen, filled the kettle with water and put it on to boil, took out the teapot and two beakers and looked in the fridge for milk, the cupboard for tea. 'Then what happened?' she called out.

'He brought Nina home on his next leave and your gran took an instant dislike to her. I shouldn't really be saying this, should I?'

'Oh, I think I guessed. They were always at daggers drawn. I noticed even when I was little.'

'Yes? Of course, when I met her I could see why he'd fallen for her. She was lovely; tall and slim, shiny black hair. She looked gypsyish, exotic-looking and very vivacious, and always wore brightly coloured clothes. Your dad was very good looking, too, broad-shouldered and his hair much redder than it is now, and he always had a smile in his eyes. They made a handsome pair. Well, I decided that if she was Gilbert's choice then I would have to make a friend of her, because if I didn't I'd lose him altogether.'

'That was brave of you.' Liz carried the tray through and put it on the floor by the fire. 'I found some biscuits, is that all right?'

Dot nodded, and poured some milk into her saucer for the cat. 'And of course that was the best thing I could have done, because she didn't have any friends when she came here; and your gran didn't make it easy for her, and neither did my mother. But strangely enough I liked her, and as you know we were good friends, right to the end.'

'But you were happy with Gordon?'

'What's happy?' Dot meditated for a second. 'We were all right. We understood each other. I missed him a lot when he died.'

'Do you think Mum knew? About how you felt about Dad, I mean?'

'Oh, I think so. But she trusted me; I think your dad had told her about me, that I had been his best friend or something, and she knew I wouldn't betray her. She was like that: people didn't go against her; she had a strength that you didn't cross. Which reminds me of what I began to say before I started rambling on. Your dad was the only one she couldn't budge, not once he'd made his mind up about something. And one of the things guaranteed to make sparks fly was a discussion about 'Reedbarrows – nearly broke them up, that did.'

'Which is where I came in,' Liz murmured. 'The name is a real thorn in the side, isn't it?'

'Yes, it is, and it's about time something was resolved. It's gone on long enough. Just reach me the phone, will you, and I'll have a word with your dad.'

Puzzled, Liz got up and brought the telephone over, stretching the flex to its maximum length. She watched whilst Dot dialled the number and listened to half the conversation.

'Yes, she's here. Where else would she be? Oh, is he? Yes, I'll tell her. So what are you going to do, Gilbert? You know what about. Don't prevaricate – there's no sense to it, not any more. You know what I'm talking about! Do you want me to spell it out for you? Or shall I spell it out to Liz? Yes, that's what I'm talking about! Well, I've always known! Your mum, of course. Who else?' As she put the receiver down there was a knock on the door. 'That'll be Chris looking for you, Liz. Your dad said he was on his way.'

Liz opened the door. Chris was standing there looking

windblown, his scarf pulled up around his ears. 'I've come to collect a runaway.'

She didn't smile. Why hadn't he phoned her to tell her about Steve's phone call? 'I hadn't planned to come back yet,' she said, stony-faced. 'I'm talking to Dot.'

'Come in, for heaven's sake,' Dot called out. 'It's freezing with the door open.'

Chris looked questioningly at the tea tray. 'There isn't another cup, is there? I came straight from college.' He glanced at Liz. 'I phoned your office, but Susan told me you'd left early.'

She didn't reply, but went to fetch another teacup while an unspoken question passed between him and Dot.

'We were having a natter,' Dot said. 'At least I was doing most of the talking. I was just telling her a few things that need resolving.' She raised her voice. 'And when you go home, Liz, your father is going to do some explaining.'

'About what?'

'You'll have to ask him that. Ask him to tell you about 'mill and Carl Reedbarrow. And you tell him you're a big girl now and have a right to know.'

CHAPTER TWENTY FIVE

They walked silently back to the Ship, side by side but not touching, Liz keeping an arm's width between them. It began to drizzle, a gossamer-light shower which wet her hair and trickled down her collar, making her shiver and even more ill-humoured than she already was.

Chris finally broke the silence. 'What's wrong?'

'You know what's wrong! The mill house!'

'You sound as though you're feeling pretty sick about it.'

'I seem to be the only one who is. But it's a big chance for you, isn't it? You must have been ecstatic when you heard. You knew before anybody.'

'Ah! That's the reason for the stony silence. You're mad at me! But you can't blame me for any conspiracy, I'm just a bystander who happened to get caught up. I couldn't understand why Steve Black was ringing me—'

'Why didn't you call to tell me?' she broke in. 'Didn't you realize that I didn't know?'

'Hang on. Hang on a minute. What's going on?'

She heard shades of irritability, of thinning patience, but she blundered on. 'Surely you must have known that I didn't know, or I would have told you when you were here at the weekend.'

There was an edginess in his reply when he stopped outside the back door of the Ship and turned to confront her. 'Just a minute – just let me explain something, will you? Steve Black telephoned me at half past ten on Sunday night. He asked me if I was still interested in an old property. I said yes I was and he said he had one coming up. When I asked him where it was he said he would only tell me if I agreed not to tell anyone about it, as details hadn't been finalized. So I said all right.'

Liz didn't look at him but kept her gaze firmly on the distant horizon. 'Steve Black's a scheming . . .'

She swore beneath her breath. *I'm in the wrong job.*

'Then he said it was the mill! When I said I was surprised you hadn't told me about it, he said that he particularly didn't want you to know because it was the express wish of the vendor. Well, I jibbed at that and told him I couldn't go along with it. He hummed and hawed and then asked if I'd give him until Monday lunchtime when he'd had a chance to tell you himself.'

'So why didn't you get in touch then?'

His voice rose. 'Because your damned office phone was engaged all afternoon, that's why, and I do happen to have a job to do. When I finally got through Susan said you'd gone home!'

'I'm sorry,' she whispered, totally demoralized. 'I've been blaming everybody – Steve, Dad, you – and it's nobody's fault. Only mine for being so stupid.'

'You're not stupid.' He took her by the shoulders. 'But you have to forget about the mill and the house. It's only bricks and mortar, for heaven's sake. It doesn't matter that it once belonged to your family. You can live in some other property and make it your own. You have to get rid of this obsession before it overpowers you.'

'Yes, but I don't know how!'

The door opened and her father looked out. 'I thought I

heard voices. Come inside. Liz, what about something to eat? There's some chicken left, and I was going to cook some rice. Chris, will you have something?'

They stepped inside the warm kitchen, but Liz said she wasn't hungry and Chris said he would be heading back.

He looks so drawn. Liz glanced at him, and saw his mouth was pinched and tense. *Oh, heavens. He's the last person I want to upset. He's the only one I've ever spoken to about this – this passion, this* obsession. *Yes, that's what it is – he's right. And he's the only one that I thought would understand and now I'm driving him away.*

'Won't you have a warm drink before you go?' The words came out cool and abrupt and not the way she intended.

'Yes, stay.' Her father sounded anxious. 'And in any case, you'd better hear what I have to say about 'mill house.'

'It doesn't concern me.' Chris's voice was cold and flat. 'I'm not an interested party. I shan't be buying it, not at any price.'

'Oh, but . . .' Gilbert looked from one to the other. He seemed flummoxed and unhappy, his forehead furrowed. 'You don't understand. The mill isn't for sale. It never was.'

Liz watched him as he fumbled for words. *He's like a man on a tightrope. What's happened? Is he ill?* 'Dad! What do you mean? How do you know?'

He sat down heavily at the table and spread himself, his freckly hands fiddling nervously with some cutlery. 'You'd have found out at 'end of this year anyway,' he mumbled. 'But it seems my hand's been forced. I'd have told you before, onny, well, I daren't risk it. Your mother allus wanted them out and I was bothered that you'd be 'same. I couldn't do with 'aggravation, Liz. Not again.'

'Why don't you tell me what it's about?' She sat down beside him and put her hand over his. Suddenly he seemed older and vulnerable and she wanted to protect him, reassure him that everything would be all right.

'The mill is ours. Carl Reedbarrow is a tenant – at least his mother is, has been for years. I never bothered to get 'tenancy changed over.' He exhaled a huge gusty breath. It was as if he had kept it stopped up for years and in releasing a valve the pressure dropped and he became calmer.

'I don't understand.' There was a hammering in her ears. She felt herself go hot and then cold. 'What are you saying?'

'The mill has gone between 'Fosters and 'Reedbarrows for generations, but it started off as Fosters' right from the off. I believe it was a Foster who built it originally, and then – I don't know exactly, but 'Reedbarrows had it at some time in 'past and it was theirs in my grandfather's time and then my father, your granddad, bought it back from Paul, Carl's dad. Paul had told him he was in debt to 'moneylenders and asked him for a loan, said he didn't know what else to do or who else to go to, and 'bailiffs were coming in if he didn't pay off 'debt.

'So Dad loaned him 'money, but then Paul came back again and said he couldn't pay back 'original loan but if Dad would lend him some more, he'd give 'mill as security. Dad thought 'onny way to get him off his back was to tell him he'd buy it from him, but there'd be no more money after that. And that's what happened.'

It was just sinking in. *It's ours. It's ours, It doesn't matter that the Reedbarrows are living there. It belongs to us.* Liz suddenly had a vision of her mother talking to the woman at the mill – Carl's mother – who was crying. She glanced at Chris, who was standing frozen-faced, his jacket zipped up as if ready to leave. She motioned for him to sit down but he gazed stonily at her and didn't move as Gilbert continued his tale.

'Well, of course, Paul hummed and hawed to begin with, saying he'd pay back 'loan, but Dad knew he wouldn't, and he never did pay any of it back; money just ran through his fingers like water. He was forever gambling: horses, dogs, anything. His wife – Joan – never had a penny to call her own, so in the end Paul gave in and Dad bought 'house and 'mill. They did a cash adjustment and 'property was legally signed over to him not long before he died.' Gilbert looked searchingly at his daughter. 'Thing is, Liz . . . I told you, didn't I, that two promises were made. One was by my father to Carl's mother, that he would never turn her out of 'mill house; she'd allus have a home there for as long as she wanted. And 'other one was made to her by me when she left to go into that residential home. I promised her that I wouldn't turn Carl out.'

Liz's cheeks burned, and she put her cold hands against them to cool them down.

'But I agreed a proviso,' Gilbert went on. 'I had to, because the property went from your granddad to your granny, and your granny willed it to you and Bill. The promise I made to Carl's mother still stands, of course, but I couldn't promise for you and Bill. I've been holding the property in trust for both of you since your gran died, and that trust expires at 'end of this year.'

Chris moved across and sat down with them and absently rubbed his hand. Liz noticed a cut between his thumb and forefinger; he must have caught it on a woodworking tool. I hope he put something on it, she thought, because it looks really red and sore. *I love you, Chris.* 'Does Carl know about this?' she said aloud.

Gilbert hesitated. 'I don't think so. I don't think his mother ever told him, but somebody's going to have to.'

'So why does he dislike us so much, Dad? Why the animosity towards us?'

Gilbert shifted awkwardly. 'Oh, I don't know. Something that happened a long time ago. He's a strange chap; he can't help it.'

'Why does everybody stick up for him?' Liz burst out. Her emotions were on the boil, ecstasy and confusion vying for prominence. 'Jeannie gets beaten up and makes excuses for him. You say he can't help having a grudge. He's supposed to be not very bright, but he's clever enough to make a fool of Steve Black. He's also malicious and a bully. Did you know that he once tried to throw Bill from the top of the mill?'

'No! No, I didn't know that.' Her father looked shocked, as if truth was facing him for the first time. Chris scraped back his chair. 'This doesn't concern me, so I'll be going.'

Liz had the beginnings of a headache, or a migraine, a heaviness hanging over her eyes. 'Won't you stay, Chris? Have some supper?'

'No.' He was abrupt. 'Thank you.'

I don't understand the look in his eyes. He's not seeing me. It's as if I'm not here. She began to feel tense, a knot in her chest and her throat dry. *Doesn't he understand how I feel? The mill is ours!*

'You don't need me around,' he said, tight-lipped. 'You've got what you wanted.' In two long strides he was at the door before she could draw breath to reply. 'Goodnight, Gilbert.'

He didn't say goodnight to her. No kiss, no hint of a smile, only a cursory nod as he opened the door. She didn't speak, and there was a flash of anger in his grey eyes which quelled her, a silent accusation. But why? What reason had he to be angry?

He turned back from the door and she felt the cold draught whistling round her ankles, dissipating the heat from the kitchen, and she shivered.

'You might have a slight problem throwing the Reedbarrows out into the street,' he said icily. 'But given your single-minded determination I'm sure you'll manage it eventually.'

Liz and her father stared at each other when he'd gone. They heard the sound of his car engine revving and the car moving off. Why did he say such a thing – and why didn't she feel

195

elated? This is what she'd lived for; for as long as she could remember this had been her aim.

No! No! That wasn't true! Not all of her life. No. It had been her mother's dream. Only since her mother's death had she had this . . . preoccupation.

This obsession. That's what Chris had said. And now it was over. All this time she had been dominated by this phobia and there had been no need. Worrying unnecessarily about Carl Reedbarrow selling or destroying the mill and the house, and it had belonged to her and Bill all the time.

'Why?' she whispered. 'Dad, why did you take so long before telling me?'

His brow creased and there was a pleading in his eyes. 'You wouldn't do that, Liz, would you?' He seemed not to have heard her question. 'You wouldn't turn them out? Would you?'

CHAPTER TWENTY SIX

Chris put his foot down hard on the accelerator and drove out of the village. He speeded on for another mile and then braked. He'd seen the look in her eyes, a plaintive, childlike appeal which he'd deliberately ignored. She wasn't a child!

Oh, damn it. Should I go back? No, damn it, I won't. She's got what she wanted. The only thing she wanted. The blasted mill and the cliffs, that's all she's interested in. She's obsessed!

Well, she's got the mill now, or will have, and heaven help the Reedbarrows – and the Ministry of the Environment if the erosion appeal gets as far as them! She's like a Yorkshire terrier with a bone, she won't let go once she's got her teeth in something.

He started up again and drove on slowly, mulling over an idea, and then, peering into the darkness, he started looking for somewhere to turn round.

He found a gated entrance to a field and reversed into it; he felt the soft mud slipping beneath his wheels and held his breath, praying he wouldn't get bogged down. To his relief, the wheels held firm and he drove back into the village, braked briefly when he reached the Ship, and then drove on towards Dot's.

He knocked on the door and waited, listening to the monotonous beating of the surf on the cliffs. Dot too was vulnerable, living here in her bungalow facing the sea, even though she had a long garden between the house and the cliff edge.

'It's Chris,' he called as she lifted a curtain to see who was there.

'I'm doing well for company tonight,' she said, opening the door. 'Perhaps I should stay home more often! Come in.'

'You get plenty of company at the Ship, don't you?'

'Oh yes, but it's not 'same as at home, is it? When people call here, I know they've come to see me; at 'Ship they're there for a night out.'

She switched off the television set and sat down in a fireside chair, motioning him to sit opposite her.

'Am I disturbing you? Were you watching something?'

'No. I'd only switched it on for the news, but I'd missed it anyway. So what happened? Did Gilbert talk to Liz?'

He stretched his hands towards the fire. 'Yes. Yes, she's got her heart's desire. All she needs now is to get the tenants out, get a wall built, and there's one deliriously happy lady.'

'And one miserable man? What's bugging you?'

He shrugged, but didn't answer.

'Come on, you'd better tell Aunty Dot and get it off your chest.'

'I can't understand,' he said heatedly. 'I can't understand why her father didn't tell her before! Why did he keep her waiting all this time?'

'But that isn't what's bothering you – you're not mad at Gilbert.' She gazed at him with frank open eyes, forcing him to look at her.

'No.' He got up and walked about the small sitting room. Absently he picked up an ornament on the sideboard, looked at it and then put it back again. 'No, I'm not. I'm mad at Liz.

I'm seeing her in a different light, whereas before I just wanted to help her find herself, bring her back to reality and not live in the past. I'm afraid that now she won't think of anything else – that she'll turn the Reedbarrows out. I know he's been vindictive, but even so . . .'

'And you think that's what she'll be?'

'I don't like to think so, but – yes, possibly.'

'Then you don't know her. Oh, you might think you do,' she added, as he started to protest. 'But you don't. I've seen the way you look at her – seen the way you've looked at each other. I'm not so old that I've forgotten what it feels like.' She gave a sad lopsided kind of smile. 'But you still don't know her. You might never; she might always be a mystery to you. But that's part of her charm. But I'll tell you,' she waved a finger at him, 'and I *know*, that she isn't vindictive. It isn't in her. She's her father's daughter and it isn't in their nature.'

She patted her fingers about her mouth and studiously contemplated him. 'Now – her mother,' she said slowly and almost, it seemed, reluctantly. 'Now *she* was something different entirely.'

'Should I know about this?' Chris hadn't wanted to hear detrimental gossip about Liz's mother. She was dead. There could be no relevance between what was happening now and what had happened in her lifetime, but Dot had been insistent.

'I only want to explain about her, so that you'll understand why Liz feels the way she does about the mill and the house.'

He had taken off his coat and sat down again. It was a large chair and embraced him comfortably; he could imagine it had been Dot's late husband's favourite seat. He could still hear the soft sigh of the surf and thought he could feel the beat beneath his feet. *I wonder if one ever gets so used to it that the sound recedes?*

'Right from when Liz was a little bairn, Nina used to walk her by the mill and tell her that it had once belonged to the Fosters and that if Mary Foster hadn't married a Reedbarrow it would still be theirs.' Dot shook her head and sighed. 'She was allus on about it, making out that they'd been cheated, that by rights it should belong to them.'

Chris frowned; surely, he thought, no matter who Mary Foster had married or even if she hadn't, it wouldn't have come to the Rayners.

Dot was silent for a moment, and Chris didn't fill the break with more questions. 'She was keen on succession, was Nina; she was also very acquisitive. She'd never had much when she was a girl – her family had been quite poor, I think, and she was always wanting. Possessions meant a lot to her.'

She got up and limped across to the sideboard, brought out a bottle of sherry and held it enquiringly. Chris shook his head, so she only took one small glass from the cupboard and half-filled it.

'Before Nina came nobody knew, not even Gilbert, that Granddad Rayner had bought the mill. He never really wanted anyone to know. He was a nice old stick, a real gentleman, and he wouldn't have wanted to embarrass anybody, particularly not Joan, Carl's mother, but it came out when he died and his Will was read.'

She pursed her lips and took a sip of sherry. 'I only know all of this cos of my mother and Gilbert's mother being friends. Nobody outside of 'family knew; but Nina was over 'moon when she heard, cos she knew, obviously, that Gilbert would get it eventually; she never liked 'pub and she started making plans about what they'd do when 'mill was theirs; make it into a hotel or build bungalows on 'land, and like a fool she said as much to Granny Rayner.'

'So Liz never knew anything about all this? How did they manage to keep it secret?'

Dot shook her head. 'I don't know, but they did, and there was never a whisper. As I say, I only knew because of my ma, and later on because Granny Rayner confided in me. She never liked Nina and turned 'tables on her. I suppose she realized that when she was dead and gone Nina would try and get 'Reedbarrows out. She was always there, up at 'mill, harassing Joan, insisting that they were unwanted, that she'd like them to leave.'

Her mouth turned down. 'As if Joan hadn't enough to put up with, with Paul and Carl; she was just a simple trusting soul, and she couldn't cope with threats like that. So when Granny Rayner got wind of what Nina was up to she changed her Will and left 'property to Liz and Bill, with Gilbert as trustee. She wanted to be sure that they were grown up enough to do as they wanted with it, and not what their mother said.'

She drained her glass and put it down. 'What she didn't realize, of course, none of us did, was that Nina wouldn't be around anyway; that she'd be in 'churchyard alongside her.'

'You don't mean . . .' He felt an uncomfortable tingle down the back of his neck. 'Not in the same grave?'

'Bless you, no! They'd neither of them rest easy like that! No, just near enough for them to keep an eye on each other!'

'So you think that Liz's mother planted this obsession? But there was no need once it had been willed to her and Bill.'

'Ah, but it was too late by then: 'worm was in the apple, in a manner of speaking. It hadn't worked with Bill; he wasn't interested. All he ever wanted was to go to sea and travel. But not Liz; Nina'd caught her early. She was always a dreaming child, full of visions and flights of fancy.'

Chris nodded thoughtfully, musing on what Liz had told him about Sarah, and the man she thought she'd seen in the High Street building.

'Nina nurtured her own ambition within Liz. She never let up, always reminding her. I know cos Liz used to come to me.

She was often confused about injustice when she was little, and even when she was older – about what was right and what was fair.'

'Poor kid,' he murmured. 'So this is why Carl Reedbarrow is so antagonistic towards Liz and Gilbert?'

'What?'

'I suppose he knew that Liz's mother always wanted them out of the mill? That would give him a grievance.'

Dot hesitated. 'I suppose so.' Then she glanced at the old clock on the wall. 'Good gracious! Is that the time? My tongue does run away with me, and now I've kept you all this time and you're probably wanting to be off home!'

He got up from the chair; her sudden agitation had given him a sneaking suspicion that she'd said more than she'd intended. 'But he's a conman, isn't he? If he knew the mill wasn't theirs – and I can't imagine that he didn't know, in spite of what Gilbert said to the contrary – then he's taken money from Steve Black under false pretences.'

Her mouth was clamped into a thin line. 'It's not for me to say! You can ask Gilbert if you want, but I doubt that he'll tell you.'

CHAPTER TWENTY SEVEN

I'll have to apologize, I suppose. I shouldn't have stormed out of the office like that. It wasn't Steve's fault. Liz parked her car and walked down the High Street. There was a smell of diesel fumes drifting from the entries running up from the river where fishing boats were moored, but there was also another intermingling, fresher smell: one of the sea, of salt and sea-weed. A gull wheeled above her, followed by another, screeching raucously as it pursued a stolen titbit.

She felt a nervous excitement when she thought about the mill, and yet agitated, for what could be done about Carl and Jeannie? Nothing, she reflected. Not unless somewhere else could be found for them to live. Jeannie would be glad to move out of the village, but Carl, she was sure, would want to stay in the mill house just out of sheer cussedness.

She sighed. *I couldn't insist that they go; it's Carl's home after all, and Dad wouldn't be happy about it.*

Still, she thought, *it's not ours yet. The end of the year, Dad said. I'll have to write to Bill and tell him.* And there was another problem looming, she mused. *Bill won't want the mill house or the mill, but he'll want his share. What do I do about that? Quite apart from the fact that I haven't got the* money to buy his half, it would mean valuation, and I know how tricky that can be.

And now, how do I tell Steve, she thought, and took her keys from her bag. How do I tell him he's been conned?

The front door was unlocked and she pushed it cautiously. Susan was rarely in before her. She saw that her office door was open, and as she slowly climbed the stairs she saw Steve sitting glumly at her desk thumbing through some papers. He looked up as she came in and let out a huff of relief. 'You're back! Oh, thank you, God. You are going to stay? You're not leaving?'

She had to laugh. She had been prepared to apologize for her behaviour, and here he was welcoming her, literally with open arms.

He gave her a hug. 'I'm so sorry, Liz. I know I'm the worst chauvinist ever, but I don't mean anything and I promise I'll be good from now on.'

'What you need is someone who can tame you,' she said. 'Only it's not me,' she added swiftly. 'But I'm sorry too. I shouldn't have blown up the way I did. But I was shocked by what you told me about the mill, and I overreacted.'

There was a clatter of heels coming up the stairs and Sharon came in. 'Thank goodness you're here,' she said when she saw them. 'I came in early in case you didn't come in, Liz. Caroline is in the other office and she said she's had a call from Susan to say she can't get in today as she doesn't feel well.' She pulled a face. 'I don't think she can deal with discord. She's not tough like me and Caroline!'

Liz smiled. 'Well, I'm back now. Sharon, will you do me a favour? Can you stay here for an hour before you go back to the other office and field any calls for me? I need to talk to Steve,' she said, turning to him, 'and no matter how I butter it up, he's not going to like what I have to say.'

*

Steve's fury had cooled by midweek, but he would definitely sue Reedbarrow if he didn't get his money back, he'd said. He'd driven up to Tillington to look for him but there was no sign of him, and no one was answering the mill house door to his knock, which didn't surprise Liz at all, she told him.

'There might be a problem,' she said. 'The money's probably been spent, or at least most of it. But in mitigation, he might have thought that he had the right to sell; he could have thought that it was his property, or at least his mother's. Or that's what I'm led to believe,' she said lamely, not wanting to go too deeply into the complicated detail.

'What? He'd sell his mother's property without telling her and nobody knew? Where is his mother? Or did she agree that he could? I can't understand the secrecy,' he fumed. 'You're a tight-lipped lot!'

'I can't understand it either,' she confessed. 'But if you hadn't gone along with him in keeping quiet about it, then we might have found out sooner and you wouldn't have lost your money.'

'I haven't lost it yet!' His fury flared again. 'Did his mother definitely sell it to your family?'

She hesitated, then shook her head. 'Somebody did. But maybe not his mother. It was a long time ago,' she murmured. 'Years. I knew nothing about it.'

'If this gets out, I'll look a right idiot.' He eyed her in contemplation. 'I don't suppose your father would sell? No, course he wouldn't; if the village gets a wall there'll be some money to be made. That's prime building land.'

She shook her head. 'No, it's not for sale. Something to do with a Trust,' she said vaguely.

He sighed. 'Right! OK, I'll have to get in touch with my solicitor, then. See what we can do. Reedbarrow's committed a criminal offence, I feel sure, even if he didn't know about the sale!' He unfastened his briefcase and brought out a newspaper. 'By the way, did you know you've hit the nationals? I saved this for you – it's yesterday's.' He handed it to her and she unfolded it to see a photograph of herself on the second page, along with one of the breached road on Spurn Point and a favourable article on the village's plight.

'This is great,' she said, glad of a change of subject. 'That's the kind of reportage we need. Dad said it was on television last night; I missed it as it was on the early news, but we need all the publicity we can get. There's another batch of experts and surveyors coming next week to have a look, so maybe there'll be more.'

'What are they looking at? Surely they've seen it before?'

She nodded. 'They're coming to see if we're worth saving.'

By Friday she still hadn't heard from Chris, so after supper she decided to pluck up courage and phone him. Why should I feel guilty, she thought. I haven't done anything wrong, and yet there was an accusation in his eyes that I can't account for.

His voice was low and dull when he answered.

'It's me,' she said softly. 'Are you all right?'

'Fine,' he answered. 'You?'

'Yes.' She felt nervous. 'I hadn't heard from you. I wondered if you were – erm, unwell.'

'No. I've been busy.'

'Oh.' There was a silence at the other end. 'Are you angry with me for some reason?' A well of anxiety flooded over her, making her voice croaky.

'Why should I be angry?' There was a forced laugh in his voice which only served to make her more apprehensive. 'I thought you'd be pretty busy sorting out your affairs,' he went on. 'About the mill property, I mean. You'll have plenty to do, I expect, making plans and such.' He paused for a moment, but before she could say anything he asked, 'And when are the Reedbarrows moving out and the Rayners moving in?'

So that's it. A flash of annoyance suddenly stung her. He thinks I'll turn them out. As if I could anyway. Even if I wanted to, it wouldn't be possible; it's their home, and they've been there a long time. 'They've a right of tenure,' she said sharply. 'At least until the end of the year.'

'Oh, of course. But after that you'll be able to get them out? I don't suppose there'll be too much of a problem?'

She slammed the phone down without answering him; there was a veil of sarcasm in his voice which infuriated her. Why was he behaving like this? Her father, too, asking her on the very night he'd told her that the mill and the mill house was theirs if she would turn the Reedbarrows out. 'You won't, will you, Liz?' he'd said. Who do they think I am, she fumed, some kind of racketeer?

The next morning she called on the children in the village and delivered the posters which she had collected from the printers. 'Colour them however you like,' she said. 'Bright and cheerful if you want.' She scrunched up a witchlike face and scrabbled her hands at the Johnson twins. 'Or dark and dismal.' Which is just how I feel, she thought as she left them and crossed the road towards the sea.

Another barrier had been put across the end of the lane with a sign warning of dangerous cliffs, but she ducked under it and walked along the cliff path, watching the sea below. The tide was receding, and on the widening strip of wet sand abandoned plastic bottles, soggy canvas shoes, food cartons and various other material spoils lay abandoned, waiting for the next high tide to carry them away and deliver them to some other anchorage.

At least we didn't get any oil on the beach, she thought. We have to be thankful for that, I suppose. Thank goodness the wind didn't change direction. There had been nothing more in the newspapers or on local radio about the oil slick or the damaged tanker; coverage had changed to the collapsed road on the Spurn peninsula following the surge tide, and a lively debate had started on whether to allow Spurn Point to become an island.

The question is, she reflected as she stooped to gaze down at the muddy hummocks, peaks and crevices of broken earth, where will the money come from? Who is going to pay for these projects?

From the corner of her eye, a wispy shadow drifted behind her shoulder. She turned her head to see who had come so silently and intrusively to join her on the cliff path, but there was no one, only a rustle of grass as the wind ruffled it and the faint perfume of sweet-scented herbs and spring flowers stirring in the cold February air.

'Sarah?' she whispered. 'Is it you? Are you alone?'

The waves slapped and danced as they hit the shore below and she closed her eyes to concentrate. Can I hear voices? Soft and gentle murmurings from a long way off, seawards? Or am I imagining it, as always? She thought she could hear a far-off echo, like a whisper, as if she held a seashell to her ear, and sensed the presence of people murmuring, laughing, calling out to her, and wanted so badly to call back, to answer. To tell them that she had heard.

Reluctantly, she opened her eyes and gazed out to sea. Out there, she thought, that's where they had been, those other village people, living, loving, quarrelling, going about their business, just the same as we do. And now there's no trace! Not an old brick or stone, not even a picture of a cottage or a village street to show how it used to be. Nothing! Surely somebody must have something handed down from those long-gone years. She sighed. It was a long time ago.

She turned and looked behind her. Beyond the retreating wire fence which marked the boundary, grassy green meadows gently undulated inland. There were but few trees in

Holderness to impede her view, and in the distance she could see the tips of the tall towers of Hull's industrial skyline.

Turning her head, she saw Alf Wainwright's cottage still hanging on the edge of the cliff. The council were going to take it down, she thought, but they haven't yet, and if they don't soon it will be too late and that too will lie on the seabed with all the others.

She hunched into her coat and walked slowly back. Why does Sarah keep coming back here? Monkston village is under the sea. Why doesn't she lie peacefully there?

As she walked, a germ of a thought took hold. Unformed, it wriggled around, questioning, responding, discarding ... and, as she looked up Church Lane and saw Alf Wainwright swinging his walking stick with one hand and holding a shopping bag with a bunch of chrysanthemums poking their heads out of the top in the other, it finally resolved.

CHAPTER TWENTY EIGHT

'Is Chris not coming up today?' Gilbert was wiping down the bar counter, replacing beer mats and ashtrays. 'He's generally here by now, isn't he?' The pub was quiet, only a few people in for lunch, whom Dot was attending to.

Liz shrugged. 'Don't know. He didn't say.'

Her father pursed his lips and looked at her but she avoided his gaze. 'Well, then, if you're not doing anything, do you want to come to Beverley? I'm going to see Joan Reedbarrow. I have to talk to her about Carl and 'mill – I can't put it off any longer.'

She was astonished. Her father hated any kind of confrontation and she'd been sure he would need weeks to make up his mind to go and see the old lady, and have made numerous excuses to avoid upsetting her with reports of Carl's misdoings.

'You can do a bit of shopping in 'market if you want while I'm visiting her.'

'No, I'll come with you to see her. There's nothing we need just now.'

'Right. You go and get ready and I'll finish off in here. I'll not be long.'

Bright winter sunshine streamed through the car windows

and Liz unfastened her scarf and turned the heater down as they drove towards the old market town of Beverley. The countryside was softer and less barren here than on the coast, with deep scattered copses and dense woods sheltering the farmsteads. Flocks of gulls made splashes of white as they searched the ploughed earth, and shrill cawing rooks rebuilt old nests in the tall spinneys; to the west she could see the soft line of the blue-grey chalk hills of the Wolds, which like a curving backbone marked the centre of the East Riding of Yorkshire.

The Gothic splendour of the grey-stoned minster came into sight as they neared the town, and Liz remarked on the amount of building development on the approach roads since she was last there.

'That's progress for you,' her father said cynically. He made a right turn and then a left, heading towards Westwood and the Hurn, the green pastureland where cattle had right of way over traffic, hoping to find a parking place in the narrow streets in the vicinity which strangers wouldn't be aware of, which he did.

'I can recall a pal of my granddad's talking about driving sheep in from Tillington to Beverley market when he was a lad, and he meant walking them, not transporting them. Imagine doing that today with this amount of traffic!'

They cut through the narrow lanes behind Market Place to avoid the bustle of the Saturday market. 'It'll be a while since you last saw Joan, won't it, lass? Don't be surprised at the change in her.'

'It's ages,' Liz agreed. 'She hardly ever came into the village. I remember her chiefly from when I was a child and Mum used to take me with her when she visited her. That's the picture I have of her. She always seemed on the verge of tears when we called. She never seemed very happy, poor lady.'

Her father flinched, and she heard him draw in a breath. 'What's the matter, Dad?' she asked with some concern.

He shook his head. 'Nothing! Stubbed my toe on a cobble!'

She looked down at his feet in his strong leather shoes, and wondered.

The residential home was in the middle of a row of Victorian terraced houses, two houses made into one; the entrance hall was painted in a soft cream and a large earthenware jar set in a corner held several umbrellas and walking sticks. The door was locked, but a woman came immediately they rang the bell and invited them in. Gilbert signed their names in a book, and Liz followed him through the hall, snuffling her nose at the aroma of antiseptic and floral fragrance which overlay the sweet sour scent of decay inseparable from such establishments.

'Some of 'folks go out,' he told Liz while they waited for their guide to locate Carl's mother. 'But Joan chooses not to, unless someone takes her; she's too nervous to go on her own.'

Someone called out to him to 'Go along through, Mr Rayner, Joan's in the lounge,' and Liz followed him into a cosy room which had about six easy chairs and a small sofa strategically placed facing a television set, the screen bright with garish colours. Horse racing was in progress, the scene shifting between the races on the lurid green grass and the ring where red-faced trainers were examining fetlocks and smoothing gleaming flanks. Two or three elderly residents were staring at the screen, their heads nodding in response to the commentary.

'Is it Beverley races?' one of them asked, but no one answered, for most of them were sleeping, their heads slumped on to their chests. 'I'm sure it's Beverley,' she insisted, as if someone had answered in the negative.

Liz's attention was caught by another elderly occupant who grabbed her hand as she squeezed past her wheelchair. 'Is it raining?' She smiled up at Liz with a trusting gaze, her eyes bright and moist. 'I thought I might go out.'

'No.' Liz smiled back at her and patted her hand. 'It isn't raining. It's a lovely sunny day, but very cold, so you might be better staying indoors until the weather warms up.'

'Thank you,' she said. 'That's what I'll do, then, if you think it's for 'best.'

Liz glanced at her father; he'd bent over one of the chairs nearer the television and was attempting a conversation over its sound. 'Hello, Joan,' she heard him shout. 'How are you?'

A feeble voice answered from the depths of the chair. 'Not too bad, thank you. Who is it who's asking?'

'It's Gilbert,' he said. 'Gilbert Rayner. Don't say you've forgotten me?'

'Oh!' Joan Reedbarrow looked bewildered for a second, and then asked, 'Is 'rent due?'

'No,' he told her. 'That's tekken care of, don't you remember?'

She shook her head. 'No, I don't think I do. But I haven't any money in any case, onny my pension, so I'll have to pay you when I can.' A look of distress came into her face and he bent over her again.

'I haven't come for any money,' he told her. 'I've just come to see you.' He took hold of her hand. 'I've brought someone with me.'

'Is it Dorothy? She generally brings a bit of sweet cake.' She leant towards him. 'I have to push it up my sleeve so 'others don't see it,' she whispered. 'They'll all want a bit; they're greedy beggars.'

'No, Dot couldn't come today, so I've brought—'

'You haven't brought *her*,' Liz heard her say. '*She* hasn't come?' A streak of anxiety crossed Joan's face and she wrung her knobbly arthritic fingers together. 'I can't have any more visitors today. I get poorly if I have too many.'

Liz went over to the television and turned the sound down, and the wakeful residents looked at her with indifference, watching her as she rejoined her father.

'I've brought my daughter Elizabeth,' he said into Joan's ear. He clutched his throat. 'I get a sore throat every time I come here,' he said to Liz as an aside and raised his voice again. 'You remember her, don't you?'

'Yes, I do,' she said lucidly, 'and there's no need to shout, I'm not deaf. You mean 'little red-headed lassie?'

Liz smiled down at her. 'Hello, Mrs Reedbarrow. It's been a long time since we last met. How are you?'

'Not too bad.' She stared up at Liz. 'Aye, you're like your dad, and your granddad. I never did think you had your mother in you.'

She slipped into a silent meditation, her body rocking slightly and her lips moving in unspoken words; a crease appeared over her sparse eyebrows as if she was concentrating on something. Suddenly she looked up. 'Did they bury your mother?'

Liz's hand went to her mouth and she drew in a breath, looking at her father. 'What does she mean?'

'It's all right. It's all right,' he answered hastily. 'Yes.' He spoke to Joan Reedbarrow slowly and clearly. 'You remember, in 'Tillington churchyard.'

'Oh, yes. Yes, I remember now. Good.'

'I wanted to ask you if you'd ever told Carl about the mill and the house. Did you ever tell him who it belonged to?'

'You said we could stay! We've paid 'rent!'

'This is going to be difficult,' he murmured to Liz. 'Did you ever tell Carl that I owned 'mill?'

'My husband gambled, you know.' She had turned to speak to Liz. 'Lost everything.' She nodded her head and a spasm crossed her face and she looked as if she was about to cry. 'He used to tek it out on 'poor bairn, and it wasn't his fault. I know he was a bad lad sometimes, but he couldn't help it. It was my fault. I should have known better.'

'Don't upset yourself, Mrs Reedbarrow,' Liz said kindly. 'Nothing's your fault.'

'Aye, what's all this?' Gilbert patted her on the shoulder. 'We've come for a nice chat, not for tears.'

'Well, I get to thinking, you know, when I have visitors.' She wiped away her tears. 'Have you seen Carl lately?' She mentioned his name without reference to Gilbert's questions. 'Will you tell him I'm in here?'

'He knows you're here, Joan, he comes to see you. Have you ever told him about 'mill and 'mill house?' Gilbert persisted.

There was a rattle of crockery as a tea trolley was pushed into the room and Joan looked up expectantly. There was a general shuffling as residents roused themselves.

'I don't know.' She pushed her handkerchief up her sleeve and sat up in her chair. 'I can't remember. I'm sorry, but you'll have to go now. It's time for my tea.'

They walked back through Market Place and Liz idly stopped to look at a lambswool sweater on one of the stalls.

'Get it,' her father said. 'Colour will suit you.'

It was a pale green, a colour she liked to cool her fiery hair, but she looked at it dully and fingered the softness. 'Oh, I can't be bothered. I don't need another.'

'Go on, I'll treat you.'

She shook her head. 'I'm not in the mood.'

'Let's go and have a cup of tea then, before we head back. I could do with one after all that shouting.'

They found a table by the window in a small cafe, and both of them put their chins in their hands and stared out moodily.

'I'm not sure that I'm doing the right thing in visiting her, you know,' he commented. 'She prefers Dot. They gossip about people she knows, and if she forgets sometimes that some of them are no longer here Dot doesn't remind her. But when I go she always seems to be reminded about things she wants to forget. About Paul gambling and losing 'mill and then dying in the accident in 'way he did – things like that, poor lass.'

A server brought a tray of tea in blue and white china and a plate of scones with strawberry jam and cream. Liz poured the tea and passed a cup to Gilbert. 'And Carl, what about him?'

'He does go to see her, 'manager told me, although not that often. She forgets who's been to visit and when.'

'What did Joan mean when she said it wasn't Carl's fault? What wasn't?'

Her father bit into a scone and jam spurted out. He caught it with his finger before replying. 'She meant' – he lowered his voice – 'she meant that it wasn't his fault that he was illegitimate.'

'What?' Liz stared.

Gilbert nodded. 'He isn't – he wasn't Paul Reedbarrow's son. Carl was nearly a year old when Joan and Paul got married.'

'I didn't know! So, if he wasn't, who . . .' She stopped. It didn't seem right to ask.

'As far as I know she never said. She used to help my mother at one time, and I remember from when I was a lad that she was always gullible; easy to tease. Her parents were very strait-laced, though I didn't know that at the time, but I found out later that they didn't want to know her when she got into trouble, poor lass!'

Liz cringed at the term *into trouble*. 'Even though someone might have taken advantage of her?' she said carefully.

'Well, I don't know about that either.' He shuffled uncomfortably. 'Anyway, she had 'baby and went to live in Hull for a time, but she wasn't happy there, seemingly, and kept coming back to Tillington, stopping with anybody who'd have her. And then about 'same time Paul Reedbarrow's mother died and he needed somebody to look after 'house and cook his meals cos he was useless in that direction and he asked her if she would come.

'She wouldn't live in,' he went on. 'She was frightened of what folk might say about her, so finally he married her. He was a fair bit older than her, but he said he'd bring Carl up as his. Mebbe she thought they'd be safe with him, but he didn't make a good job of it, and he never did officially adopt him.'

'So do you think that's why Carl behaves as he does? Does he feel let down?' She was trying to find an excuse for Carl's bullying, particularly towards Jeannie.

'No. I'm no psychologist,' her father's mouth turned down, 'but I reckon when a child gets beaten up or is given a hiding every time his so-called father is down on his luck it's bound to make him aggressive, wouldn't you say?'

'That's why you've always felt sorry for him?'

'Aye, everybody did. Course I was away at sea for some of the time, so I didn't always know what was going on, but Dot said that folk in 'village used to make up for Paul's bullying. They'd give young Carl treats, like chocolate or money, whenever they saw him with a bruise or a black eye, instead of reporting Paul to 'authorities like they should have done.' He laughed. 'And then, young devil, as he got older he must have realized he could work it to his advantage. He used to pretend he'd had a beating – he'd put his arm in a sling or walk with a limp – just to get money out of folk.'

'But what about his mother?' Liz said heatedly. 'Surely she wouldn't stand by and watch her son being battered?'

'She didn't have any option. Paul used to knock her about too; more often than not she'd have a black eye to match Carl's. He was an ugly customer, was Paul Reedbarrow. An out and out monster.' He waved to the server for the bill. 'Shall we go? I'm feeling depressed. I don't think I'll visit her again.'

'But why haven't I heard all this before?' She put her arm through his as they walked back to the car. 'I've never heard a whisper that Carl wasn't Paul Reedbarrow's son.'

'No, you wouldn't. Not your generation. Carl probably doesn't know either, or at least he didn't, not back then, though he might know now. No, everybody wanted to protect Joan. She'd had such a raw deal that everybody conveniently forgot, or pretended to. Carl had Paul's name and, besides, it was a long time ago. It just doesn't matter any more.'

She nodded and sat silently as her father pulled into the traffic and headed out of town on the coast road. *He's not a Reedbarrow. The line has come to an end, just like the Foster Rayners' is doing. Except – no, the seed is still scattered, and if Bill gets married in Australia . . . but then he's not bothered about the Foster name; he'll always use Rayner.*

'That's why Chris couldn't find any trace of Carl in the record office,' she murmured. 'And that's why you were angry?'

'Yes.' He glanced towards her and she saw benevolence in his eyes. *He's the kindest man I know,* she thought; *he wouldn't hurt a fly.*

'Yes,' he repeated. 'There are some things that shouldn't be disturbed, Liz. They should be left as they are; you never know what box of mischief you might open once you start ferreting around.'

'You're probably right,' she said. 'But there was one thing that Mrs Reedbarrow said that made her really agitated. She said "You haven't brought *her*, have you?". She wasn't talking about Dot, so who did she mean? Dad? Are you listening?'

'Sorry, I was miles away.' He'd switched on the radio and was fiddling around with the wavelengths, making the set crackle and spit. 'I don't know. I can't think who she meant.'

Chris's car was parked in the Ship car park and Liz felt a dizzying sense of relief flood over her, followed immediately by a feeling of disquiet. He's behaved very oddly; perhaps he's come to tell me he's not staying around, she thought. It's tied up with the mill. Did he think I was obsessed by it? Perhaps I was, or maybe he's had second thoughts about Helena, maybe finds it difficult to break off with her. But I thought – well, I sensed we were becoming close, though perhaps it didn't mean as much to him as it did to me; it's difficult to judge. But, well, I hope – I don't know what I'll do if . . . She couldn't think straight. I want him to be here, she finally admitted to herself. In my life.

He'd pinned a note on the door. He'd obviously arrived after Dot had locked up and gone home. *On the cliffs,* he'd written. It seemed rather terse.

'You'd better go and fetch him back.' Gilbert unlocked the door. 'He shouldn't be wandering about there. It'll be getting dark soon; look at them clouds.' He gave a deep sigh. 'Folks don't seem to be able to get it into their heads just how dangerous it is. Them cliffs aren't stable. There's tons and tons of clay there ready to fall. No one would survive being buried under that lot.'

'I'll go and get him,' she said. 'Don't worry.'

'But I do worry.'

'Hardly anybody goes along there now. Only people who know about it, and we're always careful.'

He didn't answer, just shook his head, so she changed from her leather boots into wellingtons and went to look for Chris.

CHAPTER TWENTY NINE

He was leaning on the barrier looking out at the darkening, streaked sky and the heaving white crests on the tossing and pitching gunmetal sea, his hair ruffling in the wind.

'Dad was worried that you were walking on the cliff top,' she said as a way of greeting. 'He thinks that we'll get another fall after the winter rains.'

'And what about you? Were you not worried about me?' He folded his arms across his chest, his face impassive as he turned to face her.

'I didn't think you'd do anything foolish,' she said loftily. 'I'm sure you're well aware of the danger.' I won't let him see that I care, she thought. I'll wait; find out first why he's come. Oh, please don't say you're leaving.

'Sometimes I do foolish things,' he said. 'Sometimes I do the most stupid things imaginable.'

'Oh!' She too folded her arms. 'Like what?'

'Like misjudging you.' He loosened his arms; put his hands in his pockets. 'Blundering on under a misconception of what you might do, when if I'd thought about it logically I should have known that you wouldn't, even if you could.'

'I have no idea what you're talking about. You're not making sense. Unless,' she said slowly as understanding dawned, 'you're talking about the Reedbarrows and thought that we'd turn them out of their home?'

He took a step closer and bent his head towards her. 'I'm sorry.' He took hold of her hand.

'You're entitled to an opinion,' she said stonily. 'Even if it happens to be wrong.'

'It's just . . .' he stroked her cold, gloveless hand with his thumb, 'it's just that I thought your future was all sewn up now that you and Bill know you have the mill and the mill house and I couldn't see a place in it for me. I was just jealous, that's all; that's why I said what I did. I'm so sorry.'

'You were jealous?' She smiled. 'Of the mill? Of bricks and mortar?' She could feel summer stealing over her, warming her winter-wrapped body through from her cold toes to her pink nose.

'Ridiculous, isn't it? But it's all you ever wanted, you told me that. You wanted it back for the Fosters and the Rayners and now you've got it.'

'It was all I ever wanted then,' she said softly, wanting him to hold her. 'There are other things I want more now.'

'What sort of things?' He put his arms round her and held her close, pressing his cold cheek against hers. 'I'll give them to you.'

She whispered, though there was no one to hear or see them in the gathering dusk, 'I want you to love me as much as I love you. I don't want you to go away. I want you to stay here with me for ever.'

He kissed her fiercely and then held her away from him and laughed. 'I do love you. I have from the minute I met you. Couldn't you tell?'

She shook her head and kissed him back.

'I thought you were telepathic! Doesn't it work with me?'

He stroked her cheek and gently touched her mouth. 'Do you want us to be part of this landscape, crumbling away with the cliffs? Or part of the atmosphere, like your friend Sarah?'

'You're laughing at me,' she said tearily.

'I was never more serious,' he said solemnly, and nuzzled into her neck. 'In fact, unless you can go back to the village and find someone with a blowtorch, I am going to be here for ever, because my feet are frozen solid to the ground.'

Gilbert was anxious to find Carl Reedbarrow before Steve Black's solicitor did. According to Steve, who had told Liz, Carl had not replied to the solicitor's letters and now there was an investigator looking for him.

Gilbert went up to the mill several times but the place was locked up and not even the dog was there. No one in the village had seen Carl, but Gilbert discovered that Kevin Warner had given Jeannie a job as a barmaid and she was saying nothing.

'I don't know where he is,' she said sulkily when he went into the Raven to enquire. 'I'm not his keeper; he comes home each night, that's all I know.' Kevin Warner leant on the bar counter, drawing heavily on a cigarette, and changed the subject to discuss the army of surveyors and researchers who had been swarming around the cliff top and down on the sands all day, measuring the tidal currents and wave patterns, and armed with theodolites and levels and yardsticks, and binoculars slung around their necks. Gilbert left them to it.

'What am I going to do, Dot?' he said when he got back to the Ship. 'I don't know where else to look.'

'I don't know.' She called cheerio to a customer who was just leaving. 'But if you do find him, what then? He's fiddled Steve Black out of a lot of money – more fool Steve – but that's nothing to do with you, so what are you going to tell him? That the mill isn't his to sell?' She laughed mockingly. 'Because you're not telling me he doesn't know already. I think he's been tekkin' you for a ride. Pretending he doesn't know, living practically rent-free all these years, and for why? Just because of a hunch? A vague feeling?'

'I don't know what you mean!' he retaliated. 'Reedbarrows have been paying a peppercorn rent to Rayners since my father's day!'

'And why? Cos they felt guilty about Joan!'

He fell silent and then shrugged. 'They never told me. Mebbe I was too young, although I guessed there was something from 'snippets of conversation I overheard and didn't understand back then.'

'Well, I knew,' Dot said frankly. 'Oh, not then, of course, but years later your mother told me. It was just after you and Nina got married; your mum and me had a heart-to-heart.' She paused. 'About a lot of things.'

Gilbert looked at her steadily. 'She was allus fond of you.'

Dot looked away. A flush rose up her plump white neck. 'Yes, she was. It was then that she told me they'd always suspected that Carl was your Uncle Tom's child, and how they'd look after Joan, even though they'd no proof. And even now, after all this time, here you are still protecting them, and Carl a grown man.'

'You amaze me.' He stared at her. 'You've known all this time and never said anything?'

'It had nothing to do with me,' she answered, a slight edge of bitterness in her voice. 'Why should I discuss it? I'm not a Foster or a Rayner – it wasn't my place.'

'But you're 'same as Nina,' he said. 'You think we should have turned them out!'

'I am *nothing* like Nina!' Her voice rose. 'Don't you *ever* say that. I wouldn't have harassed Joan the way she did, making her so frightened that 'poor woman daren't come out of her own front door in case she saw her.'

'I'm sorry, I'm sorry.' Grief creased his face. 'I didn't mean it like that. You know I didn't.'

Contrite, she put her arms round him. 'Don't upset yourself, darling. I know you didn't mean that. I'm sorry; I shouldn't have reminded you. But what I mean is that you can't go on feeling guilty about them. Not about Joan, nor about the way Nina behaved. Why should you or your family go on paying for something that happened so long ago? And they hadn't any proof anyway. Joan was 'onny one who could have said and no one ever asked her.'

'They'd all have been cut up when Tom was killed,' he sighed. 'I don't think it registered with them straight away, not until Joan asked if she could have a photograph of him to keep.'

He started to switch off the lights, leaving just one security lamp on. 'I think I'll slip up to 'mill now and see if I can catch Carl. Jeannie said he comes home at night.'

She sighed. He hadn't listened, not to a single word. 'I'll walk along with you,' she said. 'And be careful what you say. He'd hate to be told he was related to 'Foster Rayners.'

He put a torch in his pocket, because the street lights didn't extend to the top of the lane where the mill house stood, but first he walked Dot home.

'Are you coming in for a minute?' she asked as she opened her door.

'Better not,' he said gently. 'It would be more than a minute, wouldn't it? And I must try and catch Carl. I'll pop round tomorrow.'

She blinked, and closed the door. She looks sad; I'm not being fair to her, he thought, still standing on her doorstep. It can't be easy for her being alone. She needs someone, but is it me? I'm just scared, I suppose, of making the wrong decision, but on 'other hand . . .

He sighed. We've been a pair for as long as I can remember.

An item, I think it's called nowadays. But would our friendship be spoiled if we married? I don't know. It's a tricky one,
no doubt about that.

The lights at the Raven were being switched off as he passed
it on his way back towards the lane. Kevin Warner was never in
a hurry to close as a rule; there was often a customer or two
still there in the early hours. He glanced through the window
as he went by, and saw that the bar was empty apart from Jeannie and Kevin, who was helping her on with her coat. His
hands lingered on her shoulders, and then he turned her
round and his hands disappeared beneath the coat.

Gilbert breathed in. She didn't seem to resist, but moved
closer to him. 'Phew,' he muttered under his breath, 'they'd
better watch out; playing with fire, I'd say.' He stepped away
from the window into the gutter and walked on towards the
mill house, going slowly in the hope that Jeannie might catch
up with him.

He waited by the locked gate. The house was in darkness,
and nothing stirred except the creaking branches of the trees
at the side of the house as the wind blew through them. Some
of them needed lopping, he thought vaguely. Clouds bumped
along the night sky and the moon appeared momentarily, sil-
houetting the mill behind the house and throwing shadows
around the yard before it was obliterated again. Gilbert
narrowed his eyes. Was it his imagination, or was someone
there, watching him?

He glanced down at his watch. Ten minutes had passed and
he was beginning to feel cold; he turned to walk back and
caught the sound of footsteps. He switched on his torch; if it
was Jeannie coming home he didn't want to frighten her.
'Hello,' he called, and the footsteps slowed.

'Who is it?' The woman's voice was wary.

'It's Gilbert Rayner, Jeannie. I wanted a word with Carl, but
'gate's locked.'

She looked nicer than when she worked for him at the Ship.
She'd always seemed dull, pale-faced and uncommunicative,
but even in the wavering moonlight he could see that she was
wearing make-up, and the hair beneath her scarf seemed
fairer. She said nothing.

'So how can I talk to him?'

'He doesn't want to talk to anybody at 'minute. He's got a
few problems.'

'I know he's got problems,' Gilbert said sharply. 'That's why
I want to talk to him, before things get worse.'

'Well, he doesn't talk to me about them. I never ask him. I
know better than that. Does he . . .' She hesitated. 'Does he
owe you money?'

'No, in all honesty I can say that he doesn't, but I need to
talk to him – to both of you, in fact, because it will affect you
as well. It's to do with this property.'

'It's his mother you need to talk to, then.' She pulled her
coat closer about her. 'It's in her name, although I don't think
you'll get much sense out of her. She's going gaga, I think.'

'Don't say that!' he said sharply. 'She's not, and it's not a
nice thing to say about anybody. But I have to talk to Carl
about it.'

'You say it'll affect me, this business?'

'Possibly, I don't know, but it has to be resolved. It can't wait
much longer and it concerns Carl more than his mother.'

'All right.' She seemed to make up her mind quickly. 'Come
tomorrow morning, about eight. Carl will still be in bed and
I'll unlock 'gate when I let 'dog out – only don't mention me
or I'll get a bruiser. I'll have to go now, or he'll come looking
for me. He's not over-keen on me having 'job at 'Raven and if
I'm late he'll be suspicious.'

'Be careful, Jeannie.' Gilbert was tense. 'Don't aggravate
him. He's allus had a fearful temper.'

'Huh,' she snorted. 'Tell me something I don't know.' She

started to walk towards the gate, but stopped and turned to face him again. 'But I'll tell you something for nothing. I've just about had enough. One of these days he's going to be sorry.'

Gilbert walked past the mill gate the next morning and stood on the rough ground of the public footpath looking out across the fields. A mist was rising steadily, sweeping its weightless ghostly vapour towards the pale sun, promising a fine day.

He let his gaze wander down the footpath, the same scene he had looked upon as a young lad when he had seen his idol, his Uncle Tom, his father's younger, rollicking, carefree brother, walking towards the copse with Joan Reedbarrow, as she was now. He hadn't thought anything of it back then; it was a regular walk around the village, and peeping lads often spied on courting couples who secretly kissed in the copse.

It was only later, when Tom's treasured motorbike smashed head on into an oncoming car on a winding Holderness road, killing him outright, that he'd thought any more about it, and even then it didn't mean much to him, in his innocence. No, he thought now, it was my mother's solicitude towards Joan and her infant Carl a while later that alerted me. It was something more than neighbourly concern. But no sense in opening fresh wounds this late in the day, he mused. It's best forgotten.

The lock on the gate was hanging free, and dropped to the ground as he pushed the gate open. Surreptitiously he kicked it to one side so that it lay out of sight amongst docks and nettles.

Ben came lurching across the yard, barking and thumping his tail. 'Hello, old lad.' Gilbert rubbed the dog's neck. 'How are you, then?' The dog barked louder in response and raced off to the house. Well, my arrival has been announced, Gilbert thought. We'll see what happens now. I'll probably be sent off with a flea in my ear.

Jeannie opened the door, a dingy pink dressing gown clutched around her; this was more like the girl he remembered, pale-faced and dowly with dark streaks showing in her uncombed hair, not bright and defiant as she'd been last night.

'What do you want?' she said, and put her finger to her lips.

'Can I have a word with Carl?' he said heartily. 'I wouldn't bother him, but it's important.'

She appeared to hesitate, and then said, 'I'll see if he's up,' and went inside.

Gilbert could hear whispers in the kitchen, so he put his foot inside the doorway and called through. 'I won't keep you long, Carl, I know you'll be busy.'

Carl opened the kitchen door and stood in the passageway facing Gilbert. He was bare-chested, unwashed and unshaven, and wearing only a pair of creased loose pyjamas.

What a mess, Gilbert thought. What a disgusting mess you are.

Carl glowered. 'How did you get in? Gate should've been locked. What do you want anyway? I haven't time to talk. I have to be off.' He ran his tongue around his teeth and then took a cigarette from a packet in his hand and put it to his lips. 'Fetch us a match,' he bellowed over his shoulder, and Jeannie silently appeared and handed him a box of matches. When she didn't immediately disappear back into the kitchen, he turned and snarled at her. 'Go on, clear off. What 'you waiting for?'

'Erm, well, if Jeannie wants to stay, I don't know, it might concern her,' Gilbert began, taking a step back outside.

'Concern her? Concern her! Just get on with what you have to say and then you can clear off too.' He turned to Jeannie and thumbed towards the kitchen. 'What did I just say to you? Get in there and put 'kettle on.' He stood on the doorstep and drew heavily on the cigarette, then coughed and spat into the yard. 'Slut,' he muttered.

'It's about this place, Carl.' Gilbert took his courage in both hands. 'As you'll be aware, when the last contract was drawn up, the end date for the agreed tenancy was in October this year, and—'

Carl's eyes had narrowed and his upper lip twitched. 'As I am aware? As I am aware of *nothing*! What 'you going on about? I know nowt about a contract. This property belongs to me and my mother!' He jabbed the hand holding the glowing cigarette towards Gilbert. 'Don't you try any tricks wi' me. I remember your bitch of a wife trying to do 'same.'

Gilbert stepped back again. 'There's no need to take that attitude,' he said firmly. 'Everything was done legally and fairly. I'm not saying you have to move out, only that circumstances will be different and we have to talk about it.' He took a deep breath and plunged on. 'I'm simply a trustee. My son and daughter will be—'

What his son and daughter would be he didn't have the chance to explain as Carl turned on him, his eyes blazing and his teeth bared as if he was about to tear him limb from limb. 'Clear off!' he shouted. 'Get off my land or I'll set 'dog on you.'

Ben, standing by his master's feet, blinked, and then obediently barked.

'We have to talk, Carl,' Gilbert began again. 'I don't want any animosity. Talk to your mother if you don't believe me. She'll explain as much as she knows. I'll go with you.'

Carl pointed to the gate. 'If you're not out of here in two minutes flat, you'll get a barrel load of shot up your backside.' Gilbert turned abruptly, his face red. He was in no doubt that

Carl meant every word. The man had a shotgun, he knew that. 'And tell that red-headed bitch that's your daughter that she needn't fancy she's coming in here either,' he yelled as Gilbert reached the gate. ''Cos she'll get just 'same.'

CHAPTER THIRTY

'I'm just off, Dad.' Liz looked up briefly, folded the newspaper which was spread across the kitchen table, drained her teacup and stood up. 'I'm going to drop these posters in at the shop and one at the Raven before I go to work. Have you seen them?' She opened one out and held it up for him to see, and saw the strained look on his face. 'What's the matter? What's happened?'

He pulled out a chair and sat down. 'I've been to see Carl Reedbarrow.'

'And – what?'

'All these years I've tried to do my best for him. He didn't have a good start in life, I give him that, but I've put jobs his way, helped him out with—' He shook his head. 'Sorted out that care home for his mother, and for what? I didn't expect thanks, but neither did I expect abuse. He's just threatened me with his shotgun.'

'What? He did what? I've said all along that he's unstable.' She banged the table with her fist, making the crockery rattle. 'He has no thought for anyone but himself; he's mean, he's a bully and a cheat and he doesn't deserve any consideration, least of all from you. You owe him nothing!'

231

He nodded and huffed out a breath. 'You're right,' he agreed dejectedly. 'I don't know why I bother. Anyway, that's it. I'm finished with it. Steve Black can do what he wants. He's the one who's lost money, not me. Come October, if he's still there and refuses to move out, then 'bailiffs will have to call.' He stretched out his hand and Liz saw it tremble a little. 'Let's have a look at 'posters.'

The posters that she had given to the children to paint had come back in a variety of colours and some with additions. One now included giant gaping-mouthed fishes which were swallowing whole people and houses; some showed blue skies and gentle white-flecked sea with seabirds flying above, whilst others had angry black and purple waves dashing against white cliffs where groups of stick people clung to one another and a huge yellow sun smiled down on them.

One young artist had added a fleet of sailing ships bobbing along on top of choppy waves, whilst down below in the depths lay the village of Tillington with three recognizable landmarks: the post office, the Raven and the Ship.

'Breaks your heart, doesn't it?' Her father was clearly moved by them all. 'If they don't do any good, then I don't know what will. General public should see them. Leave me a couple, will you? I'll show them to 'council in Beverley – see if I can have them put up there. I know they're with us, but a reminder wouldn't hurt.'

Liz left two of the posters out for him and put the others carefully back in a folder. 'I'm going to ask if we can put some up in Hull as well. People from there used to come to Tillington a lot at one time, I remember. It was always a good safe place for families. Some might like to come again once we have a wall. Are you sure you're all right, Dad? I really do have to be going; I'm running late.'

'Yes.' He made a feeble attempt to smile. 'It was a bit of a shock, that's all. I'm OK.'

She walked to the post office and handed a poster over the counter, and then went on to the Raven. She rang the back door bell and glanced at her watch. I hope he doesn't keep me talking, she thought. I'm late already.

'Hi, Liz, come on in.' Kevin was dressed in a navy tracksuit and white trainers and a sports towel hung round his neck. 'I've been out for a run. I'm a bit sweaty.'

'I can't stop,' she said hastily. 'I'm off to work, but I've brought you a poster; can you put it somewhere prominent?'

'Will do.' He held it at arm's length to look at it, but didn't comment. 'We should hear something soon, don't you think? Mark you . . .' He chewed on his lip. 'P'raps I shouldn't say anything yet.'

'Have you heard something?' He always had his ear to the ground, but surely it was far too soon for any decision?

'Oh, not about that! No, it's just that it might not affect me one way or another, though of course I'll do what I can whilst I'm here.'

She frowned. Get on with it, she thought.

'It's just that I've put in for another pub, over in Bradford. It's my home patch, you know. I think it's on the cards that I'll get it, so if I do I'll be off fairly soon, but please don't mention it around just yet. It's not official.'

'Well, I hope it works out for you, Kevin. I'm sure you'll be missed here.'

She made her escape, and hurried home to collect her car. She ran lightly along the footpath towards Church Lane and glanced automatically over her shoulder before crossing. Halfway down the hill a pick-up truck was moving slowly down, giving her ample time to cross.

She had taken only a few steps across the lane when the sound of hard revving and crashing gears alerted her. The truck had accelerated abruptly and was hurtling towards her. For a second she was startled. It wasn't going to stop; should she step back or keep going forward? Was it out of control? Then she saw the driver at the wheel.

With an impulsive thrust she launched herself towards the opposite side, fear and anger lending her speed. She looked back and saw quite clearly the addled grin on Carl Reedbarrow's face. 'Idiot!' she yelled. 'What do you think you're playing at?'

She heard the squeal of the heavy tyres and saw the motion of his hands as he turned the wheel in her direction. She shook in a cold sweat. He's going to run me over!

She set off at a sprint towards the Ship but he followed, picking up speed and veering towards the footpath. He drew abreast of her, hitting the high kerb which had been the subject of numerous complaints to the council because of its unsuitability for prams and pushchairs and arthriticky elderly knees, and for which she was now profoundly thankful as she heard the rasp and scrape of the wheels against it.

'That made you stir your stumps, didn't it? Bet you haven't run as fast as that in a long time.' He gave her a sniggering wink and she backed into a low prickly hawthorn hedge. She was confident that the truck could not actually mount the pavement, but she saw with apprehension his mocking, boorish expression. 'I bet you don't run as fast as that when 'lads are chasing you. I'd bet you're soon caught, aren't you, flashing them thighs. Red-haired bitch.'

He leant out of the window. 'Just keep out of my way, you and your father both if you know what's good for you, and don't hold your breath over 'mill or 'mill house.' Spittle gathered at the corners of his mouth. 'If I catch either of you within yards of either, you'll regret it.'

For a terrified moment she thought he was going to drive at her again after all, for he revved hard, but raising two fingers at her he swung round in a wide circle and drove off in the opposite direction.

She staggered into the yard of the Ship and pushed open the back door. 'Dad!' She felt sick and shaky.

'What's up?' He looked up from the newspaper and got to his feet. 'You're as white as a sheet.'

She took a gasping breath. 'I think we've got a whole heap of trouble coming. Carl Reedbarrow has just tried to kill me.'

CHAPTER THIRTY ONE

Joan Reedbarrow sat quietly dozing. She was warm and comfortable and had managed to get to her favourite chair before anyone else did. She'd had a good breakfast of porridge and toast and marmalade, and then watched the news on television, though none of it made much sense.

Soldiers in tanks were fighting in the mountains. Well, she thought they were soldiers, though they were dressed very strangely and wore turbans on their heads. I hope they're not fighting round here. She peered at the screen. There are no mountains round here, except in Scotland. There were mountains in Scotland; she'd seen pictures of them, though she'd never been.

Never been anywhere much, only Hull where I went to live after I'd had Carl. My mam and dad didn't really want me in Tillington. I've been to York once – oh, and Beverley, yes, I've been to Beverley quite a lot. Paul used to let me go with him sometimes when he went to 'cattle market on a Wednesday. I think it was a Wednesday.

I didn't care for it, though. I didn't like to hear 'squeal of 'pigs in 'back of lorry, an' that time he took that lovely little heifer that I'd been fond of. I'm sure it knew where it was going; and then I allus worried that Paul would go home without me, that he might have forgotten I'd gone with him, and I'd worry about Carl getting into mischief when he came out of school.

She unbuttoned her cardigan; it's lovely and warm in here. I hope I won't have to pay extra for heating. *He* wouldn't let me have much heat on. Plenty of wood outside if you want a fire, he'd say. You just have to fetch it.

Not that I minded that. Liked it, in fact. It was a chance to get out of 'house away from him. I went twigging, like I used to when I was young, picking up twigs or fallen branches, and I'd drag them behind me to 'mill and stack them ready to start a fire. Sometimes he'd bring logs home that somebody had given him and he showed me how to chop them, you know, with a metal wedge so that they'd split easy and then I'd have a really good fire.

She reminisced frequently, thinking about when she was a girl living at home, going to school, and then at four o'clock walking slowly back home, cutting away from the roads and crossing over those ditches that weren't too wide or deep and filled with rain water and going into the fields; she knew she hadn't to walk across where crops were growing, but the edges were scattered with scarlet poppies and primroses and just after winter she'd see snowdrops and then bluebells coming up and always a fresh sweet smell. Nothing has a scent any more, certainly not in here, except at dinner time.

I wasn't a bad lass, though, not like some I could name. She eyed the other occupants in the room for confirmation of the fact and nodded her head in justification. It was onny ever that once and I didn't really know anything and he did say it would be all right. I dare say it might have been if—

The rattle of crockery roused her from her meditations and she moved some magazines from the table at the side of her chair to make room for a cup and saucer. She watched as the carer moved from chair to chair giving out drinks and biscuits, waking those of the residents who were sleeping. She waited anxiously. Once they had run out before they got to her and said they'd come back, only they didn't, and she was gasping for a drink by dinner time.

'Will you have tea or coffee, Joan?'

'I'll have coffee, please, and a biscuit if there're any left.'

'There're enough to go round,' the woman mumbled. 'Everybody gets 'same.'

Joan took the cup and saucer from her and reached into the tin. 'I'd like to go for a walk after,' she said brightly. 'It looks nice out.' On the television screen the sun was shining and a man in his shirtsleeves was cutting flowers in a large garden. She bit into the biscuit and crumbs fell down the front of her chest and into her lap. She brushed them away, afraid of making a mess on her clean dress. 'I'd like to go for a walk on 'sands later for a bit of fresh air.'

'You'll have a long walk, then.' The carer pushed the trolley away. 'I hope you don't want me to tek you.'

'But I can't go on my own!' She stared after the pale blue shape. 'I might see *her* and she'll go on at me again.'

She put down the cup when she had finished and looked round the room. It was very comfortable. She'd done well to get such a nice place. I think I might stay. Carl can manage without me now that he's got that girl. I think it was her who said I had to come here. What did she say? *I can manage him better on my own. I can't be responsible for you.* Yes, well, mebbe she thinks she can manage him.

She settled back into the chair, yawning. Yes, well, we'll see, won't we? I never could. Never ever. Didn't know how to. He was always such a little devil, even when he was a bairn. Kicking and screaming and carrying on. Mebbe it was my fault. I used to give in to him, I know.

What a funny old life. I only ever did one thing wrong in my life and I'm still paying for it! But he said – he said that it wasn't wrong. He said I'd made him very happy, though I can't think how. Anyway, I'd never made anybody happy before, nor since, so mebbe I'll be forgiven.

But Carl! Can I be forgiven for bringing him into the world? He's a bad lad, no doubt about that. I have to say it though I'm his mother. I did everything wrong there. I must have done, otherwise why is he like he is? He was never happy, always wanting, always angry even when he was little. I could never do anything right for him, and he was always scared of his dad, except that he wasn't his dad, was he, and I was allus frightened that one day he'd turn.

She dozed fitfully with flickering dreams of a young man beneath the swaying shadow of a tree, his features vague and indeterminate, who smilingly beckoned her to come closer, and as she willingly did the smile became the leering grin of her son.

She jumped when she woke. She'd repeatedly had a fleeting moment of fear on waking, even when she was a child, and unceasingly once she had married Paul. Since she had come to live here it had been a transient thing, and the sight of a comforting cup of tea brought to her every morning was a constant source of wonder.

But something was disturbing her now. She burped loudly; she'd had terrible wind round her heart this morning and she'd got it again now. I'll have to tell 'doctor when he comes next time.

The rattle of pans and crockery and a lovely smell coming from the kitchen told her it was nearly dinner time. I'd better go to 'lavvy first and get comfortable. She reached out for the walking frame to pull herself up; she didn't really need it but they insisted on her using it. A hand took hold of it to steady it. A large hand, with dark scattered hair on the back and dirty fingernails.

'Oh!' She sat down again with a bump. 'It's you!'

'Now, then, Ma!' Carl pulled out a chair and turned it to face her. She was trapped.

'I was just going to 'lavvy,' she dithered.

'I'm not staying long.' He didn't look at her but dipped his hand into his jacket pocket and brought out a tin of tobacco and a packet of cigarette papers and started to roll.

'You're not allowed to smoke in here.' Her heart began to flutter. She could almost wish that he didn't come, he made her so nervous.

'Who says?' He glanced around at the other sleeping occupants and licked the edge of the cigarette paper. He grinned. 'I can't see anybody in here who's going to stop me.'

'It's just the rules.'

'Rules are made to be broken, Ma. Even you've broken one or two in your time, haven't you?' He stared into her face and she leant back. 'Come on,' he grinned. 'Admit it. Now and again you've done summat you shouldn't have?'

'I – I don't know what you mean – will you go and get somebody? I want to go to 'lavvy. I'm going to wet myself.'

He drew in a deep lingering breath on the cigarette and shed a thin stream of smoke through his nostrils. 'I had a visit from Gilbert Rayner this morning. Wanted to talk about 'mill and our house. Seemed to think he can have 'em at 'end of 'year.'

She stared at him. Surely not, not yet. I've paid 'rent. I told Gilbert when he came that 'rent was paid. I couldn't sleep for thinking about it after he'd gone. I'm sure it's paid. I hope it doesn't mean I've to move from here – not when I've just got settled.

'So what we going to do about it, then? Cos they're not having them, I'll tell you that for nowt!'

'Gilbert won't move me out of here,' she protested. 'He's not like that.'

'Hah! That's what you think, is it? You think that Rayner's

made you nice and safe in here?' He leant towards her and she flinched as he whispered, 'But what about his bitch of a wife, eh? Do you think you're safe from her?'

'Stop it!' Fear engulfed her. 'Don't talk like that. She's dead. She's buried in 'churchyard. I asked him.'

He took her by the arm and bent towards her. 'She might come and haunt you, though, mightn't she?'

There was a clanging going on in her head. Like the muffled sound of a church bell. Like the reverberating toll she had heard from her door when they'd brought Nina Rayner up the lane to the church.

She hadn't gone out to pay her respects like the other villagers; she'd closed her curtains and stayed indoors and felt the mantle of fear which she'd had of that embittered and disillusioned woman dissolving and disappearing from her shoulders, and she'd gone upstairs and sat alone in her cold cheerless bedroom, listening to the muted voices of the congregation returning to their own lives.

'Why did she keep on at you, Ma? Did she know summat about you?'

She shook her head. 'It was about 'mill and 'mill house.' She felt very tired. 'She wanted us to move out, said it was theirs.' The clamour was increasing and so was the tightness around her ribs. *I'm going to be sick. I wish somebody would come.*

'Carl,' she whispered. 'I've got something to tell you. About your dad.' *I'll have to tell him,* she thought wearily. *Before it's too late. I should have told him before, onny I was too ashamed. I was always afraid of what he might think or do.*

'I've telled you afore never to mention his name, haven't I?' he hissed. 'I hope he's rotting in hell, getting what he deserves.'

'He was wicked,' she whispered. 'To both of us.' She was having difficulty in forming her words. 'It used to upset me when he beat you. That's why I want to tell you—' she wanted to swallow but her tongue seemed swollen, closing her throat, 'that's why I want to tell you – to tell you that he wasn't your father; not your real father. He said he'd look after us. Adopt you, only he never did.'

She saw him grin and she trembled. She knew that look; it always preceded some mischief, some hurt. He was worse than Paul; she always knew with her husband when the blow was going to fall, a quick burst of temper and a strike, but Carl let the moment linger, enjoying it, savouring the distress that he knew he was giving.

'You think I don't know that?' He glanced round the room and then leant over her, a lock of dark greasy hair brushing his face. 'I've known for years. Shall I tell you when I found out?' He sniggered. 'You'll laugh when I tell you.'

She started to shake. The pain in her chest was getting worse. Why didn't somebody come and send him away? *I don't like him.* Tears spilled over on to her cheeks.

'It will have to be our little secret, Ma. You mustn't tell anybody else.'

She shook her head and then nodded. She'd promise anything if it meant he'd go away.

'It was like this.' He took the smouldering cigarette from his mouth and stubbed it out on the sole of his shoe and threw it across on to the window sill and folded his arms across his chest.

'Do you remember 'day he died?' he whispered. 'What a tragedy, wasn't it?' His grin grew wider and she saw the broken front tooth from when he was ten and fell off his bike; the bike he'd nattered for and she'd had to scrimp and scrape to get and he'd kicked it when he'd fallen off as if it were the bike's fault.

'You remember 'day he died, don't you?' He leant towards

her. She hadn't wanted to remember, had removed it from her memory, but it came back, time and time again. Paul lying in a heap on the mill floor, his neck broken, and she'd turned away from the sight.

'What was it that 'coroner said? A terrible accident. A one in a million chance. Course they knew he'd had a drink or two at dinner time. I had to tell 'em, hadn't I? Onny right that they should know. Anyway,' he glanced around the room again and lowered his voice, 'that was 'day he told me. We were out in 'yard and he'd just landed me one, said I wasn't shifting stuff fast enough, and I socked him right back under his chin.'

She saw his hands start to shake. 'He was so surprised,' he went on. 'Didn't expect that at all, but I was strong even though I was onny just fourteen, and then he started shouting at me that I was a bastard, but I wasn't bothered about that cos that's what he allus called me. Then he laughed and started jabbing his finger at me and said that was what I really was, that I was no son of his, that you'd had a fancy man who didn't want you and he'd tekken us in out of 'goodness of his heart.'

He took a handkerchief out of his pocket and she watched dully as he pressed it to his wet mouth to still the tic above his top lip. She sank further into her chair and felt the warm dampness beneath her dress. The room was growing dark and misty, there was a black patch in front of her, they must have pulled the window blind down. Soon they'd put the lights on and then perhaps they'd let her go back to bed.

'Goodness of his heart,' he repeated. 'He didn't have a heart, nor any goodness.'

His face was grim, the smile wiped off but the tic still there, and he seemed to be talking to himself, nodding and muttering. 'Later that day I shouted to him from 'top floor. Telled

243

him there was a crack in 'cap, letting 'rain in, said he'd better come up and tek a look.'

The tic moved faster, distorting his nostril now. 'Hah! And then I got him. I gave him a real thrashing. You should have heard his jaw crack. He was dead scared and tried to mek a run for it down 'steps but I caught him on 'grain floor and hung him head first over 'edge of trap door. I telled him that if anybody was a bastard it was him.'

Pure malice shadowed his face. 'Do you remember, Ma, on 'floor below where 'millstones used to be? That big gap where 'staging was rotten? I told him what I was going to do and he was begging, promising me owt I wanted. What a joke. As if *he* had owt that I wanted. I let him splutter and shout for a minute or two and then I shoved him over. *Splat!*'

He stared at his mother, his face slack, the tic stopped, and she stared glassily back.

'He was groaning when I got down to 'bottom floor, so I shut 'outside door so's you and me couldn't hear him and then went and found some of 'lads in 'village and larked about so's they'd remember me being there, and we didn't find him 'til late, did we?'

He took out the tobacco tin again and crumbled the flaky mixture between his fingers and sniffed it, then returned it to the tin.

'Do you remember when we found him, Ma? Dead, wasn't he, when we found him? Ma! Do you remember? Ma! Why did you cry?' He bent forward to look at her and snapped his finger and thumb in front of her.

He slid the chair backwards and hastily got to his feet. His eyes roamed the room. 'Ma! What 'you doing? Can you hear me? I'll come back another day. We have to talk about 'mill and 'house'n that. Was there a contract or owt?' He backed away. 'I'll come back next week, when you're up to talking, and you can tell me who my dad was. Ta-ra.'

He almost fell over the old lady in the wheelchair who was trundling through the doorway as he turned to look back at his mother. 'Is it raining?' the old lady asked brightly. 'I thought I might go out.'

Resentfully he glared at her for a second, and then pushed past her. 'Daft old bat,' he muttered. 'What 'you asking me for?'

CHAPTER THIRTY TWO

'What upsets me is that somebody should dislike us so much.' Gilbert ran his fingers through his hair, making it stand on end. 'I mean, what did I do? What did Liz do, what did my father do? He wouldn't have hurt a fly, he helped 'Reedbarrows out in his time, and yet Carl is full of hatred and bitterness towards all of us.'

'I think he's off 'wall, to be honest. I do, I think that he's on 'point of cracking up.' Dot picked up a tea towel and dried some dishes on the draining board. 'He's going to do something terrible if he doesn't get help soon.'

'Who's going to help him?' Gilbert asked no one in particular. 'Because I'm not going near. I'll do all 'talking through my solicitor from now on.' He went across to the telephone. 'I'll try and get Steve Black again.'

'I'll talk to Steve, Dad,' Liz said. 'He'll wonder where I am.'

'No,' her father said. 'I need to have a word. I'll ask him what he's going to do.'

Steve answered the phone himself and Gilbert explained what had happened with Carl Reedbarrow, and that he had threatened him and Liz. 'Don't try and handle this yourself,' Liz heard her father say. 'He's a dangerous man.' Then he listened, nodding his head and raising his eyebrows, and although she could hear Steve's raised voice at the other end of the line she couldn't catch the actual words.

'So what did he say?' she asked as her father put down the phone.

'Oh, he said don't worry about going in,' Gilbert said vaguely.

'About Carl, I mean.'

'He said he's definitely going to sue him. He's phoning his solicitor now to tell him to start fraud proceedings.' Gilbert turned towards the inner door into the bar and put his hand on the latch. 'He suggested that we phone 'police about what happened this morning, about 'shotgun, and him trying to run you over.' He blew out a long breath. 'What a mess!' he said bitterly. 'What makes somebody so full of hate? It's such a waste of a life. It beats me.' He shook his head. 'I must get on,' he muttered, and went into the bar.

'I hate it when he gets upset,' Dot murmured. 'I don't like him to get hurt and he's been hurt so many times with this palaver.' She spoke so softly that Liz looked up, wondering if she had heard correctly.

'He won't want to call the police,' Liz said. 'He won't want to get Carl into even more trouble than he's in already.'

Dot turned to look at her. 'Nothing to stop you telling them what he's like, though, is there? The man needs help, and if nobody tells anybody what he's done or is likely to do, he won't get any, will he? Why Jeannie stays with him I just don't know.'

'She thinks there's nowhere else for her to go.'

'I'm going out for a walk,' Liz called through to the bar where her father and Dot were preparing for the lunchtime trade. 'There's no point in going into work now.'

She took her regular route towards the rutted lane where

her grandparents' cottage stood waiting for its inevitable end, passing other abandoned houses on the way. I don't know why I keep coming, she thought gloomily. They're never going to be saved, and it only makes me sad.

She walked on to her grandparents' cottage and instinctively picked up their wooden gate, which was lying on the ground. She propped it up, then wondered why she'd done that. Nobody was going to fix it.

The back door was swinging open, exposing the cold, bare kitchen with its mildewed walls and flapping wallpaper, and ivy growing between the quarry tiles; a spider's web festooned the grate of the old-fashioned cooking range that her grandmother had refused to relinquish. She stood quietly, remembering. I mustn't forget, I must always remember, so that I can pass it on. Strange, she thought, that the past had always seemed to her to be so solid and dependable, and the future so indeterminate and unpredictable.

The garden was overgrown with bramble. Young nettles pushed through the solid clay, and here and there the straight green spears of daffodils stood on the brink of unfolding. *'Daffy-down-dilly is come up to town in her yellow petticoat and her green gown.'*

Where did that come from, she wondered, and thought that in a month or two the garden would be a riot of elegant foxgloves, red campion, sweet-smelling wild hyacinth and myriad others. She closed the door, knowing it would blow open again, and walked carefully to the cliff edge, thinking of the time when she had played here with Sarah.

Or had she? Was Sarah just a figment of her childish imagination? Yet she had no real doubts. Perhaps she was psychic and able to cross the misty edge of time, or perhaps – and more likely – Sarah could.

She felt disconsolate and somehow uneasy. The morning's

events had unnerved her and she worried about what might come next, for the problem of Carl had to be resolved.

He could stay, but is he stable? Does he understand the situation? Clearly he doesn't or he wouldn't have threatened Dad or tried to run me down. Should I speak to Jeannie about it; will he listen to her? His mother couldn't make a decision for him; he wouldn't allow it for one thing. Is Dot right? Should I tell the police?

There had been a fresh fall overnight. Halfway down, the cliff face was tangled with wire and the wooden posts that had marked the boundary. Liz cast her eyes further along the beach towards the village, frowning as she saw new heaps of rubble, bricks and timber scattered over the craggy mounds of clay and sand.

Where had it come from? What was it? She lifted her head and saw the curve of the cliff and Matt Wilson's chicken house and beyond that the long sweep to Hornsea and Bridlington Bay. For a second she was confused, as if she'd lost her bearings and come out on a different headland. Something wasn't quite right. Then she realized that from this point Matt Wilson's chicken hut was usually hidden by Alf Wainwright's cottage. It was Alf's cottage, flung from its foundations, that now lay at the bottom of the cliff.

She made her way towards the chicken hut, skirting patches of bramble and broken fencing and turning inland into the abandoned cottage gardens where the cliff path had disappeared, until she came to the spot where Alf's house had stood the day before. All that now remained was a broken brick wall and a swinging door.

A group of men were in earnest discussion as she reached the main Hornsea road. Matt Wilson had his hands scrunched into his coat pockets and a woolly hat pulled around his ears and was listening to another man who was pontificating to his audience and gesticulating with his fist towards the sea.

'Have you seen Alf's place?' Matt called to her.

She nodded and went towards them. 'Yes. Does he know?'

'I was about to find him to tell him.' His blue eyes, usually so merry and smiling, were dull and anxious.

'It'll be your place next, Matt, I'm telling you,' the orator chipped in. 'There'll be more going over at 'next high tide, mark my words.'

'Aye, it were a mistake for you to buy a place so close to 'sea,' said another. 'That's why nobody else wanted it.'

'Tell me summat I don't know,' Matt muttered to Liz, who raised her eyebrows. 'Aye, well, I've no regrets,' he admonished the speaker. 'I'll just have to move further back.'

'I'll go and find Alf,' Liz said. 'Could you phone the council, Matt? They'll need to bulldoze the rest of the cottage. It's too dangerous as it is.'

'Aye,' he sighed. 'I will, and then start dismantling 'chicken house and find somewhere else to put it. Can't afford to lose that, or my hens.'

There was a wooden seat recessed into the wall at the back of the church, and it was here that Liz found Alf Wainwright, with his cap pushed to the back of his head, ponderously scoring patterns on the earth path with the tip of his walking stick.

He looked up as she approached. 'If you've come to tell me summat, you're too late. I've already seen it.'

She sat down beside him. 'I'm sorry. It must be hard for you.'

He stuck his chin in the air. 'Well, if I'm honest, I'm a lot better off where I am. That there was allus a cold draughty house. When 'wind blew there was many a time when I could have sworn I was back at sea again; 'windows used to rattle and there was allus a howling gale coming in from under 'front door. Still . . .' He gazed into somewhere a long distance beyond the dark yews, and his voice fell. 'Wife allus liked it.'

She remembered once more, as she sat quietly next to him, the germ of an idea that had come to her on the cliff path. 'Do you think you could help me?' she began. 'I want to find an old grave.'

'Aye, I reckon so.' He scratched his head and pulled his cap forward. 'I used to know all of 'graves at one time. I allus kept 'graveyard tidy. Now I just look after our own plot.'

'I'm not sure if it's here, but it's one of the Foster or Rayner graves.'

He heaved himself up. 'Let's go and have a look, shall we? It'll be over here if it's anywhere.'

She followed him to the side of the churchyard where there were two rows of graves, one in front of the other. The ones at the rear which sheltered beneath ancient horse chestnut trees were variously furnished with old and leaning headstones or disintegrating tombs, whilst the front row was newer monuments of marble or granite, or simple wooden crosses.

'Who was it you said you were looking for?'

'Her name is – *was* – Sarah. Sarah Rayner, or Foster Rayner.'

'Can't say I remember that one, but my memory isn't what it was. Doing family history, are you?'

'Yes,' she told him. 'That's it exactly.'

They walked between the graves, peering at the inscriptions. Some of the names were almost obliterated, others etched as clearly as the day they were placed there, but they couldn't find Sarah's.

'I don't know if it's even in here,' she said, disappointed. 'It might have been in the old Monkston churchyard.'

'Monkston!' He lifted his head. 'Ah, you should have said.' He pointed with his stick. 'You come wi' me. There are some

Monkston graves over here. Some of 'em were re-interred from 'old Monkston churchyard before it was lost, so I was told.'

The churchyard sloped gently down towards an old mixed hedge which butted on to the footpath beside the main road. From the higher ground they could see the white crests of the sea and hear its sigh, and here were perhaps twenty or thirty old graves, many with headstones leaning or fallen, the carved inscriptions illegible.

'These were all Monkston folk,' Alf murmured. 'I reckon this was as near as they could get to home.'

Liz felt a lump in her throat. It hadn't occurred to her that there would be so many Monkston people buried here. She felt conviction stir, and blessed whatever it was that had made her mention it to Alf.

'They used Tillington church after their own fell into 'sea,' he continued. 'It would've been a good walk, but I don't suppose they thought owt about it. Folks were used to walking in them days.'

'How do you know all this? Is it written down somewhere?'

'You young people! You go about with your eyes closed half the time. Don't you go to church?'

'Sometimes,' she admitted, thinking that the last time was for a friend's wedding several miles away.

'Well, if you go and look in our church, you'll see that some of 'carvings are from old Monkston church, and one of 'painted glass windows commemorates Monkston. My old da told me about it and I expect his told him; he used to thump 'organ in this church, did my grandda, so he would know.' He pulled out his pocket watch. 'I'll have to leave you now, Elizabeth. It's nearly my dinner time and I have to go to 'shop.'

'Thank you for your help,' she said. 'I really appreciate what you've told me. I'll stay and see what I can find.'

A monolithic pillar guarded one grave, and curiously she

went towards it. She had seen it from the roadside many times, it was part of the landscape of the churchyard, but she'd never come close enough to read it before.

Isaac Masterson, shipowner of Garston Hall, Monkston. She trembled as she read the inscriptions of his wife and daughter, his nephew, and others who were dear to him, and put her shaking hand to her lips. What a much-loved gentleman he must have been. And then she smiled, because everything was slipping into place.

Next to him, beneath a leaning stone with faded lettering, was Maria Foster, beloved wife of the late William and dearest mother of Thomas and Lizzie, Alice and Sarah. Other ancient Foster and Rayner graves were near by, all indicating that they had been residents of that long lost village, so it was with a sense of inevitability that she found at last the grave she was looking for. Below the name of John Rayner of Garston Hall, Monkston, was etched *Also his loving wife Sarah Foster Rayner.*

It was an instant revelation; the opening up of a whole new world. Images of her forebears appeared within her subconscious and turned the pages of time. 'They're all mine, these people,' she breathed. 'They've shaped me, formed me, made me what I am. And Sarah,' she whispered. 'What of you? Are you reaching out to me in sisterhood, into this world? Have you slipped out of your time into mine? Or are you my alter ego?'

A sudden wind blasting straight off the sea on to the open site buffeted her and tore at her hair, but she felt only warmth engulfing her body and a wave of energy filling her mind as the great forces of nature spun about her. Soft voices carried on the wind called to her; laughter, like gentle lapping surf on the sand, rang a memory in her heart. Her gaze passed over the churchyard, across the village and the crumbling cliffs, out across the grey-green watery wastes until, in joyful recognition, it met the heavy swell of turbulent water which once was Monkston.

CHAPTER THIRTY THREE

'Do you want the bad news? Or do you want the bad news?'

Liz threw herself on to the sofa and covered her eyes as her father greeted her on her return from the office the next day.

'Oh,' she groaned. 'Let's have the bad news.'

'Well, 'bad news is that Joan Reedbarrow has had a stroke.'

She sat up. 'Oh, no! Poor lady.'

'Matron phoned me from 'nursing home. She can't get hold of Carl or Jeannie. Nobody's answering 'phone.'

'Why doesn't that surprise me? Should we go and tell them?'

'That's what 'matron asked me; she's anxious to speak to Carl. I didn't like to say we weren't on speaking terms. Strangely, though, she said that Joan had been all right until she had a visit from Carl. I wonder if he had told her that I'd been to see him?' A frown creased his forehead. 'I wouldn't like to think she'd been upset on my account.'

'Oh, Dad! You can't take on responsibility for everybody. It's more likely that Carl said something to distress her; maybe he told her he'd threatened to shoot you and tried to run me down. She wouldn't like that. How bad is she? Will she be all right?'

He shook his head. 'They don't know yet. She can't speak and she's paralysed down one side, but the doctor said she could recover from that. They've taken her in to Hull Infirmary and say she's comfortable – whatever that means.'

She sighed. 'That's so sad. But if that's the bad news, what's the bad news?'

'The bad news, I'm afraid, is that the report on the cliffs isn't favourable. I've had a call from George Bennett. They're saying that 'cost of shoring up 'coastline will be too high.'

She picked up a cushion and flung it across to a chair. 'What they mean is that the village isn't worth it. That the land value is less than what it would cost to build a wall!'

'No. What they're saying is that 'word from 'county is there isn't enough money available.'

'But we already knew that,' she argued. 'What are they playing at?'

'They're saying that we must look elsewhere.'

'You mean that we, the villagers, must lobby Westminster?'

Gilbert raised his sandy eyebrows and waited significantly.

'Brussels?'

He smiled. 'Do you think we could tackle it? It could take years. Think of 'paperwork. Think of 'hassle!'

She got up from the sofa and picking up the abandoned cushion began to walk round the room with it tightly clutched to her chest. It has to be done, she thought. When I think of those Monkston folk, our folk, lying in Tillington churchyard instead of their own ground . . . They had no choice, but we have! We have the right to fight for what we want. The whole of Holderness coastline is crumbling, not just here, and somebody has to make a start.

She smiled back at him. 'What are we waiting for? Let's get on. There's a lot to do.'

*

Gilbert tried telephoning Carl, but again there was no answer. Liz said she would call in at the Raven to see if Jeannie was there and tell Kevin the news from County Hall.

There were forty-two houses, plus several smallholdings and farmsteads, in and on the edge of the village, and she and her father and Dot divided them up between them. Liz said she would make a start that night by visiting those who would be bound to come to an urgent meeting at the Ship the following evening. Her father and Dot would do the rest the next morning.

Liz quickly made herself a sandwich and put on her coat again. 'Don't go anywhere near Carl,' her father warned. 'He's unstable, I'm sure of it.'

'I won't,' she said emphatically. 'Don't worry.'

She strode swiftly down the village street, feeling buoyant, hopeful and extremely determined. She'd phoned Jim Jackson on his home number before she left and given him the latest news. 'Keep mentioning us, Jim, won't you?' she'd pleaded. 'We need to be kept in the public eye.'

He'd promised a piece in his column at the weekend if he couldn't get front-page coverage before then, and said he would write a longer article on the whole question of erosion within the next two weeks.

She knocked on the back door of the shop and told them of an extra crisis meeting at the Ship the following evening. 'Tell everybody,' she begged. 'We must have a full turnout.' In the main street she got four assurances of attendance and one reluctant decline, and then she called at the Raven to speak to Kevin, who was just opening up.

'It's all very well,' he grumbled, 'but if my customers go to a meeting in your place they're not going to come back here to buy a pint, are they? It'll affect my trade.'

She was taken aback. 'Well – erm, we could hold it here, but it means I'll have to go back to the people I've already spoken to. I'm sorry, I didn't think. I just wanted to get things moving, alert everyone to what's happening.'

'Oh, never mind. Leave it. It just means that I won't be there and I'm supposed to be the chairman.'

'Wouldn't Jeannie stand in for you? It won't take long,' she said. 'We just have to arrange a date for lobbying in Beverley.'

He bent down to pick up a cloth that had fallen from the bar counter. 'Leave it with me,' he said, giving it a shake. 'I'll see what I can do.'

'I need to see Jeannie,' she said. 'I've got a message for Carl. Will she be in later?'

He shrugged. 'Maybe. She doesn't have regular hours. She comes when she can.' He seemed unwilling to chat as he usually did, and she turned for the door, but he called her back. 'By the way, you haven't told anyone about me moving, by any chance?'

'No. You said not to.'

'That's all right, then.' He gave her a weak grin. 'I don't want it to get out just yet. Not 'til it's been confirmed, you know.'

She stared at him, her hand on the door sneck. So why tell me, she wondered. I didn't need to know.

As she came out into the street, she saw Jeannie walking slowly towards the Raven and called out to her. 'I was looking for you, Jeannie. I've got a message for Carl.'

'Oh, yeh.' Her voice was dull and indifferent. 'I'm just going to work. Kevin's expecting me.'

'Is he? Well, can you tell Carl his mother's ill? Matron at the home's been trying to contact you. She's been taken to Hull Infirmary.'

'Carl's been to see her,' she said defensively. 'She was all right then.'

'She's had a stroke,' Liz told her. 'It must have happened after he'd visited. Dad took the message; they have our telephone number. Will you tell him?'

Jeannie looked blankly at her. 'I shan't see him 'til late.' Then a frown creased her pale forehead. 'I'm sorry. It's not that I don't care, but I've got a lot on my mind just now. Is it bad? Did they say?'

She seemed nervous, and Liz felt sorry for her. It must be a nightmare living with Carl. 'I don't know. They said they needed to speak to Carl, so it's probably important, otherwise why would they phone us?'

'I'll tell him. I'll try and get to see her. Mebbe Carl will tek me when he next visits.'

'Well, don't leave it too late.' Liz's compassion evaporated. 'If she's had one stroke, she could have another.' She saw Jeannie's guard come up again and said hurriedly, 'I really need to talk to you, Jeannie. Carl won't speak to us and I'm almost afraid to approach him. He's actually threatened me and my dad.'

Jeannie fiddled with the strap of her shoulder bag. 'I heard him shouting at your dad, but I don't know what about.' She fingered her neck and swallowed, her voice almost a whisper. 'I don't know what to do, Liz, honest to God. I'm at my wits' end.'

'Can we talk now? There's only Kevin in the bar, no customers, so perhaps he'd give us five minutes?'

Jeannie nodded. 'I won't have to be long – and I don't want him to hear. He can be a nosy beggar at times can Kev; he likes to know what's going on.'

Liz smiled. 'I'll be the soul of discretion.'

Jeannie led the way into the Raven and Liz waited in the lounge area whilst she spoke to Kevin. Liz saw him smile and then slide a cigarette into his mouth before offering one to

Jeannie, murmuring something. Jeannie's mood obviously changed and a tinge of amusement played around her lips, but she became sullen and impatient again as she sat down next to Liz. 'So what's it about? He says I've not to be long. I've got to set up 'bar.'

Liz explained the position as concisely as she could about the ownership of the mill and the mill house and the pepper-corn rent that the Reedbarrows had been paying for so many years, leaving out the long history of the Foster and Rayner connection and not even mentioning Carl's parentage. She could see no point in adding to the dismay that was now show-ing on Jeannie's face.

'So what you're telling me,' she said, her voice rising to a resentful querulous pitch which she immediately moderated, 'is that his mother doesn't own 'property like he told me but you and your brother do; and that we're onny 'tenants 'til 'end of 'year and then we have to move out?'

Liz nodded, feeling vaguely guilty. 'I'm sorry. The answer's yes and no. It seems that the arrangement between our family and Carl expires then, but we can renegotiate it, except that Carl won't talk to us. In fact he's been downright aggressive, and I think you should know that he's probably in serious trouble over fraud.'

'That's it.' Jeannie held up both hands as a barrier between herself and Liz, the smoke from the filter tip curling between her fingers. 'Don't tell me any more. He told me that after his mother's gone the property will be his and he'll sell it all for building and we'll mek thousands.' She gave a short, bitter laugh. 'Why do you think I've hung on all this time?'

She stared through Liz and nibbled a piece of loose skin from her thumb. Then her eyes narrowed. 'But seeing as you've asked me I'll tell him about his mam.'

She glanced across at Kevin, who was standing at the end of the bar with his back to them, looking out of a window on to the street. 'And I might tell him a few other things as well that'll make him sit up.'

Liz knew exactly what she meant, and reached out in alarm. 'Don't,' she said. 'You've felt the brunt of his temper before. Don't give him another excuse for violence.'

'He doesn't need an excuse,' she said bitterly. 'If anything should ever happen to me, you tell them he's hit me time and time again when I've done *nothing*. He's woken me up and dragged me from my bed and given me a beating.' She inhaled deeply on her cigarette. 'He even locked me out of 'house one night cos I'd burnt his dinner, and I had to sleep in 'shed.' Her eyes filled with tears. 'But he would always sweet-talk me out of leaving. He'd beg me not to go, and made me feel sorry for him because he said that nobody but me had ever cared for him.'

She gave a small sob and rubbed her nose with the back of her hand. 'I allus knew at 'bottom of me that he was lying. His mother cared for him, I could tell, even though she was frightened to death of him; that's why I asked your dad to help me get her into that home in Beverley. I thought – I thought that if we were on our own I'd be able to change him. But I can't. Nobody can. He's bad. Bad right through, and I'm finished. I've had enough.'

'I'm so sorry, Jeannie.' Liz could hardly trust herself to speak, but what could she say that would help? 'Really sorry. If you want somewhere to stay, I hope you know that you can always come to us.'

'That would add fuel to 'fire, wouldn't it?' Jeannie mocked. 'Thanks anyway, but I'll make my own arrangements. I don't want to involve you or your dad. I can see now why he hates you. He'll feel patronized knowing that he's only living at 'mill because of your family's goodwill, especially when his mother was always saying how good your dad was. No wonder he's got this massive big chip on his shoulder.'

261

Val Wood

'If he knows! We don't know for sure that he does.' Why am I defending him, Liz wondered. 'I didn't myself, so he might not have either.'

Jeannie stood up. 'Come off it,' she scoffed. 'Anyway, we shan't find out. Only his mother would know the ins and outs, but it sounds as if she's in no fit state to tell us anything, and *he's* such a liar he'll say anything.' She took off her jacket and slung it over one shoulder, and Liz thought how young and vulnerable she looked in her sweatshirt and jeans. Jeannie probably wasn't much older than she was, yet she had so much more experience of life.

'But whatever happens it's nothing to do with me any more,' Jeannie went on. 'I'm finished. I've had enough. I'm looking after number one, starting right now.'

The inner swing doors whooshed behind her as she left. Liz waited a few moments before she followed her through, and as she put her hand on the outer door the momentum swung the inner ones open again and she heard Jeannie call out, 'Kev, I've got to slip back home for a minute. I won't be long. Ten minutes max.'

'What 'you going for?' Kevin called back. 'Customers'll be in soon.'

'I've got to leave Carl a note. His mam's poorly. I won't be long . . . and I'll bring my bag this time!'

'You what?'

'You know! Like we said!'

Liz opened and closed the door quietly and crept out. I just hope she knows what she's doing. Talk about out of the frying pan into the fire!

Chris teased his fingers through Liz's hair. They were in the private sitting room of the Ship, talking quietly of this and that.

262

'Why don't you grow it long?' he said. 'It's such a lovely vibrant colour, as if it's on fire.'

She smiled and leant her head on his arm just as the telephone pealed behind them.

'I'm sorry to disturb you so late,' said a precise, unknown voice, 'but I'm trying to contact Mr Reedbarrow and I've been given this number.'

'Are you from the infirmary? I'm sorry; he's difficult to get hold of, but I've passed the original message on to his partner. May I ask – is Mrs Reedbarrow worse?'

The voice hesitated. 'Are you a relative?'

'No, a concerned friend.'

'I see – well, we really do need Mr Reedbarrow here. Is he her only relative?'

'Yes, he is. I'll try again, and leave another message. He might be on his way to you, of course. Thank you for calling.' She put down the receiver. 'I'll have to go and find Jeannie again, Chris. Sounds as if Carl's mother's worse.'

He uncurled himself from the sofa. 'I'll come with you – I shouldn't like you to bump into Carl. Then I'd better make tracks for home.'

It was a clear, still night, with barely a breath of wind and myriad stars littering the dark sky. As they walked towards the Raven they could hear the constant murmuring of the sea.

'It's settled tonight,' Liz whispered.

'What's settled?'

'Shh. The sea. Listen.' She slowed her steps and put her finger to her lips.

They stopped and listened. A car roared past, disturbing the moment, and as its drone diminished the silence closed in again, dropping about them, enfolding them as if within an invisible cloak.

'Can't you hear?' Her voice was faint, and he bent his head

to listen. 'It's like the breathing of a sleeping child. Calm, settled for the night, and peaceful. It's not often like this.'

'Can I say something?' Chris whispered croakily.

She laughed. 'Of course. Don't mind me. You know what I'm like.'

He put both arms round her and gave her a hug. 'I'm only just beginning to. Dot said I might *never* know you.'

'Dot said?'

'Yes, but never mind that now. I was going to say that I suddenly felt very strange. The silence got to me. It was as if time was slowing down – lingering, even. It's so quiet here, and yet I know that inside the houses there'll be noise, conversation – rows, even; family dramas going on everywhere.' He laughed. 'Yorkshire must have good builders,' he joked. 'Insulated houses.'

'What about the listening? Did you hear the listening?'

He shook his head. 'I don't know what you mean. How can you hear listening?'

She paused; she hadn't told him much about her experience in the churchyard with Alf; only that she had found the Monkston graves. She knew that she couldn't tell anyone. It was her secret; a secret that couldn't be shared because she couldn't be sure it had happened.

Had she really felt the aura of that lost village? Had she wandered in spirit through rutted lanes and been watched in friendship from cottage doorways? Had she smelt the sweetness of a gathered harvest and heard the jangle of harness on horse and bullock? And had she known the bitter cold of their winters as she walked the frozen fields, and felt the welcome warmth of their smoky fires? Or had it simply been her fertile imagination?

She took his hand as they walked on. 'Sometimes,' she murmured, 'if I'm out here on my own, I feel that someone's listening. I can hear them. There's no sound, just an awareness that I'm not alone. Something intrinsic in me, I suppose.'

He squeezed her hand. 'It'll be your ghosts, I expect, watching over you. Making sure that no harm comes to you.'

The door of the Raven opened, spilling out a stream of light, noise and people on to the footpath. 'Don't laugh at me.'

'I'm not laughing at you,' he said. 'I'm perfectly serious. You believe in them, so why shouldn't they be there for you? Immortality is imponderable. Why should we scoff just because we don't understand it?'

Liz recoiled as the cannon-shot of noise hit them like a blow as they entered the Raven. Queen was playing on the juke box, and three youths were rowdily harmonizing to 'We Are The Champions' whilst a barrage of abuse was thrown at them by their companions; the fruit machine rattled and wheezed and spewed out a clatter of coins to the accompaniment of loud cheers, and above the din Kevin shouted, 'Last orders, *please*.' Liz pushed her way to the bar and spoke in an undertone to Jeannie.

'I've told him,' Jeannie mouthed hoarsely. 'At least, I left him a note on 'kitchen table. He'll have seen it. He'll be there now. I told him to go straight to 'hospital. I can't do more than that. I'm sorry about his mother, but she's his responsibility, not mine. I can't stop. You can see how busy we are.'

Liz marched out of the pub, her cheeks blazing, Chris hurrying after her. 'I know she has a lot to put up with,' she said, 'but even so, you'd think she'd show a bit more concern.'

'No.' Chris took her arm to slow her down. 'When it comes down to it, most people want to save their own skins. You can't blame Jeannie. Carl's made her like that. She probably is concerned, but from what you've told me I'd say she's simply cutting herself off from him. She's looking after herself now.'

'Yes, you're right.' Liz was dismayed at the thought of the potentially disastrous scenario. 'That's exactly what she said. Poor Jeannie.'

'I'll come to your meeting tomorrow, if that's all right?' Chris fastened his seat belt and switched on the ignition. 'And then I want to talk to you.'

'Of course it's all right,' she said. 'The more people there the better. But what do you want to talk about tomorrow that you couldn't talk about tonight?' She laughed, and then shivered as the night air put goosebumps on her arms. She'd stepped outside to say goodbye without putting her coat on again.

'Go inside,' he said. 'It's a biting wind. I want to talk to you about this long drive to Hull that I do several times a week.' He reached out from the open window and touched her cheek. 'I want to be with you, to take care of you, in this world or another.'

'Go home.' Elation bubbled inside her and she bent to kiss him. 'I'll see you tomorrow.'

CHAPTER THIRTY FOUR

As Liz signalled to turn into the Ship car park the following evening, she saw Carl on a battered old bicycle pedalling furiously in her direction. She parked and came towards him, impulsively calling out, 'Carl. How's your mother?'

He slithered to a halt, stamped one foot on the ground, swung the other leg over the torn saddle and dropped the bike to the ground. 'Who's asking?' His eyes glinted, and with no warning he poked her in the chest. 'What's it to you?'

She knocked his hand away. 'Keep your hands to yourself!' She backed off, wishing she hadn't asked. 'I'm concerned. Anybody who knows her will be.'

'Huh, and you think I'm not. Is that it?' He peered into her face, his dark eyes glittering.

'I didn't say that, but if the cap fits . . .' She turned away from him, her hand on her chest, but he grabbed hold of her arm.

'Well, she's dead!' He ground his teeth together. 'I was there all night and all morning and she went at two o'clock this afternoon, so don't you say I don't care. I haven't even had me dinner yet. They onny gave me cups o' tea at 'ospital, and that bitch has gone off and left me nowt to eat.'

She pulled her arm away from his grip. 'I'm very sorry about your mother. Everybody will be.'

He eyed her suspiciously. 'Don't think it'll mek any difference. Tha'll not get us out of 'house, so don't go banking on it. We've got our rights. Is *she* here? She's not at 'shop and not at 'Raven; I've just come from there. I'll kill her when I find her!' When Liz didn't reply, he hauled up the bike and swung on to it. 'Not so much as a sandwich. I'll stop her gallivanting about. If you see her, tell her to get hersen home,' he ordered. 'Or else!'

'Carl never calls Jeannie by her name, have you noticed?' Liz and her father were arranging chairs in the pub lounge for the meeting. 'I wonder where she is. He said she wasn't at the Raven, and yet I was sure I heard . . .' She paused. She was sure that she'd seen the brightening look on Kevin's face when she'd heard Jeannie say she'd bring her bag, as if to pacify him. But more likely, she thought, Jeannie hadn't yet plucked up the courage to tell Carl she was leaving.

People started to filter in just before seven o'clock. Chris had telephoned to say he'd been held up in a staff meeting and would be there as soon as he could, and by seven thirty the seats were full, leaving standing room only.

The atmosphere seemed to be different from the meeting at the Raven. Then the villagers had been buoyed up and eager to get things moving; now they were frustrated, their pride dented and their egos flattened.

'When you think how much money 'government wastes,' said one man. 'Aye, when a couple o' million is nowt to some folk,' said another. 'Yeh, think of industry,' came a third comment. 'Some of those big companies wouldn't miss the amount we need!'

Others frowned, shaking their heads in disagreement. 'Why should industry give us money? We mean nowt to them; they've never even heard of us. We're just small fry.'

'We should get 'Farmers Union on our side,' Matt Wilson chipped in. 'They'd support us. It's about losing land.'

Kevin came in and sat at the back, glancing at his watch. Liz noticed the gesture and rapped on a table. 'Can we get on?' she called over the hum of chatter. 'I know you're all busy people, and I'm glad to see that you're all concerned enough to turn out again.'

Alf Wainwright tapped his way in, leaning heavily on his stick. He doesn't look well, Liz thought. I wonder if he's heard about Joan Reedbarrow? He sat down next to Kevin, who was looking at his watch again.

'What we need,' Liz went on, 'is a show of hands so that we know how many we can count on to come to County Hall next week. We know that the councillors support us, but we need to show them that we still mean business despite the recent setback, and that we're not going to be put off by any adverse comments about cost.'

'Hear, hear.'

'So the committee has agreed that next Wednesday at ten o'clock would be a good time. It's Market Day, so there'll probably be a lot of people around if the weather is fine.' She looked at the intent faces in front of her. 'It might be an awkward time for some, but we can't please everyone. We all have work to do.'

'I don't,' somebody shouted, 'I wish I had!'

'So you'll be there, then!' Liz smiled. 'Come and see me afterwards and I'll give you something to do.' She saw his startled glance and guessed that he wouldn't.

'It will be an orderly rally. We don't want a slanging match, though I think we can chant.' She looked across to her father and George Bennett for confirmation and they both nodded. 'So a show of hands, please.'

The hands went up and she counted roughly thirty. Alf Wainwright put his hand up. 'I'll go if somebody'll tek me.'

Several people volunteered, and Liz asked if a list could be made of available cars. She was very pleased with the numbers, and although she knew a few people would drop out on the day there would still be a considerable turnout.

'Next we need a band of volunteers to make banners and we need them urgently. We need wood, and old sheets that can be made into squares or oblongs, starched and dyed, and have slogans painted on them. Paper or card isn't sturdy enough and disintegrates when wet. Our banners must be strong and well made because . . .' – she paused to gather breath – 'because after Beverley . . . after Beverley . . . we're taking them to Westminster!'

A great cheer went up, and she raised her voice to be heard. 'And if we don't get satisfaction there . . . then we're off to Brussels!'

There was an explosion of noise as people clapped and stamped their approval, until the crash of the opening front door made several of the crowd turn round. Gilbert looked to see who was treating his doors so roughly, and dashed forward with a sharp exclamation. Kevin too turned round, and with several choice expletives immediately clambered over Alf Wainwright's knees and rushed after him. In the doorway slumped the inanimate figure of Jeannie Reedbarrow.

Jeannie had called to Kevin as he was leaving for the meeting. 'You won't be long, will you, Kev? I'm terrified he might come looking for me.'

'He won't come in here; he won't dare. Anyone who onny beats up women is a wimp.' Kevin glanced in the mirror over the bar and adjusted his jacket on his broad shoulders. 'Anyway, he doesn't know you're here, does he? I told him I hadn't seen you. I shan't be long. If you get a rush on, ring me at 'Ship.'

Jeannie stared after him and silently swore. Another selfish self-serving barbarian. *He's onny bothered about losing trade.*

She had sighed and lit a cigarette, and turned to check the optics. She caught sight of her face in the mirror and peered more closely. What a mess! Her eyes were heavy, with dark shadows beneath them, and fine lines were traced above her nose and round her mouth. *I must stop smoking. I'll get my hair bleached, I think, and cut short. I'll ask Kev for the money. I wonder if I could claim from 'Social? I never have. Carl always said we'd manage without.*

As she thought about Carl, she felt a sickly trepidation and glanced nervously towards the door, wishing Kevin hadn't gone. He didn't have to, but he'd told her he'd said he'd be there cos he was chairman or something. He'd said that nobody would be in the bar until later, because everybody would be in the Ship. Well, Carl won't be at the meeting, that's for sure; he won't set foot in the place and I can't say I blame him, she thought now. Fancy them owning our place all this time. I can't believe that Liz Rayner didn't know about it, even though she said she didn't; *and* she said that Carl might not know but I don't believe that either: surely his mother would have told him, unless she was too scared to. I wonder how she is? Poor old lass!

Oh, cripes, I wonder if he's found that note on the bed. He must've found it when he got back from 'hospital – unless he slept downstairs on 'settee, like he does sometimes. He'll go mad when he sees it. He's told me to go often enough – but when he finds out I've gone . . .

She stubbed out the cigarette end and lit another and sat on a stool behind the bar. She inhaled deeply, closing her eyes and leaning her head back; then she got up and went to the till, and pressed a key to open it. Idly she counted up the money that Kevin had left for the float; one-pound coins, fifty-pence pieces, some smaller silver and copper and thirty pounds in five- and ten-pound notes.

'Caught you wi' your hands in 'till, have I? What'll your fancy man think o' that, eh? Or is that payment for services rendered? Eh?'

She licked her lips and swallowed; she saw beads of sweat on Carl's top lip as he leant over the counter towards her.

'I'm – I'm checking 'float, that's all,' she stammered. She could feel her heart hammering in her chest, her throat tightening.

'I got your note,' he said casually. 'It was nice of you to write.'

'I'm sorry, Carl; I just can't take any more. I've had enough. You don't need me, you've said so often enough. You've never needed anybody, have you? You'll manage better on your own with no one to hassle you.'

She was starting to shake. *Let him be reasonable for once.*

'I've been looking for you, but nobody knew where you were; that's what they said, anyroad. I've been at 'hospital, you know, with me poor old ma.' He nodded his head as he watched her and she saw red flecks in the whites of his eyes. 'Did you forget that's where I was?'

'No! No, I didn't forget. How is she?'

'She's dead.'

'Oh no. Oh, no!' Stunned, she came round to the other side of the bar where he was leaning, his chin propped in his hand. Diffidently she put her hand on his shoulder. 'I'm so sorry, Carl. I was fond of your mam.'

'Was you?' He turned towards her and put his large hand over hers. 'Was you? Why did you send her away, then? Why did you fix it for her to go into that home, then, eh?'

She screamed as he squeezed her fingers. 'You're hurting me! Stop it. Stop it!'

He stopped squeezing but kept hold of her wrist and gently stroked her face with his other hand, his fingers moving down to her throat until they stopped at her windpipe where he applied some pressure, his nails cutting into her skin.

She jerked her head backwards and he caught her other hand. 'Kevin will be back in a minute,' she gasped. 'You'd better go whilst you can.'

'Oh no he won't!' He gave her a sly wink. 'I saw him going into 'meeting. He'll not be back for a long time. We'll be able to have a nice little chat, you and me.'

'Please, Carl, don't.' She twisted her wrists in an attempt to release them, but he increased the pressure. 'You know you're always sorry afterwards.'

'I'll not be sorry this time. I'll teach you to run off with that pimp. Run off and leave me when I was with me dying mother.' He fetched her a whack across the face, right, left, right, and she felt her teeth cut into her cheeks.

'Dear God, I never did.' She sank to her knees, but he hauled her up again. 'I swear I didn't know that she was so ill. I wouldn't have left if I'd known. Carl, please – don't. It was only when I found out about 'mill and 'house not being ours – yours, I mean – that I decided to go. It wasn't about Kevin. He doesn't mean anything.'

He pinned her against the bar, bending her backwards so that she felt her back would break, his legs straddling hers so that the weight of him held her down.

'What about 'mill? What did tha hear?'

'Onny that it belonged to 'Rayners. Liz Rayner wanted to talk about renewing 'tenancy, but I didn't know anything about it. You and your mam had never said.'

Her voice was strained and she thought she was going to choke; she tried to lift her head but he pushed her back again and swore. 'Rayners! I might have known they'd be at 'bottom of this mess.' He struck her in the midriff with his fist. 'That's for associating with 'em.'

She retched, keeling forward, and he fisted her under the

chin. 'And that's for whoring with somebody who doesn't mean owt.'

He let go of her and she fell to her knees, tasting the blood in her mouth and knowing that this was just the start. That this was the big one he had been leading up to for all those years when he managed to stop himself from beating her senseless. Now she knew that he was out of control; that once he'd begun he wouldn't be able to stop, and the more she pleaded the better he would like it. Only half conscious, she screwed up her eyes tight and instinctively put her arms about her head and waited for the next blow.

'Hello, hello? What's going on here?'

As she felt the pain from the latest kick of his boot, she had heard the swish of the door and the sound of raised voices, and she opened her eyes as much as she could to peer up between her folded arms.

'What the hell's going on 'ere, like? Beating up a woman, are we?'

She saw two pairs of grubby white trainers and two pairs of denim-clad legs, and as she lifted her head she recognized two youths who regularly called in to the Raven with their pals; youths who, she suspected, were not averse to enjoying a fight of their own making, except when Kevin was there.

'No!' Carl backed off. 'I gave her a slap and she fell. I didn't mean to – you know. She's been carrying on behind my back.' She could hear the tremor in his voice and tried to lift herself from the floor. 'She's been carrying on wi' landlord. Caught 'em, didn't I? He's cleared off. Daren't face me, dare he?'

'You wha'? Kev scared of a wimp like you? You've gotta be joking, mate. Here, missus. Let's have a look at you.'

One of the youths lifted her swollen face towards them. Her eyes were beginning to close, and when she touched her mouth she felt the stickiness of blood.

'Well, you're in a mess and no mistake, aren't you? Got that for being a bit naughty, did you?'

The pair stood looking at her, their arms crossed over leather-clad chests, and for a moment she felt a fleeting sensation of fear, until as if with one mind they both turned towards Carl.

'OK, pal. If it's fightin' you're fond of, how about fightin' us? We like a bit of a brawl, don't we, Sean?'

Jeannie crept painfully across the floor on her hands and knees, and as she reached the door she heard the first crack and groan as bone met bone.

CHAPTER THIRTY FIVE

There was a minor panic for a moment as everyone rushed over to Jeannie, jostling and crowding around her as she lay on the floor. 'Move back, will you! Give her some air. Somebody ring for an ambulance.' Gilbert gave out orders as he and Kevin lifted her on to a bench seat.

'I don't want an ambulance. I'm all right,' Jeannie mumbled through swollen lips. She clearly was not. Someone had attacked her.

At the back of the crowd Liz hesitated, but at her father's nod she went to the telephone. Turning her back on Jeannie, she dialled 999 and asked for an ambulance and the police.

'We'll just let them have a look at you, love,' Gilbert said. 'Just as a precaution. They won't take you to 'hospital if they think you're all right.'

'They'll have to make a report.' She started to cry, and then to retch. 'I don't want to say anything.'

'Where is he?' Kevin straightened up. 'Where is he? I'll sort him out.'

She shook her head, and somebody handed her a clean handkerchief as blood and mucus ran from her nose. 'Somebody's doing that already.'

Kevin was suddenly alert. 'Who's looking after 'pub? Is there anybody there? Jeannie?'

She bent double. 'I'm going to be sick.'

'Is there anybody behind 'bar at 'Raven? Jeannie?'

'No, there damned well isn't! Onny Sean and his pal.' She retched and held her hands to her mouth. 'They were setting about Carl when I left.'

'For God's sake,' Kevin yelled. 'There'll be nowt left. I know those two,' and he shot out of the door.

'Thanks, Kev,' Jeannie mumbled. 'Thanks a lot.'

Dot brought a box of tissues and handed several to Jeannie, then took off her cardigan and put it round Jeannie's shoulders. She folded her arms and looked at Liz, murmuring, 'Well, we know his priorities, don't we?'

'Jeannie, can you manage to get up?' Liz bent over her. 'You'll be more comfortable if we go through to the sitting room.' She helped her to stand. 'Meeting's over, folks,' she called out. 'Don't forget, Wednesday, ten o clock.'

The ambulance men arrived quickly and persuaded Jeannie to go with them. 'You'll need a check over; mebbe an X-ray. They'll probably keep you in overnight, and then you can go home.'

'Can I?' she muttered. 'That'll be nice, won't it?'

Gilbert waited outside the Ship doorway and watched as the police car drove in front of the ambulance, leading the way out of the village towards Hull with the blue lights flashing. The ambulance too flashed warning lights, though there was little other traffic in the villages after dark. He heaved out a great breath and then sniffed. Somebody's chimney was smoking, so he went inside and closed the door behind him. The phone was ringing. What a night.

Liz picked up the phone. It was Kevin. 'There's no sign of

Reedbarrow or the lads; they must have kicked him out. They've emptied the till; fortunately there was only the float in it, so they didn't get much, but I suspect they've tekken some cigs and bottles of whisky; shan't know 'til I've checked.'

She held the phone at arm's length, not in the least interested in what he might have lost, and then left the receiver hanging by its flex. 'But at least they didn't wreck the place,' she heard him say, 'so I've been lucky.'

She walked away, and Dot picked up the receiver as Kevin carried on. 'Did the ambulance come? Has Jeannie gone to hospital? Liz? Hello, are you there? I'll give them a call later, see what's happening. Can you smell burning?'

'No,' Dot said. 'Have to go.'

'By heck, I can. Somebody's having an almighty bonfire.'

Dot hung up, and Liz turned to her. 'I feel so sickened. I wish I'd never told Jeannie about the mill and the house belonging to us, but I thought we might be able to discuss the tenancy agreement. If we had she might not have decided to leave Carl, although I suppose I'm glad that she did. I wish I'd left it to the solicitors. It's such a mess; I shouldn't have interfered. Poor Jeannie.' Liz gulped down a sob. 'She doesn't deserve this. He could have killed her, and she'll be no better off with Kevin. He won't stand by her, I know he won't.'

'It's no use blaming yourself,' Dot said. 'It's not 'first time Carl's given her a beating.'

'I know, she told me.'

'And I suspect he wasn't a loving son either. I'm not saying he hit his mother, cos I don't know, but there's such a thing as mental cruelty.' She pressed her lips into a tight thin line. 'Joan was always a nervous troubled soul, God bless her. Well, she's out of it now.' She fumbled in her skirt pocket for a hanky and blew her nose.

'Come on. There'll be thirsty folk coming in, and 'news will have spread an' they'll want to know what's been happening.'

The chairs had been put back in place and Liz gathered up her notes, which she'd barely had time to refer to, but people had added their names and telephone numbers to a list of car-owners offering lifts into Beverley. She was reading down it when for the second time that evening the door crashed open.

Gilbert looked up with a rebuke on his lips. 'Watch those doors, *please*! Oh! What's up?'

'Thank heavens you're all here. Has anybody phoned the fire brigade?' Chris was breathless. 'You can see the flames from miles back.'

'What? Flames from what?'

'Phone the fire brigade! It's the mill or the mill house or both. Dear God, I just hope there's nobody there. Have you seen Jeannie or Carl?'

Liz felt the blood drain from her face and her heart hammered so fast she thought she was going to pass out. She clung on to a chair back and watched numbly as Chris, seeing Gilbert, Dot and herself standing as if made of stone, dashed behind the bar to pick up the phone and dial 999.

Before he finished speaking, they heard the wail of a siren coming closer for the second time that night, the strident alarm of the fire engine getting louder as it neared the village, the flashing light illuminating the windows as it turned to go up Church Lane, and the resounding cacophony deafened their ears.

'You go, Gilbert,' Dot urged. 'I can manage here. There won't be many coming in, not yet, anyway. Take your coat!'

'No, nobody will be coming. They'll all be watching.' He

gazed vacantly at her, and then darted for the door. 'Are you coming, Liz? Chris?'

Liz hesitated. 'I don't know. I'm scared. Yes, all right. Wait for me.' She turned and rushed to the small hallway behind the bar to pick up her coat and one for her father, then raced after the men. Groups of people were heading up the lane, alerted by the acrid reek of burning, the cracks and sparks of blazing old timber, and the warning alarm of the second siren of the night.

'Thank heavens Jeannie isn't there,' Liz gasped as she ran up the lane with her father and Chris, and then she put her hand to her mouth. 'What about Carl? Dad? Do you think he'll be in the house?'

'No I don't,' said Gilbert. 'He'll be nowhere in sight. He'll have skipped, take my word for it. He won't hang around here.'

'What's happened?' Chris asked. 'Have I missed something?'

Liz nodded, but didn't answer, and Gilbert elbowed his way through the small crowd waiting at the open mill gate. 'Can I come through, please? Stay here with Chris,' he said to Liz. 'We'll tell you later, Chris, not out here!'

He pushed his way through and dashed across the yard to the fire engine to speak to a fire officer. Liz watched with frightened eyes as sheets of writhing flames leapt through the smoke into the night sky and showers of gold and crimson sparks crackled and burst like a firework display.

'I nearly broke my neck getting here.' Chris put his arms round her and gratefully she leant into him, only half listening as she watched the dark figures in the mill yard working swiftly and methodically in their allotted roles. The firefighters were concentrating mainly on the house, which was ablaze with tongues of flame, and shooting jets of gushing water through the exploding windows. 'I was confused to begin with,' he went on. 'The sky was lit up, all red and gold like a sunset, and then I thought, I'm travelling east not west and it must be a fire! I was so scared that it might be the Ship.' He exhaled intensely. 'It's a wonder I didn't finish up in a ditch.'

She squeezed his hand. 'I'm sorry you were worried. We've had a terrible night. I've got an awful sense of guilt as if I've done something wrong, even though I don't think I have, but I'd told Jeannie about the property. I mean, well, I've only just discovered that it was ours after all' – she was babbling, she knew, but she couldn't stop – 'and I was going to tell Jeannie we could negotiate another tenancy agreement, because we couldn't speak to Carl, and I'd guess that he didn't know it was ours until she told him, and then he found her at the Raven and beat her up.'

'*What*? He did what?'

She stifled a sob. 'She's in hospital; we had to call an ambulance she was in such a state. She'd told him she was leaving and it was only two lads happening to go into the Raven that stopped him. He might have killed her.'

'How can you blame yourself for that?' he said sharply. 'Did you call the police? Where is he now?'

'Yes. We don't know where he is; the two lads in the Raven set about him and he hasn't been seen since, as far as I know, and then the fire broke out. Oh, Chris!' She began to sob in earnest. 'Do you think it was deliberate? Carl would have such a grudge – against us, I mean – and he'd realize that everyone would know what had happened to Jeannie.'

He shushed her gently. 'The police and the fire chief will find out soon enough.'

Gilbert came back to them, his face crimson from the heat and scattered with grey freckles of ash. 'I've told them that Jeannie's in hospital and they said that if Carl was in the house then he wouldn't have stood a chance; they can't get near, and the inside had completely gone by the time they got here. But it's hardly likely that he would have been there, as it was a deliberate fire!' he said bitterly. 'There's a strong smell of petrol.'

Liz felt her legs weaken, and she took hold of her father's arm so that she was held firmly between the two men.

'Are you all right?' Chris looked down at her. 'Do you want to go home?'

'I think so. Do you, Dad?'

She really wanted to run back to the Ship and hide beneath the sheets and pretend that none of this was happening. To stand and watch the mill and mill house burn and see the culmination of her aspirations go up in smoke instead was devastating.

'They'll not save 'house.' Gilbert stared at the fire. 'There goes 'roof.'

'They might,' Chris murmured, even though there was an enormous crash as the slates fell. 'The bricks and boulders won't burn and you can get a new roof; it's not the original.'

Gilbert glanced at him. 'They said that 'mill will stand.' He turned to Liz. 'Inside timbers have gone, 'steps and 'floors and 'old driveshaft, but there's nothing left to burn; bricks'll be blackened, but 'fire will die down now.'

She looked towards the dark shape silhouetted against the reddened sky. The glassless windows and open doorway were lit from within, and it reminded her of an advent calendar she'd had when she was a child: windows glowing red and yellow when she opened the tiny paper shutters.

Gilbert shook his head. He looked tired and sad, and put his hand over his eyes. 'I don't know what's going to happen now, Liz.' He rubbed his nose. 'There was a strong smell near the house, paraffin or petrol, and 'fire chief gave me a funny look when I said I was the owner. I didn't bother to explain the ins and outs. I didn't think he'd be interested at this stage. But he did ask if I was insured.'

'Surely you are?' Chris asked.

He gave a brief nod. 'Buildings and third party. Not contents. So if Carl wasn't covered, then he's lost everything. Come on, we can't do anything here. Let's go home.'

CHAPTER THIRTY SIX

Liz could smell smoke in her hair; she thought she should have had a shower before getting into bed. She had just said goodnight and come upstairs; couldn't wait to crawl under the sheets and hide. She thought she had slept part of the time, but kept waking and looking at the clock. Three o'clock, four fifteen, five o'clock.

Her mind was running with terrifying thoughts of the fire, of crashing, burning timbers, when suddenly she shot upright. Ben! Where was Ben? Oh, surely the dog hadn't been in the house! But no, he wasn't allowed, not by Carl anyway, and Jeannie hadn't been there.

She got out of bed, sleep having finally deserted her, and padded downstairs. She filled the kettle with water and put it on to boil. Surely, if Carl had started the fire and left it to burn – and she told herself that she shouldn't judge him, but if he had – then he would have taken the dog with him; and if it was accidental the dog would have run away, frightened by the fire and the noise of the fire engine.

She sipped her tea and worried about Ben and about Jeannie and what she would do when she had recovered, and then wondered where Chris was sleeping; perhaps in the bedroom he had slept in the last time he was here. She assumed he had just made himself at home, unless he had gone home with Dot, who had waited in the Ship for them all to come back.

She reached across the kitchen table and picked up an envelope addressed to her with an Australian stamp on it. Bill. She scanned the contents and on the second page he had written, *Were you thinking of coming over for the wedding? We've decided to put it off for now until we have a bit more money. Now that we're going to be property owners we'll be able to splash out a bit more. Great news about the mill house and the mill, so let me know when it will go on the market. Nadia's thrilled to bits and is talking about us buying our own place with the money. How much do you think we'll get?*

She threw the letter on to the table. Not a lot, she brooded, and not yet. Sorry to tell you this, Bill, but your inheritance, which I seem to recall you didn't want, has gone up in flames. You'll have to wait quite a while before the insurance company pays up; there'll be a few questions to answer first, especially if it's found to have been deliberate. 'Arson,' she breathed. It could take a long time to resolve, and if it was Carl – though I mustn't assume it was – he will be imprisoned.

She folded her arms on the table and rested her head on them. Who else? Surely no one else could hate us as much as he did, but *why* did he? This must have been simmering from a long time ago, and maybe, just maybe, it isn't anything to do with us, but something else entirely.

I'm a fool, she thought. Bill was right when he said I've been living in a dream world. I've always imagined that one day I'd own the mill, run a rural museum, grow a herb garden – and it was total fantasy.

How did it all begin? Was it my mother who nurtured this obsession? She said that the Reedbarrows only had it by accident from a long time ago. Or was it Dad, who told me to leave it, we have to be satisfied with what we have, and so made me more determined than ever to have it? And all the time there was no need; it was ours. I don't understand, and I'm not sure, now, if I even care.

Fourteen cars and Matt Wilson's Land Rover left the village on the designated morning. The jeep was stacked with placards and banners, a wheelchair borrowed from social services for Alf Wainwright, and four exultant giggling schoolchildren, two girls, two boys, who had been allowed to miss lessons to join the demonstration.

Following the theme of the posters, the children were adorned with lurid green plastic seaweed on their heads, which Liz considered wasn't strictly appropriate, but she hoped the townspeople would understand the message they were trying to convey; the villagers wore rubber rings and armbands, and one small boy a snorkel and mask and rubber flippers on his feet which were causing him some difficulty in walking.

Gilbert, not wanting to degrade his standing as a parish councillor, lent Matt his Neptune crown and trident, and as they drove off through the village, waving to those left behind, Matt broke into a rollicking rendition of old sea shanties.

'This is supposed to be a serious occasion,' Liz grumbled, but smiling in spite of herself at the sight of Matt's skinny legs draped in strips of old sheets dyed green to look like seaweed. 'I'm not sure that dressing up was a good idea.'

'It'll make folks notice us, if nothing else,' her father said. 'And that's what we want.'

She nodded. I'm turning into an old sourpuss, she thought. Where's my enthusiasm gone? She'd felt so downhearted since the fire that everything seemed an effort. She'd put off making the placards until the last minute and then had to work on them through late evenings to get them finished.

Everyone met in a car park and unloaded the banners and

home-made flags depicting the sea with the words HELP: WE ARE DROWNING in bold red lettering. The children in front simulated swimming and three men behind them walked in a row, each carrying a banner adorned with a single letter, two Ss and an O, whilst behind them were women carrying placards reading SAVE OUR HOMES FROM A WATERY GRAVE and OUR FEET ARE WET and BUILD US A WALL – NOT AN ARK.

A child standing near by watching the antics of Matt Wilson suddenly pointed at him and asked, 'Who's that man?'

'It's Father Time, I think,' the woman with him said vaguely.

'No I'm not,' Matt snorted indignantly, 'I'm Neptune, king of the sea. This is a trident, not a scythe!'

The woman just shrugged.

Dot, walking behind him dressed in a black sheet with a grinning death mask over her face, laughed as she held up her placard which proclaimed DAVY JONES, SPIRIT OF THE SEA, and said, 'I hope folk don't think we're from a travelling circus.'

Bringing up the rear, Liz hoisted up her placard and wished that Chris could have been there to help her carry it; he'd wanted to, but said he didn't think that the education authority would have been pleased if he had taken time off to join a demo.

On her square bleached sheet she had painted a deep blue sea with the tip of a church tower showing above tumultuous waves; towering above them was a sheer cliff with what looked like the face of a child impressed into the rock – where had that come from? – and around the edge were the names of lost villages, AUBURN, DIMLINGTON, RAVENSER ODD, OWTHORNE and MONKSTON. At the bottom she had painted IS TILLINGTON NEXT in large lettering, followed by four question marks.

The procession met up with its police escort and circled the town in an orderly fashion, marching into the Market Place and circling it twice whilst chanting loudly to curious onlook-ers 'Save Tillington' and 'Don't let us down. Don't let us drown', before making its way through the pedestrian shop-ping street to County Hall.

Liz, as the chosen representative of the village, sat in the council chamber listening quietly as the issue was discussed. There was general agreement that although Tillington was an urgent case the whole coastline, stretching over thirty miles, was at risk.

'We have all the figures here and I'm afraid we just don't have the money for this kind of commitment,' said one coun-cillor. 'We're already fully stretched.'

'This should be a test case,' said another. 'We've got 'worst erosion in Europe. Government should be asked for funding.'

Liz held her breath in dismay as someone else argued that the plan for a wall was not economically viable and suggested that a bypass should be built at the back of the village and the tides left to do what they must. 'We can't hold back the sea,' he said. 'It's impossible.'

'The Dutch did,' came back a sharp reply.

Another meeting was arranged to discuss the issue further, and a statement in conclusion, addressed to the villagers, con-firmed what they already knew: that although they had the sympathies of the council chamber, after the costings report there wouldn't be sufficient money available to fund the project.

'So that's that!' Liz felt frustration building up. 'Back to square one.'

'Can I quote you on that?' Jim Jackson came up at her side. 'Or have you got more to say?'

'I've got a lot more to say,' she asserted, feeling the fervour of passion pounding inside her. 'And you can quote me. You can say that we are not finished yet; that just because we are little people it doesn't mean that we can be forgotten. We shall fight for our existence in Tillington; we will *not* become another name in the list of lost villages.'

She took a huge breath and Jim Jackson paused, his pencil poised above his notebook as he waited for her next words. 'Say that this campaign will be the start of something huge in the history of our crumbling coastline, and that this time the sea will not win!'

CHAPTER THIRTY SEVEN

Chris came over that evening and listened without interrupting when Liz related what had happened at the demonstration. 'Jim Jackson said we should hit the national newspapers, and there was one local television channel there – which is good,' she said quickly, 'but what we want is national TV coverage, so how do we get that?'

'Go to Westminster,' Chris said at once. 'You said that you would. Go soon, whilst everybody is still enthusiastic; don't wait for officialdom. Write letters to your MPs. Get your petition organized, but do it now.'

'Yes. Yes, you're right,' she agreed. 'I think I'll take next week off work; I'm due some holiday. Come on, let's take a walk whilst it's still daylight.'

Inevitably, they headed seawards and breathed deeply in the salty air. 'It's going to rain,' she said. 'There's a storm brewing.' The sun that had been bright most of the day had not yet set and puffy cumulus clouds were dotted over the darkening sky. 'Wispy white tails,' she murmured. 'It will be cold up there.' She lifted her head to watch them. 'That's what Dad used to say when I was little.'

In the far distance flashes of lightning lit up the toy-size shape of a tanker barely moving against the horizon. Liz stared out across the span of sea and listened for distant sounds but heard only the rush of the tide and the screech of black-headed gulls.

'Can we get down to the sands?' Chris asked. 'It seems ages since we walked along the beach.'

'It is.' She smiled at the recollection. 'But we'd better not risk climbing down tonight. Do you remember when we talked about the seals and the drowned forest? I still haven't taken you to Spurn Point, have I?'

'No. Nor found me a house.' He looked long and hard at her, and then quipped, 'I was wondering if Dot would take me in as a lodger.'

'Oh!' She felt a shivering sensation of disbelief. Was this what he meant when he'd mentioned the long drive from Hull? 'I don't know,' she answered casually. 'You'd have to ask her.'

He nodded, and then asked, 'What's happened to Jeannie, do you know?'

'She's out of hospital.' Liz was glad to change the subject. 'She's gone into a women's hostel for a few days, just in case Carl should try to find her. Not that he's been seen since the fire; it seems as if he's completely disappeared. The police are looking for him, and Dad thinks he'll be charged with arson. Ben hasn't been seen either,' she added. 'It's very sad.'

'Is it sad about the dog, or Carl and Jeannie?' He took hold of her hand.

'Everything,' she sighed. 'It's a very gloomy prospect for Jeannie and Carl.'

'Perhaps she'll get back with Kevin.'

'I hope not. That would be the worst thing she could do.'

'Have you been inside the mill since the fire?'

'What?' She grimaced. 'Since the fire? I've never been inside the mill.'

'What do you mean, never?'

She shrugged. 'What I say. Bill has, but I have never, ever, been inside the mill. Never in my life.'

'I find that astonishing! Why not?'

'I don't know.' She considered. 'Whenever I went with my mother, we were never invited into the house, hardly ever got past the gate; and as I got older I was scared of Carl and his father – who it turned out wasn't his father in any case. It was only after Jeannie came on the scene that I went to the house, but I never went into the mill; there was no reason why I should.' She shrugged. 'I've been into Skidby mill,' she added, 'but that's a working mill.'

'Let's go now,' Chris suggested. 'I admit I'm curious.' He seemed almost eager as he took her arm and about-turned towards the village.

'It's getting dark. We shan't be able to see much.' Something like panic gripped her. *I don't know if I want to. I'm not ready. I have to prepare myself.*

'It's not for sale,' she said in a rush. 'You do realize that, don't you?'

He nodded and gently squeezed her hand. She swallowed hard. *Damn the man, why does he make me feel the way I do?*

'Look!' He pointed across the road. 'I thought you said she was in hiding.'

Jeannie was standing at the open door of the Raven, looking down the street, and they crossed over to speak to her. Liz spoke first.

'Jeannie – it's good to see you! Are you all right?'

She looked very pale, and a dark ugly bruise showed along her cheekbone. She narrowed her eyes as she drew hard on a cigarette, nodded to Liz's question, and then looked up the road the other way. 'You won't tell Carl you've seen me, will you? If you should happen to bump into him, I mean?'

'He won't come back here, surely?'

'He might,' she countered. She was remote, yet her eyes

were watchful, darting uneasily between them and into the distance. 'If he thinks I'm here he will, and then he'll want me to go with him – and I don't know if I can.'

She will, Liz thought. She will. She'll go with him. That's why she's here, in case he comes looking for her; she's not in hiding at all.

'No, we won't tell him,' she answered calmly, her manner tolerant and indulgent as if speaking to a child. 'But perhaps you should go inside, just in case?'

As Liz and Chris reached the mill gate there was a distant rumble of thunder and Liz hesitated. 'Shall we leave it for now? We're going to get wet.'

'We needn't take long,' Chris said tolerantly, stepping forward.

'There's a paddock at the back, and a small copse behind it,' Liz told him. 'You can see it from the footpath. That's where I'd imagined the herb garden would go. It's sheltered from the wind; catches the sun—' But her words came out sharp and breathless as she saw from this angle the burnt-out shell of the house, and the pools of muddy water and bits and pieces of smashed furniture, scorched chairs and a blackened mattress that littered the back yard. The acrid smell of burning still lingered and she turned away. 'I can't bear to look. It's devastating,' she muttered.

'It is terrible,' he agreed. 'But no one was hurt. Bricks and mortar don't feel pain. Another house could be built.'

The area at the back of the house had not been touched in years, it seemed. The undergrowth was a tangle, a knot of briar and dock and waist-high nettles growing through rusty machinery; car tyres, a wire-sprung mattress and here and there wild roses and ash saplings. Two dead elms hung over the fence and spread their leafless branches against the darkening sky.

'How do you feel now?' Chris asked carefully, his eyes anxious.

'Better, I think.' He knows I'm tense. How does he know? I didn't think it showed. But it's true, I do feel calmer after coming in and seeing what's here, and yes, he's right, perhaps it's not impossible; perhaps something can be salvaged after all, even made into a home again, though the original house and its memories have gone for ever.

'Let's go, then; we'll look at the mill some other time. You're right; it's too dark now to see anything.'

'No, come on, I'm being silly. We'll just look inside. Dad came the other day with the fire assessors. He said all the floors had burnt away, only the hoist chains and pulleys and the ironwork are left. The stones were removed years ago; we have one in the yard at the back of the Ship. Don't know what happened to the others.'

The shadows were deepening as they crossed the yard, and the sound of thunder grew ominously nearer. Liz unzipped her jacket. 'It's so close, isn't it? We could do with some rain to clear the air.'

Chris didn't answer. He was staring towards the double mill doors, and put his finger to his lips. 'I thought I heard something. I think there's someone inside.'

She felt a sudden sensation of fear. Not Carl! Her heart pounded. Perhaps he's hiding, but why would he come back here? Surely he'd realize the police are looking for him. No, it'll be someone having a look round to see if there's anything worth taking. But she thought of when Carl had threatened her father with the shotgun and felt a sudden panic.

'No,' she whispered as Chris moved stealthily towards the doorway. Suddenly he hunkered down and extended a hand.

'Come on, then, old fellow,' he wheedled, his voice soft. 'Come on.' He glanced back at her. 'It's all right. It's the dog. What's his name?'

'Ben!' She came quickly to his side. 'Oh, is it Ben?' She called coaxingly to the dog, who stood slavering and panting in the doorway. 'I wonder why we didn't see him before? Or why he didn't bark?'

'I think he's only just got here. Look at him: he's exhausted. He's lathered in sweat and he's been tied up somewhere – the rope's still fastened to his collar.' Chris got to his feet and walked slowly towards the doorway, but as he got nearer Ben backed off and bared his teeth.

'Let me try,' Liz suggested. 'He knows me. Ben! Come on, old lad, come on.'

Ben wagged the tip of his tail and moved a few steps forward; Liz gingerly put her hand out and stroked the top of his head, talking softly, calming him. She slipped her hand beneath his collar and held him. 'I suppose we could take him to Jeannie.'

Chris didn't answer. He moved nearer to the doorway, but Ben turned his head and snarled at him again, his hackles raised.

'I've never seen him like this,' Liz protested. 'He's usually so friendly. Something's frightened him.'

'He doesn't want me to go inside. I think that's what it is. Perhaps this is his shelter, and he's protecting it.'

'No, he has a kennel.' She looked round the yard. 'It's still there.'

'Try to hold him while I step inside; there's definitely something in there that's bothering him.'

She held tight to Ben's collar, turning him to face her and talking gently whilst Chris opened the mill door wider and looked inside.

She saw him bend down to the floor and pick something up, and as he straightened she heard his suppressed gasp. 'What is it, Chris? Is someone there? Chris!' Suddenly the dog broke free from her grasp and almost knocked her over as he raced towards the door and past Chris into the dark interior of the mill, where he set up a frenzied howling and yelping.

'What's happening? Why is he barking?' Alarmed, she took a step nearer, and Chris turned quickly.

'Get back,' he hissed, his words almost drowned by Ben's frantic barking. 'Get back! Run home.' He cupped his hand over his mouth. 'Ring 999. Get armed police, ambulance, everybody. It's Carl. He's got a shotgun.'

'I can't leave you!' She didn't want to, but knew she had to. She backed away and ran towards the gate, and to her astonishment Ben raced to her side. As she reached the gate and opened it she saw Matt Wilson's old van trundling towards her; she grabbed the dog and Matt braked just in time as she shot towards him.

'Stop! Stop! Matt, Carl Reedbarrow is in the mill and he has a shotgun. Chris is there. Will you go back and dial 999 for the police? You'll be quicker than me. Maybe the Raven – it's the nearest phone.'

He pulled to the side, away from the gate, and braked. When he opened the van door he was holding something in his hand. 'I'll do better than that, m'dear,' he said, pressing a number three times on his mobile phone and handing it to her. 'Only bought this last week.'

She spoke to the operator and quickly answered their questions, saying there was an armed man, giving them his name and location, and telling them that Chris was with him. She was shaking when she handed the phone back to Matt. 'Thank heavens you came when you did. I must get back to Chris.'

'I'll come with you, love.' Matt took her arm. 'Or you can sit here in 'van 'til 'police get here. If it's an armed response I shouldn't think they'll be long.'

*

When Chris had looked through the mill door the first thing he saw was a white envelope on the ground immediately in front of him. It was held down by half a brick and Chris was able to read just one word. STOP. He bent down to pick it up, and as he straightened and lifted his head he saw Carl Reed-barrow standing halfway up a long ladder with a rope over his left shoulder and a shotgun held in both hands. Then Ben had raced past him into the mill and distracted Carl, and by the time the dog raced outside again Chris was able to face the other man calmly.

'Whoa!' he said. 'I hope you're hunting rats and not pointing that at me?'

Carl sneered. 'I've no grouse wi' you, even though you sound like a toff, so if you want to clear off now you can do.'

'I can't help sounding like a toff, it's where I come from,' Chris said, trying to sound as if he wasn't terrified. 'I'm just a schoolteacher, nothing else, but I'm a bit more bothered about that rope than the shotgun. What were you intending to do with it?'

He saw Carl take a breath and glance up to where a beam ran the full width of the building.

'If you were intending to throw it over that beam and hang something on it, I think you'll find it won't take much weight. I'm a woodwork teacher, did you know?' Chris went into schoolteacher mode. 'That beam is probably well over a century old and as such is probably full of woodworm. Any weight on it and it'll come crashing down. You weren't, erm, you weren't thinking of – not . . .? You can get help, you know. Life's a bastard sometimes, I know, but you don't have to give in to it.'

Carl threw the rope to the ground and pointed the shotgun not at Chris but, awkwardly, at his own head. 'I'm not giving in,' he muttered. 'But I'm not going to rot in jail either. Nobody'd be bothered either way.'

'I think you've got that wrong.' Chris heard the sound of motors and the screech of tyres and kept talking. 'I think a lot of people would wish they'd offered you some help, and I know Jeannie would be devastated.'

'How do you know?' Carl swung the gun round to point it at Chris. 'You don't know her!'

'I don't know her at all, but I do know that she's come back to Tillington to look for you. She's worried about you, so I heard.'

Carl frowned, and at that moment the door crashed open, Chris dropped to his knees. The place was full of police, all pointing weapons at Carl, who dropped the shotgun to the ground and raised his hands.

CHAPTER THIRTY EIGHT

'Shall we run you home, sir? Do you live in 'village? Lucky we were so close, I'd say.'

Chris shook his head. 'No, but I'll probably stay at the Ship. The millowner is a friend of mine. In fact he's here.'

Gilbert was standing at the gate with his arm and his coat round Liz's shoulders. A small crowd had gathered, alerted by the sound of emergency vehicles coming into the village, and rumours abounded until Carl was brought out of the mill handcuffed to a police officer and with a blanket covering his head and shoulders. Chris was talking to one of the other officers, and Gilbert heard the sergeant say, 'If you would keep yourself available for questioning tomorrow morning, we'd be obliged. We'll come out to you.' Chris nodded mutely; he was beginning to shake. He'd already answered some questions, and had gathered that he certainly wouldn't be going in to college the following day. He had given the policeman information about himself and told him that he hadn't been threatened by Carl Reedbarrow, who, it had seemed to him, was bent on suicide, and had handed over the note he'd picked up from the mill floor where Carl had left it.

'Seems like you got there just in time,' the sergeant went on. 'We were looking for him, as a matter of fact.'

Chris made no comment. He didn't want to be embroiled in the matter and felt he had nothing to add that might help or hinder an already tragic story. He was quite sure that Carl would be committed to prison or hospital; how long he would be at either was debatable.

There was a commotion at the gate and Chris turned to watch as a woman tried to break her way through the specta-tors, insisting that she speak to Carl. The sergeant frowned. 'Who's this?'

'It's Reedbarrow's wife – or partner,' Chris told him. 'They lived here at the mill house. It was their home.'

'What? He's accused of burning it down.'

'Well, somebody did.' Chris decided to stay neutral. 'I wouldn't know.'

Jeannie wasn't allowed to see Carl, who was now in the police vehicle, but the police took her details and said they would speak to her the next day. When they asked for her address she gave them the Raven's.

Dot had milk warming on the cooker, mugs out ready for tea or coffee and a brandy bottle standing by when they all trooped back to the Ship. 'What's happened, then?' she asked. 'Everybody left after somebody looked in and said that Carl had been found in 'mill, but nobody knew what he was doing there, except probably trying to fire it.'

Chris shook his head. 'He wasn't,' he said. 'Definitely not.' He said nothing more, except that he didn't want to talk about it, but he followed Gilbert when he went to the deserted bar to lock up and said quietly, 'He needs help.'

'I've allus known it.' Gilbert turned to him. 'But he wouldn't accept any. He was hell bent on doing everything in 'way he wanted to. I'm glad his ma isn't here to know what's happened – or nearly happened; she would have been devastated about 'mill house going up in smoke, as I am, when I think of 'work that's gone into it over 'years. It's been a family home for generations, and now it's nothing but a shell; and Carl will have to serve time for it. He's had this great big grudge on his shoulder for years, but mebbe his step-dad's behaviour towards him didn't help. He was a right bonny lad when he was little.' He sighed. 'Sometimes things just don't work out.'

'Is it all right if I stay the night?' Chris asked. 'The police want to interview me again in the morning and I'm afraid I told them I'd be here.'

'Course you can; you don't need to ask. I'm going to lock up now. Don't think anybody'll be coming in.' But he was wrong on that count, for just as he was about to lock and bolt the door someone came up the step. 'Jeannie!' he said, opening the door again. 'What's up?'

'Can I stay the night?' She looked on the verge of tears, and he opened the door wider.

'Course you can. What's happened?'

'Kevin said I can't stop at the Raven any more. If 'owners find out there's been another incident they might not let him have 'other pub. He doesn't want to lose his *reputation*,' she scoffed. 'Hah! I could tell 'em a thing or two about that.'

'Don't!' Gilbert said. 'Walk away from it. Liz'll find you a bed.'

She also found one for Chris. She had hoped he might have chosen to share hers, but he kissed her goodnight saying he knew he wouldn't sleep and wouldn't mind just being in a guest room; he did not say that the image of Carl halfway up a ladder in the gloom of the mill carrying a rope and a shotgun, and thinking that either one of them could have been meant for him, was becoming more real than it had been when he was actually there, talking to Carl and trying to persuade him to step down.

But at midnight, as the church clock was striking, she slipped out of her room and opened the door to his in the guest annexe, and saw him sleeping soundly with his arms flung out over the covers, and she smiled as she thought of Dot, who had told her she'd tipped a little extra brandy into his mug.

Gilbert and Dot had sat on in the sitting room after everyone else had gone to bed. Liz had put a hot water bottle in Jeannie's, even though the room wasn't cold; but it's comforting, she thought, at least I always think it is. She'd also brought Jeannie a nightdress and dressing gown, not knowing and not wanting to ask if she had one. Jeannie had said that she'd stormed out of the Raven leaving her few belongings behind, and accepted the nightwear gratefully.

'Well, I'm beat,' Dot said, putting her empty mug on the small table next to her. 'I'm ready for my bed. I hope there won't be any more incidents like 'ones we've been having. Mebbe things will get back to something like normal. Give me a shove, will you? This sofa's too soft for me to get out of.'

Gilbert put his arm round her. 'Why don't you stay?'

She turned towards him. 'What? Here, do you mean?' She tried to keep her voice neutral; she had never spent a night in the Ship. Gilbert had always come to her.

'Yes. Will you?'

A flush came to her cheeks. She felt suddenly shy. 'All right.'

He lent her his bathrobe, and as she washed and cleansed her face, and cleaned her teeth with her fingers and tooth-paste, she contemplated on his reasoning. It must be because of Liz and Chris, though they're in separate rooms, or because he's upset about Carl being locked up. She sighed. Heaven knows I wasn't looking forward to being alone tonight. Poor Jeannie, I wonder if *she's* sleeping.

'Do you want a pyjama jacket?' Gilbert took off his dressing gown, kicked off his slippers and sat on the edge of the bed.

'Why should I want a pyjama jacket? We don't usually dress for bed.'

'I know,' he said sheepishly. 'It just seems different here.' He smiled and drew her towards him. 'But sometimes you wear that black nightie, 'one with 'thin straps.'

'I only wear that for you,' she whispered and pulled at the cord around his waist. 'I bought it specially. I don't wear it when I'm sleeping alone.'

He nuzzled into her cheek. 'And when you're sleeping alone, is that when you take Valium?'

She stiffened. 'No. I've had them for a long time. I only take them now and again, when I feel 'need.'

When I feel that we're going nowhere, she reflected. When I think of the wasted years when I've hankered after you, and known that you'll never belong to me. But then she recalled that first time, when they had been reminiscing together about Nina and Gordon and about how lonely life could be when your life partner had gone, and she had started to cry and he'd drawn her towards him and kissed her, oh, so tenderly, and then he too had cried and she had comforted him, and there they were crying and kissing and loving, and saying how they had always loved the other, ever since they could remember, and so it had begun.

But always there was Nina, casting a shadow, her presence always felt, always there between them.

He pulled her gently on to the bed. 'Perhaps you wouldn't feel 'need if you didn't sleep alone.'

She didn't answer but ran her fingers through his hair and he kissed her and looked into her eyes and she gazed back into his; she saw the flecks of amber and his fair bushy eyebrows. She felt she knew every part of his face, every freckle, every hint of a wrinkle.

'So what about giving up your bed and sharing mine?'

Goose pimples ran up and down her arms. 'What do you mean?' She hardly dared hope. 'I am sharing your bed,' she bantered.

'I mean permanently.' An engaging grin creased his face. 'Don't you think it's about time?'

'But why?' She was bewildered, wanting to be happy, but aware that something was holding the happiness back.

'Oh!' He fell back on the pillow beside her. 'I just feel . . . I don't really know how to explain it, but after 'fire at 'mill house and then tonight when we heard about Carl and that he'd done it, well, I was devastated about what he'd done and then somehow – I don't know, I felt a sort of release from 'past. As if I had been responsible in some way for everything and everybody, and as if it was holding me back, and suddenly it was gone. There'll be no more pressure about 'mill, or 'mill house; no more secrecy, no more remembering about 'arguments that Nina and I had for so many years. Mill and 'mill house was such a bone of contention between us, always a barrier – and now that barrier has gone. Even 'memories I have of Nina will be different now.'

'What you mean,' she said, her heart sinking, 'is that you'll only remember 'good times?'

'Yes.' He nodded in agreement. 'All of 'aggravation has disappeared. I feel as if we, you and I, can start afresh.' He turned to her and smiled, the smile lighting up his eyes, the amber flecks glinting. 'So what about it? Isn't it about time I made an honest woman of you?'

'I don't know,' she said. 'I'm going to have to think about it.'

CHAPTER THIRTY NINE

Liz drove home from Hull every evening after work, and every evening she saw the mill standing stark and desolate against the skyline. She knew that she still wasn't ready to go inside; the last incident, when Chris had found Carl intent on ending his life, had set her back considerably.

She knew that Carl wouldn't be coming back to Tillington for a long time, if ever; he was being held somewhere safe and secure until he was fit to appear in court. Jeannie had made several attempts to visit him and been refused permission, but had been told she could write to him and the letter would be delivered.

'Can't do that,' she told Liz. 'I'm no good at writing letters.'

'Send him cards, then,' Liz suggested. 'Something bright and cheerful, maybe with cars, or tractors, or dogs on them. Then you just need to write your name on them and it'll show that you're thinking about him.'

'I'm thinking of leaving Tillington anyway,' Jeannie said, as if she hadn't heard. 'Why am I stopping here? Nobody talks to me; no one knows what to say and some, even them that used to come into 'Raven, cross over 'street when they see me.'

'My dad would give you a reference if you asked him – if you were thinking of doing bar work again, I mean.'

'No,' Jeannie said. 'I'm going back to 'women's hostel, I think. They said they'd help me.'

'Then try it,' Liz said. 'You know that Carl is going to be away for quite some time. You have to think of yourself now, and decide what you want to do with your life. I can drop you off at the hostel on my way to work, if you'd like. I'll give you my work telephone number so you can keep in touch.'

'Yeh.' Jeannie nodded. 'Yeh, I'll do that.'

Liz hoped that she would. She wanted to help her, but she also wanted to continue with the project of trying to build up support for a sea wall before it was forgotten.

Every evening when she came home, she showered and changed into something comfortable, ate a meal with her dad and Dot – who to her delight was eating with them most evenings – and then she went into the small living room and began drafting letters to politicians, government departments, environmental bodies, local conservation groups and industrial bodies, asking for their support.

Early one Saturday morning, she had her word processor, a fat file and a pile of newspaper cuttings which she was clipping together in date order in front of her when Chris arrived.

'You're early,' she said, and lifted her cheek for a kiss, which he gave her. 'I've been thinking that we should make a big push to organize a Westminster demonstration before the summer recess. If it's left until September the enthusiasm will have gone off the boil.'

'I was thinking the same thing,' he agreed. 'And I can help at the London end, if you like. I know just the person to sort out the red tape.'

'Helena?' A shade of jealousy touched her. 'I suppose she'd know what to do and all of 'right folk to ask.' Deliberately she exaggerated an East Yorkshire accent.

'Now now!' Chris grinned. 'Just because she's blonde and beautiful.'

She shrugged, and when she didn't answer he bent towards her and whispered, 'You should be flattered that I'm only ever seen with beautiful women.' He tugged gently on her hair. 'But whereas some are beautiful and practical and see only in black and white, there are others who are beautiful and elusive – like the dreamer I can't catch hold of.'

'What brass nerve! And I am practical,' she complained. 'Just look at all these letters! If those are not showing that I'm practical, then I don't know what would.'

'An idealist,' he persisted. 'That's what you are. You become practical when you reach out to grasp your ideals.'

'So am I wasting my time with all this? Is that what you mean?' She cast her hand impatiently towards the pile of letters and files on the table.

'No! Don't get cross! You know that's not what I meant! It's just that sometimes I feel that I need to catch hold of you by your coat-tails – or the hem of your jeans – to haul you back to earth! I want to shield you from becoming demoralized if what you want doesn't happen.'

'Like the mill, and the plans I once had.'

'Like the mill,' he said quietly. 'Which you have to face sooner or later.'

She decided to face it the following Saturday. She rolled out of bed and stood at the window, watching the milk float rattle down the road and Matt Wilson's old Land Rover cough and splutter as he drove his wife to Beverley Market. The sea in the distance sparkled with frothy silver crests, and white cotton-wool chocolate-box clouds drifted across a brilliant blue sky.

If I'm to go at all, today is the day, she considered. It's an innocent, innocuous sort of day. The sort of day on which we would think that nothing bad could happen. There'll be no wars today. No murders committed. No crime. It's a picture postcard day – having a nice time, wish you were here kind of day. I'll go! I must. Then when Chris comes – she drew in a breath – I can tell him.

She showered and dressed and raced downstairs. She dithered over whether to have breakfast first or later. First, she decided. If I have to face up to going inside the mill, then I must fortify my body as well as my mind. She made coffee and toast, eating and drinking quickly, walking about the kitchen, not sitting down, trying to keep a sense of urgency so that she wouldn't change her mind.

A cool breeze hit her as soon as she stepped outside. It wasn't as warm as it had appeared to be from inside, a northeasterly breeze keeping the temperature down. She looked both ways and in the distance, heading out of the village, was a familiar figure, her shoulders lopsided under the weight of a large bag.

Liz ran after her. 'Jeannie!' she called. 'Jeannie, wait. Where are you going?'

Jeannie put down the bag and looked at her with sullen, shadowed eyes. 'Hull.'

'Not walking!'

'I'm going to try and cadge a lift.'

Liz looked down at the bag. 'You're obviously not going shopping.'

'You're a nosy tart sometimes, aren't you?'

'Sorry.'

'If you really want to know, I'm leaving this godforsaken hole and I'm not coming back. As far as I'm concerned Tillington doesn't exist. It can fall into 'sea for all I care.'

The day was beginning to lose its brightness. 'What's happened? I said I would drop you off at the women's hostel whenever you were ready to go.' It dawned on Liz then that Jeannie hadn't stayed at the Ship last night as they'd said she could whenever she wanted to; she didn't have to ask. So where had she been?

'I changed my mind, didn't I?' she said. 'I decided I would walk out of here on my own two feet.' She heaved her bag off the ground. 'Folk can say what they think about Carl, but he wouldn't have left me – not for anybody else, I mean; he told me to clear off many a time when he was in one of his moods, but he didn't really mean it. And then when I did go, he couldn't cope, but – but I would allus have gone back to him, you know, eventually.'

She gave a wistful grin. 'One of 'world's losers, that's me! I suppose I've onny got what I deserve.' She stared straight at Liz. 'I stayed at 'Raven last night, in case you were wondering. Kev's moving out on Monday. He's got some woman waiting for him in West Yorkshire and she's welcome to him.' She swung the bag over her shoulder. 'Ta-ra!'

'But – but where will you go? Can I give you a lift somewhere?' Liz felt desperate, but not as desperate as Jeannie must have been feeling.

Jeannie began to move off. 'I'll try and register as homeless first and then get a bed for 'night at 'hostel. Then, who knows. I might join a circus,' she joked. 'I might become a traveller – a gypsy. The world's my oyster – I've never tasted one.' Tears began to trickle down her cheeks and she dashed them away. 'But I'll begin in Hull. Cheerio, Liz. All the best!' She raised her free hand. 'And thanks.'

'For what?' Liz swallowed and felt her voice crack.

'For friendship?'

CHAPTER FORTY

The sky was still blue, but somehow the morning had lost its glow. Liz had walked back to the Ship and lingered, quite put off her original intent of going to the mill. Then she came out again, dithered on the step and almost went back in, then made herself walk on and turn up the lane towards the church and the mill.

She pushed open the churchyard gate and crossed over the graves towards the Monkston burial ground. She gazed down at the inscriptions, at Sarah's and John's, at Maria's, who was Sarah's mother, and bent down and scraped with her finger-nail at another leaning green and mossy stone.

Thomas Foster and his wife Elizabeth – she searched the ground for a pebble to scrape the stone – *of Tillington Mill.* Was he the first, she wondered? The first Foster of Tillington? If I can keep that in mind, that others have lived and worked at the mill and the mill house, then it isn't so frightening after all. But the creaking branches of the ancient yew trees swaying above her made her shudder, and she shook her head as they showered dark green needles into her hair.

The gate to the mill was closed and she unhooked it and left it open; just in case I have to run, she mocked herself; in case the ghosties chase me. But she was fooling herself; her fears were real, and if there were ghosts here then she would know them; they would reach out to her just as Sarah did. *I'm the crossing point, the axis on which they spin.*

She approached the mill door, which was also closed. There was no Ben this morning; perhaps Alf had let him out. It's just an ordinary day, she convinced herself. A Saturday, market day, gardening day, nothing special about it, and she lifted the latch and stepped over the threshold and held her breath, then exhaled slowly as she realized that this was no tower of darkness, no sinister black cavity; the sun was filtering through the cracked cap and dust particles were sliding and dancing down the long shafts of silver light, flickering like jack-o'-lanterns on the inclining walls.

Her eyes as she turned away from the glare focused on a mosaic of red, purple and black spots that filled her vision, so that for a brief moment she couldn't see past them and had to stare hard at the black walls to clear them. As her sight came back she saw a grey circle on the floor opposite, dense and solid, and crossed over to look at it.

It was a millstone, identical to the one in the yard at the Ship except for the tub of flowers in the middle of it. But this one was dark, its radial grooves filled with dust and soot. She crouched down and ran her hand over it, feeling the indentations that had crushed and kibbled the grain, the cracks and holes that time and age had wrought, and below her fingers some lettering or pattern.

Someone had chiselled out a name between the grooves and she spat on her fingers and rubbed them over the lettering. *Carl Reedbarrow.* The name jumped out dark and prominent and she almost fell backwards as if she had been struck.

She shivered, feeling suddenly cold, and looked up and saw that the patch of sunlight was no longer bright but covered in cloud. Lowering her gaze, she stared at the name. It was the writing of a child, she convinced herself, yet in her head she could hear his mocking laugh. Something rattled above her and she jumped, her eyes roaming the tower. The pulley on the wall was moving, the wheel rotating as a gusty breeze gathered in the space above it.

A whooshing sound as a breeze rose in the trees behind the mill caused her to think of past millers setting the sails; of the white canvas shades capturing the power of the wind and slowly turning, their convolution increasing as the wind grew stronger; thought too of the huge stones ponderously grinding the corn, and the clatter of feet as millers of many ages ran up and down the narrow steps to the various stages: the dusty meal floor, the creaking stone floor and up to the top where the grain began its journey.

Think of the millers who were once here. Think of the other Fosters and the children who had played in the yard; of Alf Wainwright and my grandfather who swung on the sails and couldn't get down. Stay. Don't run away!

But sounds were gathering and she wrapped her arms about her head and stopped up her ears and closed her eyes, for she could hear a keening tone like that of a child crying. *I want. I want. Don't. Don't.*

The keening fell lower, becoming softer, disappearing into a breathing murmur which could have been the sigh of a breeze as it swept into the doorway and gathered up the dust from the ground and blew it around her feet.

She took her hands from around her head and cautiously peered about her. The mill was empty as before, shadowy now that the cloud had blocked out the sun and uninhabited by illusions and displaced phantasms, bare but for the millstone and charred pieces of timber and rusting cast-iron cogs and bolts.

She heaved a great sigh, and then tensed. What was that? A sound came from behind her by the door. A whimpering whine, a snuffling grunt. Swiftly she turned, an exclamation on the tip of her tongue which turned into a laugh as she saw Ben blocking the doorway, one ear tipped pleadingly as he nudged his bowl towards her.

'Oh, Ben!' She flung her arms round his neck and hugged him. He submitted for a moment and then, freeing himself from her grasp, he raced out of the mill towards his kennel and nosed at a bag of dog biscuits that was leaning against it.

She picked up his bowl and followed him out to his kennel. She scooped some of the biscuits into the bowl and he crunched and chomped his way through them and then waited expectantly for more. She put a handful in her pocket. 'Come on home with me and then you can have these,' she wheedled, and walked to the gate. The dog looked at her as if puzzled, but stood his ground and put his nose into the empty bowl and pushed it towards her.

'No,' she explained. 'You either come with me or wait for Alf to come.'

The dog stood watching her as she went out of the yard, but made no attempt to follow her. She turned to look back at him; he was standing watching her, his ears pointing and his tail hanging motionless. She rattled the biscuits in her pocket, but his response was to sit down and put his head on his front paws.

I'll come back later and try to persuade him to come home with me . . . although perhaps he could stay. He'd guard the place, he wouldn't let strangers in, and he could sleep in his kennel. We have to decide what to do about the house: pull it down and build new, or . . . I must speak to Bill and – she hesitated – yes, to Chris. Her spirits rose at the thought and then went down again, because he hadn't really spoken of his intentions; I think he's waiting for me to make my mind up about . . . things.

I'm calmer now than I was; I've blotted out the vision of

Carl halfway up that ladder. Chris doesn't know that I saw him, but I did, and understood his intentions, but the police arrived just in time. Would he have used that gun?

Don't think of it, she told herself. Think of the petition, think of the wall. Think of saving the village from destruction. With these censures firmly in her mind she crossed the road and headed down the old lane towards the cliff top, where, in spite of the fact that she regularly saw such changes, she was still startled to see that the land that had held the iron barrier had slipped away and was now newly positioned as a ledge five feet down.

We haven't had any exceptionally high tides recently, she thought, peering over the edge, yet the sea is just eating steadily away, eating and swallowing.

She walked further along the cliff, making a new path past where the old one had disappeared; above her the sand martins flew in streamlined flight piping their shrill cry, and in the distance she could see figures on the cliff, most likely fishermen making their way down the slippery steps that had probably been made out of bits of old planking found abandoned on the beach.

The tide was pounding a surge of potent energy at the base of the cliff before falling back and leaving a froth of creamy edging in its wake. Here and there along the sands small bays and narrow inlets had been formed by the fall of clay and boulders, and in them she could see plastic bottles buried to their necks, a sock, an assortment of plastic bags and crisp packets and, in a narrow strip of damp sand, a small seal.

It was lying perfectly still behind a protruding spur of clay with the sea lapping around its stumpy tail, and she couldn't tell from where she was standing if it was dead or merely basking. She looked down the cliff face. I wonder. Can I get down to have a better look at it? It was rare to see them quite as close as this; usually they were seen only in the distance, out on the mud flats near the tip of Spurn Point, or sometimes just as the top of a dark head swimming in the sea.

She hurried further along the path, anxious to get down before the seal, if it were alive, would flip its way back into the receding water and swim out of her sight.

Below her was a narrow jagged platform of grassy clay and she surveyed it, assessing whether or not it was too far to lower herself or whether she could jump, for there didn't appear to be any place for footholds.

'If I ease myself over, and then just a short drop,' she muttered, 'it shouldn't be too difficult.'

Instinct told her she was crazy, that the cliffs were unsafe, and if anyone else had suggested that she should climb down the unstable surface she would have laughed at their stupidity and ignorance, yet because of her knowledge of the cliffs she felt confident and assured enough to attempt it.

After all, she reasoned as she turned her back to the edge and knelt down, the fishermen do it all the time. She eased herself over and dangled first one leg and then the other over the side. She grabbed a long tuft of grass with one hand and with the other scrabbled for a handhold in the sticky clay; then, taking a quick look at the landing place, she launched herself down.

Oh! Easy! Breathless yet triumphant, she picked herself up from her hands and knees, ignoring her sand-scrubbed palms; the next bit will be no problem.

The next descent was a rough incline of sludgy humps and quaggy hillocks, and though her trainers clagged and stuck in the viscous clay she jumped and leapt and slithered, catching handholds where she could, until she landed with a thud on the wet sands.

She ran along the sands to where she had seen the seal, waiting for each powerful breaker to expend its force against the base of the cliff, and then dashing on as it withdrew. She crouched to examine the creature without getting too close and disturbing it.

It's only young, she thought. Its smudgy mottled coat was damp but drying, so she hazarded a guess that it had come in with the tide and had since been resting, for it was certainly alive and gazed at her from mournful eyes, which had beneath them a round wet patch where perpetual weeping had salt-stained the pelt, and she thought of the wooden seal that Chris had made for her, which was now filling the wide windowsill of her bedroom.

She nudged it gently with her fingertips to feel the texture of its coat. The hair was smooth as she stroked it with the lay, rough and harsh against it. How could anyone hurt such defenceless creatures, she wondered, and then began to worry about it missing the tide and being stranded on the shore.

The seal flared its nostrils and gave an explosive hostile grunt and she moved back. Not so defenceless after all, she decided. It arched its back and raised its chest from the sand with its front flippers, and with a sudden thrust forward with its hind end hitched clumsily towards the water and away from her unwanted intrusion.

She watched as its blundering propulsion made long tracks in the wet sand and into the shallow water; and then, snorting into deeper troughs, it darted smoothly away until all she could see were ripples on the surface of the sea.

Walking along the beach she kept watch on the ebbing tide; the waves rolling back threw up frothy sandy white surf that gushed and slapped into ever-deepening channels. Then she spotted the seal's flat head rising above the surface and she stopped to look and the seal seemed to stop too, its head bobbing in a straight line from her. Are you watching me watching you? She walked a little further, and the seal kept pace with her.

So absorbed was she in the game they seemed to be playing

that when she eventually looked away from the sea she realized that she had walked too far; that the cliffs here were higher and jagged and she wouldn't be able to climb them. She turned about and headed back the way she had come, giving a last glance towards the sea.

'It's turned back,' she laughed aloud. 'The seal is following me.'

She looked up towards the top of the cliff. There were no landmarks to show where she had come down; everywhere steep ridges and pinnacles of soft boulder clay ran with streams of sludgy brown ooze, barring her way. Damn! Where did I come down? I've moved away from the village.

She stood with her arms folded as she pondered. I know these cliffs so well. Something has changed. The small bays and inlets she had seen from the top looked different from down here on the sands. Gosh, how stupid I am. I was so eager to see the seal up close I didn't take notice.

A slurry of sand and mud and stones slithered down the incline and landed at the foot of the cliff, forming a small mound in front of her as if intentionally barring her path, so she moved away to try another. Soon she was feeling frustrated and just a little tense; each time she thought she had found a way up, the clay sucked at her trainers and she had to move crablike to avoid boulders and find a handhold. At this rate, she thought impatiently, I'm going to be halfway to Bridlington before I can climb to the top.

But up she went again, her trainers heavy with clay, and she tried to wiggle her feet to shake off the excess, but at the next step, as she raised her left leg to feel for another foothold, her foot pulled clean out of the trainer and she put it down in the cold wet clay.

She sat down to pull her muddy sock off and put it in her jacket pocket; the trainer lay a tantalizing stride away. They're a new pair, she deliberated. Do I go back for it or leave it?

As she tried to decide she glanced out to sea and narrowed her eyes; where there had been one dark head there were now two, side by side at the same angle, as if watching her. 'So you've brought a friend to see the show,' she muttered. 'Well, it must be very amusing.'

She put her hand down to ease herself upright again, and looking up she realized that she was less than halfway up and an overhang of cliff was almost immediately above her. She would have to move sideways, just in case. She decided to leave the trainers and go up barefoot, and bending to remove the right one she felt a slight tremor. She looked up; was it a jet's sonic boom? But the sky was clear, no wispy trailing tail of white to show that an aircraft was flying high.

And again; this time stronger. She felt the surface shift beneath her and held her breath as she looked up and saw the overhang tremble. Small clumps of sand and boulders beneath it began to slide, weakening the base, and like a building blown up from its foundations the ledge crumpled and fell, slowly at first, then gathering momentum and scooping up other debris on its descent it swept down the cliff towards the sands.

Thank goodness I wasn't just a little further along! Liz trembled at the thought; it didn't bear thinking about. She took another look to assure herself that the way she had decided on was safe. Above her a large boulder jutted out from the clay. It looked very precarious. Arrayed around it were loose clods of sandy earth with grassy tufts growing out of them, part of the cliff top footpath that had fallen away.

She bent again to remove the other trainer; once more she felt a tremor and looked up. A small stream of sand, gravel and shells had started a downward fall towards her and she stared, immobilized with fright, as she saw the boulder shift, loosening the wedge of cliff above it.

'No!' she whispered. 'Oh, no!'

She had a confused feeling that the moment was frozen in time as she watched the boulder ease out of the hollow nest of clay where it had rested for perhaps thousands of years. She saw it roll steadily down the cliff, leaving behind it an empty cavity that was already beginning to fill with falling debris as the mass of clay above it began to disintegrate.

Fleetingly she thought of earthquakes in San Francisco and Mexico: collapsing buildings, people buried alive, causing suffocation as they breathed in the choking dust. She heard the resonance, like distant rumbling thunder, as the boulder gathered speed, and the sound of her own frantic cries as she crouched herself into a ball like a frightened animal and was sucked up by the amassing heap of solidified ooze, the moraine of glacial deposits, and flung down into blackness.

CHAPTER FORTY ONE

Somebody was hammering a wedge into Gilbert's head. Don't do that, he kept telling them. Stop it. But they wouldn't listen, and each time a blow was struck small splinters broke off and lodged painfully behind his eyes and temples.

He groaned and turned over to escape his assailant, but now they were trying another form of torture: machine-gun fire was being aimed at him. He could hear the sharp rattle of ammunition as it flew from its belt.

Wretched, he opened his eyes. The sun was bright behind the bedroom curtains, and he rolled over and tried to focus on the bedside clock. He groaned again. He felt rough, and he could still hear the rattle of the gun. What gun? He shook his head and listened. Somebody was throwing stones at the window.

He dragged himself out of bed and staggered towards the window. Dot was standing below, getting ready to aim another handful of gravel towards him. 'Are you ill? Do you know what time it is?'

He mouthed something back and pointed towards the back door, pulled on his dressing gown and tottered downstairs to unlatch the door. 'Oh,' he groaned. 'I feel lousy. I feel as if

I've been hit by a ten-ton truck.' He turned into the kitchen and sat down unsteadily. 'Mek us a pot o' tea, will you, love?'

'It's gone half past ten.' Dot filled the kettle. 'I've been hammering and hammering on 'door. I was getting worried. Where's Liz? It's a wonder she isn't up and doing!'

'I don't know. Is she still in bed?'

She shook her head. 'There's a cup and plate in the sink. Was the door bolted or was it just on 'latch?'

He gazed blankly at her. 'What do you mean?'

'When you opened 'door to let me in.' Patiently she spelled out her question. 'Did you unbolt it, or was it just latched?'

'I think it was just latched. Yes.' He remembered. 'It was.'

'You'd better get yourself back to bed. You're not fit to be up; you'll be no use to anybody as you are. Go on, I'll bring your tea and toast. Do you have any paracetamol?'

He nodded. 'Aye, somewhere.' He shivered. 'I feel rough. I bet I've got this from old Alf. He said he didn't feel well when he was in 'other night. He had whisky instead of ale.'

'It's probably this twenty-four hour flu that's going about.' Dot frowned. 'I wonder if anybody's seen him since then? That'd be Thursday, wouldn't it?'

'P'raps better phone him,' Gilbert said vaguely as he shuffled back to the stairs. 'See if he's all right. I wouldn't like to think he's feeling like this.'

She took up a tray of tea and toast and plumped up the pillows behind him. 'Take the paracetamol,' she instructed, 'and stay in bed. I'll phone Jack and ask him to come in. I can't manage 'bar and lunches on my own. I don't know where Liz is. She's not in her room, I've just looked.' The room was stuffy, and she opened the window. 'Are you warm enough?'

He gave a weak grin. 'Why? Are you going to climb in and keep me warm?'

'No I'm not. I don't want to catch whatever you've got,

thank you very much. Besides, I've got a pub to run whilst you lie there shamming!'

He gulped down his tea, but left the toast; his throat was too sore to eat it. 'It'd be a lot easier if you were living here,' he said, and slid down beneath the sheets, pulling them up to his chin. 'Have you made your mind up yet?'

The subject of marriage hadn't been mentioned again, but he was a patient man. He didn't want to press her.

'It'd be easier for you, you mean. You only want me to look after you cos you're feeling sorry for yourself,' she chided.

'Well, I'd look after you if you were poorly,' he said plaintively.

'I'm never poorly.' She patted the top of his head. 'We'll see. Rest now, and I'll pop up a bit later.'

Back in the kitchen she turned on the oven and then telephoned Jack, who said he would come in. She might as well be living here, she thought; it was like her second home. But she was getting anxious: it was late and she still had lunches to prepare. She cast around in her head, wondering who else she could ask to help out. Where *was* Liz? Her car was still there so she hadn't gone off to meet Chris. Not like her not to leave a note.

She washed her hands again and rinsed salad things and gave them a shake, then put them to one side. She took out a leg of pork and topside of beef from the larder, unwrapped them from their covering of muslin and adjusted the oven temperature; then she remembered Alf Wainwright, washed her hands again and went to the telephone. There was still no answer from the number she'd dialled and she rang the Raven number.

'Yep?'

'It's Dot Gowers here at 'Ship. Did Alf Wainwright come in last night?'

'Mm, no, I don't think he did; in fact, no he didn't when I

think about it. I didn't notice at the time, but it was a busy night.' Kevin Warner's voice sounded gravelly. 'I had a bit of a send-off. I'm leaving, you know.'

'Yes, I heard. All right. Thank you.' She hung up. 'Good riddance,' she muttered. 'You won't be missed. Now, what to do about Alf?'

Jack came in and attended to the bar and she continued preparing lunch, turning up the oven temperature a touch, mixing horseradish sauce and beating up batter for the Yorkshire puddings. Then she stopped, washed her hands again and rang Matt Wilson's number, but there was no reply. She opened the front door and looked out. It's like Dodge City, she thought. There's not a soul about. Where is everybody? Then she heard the sound of an engine labouring up the road.

'If I stop I shan't get it started again,' Matt called out to her as she signalled to him.

'Oh, stop the damned thing,' his wife said, opening the door of the Land Rover. 'I'll be glad to get out. I'll not come in it again until you get it fixed,' she warned him.

He shrugged and pulled a face, and then grinned at Dot, rammed grindingly into first gear and chugged off again.

'Wait!' Dot shouted after him. 'Can you help in the bar? Gilbert's poorly!'

He waved his hand, which she took to mean yes, then his exhaust backfired, and the two women jumped and laughed. 'I'll go and knock on Alf's door,' Gwen Wilson said when Dot had explained the situation. 'And I'll phone you and let you know when I get home again. Shan't be long.'

Feeling easier in her mind, Dot went back to preparing lunch, and was cooking quiches and arranging salads when the phone rang. 'Ship Inn,' she answered.

'Hi, Dot. It's Chris. Is Liz about?'

'No.' She was puzzled. 'I thought she must be with you.'

'We were going to Spurn Point today, only I've been held up. Will you tell her I'm leaving now?'

'I don't know where she is.'

'Doesn't Gilbert know?'

'He's ill in bed. Got flu, we think. He hasn't seen her at all this morning. I assumed she'd gone out early to meet you, but she can't have done as her car is still here.'

'It's nearly twelve o'clock. Where can she be?' There was a note of anxiety in his voice. 'Anyway, I'll come now. I'll be as quick as I can.'

The quiches were cooked and out of the oven, and in their place she put apple pies and gooseberry tarts. 'We're going to be late,' she intoned. 'We're not going to be ready. Liz, where are you?'

The telephone rang again. It was Gwen Wilson to tell her that they'd had to break the lock on Alf's door. They'd found him lying unconscious on the sofa and she'd called an ambulance.

'I'll stay with him until it comes,' Gwen said. 'Matt's on his way.'

CHAPTER FORTY TWO

Liz opened her eyes. Her vision was blurred and indistinct, but she saw before her a stark moonscape of deep ridges and smudgy purple and grey mud patches on what looked like a small mountain or large hill towering above her. I'm lying in a deep hole, she immediately thought. I seem to be in another world. How will I climb out?

Then she remembered some of what had happened. There had been an earthquake and she had been in the middle of it. *But I'm alive*, and the relief of it made her cry.

She was lying on her right side and couldn't move her right leg as it seemed to be trapped, but she managed to ease herself up on to her elbow and hip and with her left hand reached into a pocket, hoping there was a handkerchief. She winced as she moved and felt soreness across her chest, but found a handkerchief and tried to blow her nose to clear it, but it hurt when she did.

Carefully she felt her forehead, her temples, her chin and then the back of her head, which felt sticky with either mud or blood, she couldn't tell which, and there was a tender lump on her crown.

I think I'll live. I can't tell if anything's broken. The enormity of what had happened brought tears to her eyes. Maybe

I'm in shock. How can I get out? What do I do? She wondered how it was that she was in one piece, if indeed she was.

She could move her left leg even though it was covered in layers of sand and clumps of clay, and she pulled and jiggled it free and saw that her foot was bare and bleeding and wondered where her trainer was. Her right leg was completely hidden in a pod of dense clay, and although she tried to wiggle her toes and stretch her calf the leg was immovable and painful.

She looked down towards the sands and wondered how long she had been there and whether the tide was coming in or going out. There was a huge boulder resting on the sands and she vaguely remembered seeing one above her; she glanced around and up, and everywhere she saw scraggy hummocks and shallow craters, peaks and crests, as if some crazy potter had gone berserk. She lifted her head and gazed as far as she could along the top of the cliff, but it made her neck and shoulders hurt.

There'll be no one in their right senses walking along the path, she considered, except perhaps the fishermen. Did I see anyone when I came out? Where have I been? Nobody will see me down here; I'm completely hidden from view. Keep calm, don't get hysterical.

She tried to remember what she'd been doing and why she had come this way. Where was I going? Her view was restricted, but there seemed to have been a huge cliff fall and she was trapped in a secluded inlet which could not be seen from above. If she could stretch her neck over the craggy fall of clay next to her she ought to be able to see the distant high chalk cliffs of Flamborough Head, but she couldn't raise herself high enough, the pain when she tried being so sharp and intense.

The sea had pulled well back by now, leaving a bay of damp sand below her, and she estimated that she was about twenty feet up from the sands, but thought ruefully that it wouldn't have made any difference even if she'd been lower, as she was well and truly trapped beneath the debris of sand and clay. Except, of course, if I'm still here when the tide turns again, I'll be in trouble. But surely somebody will miss me before nightfall.

She looked at her watch. The glass was smashed, and it had stopped at nine twenty-eight. She didn't know how long she'd been unconscious. Not long, she thought, and looked up at the sky to try to estimate the time, but above her there was no sun and the sky was pale grey and she could only hazard a guess that the next tide would be early evening.

She leant back on her elbows. She was extremely uncomfortable. Her head ached and her ribs were sore; her trapped leg was cramped and her ankle was throbbing and she was cold. A raw wind was buffeting off the sea and blowing sharp, stinging sand into her face. Sand flies buzzed around her and irritably she brushed them away.

What a mess! What an idiot I am. I tell everyone to take care, that the cliffs are unstable, and fall into the trap myself. I wonder if anyone's missed me yet? She glanced again at her watch. The time hadn't changed.

Chris will be here soon; we were going to Spurn today. Wryly, she laughed. We were going to look at the seals. *That's* why I came down! I was watching a young seal and went down on to the sands and couldn't find my way back up. That must have been hours ago. I hope he comes looking for me. Dad might not have noticed that I'd gone out. Dot might, but it will be Chris who will wonder – will he go to the mill, to see if I'm there? Will he come to the edge of the cliff?

A doubt slipped into her mind. Will he think of looking along here? It's further than I normally go; I was following the seal . . .

In a sudden panic she sat up and yelled at the top of her voice. 'Help! Help!'

Out on the horizon a deep band of vivid blue sea lit up the grey sky and reflected a canopy of aquamarine; a paling gradation of the same shades was pushing towards the shore, a harlequin cloak edged with a fringe of white and gold.

From her position she saw its beauty and thought of the posters that the schoolchildren had painted and on her own banner the image of the child she had unwittingly superimposed into the cliffs. She was suddenly afraid; had she subconsciously divined her own destiny?

She thought then of how quickly the gentle waves could change into a defiant roaring monster, devouring with greed whatever was in its path. It could crash through sea defences, breach highways, disguise shifting sandbanks and sink unsuspecting fishermen out on a day's pleasure. We can't win, she thought. Not ever. Not with our tidal barriers or our sea defences, not even our wall, if we get it. It'll pay us back, somehow, with its terrible power. We can't possibly tame it and here I sit, stuck like a limpet and all because the sea wants this bit of land back.

Above her she saw white-breasted, brown-collared sand martins as they wheeled swift-winged, searching in vain for their shattered nests in the low cliffs; she could hear the faint bleat of sheep carried on the wind from the fields beyond the Tillington road and watched the clockwork motion of sanderlings following the lapping sea as they searched for insects uncovered by the waves.

As her eyes roamed she saw a dark head in the water. The seal. 'Oh,' she greeted it like an old friend. 'If only someone else would spot you and come to look.'

She shouted again. 'Help. Somebody! Help!'

Fear ran through her once more and she looked up at the top of the cliffs. If there should be another fall I won't stand a chance of coming through it a second time. I'll be buried. I don't want to die! Not yet; there's so much I haven't done. She raised her voice again and realized that instinctively she was shouting for Chris, and for her father. 'Dad,' she sobbed. 'Dad! Come and get me!'

She pressed her eyes tight to stop the hot tears flowing, then sniffed and gulped. 'Get a hold of yourself. Somebody will come.' She picked up a handful of clay and examined it. Grains of wet sand slipped through her fingers, skeletal remains of insects, plants and animals from a pre-glacial age, fragmented rocks carried from the Wolds during a melting of an ice age. Arctic shells and fossils embedded into the soft boulder clay of the ancient deep seabed.

Thoughtfully, she squeezed the ball of clay and a thin trickle of muddy water ran down her hand and wrist. She remembered when she was a child and played on the sands and built castles and dug dykes with her brother and children from the village. She thought of her mother and grandparents, and then she thought of Sarah. Strange, she mused. I haven't thought of her lately. Does that mean that I've been more content with my life than I was? She was always there when I needed her; when I was lonely as a child with conflicting observations about life. When Mum died. She came whenever there was a crisis in my life. *So where are you now, Sarah? I'm in a crisis now. Have you left me to get on with my life?*

She looked out to sea, to where Monkston once would have been; she stretched her thoughts, her mind and her perceptive senses out to the sunken village, to her long-dead ancestors, and there was no response to her plea, no unifying bond to comfort her, and she recognized, sadly, that Sarah had gone, leaving her to reality, making her face up to life without her.

'Help! Help!' she shouted again. 'Somebody!'

As she looked up she saw that the sky had brightened and heard the screech of gulls flying over the sea – and a soft whine coming from the top of the cliffs.

'Ben!' she breathed. 'Ben. Oh, good boy!'

A black head and the upturned tips of a pair of black ears were outlined against the skyline and she called to him. He barked at her and pawed the ground and a slither of sand rushed down. 'Oh, heavens!' She panicked. 'Go and fetch somebody!'

The dog looked down at her, barked again, and raced off along the cliff top. He looked down and then raced back to the same spot.

'I can't help you, Ben. You'll have to find your own way down.' She put her hand into her pocket for the handkerchief and she saw the tip of his tail wag. She delved deeper and found the biscuits she'd taken from the bag at the mill that morning.

'Come on, then. Come for a biscuit.' She held out her hand and his ears pricked up and he barked again.

'Come on, you mutt,' she shouted, shaking her hand in his direction; he barked again but didn't move. Then, suddenly, as if he'd made a decision, he raced away along the top of the cliff and, heart in her mouth, she watched him as he found a shallow drop on to a ledge and leapt down. It took him only seconds to jump the gullies and ridges to reach her and she cried again as he victoriously panted in front of her, then obediently sat on his haunches and waited for his reward.

She was comforted simply by his being there. She put her arm round his neck as he sat there and seemed content just to stay by her side. She talked to him of anything that came into her head, about the sea wall and the petition, about going to Westminster, about her job, and a decision she had just made, and about Carl and Jeannie and how sorry she was that they'd had to go away and leave him. She asked if he'd like to come and live with her and he licked her hand and then got up and stretched and began to move away, snuffling about on the rocks and moving further down towards the sands.

'Don't go,' she said, alarmed that he would go off and leave her, and she searched about as far as she could for something she could throw to keep him occupied.

She threw a pebble and he ran for it, then dropped it and started to dig, throwing up a hail of sand until he unearthed a piece of wood and brought it back to her. 'Good boy,' she said wearily. She felt desperately tired and ached all over, and she was cold. If only someone would come, but who? There're only the fishermen who come this far.

Ben barked volubly each time she threw the stick and she prayed that someone might hear him; she threw it until her arm ached, reaching out with each throw to try to reach the sands so that if anyone should be there they would see the dog and come to investigate.

Finally she threw it far enough and Ben chased after it, but instead of picking it up he disappeared round the corner of the outcrop out of her sight. She could hear him barking, and sobbed as the sound moved further away and finally stopped.

'Ben,' she shrieked, her voice hoarse and the wind rising, catching her shouts and tossing them away. 'Come back! Help, somebody. Help!' She put her head in her hands and wept.

CHAPTER FORTY THREE

'Somebody must know where she is.' Chris faced Dot over the bar counter. 'I said I'd be here at eleven, and was late, which was why I phoned. Sorry, Dot, but I'm worried. It's not like her, is it? Not to say where she was going?'

'No, it's not.' Dot looked harassed. 'She generally shouts out where she's off to, but I wasn't here and Gilbert was still in bed.' She frowned. 'She can't have been going far or she'd have left a note, and she must be in 'village or she'd have taken 'car, wouldn't she?' She puffed out a breath. 'What a morning. We had to call an ambulance for old Alf, I've been doing lunch on my own, Jack's been at 'bar, Matt said he'd come but he hasn't, and Gilbert's poorly in bed. And you're right. Liz must have been gone a couple of hours at least.'

'Right,' he said. 'I'm going to look for her. You don't think she's gone down on the sands, do you?' He turned round when he saw Dot's vexed expression and saw the object of her annoyance; a fisherman in orange oilskins and thigh boots with a fringe of mud on the soles was standing in the open doorway with a very sandy dog attached to a frayed rope with muddy paws on the doormat.

'Is Gilbert about?' the newcomer said. 'I'm sorry about 'mess.'

Dot shook her head. 'No, he's poorly in bed. That's Ben! What are you doing with him?'

'We've just found him. He was down on 'sands. That's why I've come. He was wi' Liz, Gilbert's lass. She's trapped on 'cliffs. At least she was; we've just dug her out.'

Chris turned to Dot as he heard her moan and saw the colour drain from her face. He thought she was going to faint, but she caught hold of the counter in time, and he too steadied himself with a hand on a bar stool as he scanned the man's face for tragedy.

'It's OK,' the man said hastily. 'She's all right, but I think she's in shock, and she's injured her leg. Can't move it, but it might just be stiff cos she's been trapped for a few hours, I reckon.'

Chris moved towards the telephone, but the fisherman stopped him. 'We've done all that. Coastguard's on his way. It was my mate who found her. He went to look at a seal that had been in 'water for ages and we wondered why, and then he saw 'dog who took him up to 'young lass. We shouted up to Matt Wilson's place and as luck would have it he was feeding 'chickens in his yard, and he phoned for 'coastguard.

'Do you want to come?' he asked Chris, who was halfway to the door. 'I'm going back to see what's happening. They might have to send for 'helicopter. There's no way we can get her up 'cliffs on our own. Can I leave 'dog wi' you, Dot? And if you'll tell her dad?'

'Stay here, Dot,' Chris said. 'I'll let you know what's happening as soon as I can, and I think Gilbert's best staying where he is; no use making himself worse.'

'Yes,' Dot said in a shaky voice, and he saw she was close to tears. 'I'll go and tell him.' She put down a bowl of water for Ben, who drank off half of it and laid himself down across the floor.

As they were leaving, Matt Wilson came through the door.

333

'Coastguard's arrived.' His cheeks were scarlet with hurrying. 'They're just assessing 'situation. I've come to give you a hand, Dot. I'm sorry I'm late, but to be honest I forgot! I don't think we'll have many customers, though; they'll all be down watching what's happening on 'cliffs.'

Leaving the fisherman trailing behind him Chris raced across the road to the old path where the police vehicles and an ambulance were parked. Waiting there were two ambulance men and a police officer, who moved to stop him as he ran up.

'It's my fiancée down there,' Chris told him, exaggerating slightly. 'I have to get down to her.'

'Go on, then,' the officer agreed. 'Continue on down here, and then along 'sands, but mind where you're going. Cliff's not stable,' he called after him as Chris set off.

It was worse than when they had come before; it looked as if the whole of the cliff had taken a battering. The fisherman caught up with him and they slithered and shuffled, and several times Chris felt as if he was going to fall, but eventually they reached the base of the cliffs and saw the coastguard's jeep parked on the sands below the inlet where Liz was lying, hidden by the three figures surrounding her. Chris could only see her stretched-out legs and felt sick at the thought that she might so easily have been killed; but just how badly was she hurt?

He climbed up towards her and was relieved to see she was sitting up with a blanket wrapped round her and her legs were free. She gave a trembling smile on seeing him and he knelt down and put his arms around her.

'Are you all right? Are you hurt?' He kissed her cheek and whispered, 'What a scare you've had! We've all had! I was so anxious when no one knew where you were and no one had seen you – at least, Dot hadn't seen you; your dad is still in bed. Dot says he has the flu.'

'No! I didn't know. I went out before he was up.'

'Are you hurt anywhere? The fisherman who came to tell us said you might have broken your leg.'

'I might have, but it's a bit easier now, though my ankle hurts and my ribs are sore. I was so scared, Chris. I was beginning to feel desperate. I thought I was going to become part of the landscape if there was another fall.'

Gently he put his arms round her again and she leant into him. 'If it hadn't been for Ben,' she began to cry in relief, 'and the seal . . .'

'The seal?' How could a seal have helped, he wondered, but didn't pursue it; she was probably in shock and it was kicking in.

She put out her hand to push her tangled hair from her eyes, and he saw how much it was shaking. 'Try to relax,' he said softly. 'You're quite safe now and you'll soon be out of here, once they've worked out the best way to do it.' He moved up and sat on the sandy rocks and clay next to her and put an arm round her shoulder. She leant against him and closed her eyes, and he kissed her cheek.

Two police officers were heading back in their direction across the sands; the coastguard was talking into his radio telephone and coming up the cliff towards them.

'I've been on with 'rescue services to explain what's happened,' he said, addressing Chris. 'I've told them that we can't stretcher her out of this terrain, and there's always a risk of another fall, so they're sending a helicopter; Sea King Search and Rescue, Helicopter Flight at Leconfield have been alerted and they'll be here in ten . . . fifteen minutes at 'outside.' He smiled at Liz. 'Not much longer, love, then you'll be out of here and tucked up in a warm bed.'

Steve Adams had just made himself a coffee and sat down in the operations room with the ragged morning paper, which had been chewed by the pilot's dog, when the call from the coastguard came through. He wrote precise details in the log book and turned to scan the large map that was pinned up on the wall to find Tillington on the Holderness east coast. The three other crew members were already running down the metal steps from their quarters into the hangar where one of the four yellow Sea King helicopters was about to be towed out on to the runway when Adams received permission to go from the regional control centre in Edinburgh.

The two pilots checked their dual instruments; the radar controller and Adams, on duty as winchman, strapped themselves into their seats, and the four rotor blades and the tail rotor began to spin.

The helicopter, like a noisy, angry wasp with extra aerodynamic power, lifted its great body off the ground and soared skywards, and then, crossing the northern edge of Beverley and the green fields of the East Riding, headed over the flatlands of the Holderness Plain to the sea.

Liz heard it before she saw it. She heard the droning buzz and then watched as its source grew bigger and then metamorphosed into a hovering golden metal bird.

'I'm scared.' She clutched Chris's hand.

'Don't be.' He had to shout to make himself heard above the ear-shattering racket. 'Most people would jump at the chance of having a ride in one of these.'

'Will they let you come with me?' she shouted back.

He shook his head. 'I doubt it. There won't be a lot of room.' He turned to one of the policemen. The coastguard had gone, as had one of the police cars, but they'd been told the ambulance was still there. 'Where do you think they'll take her?'

'Hull Infirmary. There's a landing pad there; she'll be there in ten minutes. No time at all.'

'I'll drive into Hull,' Chris told her. 'I'll be three quarters of an hour max, unless there's a lot of traffic. By the time they've got you settled I'll be there. Don't worry.'

The helicopter hung over the sea before oscillating over the narrow sandy beach. The door slid open and a figure looked out; they heard the crackle of muffled speech and the machine lifted higher and swung to the cliff top.

On the cliff path a police officer spoke into his radio telephone and motioned with his arm to the ambulance men. One of them gave him a thumbs-up sign, and the crew climbed into their vehicle and drove away. 'What's happening?' Chris asked the officer.

'They're going to winch her up. They can't land on the cliff top because it isn't stable, and although they could come down on the sands they've decided against it, so the winchman is coming down. He's coming down now, so we need to move away and give him room, and he'll take her back up.'

They both climbed carefully down on to the sands, while Liz watched in trepidation as the figure in the doorway of the helicopter suspended above her strapped himself into the bosun's chair and, with one hand easing out a fine wire cable and the other holding on to a bag, was lowered slowly down to her side.

'Hi, how you doing?' Steve Adams grinned at Liz reassuringly and bent down to run his fingers round her ankle and knee. He asked if he could feel her rib cage and then spoke into his mouthpiece. 'We shan't need the stretcher. Will use a splint and bring casualty up on rescue strop. Preparing casualty now; she's in good shape apart from possible broken foot or ankle and bruised or cracked ribs.'

He opened up his first aid box and brought out a roll of blue canvas, which he unrolled and placed beneath Liz's right leg and proceeded to wrap around it. 'This splint will support your leg as we winch you up,' he told her. 'Now I'm going to put this strop over your head, like so – that's it – and now under your arm. Right; and now I'm clipping you on to my strop – casualty ready for winching,' he reported, 'and away we go.'

Liz closed her eyes in fright for a moment as she felt herself lifted off the cliff and swung high into the air; then she felt the supporting arm of the winchman around her and opened them. Below her the sea crests surged and herring gulls flew low over the water. As she swung she saw the diminishing figures of Chris, the police officer and the two fishermen on the sands, and on the top of the cliff at the end of the old lane a police car and a small crowd of people, some of whom were waving.

The winch operator helped to bring her in through the door and she was laid on the floor of the helicopter. She heaved a great sigh and held back tears. 'Are you OK?' The winchman unclipped the strop and it was wound back into its casing.

She nodded. 'Thank you,' she choked. 'Thank you very much.'

The door was closed; one of the pilots looked over his shoulder and nodded to her, Steve Adams handed her a pair of earpads to wear, and with a great roaring the helicopter swung in a wide arc, its blades silver-sharp in the sunlight.

Liz sat up and leant on one elbow and gazed out of the bubble window in the door. The machine turned and hovered over the sea, and she looked and reflected on the imperishable grandeur of the watery wastes below. Humbly she paid honour to its greatness, its power and supremacy, but as they swung over the crumbling cliffs and turned towards the city of Hull, she smiled grimly. Just because you're bigger than we are, she thought, it doesn't mean you can *always* win.

CHAPTER FORTY FOUR

Liz felt safe and comfortable in a single hospital room but longed to be at home. She was told she would stay there for at least three days. Her right foot had broken bones and needed an X-ray and probably a cast; she also had cuts and bruises over most of her body. Fortunately, most of these were superficial, as when the cliff began to slide she had intuitively wrapped her arms about her ears and head and bent low, curling herself up for protection; she was, however, kept in bed so she could be monitored to ascertain that she wasn't in shock or traumatized.

'Which you probably are,' Chris said, holding her hand as he sat by her bed on the first night.

She agreed with him; she was shaking. 'I felt so trapped, not being able to move my legs from under the clay, and I was scared too of the tide reaching me. It wouldn't have, I don't think; I was probably high enough, but it was just the thought of it. I was getting so cold, too.' She was warm now, a blanket round her shoulders and an electric blanket beneath her.

'Your father's coming to see you tomorrow. Dot wouldn't let him get out of bed today, not until he was feeling better; she told him he wouldn't be allowed in the hospital in any case.'

'Poor Dad.'

'I think I'm going to have to marry you as soon as possible,' he said earnestly, but with a twitch of his lips. 'You can't be trusted to be let out on your own.'

'I've managed until now,' she mumbled. 'You're trying to catch me whilst I'm vulnerable.'

'Dot said I should.'

'Dot said? She's one to talk!' Her words slurred.

He shrugged. 'She told me that she couldn't live at the Ship.'

'Really?' Liz slid down beneath the sheets. 'Cos of Mum having lived there, I suppose. I'll have to think about that. Maybe I'll have a think about that,' she repeated.

'And will you think about marrying me too?' He bent and kissed her forehead; he could see she was fighting to keep awake.

She smiled and slurred, 'You shouldn't ask me while I'm under 'fluence of drugs. Did you see the helicopter?'

She closed her eyes and he got up and kissed her again. 'You know I love you,' he murmured, but she was asleep.

Her father came to visit her the following afternoon; Dot insisted he wore a mask when he went into her hospital room and told him he shouldn't give her a kiss in case he was still infectious. Liz began to cry when she saw him and put her arms out to him.

'Dot said I hadn't to kiss you,' he said, his eyes filling with tears.

'You old softie,' she snuffled. 'We can have a hug, can't we, and swear not to tell her?'

'Yes, I think so. We've got to have some secrets, haven't we? But now, then, how did you get into such a pickle? It's not like you to take risks!'

'I know,' she said, shame-faced. 'It was the seal – it was only a young one and it seemed to be watching me, so I took a chance and went down to see it closer to. Then I felt the cliff shudder as I climbed back up; it was a bit like an earthquake, not that I've ever been in one, but how I imagine it would feel. And it was so sudden, too; I somehow expected it to be a slow slide but it wasn't, it came down quite fast. Dad, how long do you think it would have taken for Monkston to disappear under the sea?'

He shook his head at her; this was how she used to be when she was young, constantly asking questions when really there was no answer to give her.

'Years,' he said, 'decades, bit by bit.' He pondered. 'A century or more. You'd wonder, wouldn't you, what it looked like, the terrain, I mean. There was no mill in Monkston so I'd guess it was probably quite flat, or hummocky, and mebbe that's why our mill was built in Tillington on 'highest bit of land, behind 'church. It must have been a piece of private land, mebbe a smallholding; or mebbe 'present house was originally a cottage for 'miller and his family.'

She nodded. 'That's what I've been thinking,' she murmured. 'It wouldn't have been church land, because that wouldn't have been sold for building a mill, would it?'

'Why are you asking?'

'I don't know; mebbe because I'm lying here thinking of the cliffs and wondering what we should do about the house and the mill.'

Her father gave her an anxious glance. 'Don't—'

'It's all right,' she said, 'I'm not going doolally, I'm just interested. You've heard of Ravenserodd, haven't you?'

'Aye, course I have; we were taught about it at school. It's part of our history. Ravenserodd was a proper town with farms and businesses and even MPs in Parliament, and massive storms washed it all away.'

'Built on sand,' Liz commented. 'I was going to take Chris down to Spurn Point and tell him about it; he hadn't heard of Ravenserodd.'

'Well, no, he wouldn't have. Practically forgotten about, even out here in Holderness.'

'We could use it in our publicity, couldn't we?'

He shook his head at her and sighed. 'Just get yourself better first, will you, and then we'll start thinking of 'campaign? You've been on 'TV news and 'radio, by the way. That'll be publicity enough for now.'

'I'm not ill, Dad,' she said. 'Just a bit battered and bruised. So have you given any thought as to whether we can save any of the mill house or the mill?'

'I've given thought to nowt else,' he said bitterly, 'but I'm not going to discuss it now. And you do realize that 'fire assessors have 'first say on what happens, especially if it's ruled to be arson, which we know it was. Has Chris said if there was a note from Carl?' he went on. 'He'd intended to top himself, hadn't he?'

Liz wriggled uncomfortably. 'I, erm, don't remember, or at least I can't recall. I don't *think* Chris said, or I would remember, wouldn't I?'

'Aye, you'd think so.' He sighed. 'Well, at least he was saved; if Chris hadn't gone in when he did Carl would have been a goner, and everybody in 'village would have wondered if they'd done enough to help 'lad out.'

'Dad, he's a grown man, a lot older than me, not a lad at all. Old enough to ask for help if he'd wanted it; and he was offered it often enough.'

'I know,' Gilbert said reluctantly. 'It's just sad.'

'It is,' she agreed. 'But he might get help now, if he'll accept it.' She patted his hand comfortingly. 'Now, then, what's this about you and Dot?'

'Well, I've said I'd give up 'Ship if she can't live in it, and I'd buy a boat and we can sail round 'world if she'd like to, but I rather think she's had second thoughts. About 'boat, not about me!'

'Take her on a cruise first and see if she likes being on the water. We – that is, Chris and I—'

'Oh? You and Chris? What? Has he, erm, proposed, then?'

'It's not the same as it used to be, Dad,' she smiled, 'but we have an understanding!'

He shook his head and sighed. 'There's no romance in 'world any more, more's the pity. I was hoping I'd be able to walk my only daughter down 'church aisle.'

'Well, you still might, but let's get you and Dot spliced first, and then there's Bill and Nadia – lots going on, or will be, as well as the campaign, which we'll continue just as soon as we've counted up the votes of support and made our way to Westminster!'

Jack was setting up ready for the evening customers when Gilbert came back from visiting Liz. 'Thanks, Jack,' he said. 'I really appreciate what you've done while I've been laid up. We've had a rough time this last week, what wi' fire at 'mill and then Liz falling down 'cliff. We couldn't have managed without you; Dot's been a great help too but she couldn't have done it on her own.'

'Oh, I love it,' Jack said cheerfully. 'I really do; I like 'atmosphere, and chatting to folks. I'd like a place like this of my own, but I've no money for such ambitions, and I don't think 'missus would care for it. Not to live in, you know.'

'Well, you're 'right sort of person to run a pub; friendly, without letting folk get out of hand. Not that we have many troublemakers in here. Anyway, I'll just go and change and be with you in ten, fifteen minutes, after I've had a cup o' tea and a sandwich.'

'Tek your time, Gilbert. There won't be many folk in yet.'

Gilbert went into the kitchen, where Dot was making him a sandwich and boiling the kettle. 'How is she?' she asked. 'Has she got over 'shock?'

'Not yet, I don't think. She'll need some time off work, especially if they fit her with a plaster cast on her leg; don't know if they still do that. I'd better phone Steve Black. He'll wonder what's going on.'

He sat down on one of the chairs, slipped off his shoes and sat thinking.

'Penny for 'em?' Dot put a plate of sandwiches and a pot of tea on a tray and passed it to him.

'Oh, just thinking about stuff that's piling up; what to do about 'mill house and 'mill, for one thing, though it won't be my problem come 'end of 'year. Bill won't want it, though he'll want recompense for it. I think Liz might still want it; Chris was asking what I was thinking of doing with it. He thinks it would rebuild. And I've had another thought about you and me.'

'What!' She glared at him, and he laughed.

'I don't mean that like it sounds. I'm thinking of alternatives. You don't really want to live on a boat, do you?'

She folded her arms across her chest. 'I wouldn't mind going on a cruise for a couple of weeks, but I don't really . . .' She sighed and looked at him. 'I like my own stuff around me; you know, my own furniture and ornaments and suchlike.'

He nodded and took a sip of tea. 'I know,' he said. 'And I've had an idea.' He looked about him. There was little of what Nina had left behind; she wasn't one for wanting new furniture or curtains. She liked a picture or two, but he thought that Liz would take those if she ever did move out. But something else was niggling away: he was ready for a break, and he'd like to visit Australia to see Bill. He thought that perhaps the idea he had had just might resolve it.

CHAPTER FORTY FIVE

Liz came home from hospital on the third day and was told not to walk or put weight on her foot or leg; she was given another appointment for the following week, and told she would probably be fitted with a boot. Finally, she was given a warning not to go back to work just yet. She phoned Steve once she was home to tell him.

'What an idiot!' he said. 'You could've been killed.'

'I didn't expect any sympathy,' she responded, 'but you might at least ask how I am!'

'I'm coming to that,' he said. 'That's just not like you. What happened?'

She decided not to tell him about following the seal – he wouldn't have understood what she was talking about – but told him how quickly the cliff had come down and trapped her.

He whistled. 'Your father must have been frantic with worry. And that fellow you're seeing – is he still around?'

'Dad was ill in bed,' she said. 'He thought I'd just gone out; it wasn't until Chris phoned that anyone realized I was actually missing. How are you getting on with Susan?' she asked, changing the subject. 'Is she managing all right? I imagine she will be.'

'Yeah, she's good. Very efficient. Not as good-looking as you, but I expect—'

'Steve!' she warned. 'Have you not been listening? She'll leave if you try anything, I can tell you that for sure.'

He laughed. 'I'm winding you up, Liz. I've been very good. Turned over a new leaf! Listen, I'm guessing that I won't get any money back from that— well, I won't mention what I think of Reedbarrow; he's got troubles enough. He'll go to jail for sure, and I don't suppose he's got any of the money left in any case!'

'I'm sure he hasn't,' Liz interrupted, knowing where he was going next, 'but if you were thinking of making an offer for the land it's not for sale. We're waiting for assessors and solicitors and suchlike in any case, and I'm thinking that I might rebuild the house for myself; it depends,' she added. 'It's my brother's too.'

'Well, good luck with that,' he said cynically. 'Family matters don't always work out.'

'I know,' she said in a conciliatory tone, 'but what I really rang to say was if you'd like me to type up any letters or answer any telephone queries, I'll be glad to do that. I've only been told to rest for a while until I'm over the effects of shock.'

'Oh, I guess we'll manage, Liz. You look after yourself, and we'll speak again soon.'

They both hung up and she blew out a breath; she was glad that he didn't want her to hurry back. *I can plan the campaign; we'll make a huge effort and hope that Westminster will understand our predicament.* She punched a fat cushion into shape, and easing off her slippers she curled up on the sofa and fell asleep.

Gilbert rang Jack just after midday. The Ship was closed until six o'clock. Gilbert chose his own hours after the last Licensing

Act, and the village was quiet on a weekday except in the holiday season.

'Can you pop over for half an hour or so, Jack? There's something I'd like to run past you.'

'Erm, yeh. I'm just having a bit of lunch. Half-hour all right?'

'Perfect. Thanks,' Gilbert said, 'see you in a bit.' He looked through to the living room where Liz was fast asleep, and went in to pick up the wool blanket that hung over another chair and carefully place it over her. She sighed, but didn't wake as he closed the door behind him and went into the bar to wait for Jack.

'Nowt wrong, is there?' Jack asked when he came in.

'No, nothing at all. I want to make a suggestion, if you're interested. Let's go through and sit down.' Gilbert led the way to the smaller room, away from the bar and the door, where there were some comfy chairs. 'You said 'other day that you enjoyed working at 'Ship and wished you had something like it to run.'

'Aye, I did,' Jack answered. 'I would if I had 'money for it.'

'Well, I was wondering if you'd like to come into 'Ship as manager? I'm not anywhere near retiring age, but I'd like to take some time off now and again; not just an extra week or so for a trip to Scarborough or somewhere, but for a bit longer. My lad Bill is in Australia as you know, and intends staying there; he's met an Aussie girl and mebbe they'll be getting married soon.'

'Ah, so you want somebody to cover for you if you go? I'll allus be glad to do that, Gilbert. Any time.'

'Not only to cover for me, Jack, but to come in as manager. I'd show you how to run it, how to order from 'brewery, settle bills and that – there's quite a lot to do and it's got to be done right or 'brewery'll be on your heels. I'll pay you a manager's wage, and if you do well we can talk about shares in 'business after a bit, if you'd like.

'The downside is that you'd have to live in whilst I'm away; 'Ship can't be left empty at night. You said you didn't think your missus would like to be in the business, but she wouldn't have to be – she can do whatever she does now and we can rustle up somebody else to cover for you if need be. Ted's always reliable, he'd come in, I'm certain. And if you're going to be too busy at say Bank Holidays and such we'll have to find somebody else to do 'lunches. But I need somebody to be in charge overall. Would you like to think about it?'

'Well, she's a proper home bird is my wife,' Jack told him in a confidential manner. 'She goes to women's meetings and that, village stuff, you know, and we sometimes take a week's holiday in Bridlington. She's not bothered about holidays abroad, but she does like a change of scenery and she'd know 'folks who come into 'Ship. And another thing – she's right sharp wi' money; she could keep 'books better than I can.' He blew out a breath. 'By, that's took 'wind out of my sails all right, but it's a great opportunity, Gilbert. I'll talk to 'wife, but yes, I'm very keen. It'd be a step up for me to work full time here at 'Ship instead of 'odd jobs I'm doing now. Manager, eh? Aye, a right step up.'

They celebrated the deal over a pot of coffee, even though Jack hadn't yet talked it over with his wife, and they discussed various concerns about running the Ship, until Jack said, 'What about Dot, then, Gilbert? Is she stopping or not? Don't want to be nosy, but you keep saying "we".'

'I do, don't I?' Gilbert said, and grinned. 'But keep it under your hat for now, Jack. That's still under discussion.'

Jack lifted his thumb. 'Women, eh? Your secret's safe wi' me!'

*

After Jack had left, Gilbert went back into the sitting room, where he'd heard Liz moving about. 'Shouldn't you be resting your foot?' he asked.

'I have been resting it,' she said. 'But I have to keep moving as well, but not bear any weight. Not quite sure how I'll manage that. What are you up to, then? I've been planning the campaign and I'm about to draft some letters for support. Was that Jack I heard earlier?'

'Yes, it was. I'm just popping down to see Dot,' he said. 'A couple of things I want to ask her.'

'Oh, yes?' She lifted her gaze from the notepad on her knee. 'What sort of things?'

He raised his eyebrows at her, but didn't answer.

'Nice things? Don't make her cry.'

'I *never* make Dot cry,' he protested. 'Though I might have done in the past.'

'Heartbreaker,' she said casually, looking down at her notes again, and he saw that she was trying to hide a smile.

'I won't be long.' He headed for the door.

'Don't rush!' she murmured, not looking at him. 'Take your time.'

Women, he murmured beneath his breath. How is it they can read your mind? You don't have to say a single word but they know what you're thinking!

He rapped on Dot's door with the metal knocker shaped like a mermaid and waited. He heard her footsteps in the small hall, then the key turn and the safety chain rattle.

'What 'you doing here at this time o' day?' she greeted him.

'Are you expecting burglars or somebody, wi' your lock and chain on during daylight hours?'

This is how we are with each other, this banter. He stepped into the small hall. It's hiding something that we both want to say, and yet somehow can't say it; because we're of the age when between men and womenfolk the man has to take the leading role and the woman has to wait. It's how we were brought up, how our parents did things, and they laid out the pattern for us to follow. But I'll do as I like, he decided. I'm halfway through life; I'm not waiting any longer.

She opened the door to her living room. 'Tea?' she asked. 'Coffee?'

'No, ta, not just now. Mebbe in a bit. I've got summat to say.'

He looked round the room. If he tried to go down on one knee he'd never get up again without making a fool of himself. So he held out his hand, and with a question on her face she took hold of it. 'What?' she said, a little frown between her eyebrows.

He gently stroked her hand with his thumb. 'Dorothy,' he said, 'I've waited a lot o' years, some might say wasted them, though that's not strictly true, but there comes a time o' reckoning and making up, and I've come now specially, belatedly, to ask you to marry me; to be my lawful wedded wife and I your lawful wedded husband.'

She blinked and gazed at him, her lips slightly apart. She thought of being flippant; saying something about a sink full of dirty dishes, but no; not this time. This was what she had been waiting for for years, always thinking that it would never come and if it did she would say no, because Nina would come between them. But poor Nina was no longer here and Dot wouldn't be stepping into her shoes, because they were different people who had happened to love the same man.

Her eyes were moist as she reached up to kiss him. 'Yes,' she breathed. 'Yes, please, my darling Gilbert, I will.'

Tears gathered and fell and mingled as he gathered her into his arms and held her close. 'I've always loved you, Dot,' he murmured, kissing her cheek. 'There's allus been a place in my heart for you. Now I'll be able to show it.'

'What can I say?' she whispered. 'I've waited a long time to hear those words and they're sweeter than I ever imagined.'

They stepped apart. 'How shall we celebrate?' he said.

'I'll put 'kettle on, shall I?' She wiped away the wet tears on his cheeks with tender fingers and then her own, and they melded moistly on her warm skin. 'They say there's nothing like hot sweet tea after a shock.'

CHAPTER FORTY SIX

Liz looked up from her notes to the old clock on the wall. She had heard the murmur of voices, not her father's or Dot's, but Jack's and she thought Chris's too. She hoisted herself up, reaching for the stick she'd brought home from the hospital, and went into the kitchen to look through the hatch into the bar.

It was Chris, and he caught sight of her and smiled. 'I looked in and you seemed busy,' he said. 'I didn't want to disturb you. How are you today?'

'Rather stiff, but not bad. You?'

He nodded. 'I was just asking Jack if he wanted any help; your dad doesn't seem to be about.'

'No, he said he was slipping out. I don't suppose he'll be long. I've been making notes for the campaign, making use of my time as I can't go to work for a while. I've a few ideas I'd like to run past you.'

'OK. Shall I come through?'

'Of course.'

He came into the sitting room and put his arms around her. 'I've missed you,' he murmured. 'Lost without you.'

She smiled. 'How much?'

'How much what?'

'How much have you missed me?'

He stretched his arms wide. 'This much,' he grinned, 'even further if my arms were longer.'

They both listened as they heard the back door open. 'Dad,' she whispered. 'He's been to see Dot,' and then, alerted, she murmured, 'I think she's with him.'

Chris's eyebrows rose. 'And?'

She grabbed her stick. 'Don't know. Have you eaten?' she asked in a louder voice. 'I'm starving.'

The door opened and her father came in, followed by Dot, who stood beside him, their fingers touching.

'Ah!' Gilbert said. 'Chris, I wondered if you'd be here.'

He looked down at Dot, who nodded and looked at Liz. 'Should you be standing?' she asked.

Liz leant ostentatiously on her stick. 'I'm not putting any weight on my leg.'

Dot gave Gilbert a nudge with her elbow, and he cleared his throat. 'We've got some— something to say, me and Dot, I mean.'

Liz began to smile, and her eyes became moist; Chris looked from one to another. 'Shall I go and give Jack a hand?'

'No!' Dot said. 'No, stay. Go on, Gilbert. Get on with it!'

Gilbert cleared his throat again. 'I've asked Dot – Dorothy – to marry me and she said yes!'

Liz dropped the stick and held both arms up high. 'Oh, at last!' she shrieked, and exhaled. 'You'll have to come to me for a hug, Dot.'

Chris put out his hand to Gilbert's and they shook vigorously. 'Congratulations!' Chris said. 'That's wonderful news.'

'It is, isn't it?' Gilbert grinned. 'I don't know why I waited so long. It's a lonely sort of life for a man on his own.' He glanced at Dot, who was embracing Liz and raised her eyebrows at him over his daughter's shoulder, shaking her head. 'And for women too,' he added hastily.

'So this sounds like a great excuse for a celebration,' Chris added, before Liz interrupted.

'So, Dot, are you moving in with us straight away or are you following convention and waiting until you and Dad are married?'

'Don't know.' Dot laughed. 'We're going to have to decide what's best, but I'd like to get married in Tillington church. I don't have to be given away, but I'd like my stepdaughter to walk by my side.'

'I'd love to, Dot.' Liz put her fist to her nose, feeling suddenly emotional, tearful because of thoughts and memories of her mother, yet joyful for her father, and for Dot, whom she had loved as long as she had known her.

Chris silently watched and listened, not quite part of this family but hoping that one day he would be, although he must tread carefully with Liz. He had learnt that already, knowing now that she was sensitive, otherworldly and yet, strangely, very much of her time. I can wait, he considered. There's no rush, and I rather feel that things are falling into place.

His feeling was justified, not because of what had just happened but something else he had heard of only today; a possibility of an opportunity had been mentioned, and it was what he had come up to Tillington to discuss.

'Can I give you a hand with anything?' he asked Gilbert, whilst Dot put her apron on and went into the kitchen to speak to Jack. Gilbert sat down next to Liz and she reached over to give him a kiss on the cheek and he drew her towards him.

'Maybe later, thanks, Chris,' he said. 'Jack'll be all right on his own for now.' He turned to Liz. 'I'm making some changes,' he said. 'I've been thinking about it for a bit. I've asked Jack if he'll tek on 'role of 'permanent manager. He's thrilled to bits, but I've yet to find out if his wife approves.'

'She will, Dad,' Liz enthused. 'She'll like the prestige, and she's a good cook. She was the cook when I was at primary school; I remember her sponge puddings! Oh, how brilliant; it'll mean that you and Dot can take more time off.'

'Aye, that's what I thought, and she and Jack could live in if we want to go to Australia to see our Bill. That's a must,' he added, glancing at Chris. 'We can't leave 'Ship unattended.'

'Of course,' Chris agreed, feeling more and more positive that things were moving in the right direction. He just needed to talk to Liz about that opportunity.

Liz clapped her hands excitedly. 'So when will there be a wedding?' she asked her father.

'You'll have to ask Dot,' he grinned. 'She's in charge. Aren't they always?' He turned to Chris, who lifted his hands in denial and shook his head, catching Liz's eye.

Gilbert went into the kitchen to join Dot, and through the doorway Liz saw him lean over and give her a kiss on her cheek. 'I'm so happy,' she said softly. 'Dad's waited so long, trying to find the right moment.'

'I know how he feels,' Chris murmured. 'When is the right moment?'

'For us?' she questioned. 'Soon, I think. You know that I love you, don't you?'

He closed his eyes, holding his head back and giving a big sigh. 'No, I didn't know, not for sure. When did you know? Why didn't you say?'

'Because of my mum and dad,' she said. 'Loving someone and marrying them doesn't always work out. I'm sure they fell in love, but they weren't right for each other in marriage. Whereas Dad and Dot are made for each other.'

He laughed and put his arms round her. 'So you are a romantic after all!'

'Don't know about that, but what I do know is that when I was stuck on the cliff I thought of you constantly, and I some-how knew you'd be looking for me.'

'I would have found you,' he said. 'I'd only just arrived and was about to come down to the sands to search for you. The fishermen found you first.'

She shook her head. 'It was Ben who found me first and went to tell the fishermen. I think we should adopt him.'

'A fisherman?' His eyes grew wide.

'No.' She kissed him. 'Ben; he needs a new home.'

'I haven't got a home to offer him at the moment, but I'm working on it, and I think that maybe a temporary one might be coming vacant.'

'Oh?'

'Mustn't count my chickens,' he grinned, 'but a colleague alerted me that a primary school out here in Holderness is looking for a new head teacher as the present one is about to retire.'

'Oh! How wondrous that would be,' she gasped. 'And have you got the necessary, erm, qualifications for a head teacher?'

'I have, absolutely. Doing cabinet-making was my favourite hobby when I was young, but later I decided to add another string to my bow and did technology because I liked it. I already had English and Science as my first degree – I was a bit of a swot, I admit – and I took a postgrad course in psychology and education. And of course I have my teacher's qualification.'

'Heavens,' she said. 'Might they think you're over-qualified?'

'Don't think so; and they'll be pleased when I tell them I live here.'

'But you don't yet!'

'Well, I will be doing if Dot sells me her house when she comes to live here at the Ship. Think how thrilled she'll be: no estate agent fees to pay.'

'Yes.' Her eyes gazed out into oblivion as other matters came to mind. 'It's only a small house,' she whispered.

'I haven't asked her yet,' he murmured. 'She might prefer to let it for the time being.'

'Yes, of course,' Liz said vaguely.

'What?'

She shook her head. 'I don't know yet.'

CHAPTER FORTY SEVEN

So much to plan and do. First of all, wedding arrangements to be made; everyone agreed with Dot that early October would be a good month to be married, and it wasn't too far away. The weather was promising to be mild and the lane up to the church would still be golden with foliage not yet fallen from the horse chestnut trees.

A honeymoon touring the North Yorkshire Moors, perhaps staying in Whitby or Ravenscar. Almost on their doorstep, but never visited before.

Then we'll be able to have Christmas at home, Dot had said, and make preparations for our trip to Australia, travelling to that faraway country towards the end of April and returning at the end of May, which apparently was the best time to be there before becoming too hot. But what about Bill? Would he be able to come home for the wedding? It would depend on where in the world he might be.

In the meantime, bit by bit Dot moved her belongings from her house to the Ship, Gilbert bringing over her favourite pieces of furniture and Liz surreptitiously removing her mother's choice of paintings from the walls and asking Chris to climb the ladder into the loft to store them away until such time as they could be put on some other wall.

'And perhaps, Chris,' Dot said slowly and meaningfully, 'you'd like to stay in my house whilst we're away and see how you like living in Tillington?'

'I would love to live in your house, Dot, and Tillington is where I want to be,' he said with a grin. 'People I care for live here. Perhaps,' he added boldly, 'you might even like to sell your house to me?'

She nodded solemnly and tapped the side of her nose. 'Perhaps I might,' she agreed. 'I know someone who works at an estate agency; she'd strike a good bargain for us both, I'm sure!'

Chris, after two interviews regarding the headship, was waiting hopefully for another call; he had already cancelled the tenancy of the Hull flat even though there was another contender for the position. He would move out of Hull and live in Tillington whether he was given the headship or not, and simply reverse his daily drive into and out of Hull.

'If you're moving into Dot's house, we'll be able to travel into Hull together if you don't get the job,' Liz suggested. 'Though I really hope that you do. I'm going back to work next week; the doc says I can.'

'Then I'll drive us both to begin with,' Chris suggested. 'And we'll be able to talk.'

'What shall we talk about?' she said cautiously.

'Us,' he said. 'What else?'

Whilst Liz had been convalescing and still wearing the surgical boot, Dot had driven them into Hull to look at wedding attire, and later Gilbert drove them to the railway station to catch a train to Leeds, where they enjoyed a great day touring the clothes shops together; not something Liz had ever done with her mother, who had died before Liz had become interested in fashion. Dot had never had the good fortune to have a daughter, but now took great joy in the fact that Liz was about to become her stepdaughter.

'Dot has bought a silk dress and coat in a lovely shade of lavender,' Liz told Chris when her father was out of hearing. 'It suits her silvering hair and the sweetest smartest veiled hat you have ever seen. I chose—'

'Don't tell me,' Chris interrupted. 'I'll wait for the wedding day.'

Gilbert phoned Bill to tell him the news and asked if he could come over, but Bill said no, neither he nor Nadia could, as he'd promised Nadia's father that he'd give them a hand on the farm, and besides, hadn't Gilbert said they were thinking of coming over to Australia in the English spring? He and Nadia were planning their own autumn wedding to coincide with that. Gilbert didn't try to persuade him. Life was complicated enough, and Bill said they'd already spoken to the vicar.

Gilbert had asked an old school friend to be his best man and Chris if he would be an usher, which delighted and touched Chris, who felt honoured by the implication that he was now a close family friend. 'By the way,' Gilbert said over lunch one Sunday. 'I've booked 'Beverley Arms for our reception, and Dot and I will drive off from there up to North Yorkshire on 'following day.'

'Isn't that a bit extravagant?' Dot commented. 'Or are you better off than I thought you were?'

Gilbert put his chin up. 'Never you mind, missus,' he said. 'Nowt's too good for my wife-to-be. She's waited a long time for this.'

Dot turned her head and raised her eyebrows at Liz, who was listening in and could see the glint in her eyes. 'Well, I never,' she said. 'You mean we'll stay overnight?'

'Course we will. We can't have 'reception here at 'Ship, now can we?' he said, with a sideways glance at Liz. 'We'd have all of 'village here and us serving 'em. No, it's all arranged wi' Jack and his wife and they're going to stop here while we're away. It's onny a week and a bit, isn't it? It'll be good practice for them for when we go to Australia. I wish you were coming with us, Liz,' he added. 'Well, all of us, really.'

'You mean to Australia?' she said mischievously. 'Surely not on your honeymoon! I want to finish off the details of the Save our Village campaign once your wedding is over, do another push for supporters and send the list to Downing Street. And whilst you're away I'll be here for Jack and his wife for their first time. Even though I'll be back at the office, they can be in touch. I know where everything is.'

Chris telephoned from the flat that evening and said in a matter-of-fact voice, 'Will you tell Dot I'd definitely like to buy her house?' He heard the squeal coming from Liz at the other end of the line.

'You got it? You got the headship? Oh, how wonderful. When?'

'I begin after the autumn half term, so the beginning of November, which will be perfect!' He sounded so buoyant. 'I can move into Dot's house as she moves out. Incredible!'

He blew out a breath. He had already sorted out books and paperwork that needed to be packed into boxes where he could easily get at them. His furniture was still in store and would stay there for the foreseeable future, but whilst he was still in Hull there was another issue he wanted to look into. He looked at his watch. Too late tonight, but tomorrow morning probably, if his call was accepted. The next morning he picked up his phone.

'I'm sorry, we don't have anyone of that name here.' The voice was abrupt.

'Might I leave my name and telephone number in case she shows up? She might have changed her name? I'm sure if she knew I'd called she would ring me back.'

The call ended. He looked at the time again. He'd have to go. He had given prior warning that he might be leaving his position at college, but he needed to confirm.

He was shrugging into his coat as his phone rang. An unknown number. He gave his name.

'What do you want?' Jeannie asked from the other end, and he half laughed and shook his head. Nobody hearing her now would ever think that anyone could best her, but Reedbarrow had. Would he still be able to, if he were given the chance?

'Let's take a walk,' Chris said to Liz on the Tuesday evening, four days before the wedding. 'Let's leave the betrothed pair to talk.'

'I think they're all talked out,' Liz said, reaching for her jacket. She was now walking without the boot. 'I'm taking Friday off work to make sure the flowers will arrive on time on Saturday morning, and that Dad knows where his notes are for his speech. I'll drive Dot up to Hornsea to the hairdresser and to have her nails done to match her dress, and then, well, that's about it really. Dot's staying at her house on Friday night and I said I'd stay with her, and Jack's wife is going to come in and help button us up on Saturday morning. Dad will walk up to church with his best man and then Dot and I will follow.'

'Walking?'

'Yes; that's what Dot wants. She doesn't want any kind of fuss, says she doesn't need a car for such a short distance. The weather's going to be fine, according to the forecast, but if it isn't, would you drive us up the lane? We've booked wedding cars to take us to Beverley after the church ceremony and ordered taxis to bring us back. Somebody's going to drive

Dad's car and leave it in the car park for them ready for the next day.'

'Very organized.' He smiled. 'I wonder who's arranged all that?'

'Can't imagine.' She laughed. 'Not Dad or Dot, that's for sure.'

'Can I walk up with you? One on each arm, or will I be the only usher?'

Liz laughed out loud. 'Dad's asked Alf Wainwright if he'll stand at the door and tell people where to sit. "Bride or groom," he's going to say! So, yes please, you won't be on duty and neither Dot nor I are used to walking in heels. We'll be glad of an arm up to the church door.'

'Brilliant!' Chris said. 'That's just the way a country wedding should be.'

Inevitably, they were walking towards the mill and the mill house. As they approached the gate, Ben appeared out of his kennel, looking hopeful. 'Here, boy,' Liz called to him, and wagging his rear end furiously he galloped towards them.

'I thought Jeannie might have wanted him,' Liz murmured.

'She's looking after number one at the minute, and quite right too.'

Liz looked up at him. 'How do you know?'

'I've spoken to her. On the phone. She's still at the women's hostel, says she's helping out.'

Liz paused. 'So why did you phone her?'

'I wasn't going to talk about it until after the wedding.'

'I'd rather know,' she said.

'OK. I phoned to ask about Carl. I, erm, went to his trial.'

'Did you?' She was astonished. 'Why?'

'To find out what sentence he received. I saw when the trial was coming up, and took leave of absence from college, explaining some of the reasons why and that I had a vested interest. There was only a brief report in the local newspaper. Carl was found guilty of arson and sentenced to eight years. It would have been more but for mitigating circumstances.'

'Which were?'

'Childhood trauma. A bullying father, an unstable background; and that he thought the house he lived in was his. He said he believed that he'd inherited it from his mother; I'm not sure if anyone believed that, but it could have been true. Also that he didn't endanger any life except his own, which he tried to take. He had a good lawyer, too, who pointed out that he had mental issues.

'Anyway, I got in touch with Jeannie,' he went on, 'to find out where he would be held, and it will probably be somewhere in the Midlands where he'll get help with his psychological problems. It won't be anywhere near here, and Jeannie said that against all advice she'll visit him when she's allowed, and if he improves she'll go and live down there.'

'She'll be there for him when he comes out!' Liz said, almost under her breath.

'I think so.' He put his arm round her shoulders and she leant into him. 'He won't ever be coming back here,' he said softly. 'With help and advice and perseverance, he'll make another life.'

'It's sad in a way,' she murmured. 'There's always been a Reedbarrow here, just as there are Fosters and Rayners. But why? *Why* did you ask Jeannie these questions, or go to the trial?'

'I wanted to find out what would happen to Carl so you could close up this chapter of fear that you have, and—'

'But—' she interrupted.

'Begin to think about your own life. It doesn't matter about a name. A name doesn't make a person what they are; if you marry me you'll change yours, won't you?'

Vaguely she nodded. 'Though I'd add Foster, as others have

done before me.' Then she looked up at him to find that he was looking down at her and trying to hide a grin. Her lips parted. 'Was – was that a proper question?'

'We've skirted around it for long enough. What is it with you Rayners, or Fosters, or whatever you are, and marriage? Your dad took long enough to ask Dot to marry him. Are you going to take as long?'

'For what?' she asked.

'To answer my question.'

She took a step back and Ben sat down and yawned. 'What question was that?'

'Will you marry me, Miss Rayner, and sell me your house?'

'You're after my fortune,' she said.

He nodded. 'Yours and your brother's, I think. Remember you have to share the proceeds with him.' He took her hands in his and drew her towards him. 'Is it a deal?'

She stood on tiptoe to kiss him. 'The best I've ever made,' she said softly. 'I love you. I'll marry you with or without the house or mill. I won't ever be afraid again if I have you there beside me.'

CHAPTER FORTY EIGHT

It was the most perfect autumn day for a wedding, everyone agreed. The sun shone, highlighting the crisp golden leaves that floated down to the warm brown earth to form rich hummocky mounds that for many brought back childhood memories, of running through them, scattering them into an explosive autumn cloud.

Dorothy looked so happy, carrying a bouquet of roses, joy lighting up her face, her fair hair shining like silver and tears glistening in her blue eyes as she came up to Gilbert, who, tall and dressed in a smart pale grey suit and waistcoat, held out his hand to her, his moist eyes only on hers.

Liz, the only attendant, wore a calf-length cream silk gown and a headdress of real cream roses and freesia that she had made herself, and carried a similar bouquet. She cast a glance at Chris as they passed, their eyes smiling as they met.

Outside in the churchyard after the ceremony the bride and groom chatted to the crowd of friends who had come to congratulate them, and many said what a handsome couple they made.

Jack and his wife had announced that there were complimentary sandwiches, sausage rolls, scones and wedding cake waiting at the Ship for anyone who would like to partake of a light lunch and raise a glass to the newly-weds, and many agreed.

The small wedding party climbed into the two wedding cars, the bride and groom's suitcases already packed in Gilbert's car and on their way to Beverley.

'Well, darling.' Gilbert held Dot's hand as they both sat back and let out huge breaths. 'I think that went well.' He leant towards her and kissed her.

'I agree,' she said softly, and smiled at him. 'Best wedding I've been to in a long time.'

CHAPTER FORTY NINE

'If we were married,' Chris said, winding a lock of Liz's hair around his finger, 'we could both live in Dot's house.'

'True, we could,' Liz agreed. 'And make plans about the mill house.'

The newly-weds were due home the next day. They had telephoned some time previously to say they were going to stay on for a few more days: the weather was glorious and they loved Ravenscar and their hotel overlooking the sea. But two days later the weather had turned and a gale was blowing in from the east, so they telephoned again to say they had changed their minds and would travel home after all.

'Home from home,' Chris laughed.

He and Liz had discussed the mill house and he had persuaded her to come with him when he met the surveyor to discuss what was possible and what was not. Liz had spoken to her brother and told him approximately what the property was worth in the condition it was in.

'Not much, then?' Bill had said.

'What I'm willing to do, Bill, is get an estimate of its value as building land, but what *we* want to do is rebuild the house and live in it. You know I've always wanted to be here. So if we speak to the surveyors and assessors and get prices, and then split what it's worth down the middle . . .?'

'Really?' Bill's voice rose. 'Would you do that, sis? But would you still be able to afford to rebuild the house?'

'Chris has sold his London flat and prices are much higher there; so yes, hopefully, but we'd have to get a mortgage.' She'd kept her fingers crossed as she answered.

'And will you be OK, not scared of the odd ghost or two?' He sounded concerned. Was her younger brother becoming more caring and less flippant about others' concerns than he once was?

She wondered how she would have felt if Paul Reedbarrow had carried out his deadly intentions. Different, certainly. 'I think there might be friends around,' she answered, and heard his usual cynical laugh.

Gilbert and Dot looked so happy and relaxed when they arrived back. Neither of them had had a holiday in a long time. Liz felt a sudden ache in her heart at the loss of her mother, and yet saw the love in her father's eyes when he gazed at Dot and understood that life had to move on.

'Hi, Dad,' she greeted him when they came through the door with the luggage. 'Hello, Ma!' She hugged Dot. Somehow she couldn't call her Mum, but Ma seemed to fit, and it suited Dot, whose eyes lit up when Liz said it.

'Hello, honey,' she said in return. 'We've missed you.'

They talked of general things as Liz made tea and brought out the biscuit tin, of which Jack had said 'Wife's made 'biscuits,' and then Chris came in. He raised his eyebrows at Liz, who raised hers back and gave a slight shake of her head, then they all sat down to chat and listen to Gilbert and Dot telling them about their travels.

'I've not been up on 'North York Moors in a long time,' Gilbert said. 'Not in years. Nor has Dot, have you, love?'

'Not since I was a schoolgirl,' she said. 'The moors are lovely this time of year; 'colours are beautiful. Then we found this old untamed wooded area and picked some sloes. We've brought them back. I'm going to have a go at mekking sloe gin; my ma used to mek it.'

'So what have you two been up to?' Gilbert asked, and Liz noticed that he hadn't asked if there had been any problems with the running of the Ship. He was so much more relaxed.

'Well, I have a very important question to put to you, Mr Rayner,' said Chris solemnly. Gilbert's mouth framed an *Oh*, and Dot raised her head in her usual shrewd, astute manner. Chris got to his feet.

'Mr Rayner. Gilbert,' he said carefully, and cleared his throat, then put his hand out to Liz, who also rose to her feet. 'I have asked your daughter, Sarah Elizabeth, if she will do me the honour of becoming my wife. But also, in the time-honoured way, even though she's old enough to make her own choices, I would like to beg your permission to marry her.'

He blew out a breath and bent to kiss her; Dot clapped her hands and clasped her fingers together; and Gilbert, who had also risen to his feet, said gruffly, 'Well, what a homecoming this is! Can't think of anything I'd like more.' He gazed down at Liz and saw the mischievous smile touch her lips.

'If you give permission, Dad,' she said, 'or even if you don't, we'd like a Christmas wedding.'

Gilbert drew in a breath. 'So soon?' Then he flushed. 'But why not!'

Liz put her arms round him. 'When we saw how happy you and Dot were, well, we wanted some of that; and whilst we were all in the marriage mood we thought let's do it now and move into Dot's cottage, then we can all go to Australia in the spring.'

She took another breath and continued, 'And I made a real effort and finished the report on the state of the cliffs, and

Chris read it through and we added up the numbers of supporters, which were incredible, because not only those who
were particularly affected signed the petition but residents of
other villages, and townspeople from the West Riding who
come to the coast every year who'd read the report I'd sent to
the local newspapers; business people, like the brewers for
instance, who supply the various inns and hostelries; drivers
of coal wagons, grocery suppliers – so many who come along
our essential roads all added their names.'

She breathed out. 'And then I took the report to County
Hall, sat with them as they read it through and watched as
they counter-signed the document, made a copy, and put it in
an official envelope addressed to Downing Street.' She blinked
rapidly and added throatily, 'And I watched them put it in the
sack for posting that same day. So that's done and dusted and
there's nothing at all to delay our wedding day.'

Gilbert gazed at her. When she was a child she never gave
up on any task or project if it was important to her. Proper
Yorkshire terrier she was, he recalled; she'd hang on by the
skin of her teeth until she claimed victory. He recovered his
equilibrium and turned to Chris, holding out his hand to
shake his. 'I hope you realize the challenge you're getting
into?' he said mildly.

And so another wedding was announced in Tillington church
two weeks before Christmas; they'd chosen a Saturday, which
fortunately was bright and sunny with a scattering of snow-
flakes to give a seasonal touch. Liz had asked the Johnson
twins to be her bridesmaids, and a school friend who had married two years before to be her matron of honour. Alf
Wainwright, she agreed with her dad, would be overjoyed to
be asked to be usher again. Chris asked an old friend from his

university days to be his best man, and also telephoned Helena, who said she would come, otherwise she wouldn't believe it had happened. Wryly cynical, she'd added, 'You do know it won't last?'

'Mm, I guess you might be right,' he'd sighed. 'But I'm prepared to give it a try,' and she'd laughed.

'Take her to Paris,' she suggested.

'I've already booked,' he said in return.

Chris also rang his mother to give her the news, and there was a sudden silence at the other end of the line, until she asked warily, 'To whom? Anyone I know?'

'No one you know, Mum.' He was grinning as he answered. 'Although I have mentioned her several times. She's a Yorkshire girl through and through. You'll love her.'

'We'll see about that,' she said. But she did.

One of his female cousins brought her up to Tillington the day before the wedding, and they stayed at the Ship for three nights. As he had thought she would be, his mother was delighted that Liz still lived at home. He showed her Dot's house where he and Liz would be living and she very much approved, but was unsure about the mill house. 'A lot of work,' she said.

'Not once it's built, Mum, and you know that I like a project. So does Liz.'

Most of the village came out to watch Gilbert Rayner's lass on her wedding day; her boss Steve and two of the girls came from the office, and two of Chris's former fellow teachers from Hull College. Even Jeannie turned up, though no one knew who had alerted her. The Ship was closed until the wedding was over and would open again with free food and an extra tier of the wedding cake that Dot had made especially for the locals.

Once again, Alf Wainwright sat by the church door with Ben at his feet, directing the few who didn't know whether to sit on the right or the left, but all decided that it didn't really matter which seats they took, except for those at the front for relatives and the one that was reserved with a cap and scarf.

The sea breathed softly as it caressed the base of the cliffs and the sun shone for the first time that week, its radiance enhancing the glow of Liz's shining red hair. She had grown it long and dressed it in a soft chignon in the nape of her neck, intertwining it with a circlet of pearls, a present from Chris. Her wedding gown was of cream silk, her favourite shade, with a wide hem of pale gold and a short train; she carried a bouquet of deep golden roses. The Johnson twins and her matron of honour, Laura, wore pale gold dresses with long sleeves, pearl headdresses, and fine wool-fringed cream shawls, for it was a winter wedding after all.

As Liz, holding tight to her father's arm, walked along the aisle towards Chris as he waited by the altar, she inhaled a deep breath, overwhelmed to see him so smart and handsome in a pale blue double-breasted suit with a cream tie and a cream rosebud in his top pocket. She thought of her mother and wondered what she would have made of him, but she cast a warm smile at Dot who, she knew, loved Chris as a treasured stepson-in-law.

The reception was again held in Beverley's ancient hotel, and two days later the newly-weds flew to Paris. They stayed for four days before returning to Dot's house, which would be their home until such time as permission was given to begin the building work on the mill house, which they had decided would be known by its old name of Foster's Mill House.

ENDING

Bureaucracy moves slowly and life has to wait for officialdom, and as expected there was a waiting time for an answer from Downing Street regarding a sea wall. Chris asked Helena if she could pull any strings as they also waited for permission to proceed with the building work on the mill house.

They waited too for an assessor's valuation of the land so that Bill could be given his share, and to their delight, when the original documents were surveyed, they discovered the existence of an extra piece of land that also belonged to the property. It was at the top edge and on the opposite side of the lane, so after permission was approved they decided to sell it to Steve Black for the building of a maximum of three houses.

When that was done, a surveyor was brought in to assess the cost of rebuilding the mill house. A new roof was required first of all, and some of the interior of the house that had been affected by the fire had to be gutted. Walls had to be removed and others built, virtually turning the house around and giving them more interior space, including an open-plan family kitchen and a brand new pine staircase in the newly enlarged entrance hall.

Liz watched as walls tumbled down and wondered what the original mill-owning Foster family would have thought: three sons and a daughter of the Monkston Fosters; Tom, son of Will Foster, and his wife Elizabeth, who had no known predecessor, both born in Hull, though not in the grand house in High Street but from much humbler beginnings. *How do I know this?* She was agreeing with her intuitive self without any proven evidence. *But know it I do.*

Anything she heard, or thought she glimpsed, both happy and sad, when alone in the empty house she now accepted as part of life's rich tapestry, knowing now that she and Chris and the children they hoped to have would make their own memories, and pass them on to anyone in the future who might intuitively see or hear them: children, or grandchildren perhaps, or someone born long after the people they knew had gone from this world. The endeavour must be to create good memories and remembrances for those who might hear, see and believe in them at some future time.

It was over a year after their wedding day and Liz was pregnant with their first child when an envelope dropped through the letterbox of Dot's cottage. Chris picked it up, glanced at the address stamped on the back, and then, drawing in a deep breath, called to Liz. *She'll be devastated if they say no, as everybody from the village and the surrounding area will be.* Mentally, he crossed his fingers. Liz stood looking at him, taking in the envelope clutched in his hands.

'This is it, isn't it?' she said, croakily. 'This is yes or no?'

He nodded slowly. 'If it is no, then we'll try again.'

'I told them that someone was dragged over the edge of the cliff in a landslide,' she admitted, 'but was saved by the efforts of local fishermen and the coastguard.'

He nodded again and made his bottom lip quiver. 'Did the victim say it was the combined efforts of local people that saved her life?'

'Oh yes, and one hero in particular, and his dog.' Her lips trembled too as she tried not to laugh. 'And she married him in the end, because he'd been so brave!'

'Well, come on, then!' He held the envelope out towards her. 'Open the damned thing; we've been waiting long enough.'

She took it from him and slit it open with a table knife, and opening the letter contained within she read it and took a deep breath. 'It's from the Secretary of State for the Environment, and the subject matter is to be discussed with Brussels.' She looked up at him. 'What will it mean?'

He gave a big grin. 'It will mean that the UK will ask Europe for money to build your wall. We'll still have to wait, but it's very encouraging. Anything else?'

'Yes! There's another page; an invitation to take a delegation to Downing Street where we'll be met by the Prime Minister! They've given us a choice of two dates in the spring. March or April. We'll have to have another meeting! Alf Wainwright *must* be invited; the mayor of Holderness, Beverley councillors, George Bennett, Matt Wilson, who's lost even more land ... oh, and Jim Jackson the journalist to take photos, and *everyone* who's been actively involved.' She lifted her arms and he picked her up and swung her around Dot's small kitchen and she smothered him in kisses.

They agreed they'd have to hire a coach, because everyone who had been involved wanted to go to Downing Street and meet the Prime Minister. 'There'll be a coachful,' Dot said. 'We won't all be able to go!'

'I think we can,' Liz said. 'I'll hire a sixty-seater, and we'll ask everyone who wants to come for a contribution. Tillington

376

folk will get the first choice, then the East Riding councillors, then other villagers, and Hornsea folk; and the campsite owners who will lose their livelihood if the cliffs continue to erode can choose a representative too.'

The coach was full on that spring day; the passengers were high with excitement as at six o'clock in the morning they left the village, all waving to a small crowd who had come to see them off on the long road to London.

'Well, folks,' Liz called out when she had counted everyone on board. 'This is it. To do or die! We must prove that this campaign is important to us; that our homes and our families are at risk if something isn't done, and soon.'

'Hear, hear!' Alf's tremulous tones were heard and everyone cheered.

He had been adamant that he would be going, and sat in a front seat with a blanket over his knees, across the aisle from Liz and Chris, who were behind the driver, and Dot and Gilbert behind them. Dot had packed sandwiches and quiche and two flasks of coffee for the family and included Alf in the feast; she had also brought a tin of home-baked biscuits for everyone else to share. Jack's wife had baked biscuits too, for Gilbert had said they would close the Ship for the day.

Such incredible luck, Liz thought as they began their journey, remembering the day after she had been trapped on the cliff, when they had discovered that a holidaymaker, there for the day, had seen that something was going on further down the beach and had filmed police cars and an ambulance arriving and then the coastguard's jeep driving at speed along the sands. He had continued filming right up to the moment when Liz was winched up into the helicopter, then aimed the camera at the fallen cliff face and the heavy seas.

The video film was shown on TV late that evening, and the next morning a journalist had arrived at the hospital and asked for an interview.

Letters of support from all over the country began to come in, especially from the east coast, down as far as Lowestoft and from as far away as Glasgow, and all of this publicity was included in their deputation.

The coach stopped twice for a 'comfort stop', and at the first stop Chris and the driver brought out a wheelchair for Alf. He had never been in a service station before, and exclaimed at the size of it. 'Well, I never!' he breathed. Chris bought him a takeaway cup of tea to drink once they resumed their journey, which proved to be a mistake as an hour later they had to stop again.

Finally, they reached London and the driver headed towards Westminster Bridge, slowing down so that everyone could see the Houses of Parliament directly below. 'Less than ten minutes to Downing Street, ladies, gentlemen and children,' he called out into his microphone, mentioning the twins who were representing the youngest of the community. 'Those who are going inside, have your papers ready, as I'll have to park the coach wherever I'm sent.'

There was a general hubbub of excitement, and when the driver had shown his credentials to the police officers he jumped down and once more helped Chris remove the wheelchair from the hold. They were both patted down for security and then so was Alf, who was helped down from the coach by the police officers and said, 'Don't worry about it, lads. You don't know me and you've got an important job to do. I might be a criminal for all you know.'

The policemen stood back and saluted him. 'Thank you, sir. Very kind of you, sir.'

'Look!' Chris alerted Liz. 'There's Helena. I wondered if she'd come.'

Helena had offered her assistance in preparing official documents appertaining to the petition, and Chris had felt she had had a hand in moving things along more swiftly, though he didn't tell Liz that. But he was gratified to see Liz smile at her as they approached to thank her for her assistance and for coming on this important day.

Liz, carrying a copy of the petition, and Chris pushing Alf in the wheelchair were at the front, with Gilbert and Dot behind. Next came George Bennett, representing the local council, and others from Tillington and nearby villages who had permission to enter Number Ten. All turned to pose for photographs taken by Jim Jackson and other newspaper reporters waiting opposite the black door, then turned back again as the door slowly opened.

Liz bent down towards the elderly Tillington villager. 'Well, here we are, Mr Wainwright. Alf,' she said, handing him the petition, 'would you care to do the honours?'

ACKNOWLEDGEMENTS

My thanks as always are to the Transworld Penguin Random House team. For the patient understanding and support of both past and present of my editors as I strove to recreate this old novel; included are much-valued production editor Vivien Thompson and copy editor Nancy Webber. Not to be missed, Richard Ogle and the design team who create the lovely covers for all of my books.

Thanks too to those who understood the challenges of adapting the intricacies of the 1980s computer system to the complexities of today's technology. Also to personnel at Leconfield Airport East Yorkshire for information on the procedures of Air Sea Rescue Services (1987–89). If they should read this book they will recognize their input. Last but not least, to my local creative Divine Clark PR team, who guide me through the terrors of social media and publicity, thank you.

If you enjoyed *Foster's Mill*, be sure to read Val's
other gripping and heart-warming novels

Winter's Daughter
by Val Wood

Hull, 1856: James Ripley and his wife, Moira, have always
looked out for the poor of Hull. When, during one
stormy night, there is a flood in a nearby cellar – a
popular shelter for the homeless – James
rushes to help.

Among those rescued is a dark-haired little girl
who speaks a language no one can understand.
Some say that she came to the cellar with her mother,
but no one knows where the mother is now.

Concerned for the child's safety, James is unsure
of what to do. Where has the girl's mother
disappeared to? And what can be done
to help the homeless who have lost the
only shelter they knew?

Winter's Daughter is available in paperback and ebook now

The Hungry Tide

by Val Wood

As the sea claims the land, can she claim the love she deserves?

In the old fishing town of Hull, Sarah Foster's parents have been fighting a constant battle with poverty, disease and crime. When her father, Will, a whaling man, is involved in a terrible accident at sea, their lives became even harder.

But Will's good deeds of the past pay off as John Rayner decides to rescue the Fosters. John provides them with work and a house on the estate owned by his wealthy family. It is at this new home on the crumbling coastline of Holderness that Sarah is born – and grows into a bright and beautiful girl, and a great source of strength to those around her.

As John grows closer to Sarah, he becomes increasingly aware of his love for her. But could these two very different people ever make their love story truly work?

The Hungry Tide is available in paperback and ebook now

Annie

by Val Wood

Can her courage lead her to a life of happiness?

Annie Swinburn is harbouring a terrible secret. She
has killed a man. The man was evil in every possible
way, but she knows that her only fate if she stays
in the slums of Hull is a hanging.

And so she runs. As fast as she can, and as far as
she can – up the river, along hidden paths of the
Humber and into a new and familiar territory
where she can start a new life.

There she meets Toby Linton – a man born into a good
life but now estranged from his family. He and
his brother Matt earn a dangerous living as smugglers,
but Annie soon realizes they have more in common
than she thought. And this new way of life might
just offer her the chance of love, in spite of
all the tragedy that has gone before . . .

Annie is available in paperback and ebook now

The Lonely Wife

by Val Wood

1850.

Beatrix Fawcett is just eighteen when her father tells
her she is to marry a stranger. Hesitantly, but with little
choice, she agrees to the match – in the hope of
a good husband in Charles, and a happy
new life together in rural Yorkshire.

As Beatrix sets about making their house a home, she falls
in love with it and the surrounding countryside. But she
does not fall in love with her husband . . . Charles has
chosen her simply to meet the requirements of his
inheritance and has little interest in his young wife.

Soon, the only spark in Beatrix's lonely life is her
beloved children. But when Charles threatens to
take them away from her, Beatrix must find
strength in desperate times.

**Can she fight against her circumstances
and keep what is rightfully hers?**

The Lonely Wife is available in paperback and ebook now

A Mother's Choice

by Val Wood

For ten years, Delia has had to fend for herself and
her son Jack, and as a young unmarried mother, life
has never been easy. Every new coat and pair of shoes
was bought with what little money she could scrape
together as a singer on the stage.

But when the theatre work dries up, Delia faces a dilemma:
continue the search for employment with no knowing
whether she'll find the stability and security her son
needs, or return to the place that should be home . . .
where only spite and hatred await them.

Desperate now, a chance encounter suddenly
presents a lifeline. But Delia is faced with an impossible,
heart-wrenching choice. Can she bear to leave Jack
behind, hoping another family will care for him?
Will they ever be reunited?

**What else can a mother do to give her
son the life he deserves?**

A Mother's Choice is available in paperback and ebook now